Dedicated to Carlos Ezquerra

An Abaddon Books™ Publication
www.abaddonbooks.com
abaddon@rebellion.co.uk

First published in 2019 by Abaddon Books™,
Rebellion Publishing Limited, Riverside House,
Osney Mead, Oxford, OX2 0ES, UK.

10 9 8 7 6 5 4 3 2 1

Creative Director and CEO: Jason Kingsley
Chief Technical Officer: Chris Kingsley
Head of Books and Comics Publishing: Ben Smith
Commissioning Editor: David Thomas Moore
Series Editor: Michael Carroll
Marketing and PR: Remy Njambi
Design: Sam Gretton, Oz Osborne and Maz Smith
Cover: Neil Roberts

Based on characters created by John Wagner and Carlos Ezquerra.

ISBN: 978-1-78108-639-1

Printed in Denmark

J[★★★★★]DGES

VOLUME ONE

MICHAEL CARROLL • GEORGE MANN • CHARLES J ESKEW
EDITED BY MICHAEL CARROLL

ABADDON
BOOKS

INTRODUCTION

WHEN I FIRST told my friend Kevin about this series, he said, "What?" because he wasn't listening. So when I second told him about it, he said, rather dismissively, "Oh, so, you're doing a *prequel*, then. Did you get that idea from *The Phantom Menace?*"

Through gritted teeth, I explained that, no, this idea didn't come from *The Phantom Menace*. And it's not a prequel.

Well, not really.

In 2006, almost thirty years after they created *Judge Dredd*, writer John Wagner and artist Carlos Ezquerra finally gave us the epic tale *Origins* which relates the history of the Justice Department. It told us how the USA finally began crumbling under the weight of its own bureaucracy and internal politics, drowning in the blood on the streets even as it choked on the dust of its collapsing economy. We saw how hot-shot young lawyer Eustace Fargo was appointed Special Prosecutor for Street Crime by President Thomas Gurney. How he founded the Judge system in the hopes of applying order to the growing chaos, and how that system eventually came to completely supplant the US government.

Origins is a masterpiece, but it has a *lot* of ground to cover. The story of the first Judges on the streets—back when they were still sharing those streets with the cops and lawyers they would eventually replace—occupies just two panels out of its 132 pages.

That's where this series comes in. Who *were* those first Judges? What sort of person would be willing to throw away the fundamental concept of due process? To forfeit every other citizen's basic rights in the name of justice?

What does it take to become the physical embodiment of the Law?

Senior editor and overlord David Thomas Moore asked me to be the line-editor for the series: he knew of my love for Dredd (I'm a *2000 AD* reader from the very beginning!), and my enthusiasm for Dredd's history. I realised that since I'd be working with other writers my first task should be to create a series bible; a comprehensive document that explains the background to the series, the setting and tone, a list of dos and don'ts, lists of characters that can be used and those who are off-limits, and so forth.

But all that seemed like way too much work, so instead I wrote *The Avalanche*, the first novella you'll find in this collection, as a sort of template for the other writers. A blueprint that tells them, "This is the sort of thing we want. Do it like this. But not 100% *exactly* like it, of course. Add your own slant."

Dutifully, for they are professional, George and Charles both studied my blueprint very, very closely before deciding to carefully—almost reverentially—crumple it up, toss it aside and write their books their own way. I'm glad they did! This is, after all, why they were chosen. They each brought their own unique voice to the series, and it's all the richer for it.

I won't spoil their books for you, of course, but you're in for a treat. George Mann's *Lone Wolf* takes what on the surface might seem a clear, straightforward cop-story and applies his well-honed skills to ramp the tension way, *way* up. It's a fantastic, gripping adventure: when I was editing the first draft I constantly found myself so engrossed in the story that I was forgetting to annotate the script. I've edited thirty-something novels and I think that's the first time that's *ever* happened to me.

As for Charles J. Eskew's *When the Light Lay Still...* Well, that was initially scheduled to be the second release in the series, but Charles kept adding so many layers to it. The story—which we were receiving in chunks—was magnificent, but it was taking way too long. Editorial decision: do we rein him in, or give him the room to fly? We chose the latter option, and swapped the publication order with *Lone Wolf*, which was possible because George had delivered his book early, the absolute champion.

All that remains is for me to thank George and Charles, the awesomely gorgeous and tantalisingly exotic Abaddon crew, and of course the unbelievably talented creators of our universe, John Wagner and the much-missed Carlos Ezquerra. Thank you for letting us play with your wonderful toys, gentlemen!

Justice lies within, folks.

Michael Carroll
Dublin, November 2018

THE AVALANCHE

MICHAEL CARROLL

*To my friend John Vaughan,
Larger than life, more fun than a barrel of monks and
considerably smarter than two short planks.*

PROLOGUE

Monday, January 3rd 2033
20:47

THE UNIFORMED OFFICER was busy transcribing a handwritten statement and didn't look up from his keyboard. "With you in a second."

Charlotte-Jane Leandros looked around the open-plan office. Aside from the now-limp Christmas tree in the corner, the top half of a paper Santa Claus pinned to the wall, and an Elf-on-a-Shelf that had what was very clearly a bullet hole in the middle of its forehead, the police station of St. Christopher, Connecticut, didn't appear to have changed in the two years since she'd last visited. The officer behind the desk, however, had changed quite a lot. He'd put on weight, and his hair was now very grey, as was the thick moustache he sported.

She reached across the officer's desk and poked a pencil at his Schnauzer-a-day calendar. "So... Happy birthday, Benny."

His typing paused for the briefest moment as he said, "Knew it was you, CJ."

"No, you didn't."

He still hadn't looked up from the screen, but he was suppressing a smile. "Sure I did. You're still wearing the same

15

deodorant, and you cleared your throat on the way in. You think I don't know my own baby sister's voice, even if she's just clearing her throat? I'm a cop. I've been *trained* to notice stuff like that." Benny Leandros finally stopped typing and glanced up at his sister. "So, does Mom know you're back or is this a surprise vis—"

He jumped to his feet, and his chair skidded back across the room. "CJ, what are you *wearing?*"

CJ Leandros placed her dark-visored helmet onto her brother's desk and took a step back, giving him a better view of her uniform. Matt-black Kevlar-and-titanium-fibre tunic and pants, dark grey gloves and boots, reinforced grey pads protecting her shoulders, elbows and knees. She turned in a slow circle, ignoring the officers who had been staring at her from the moment she'd entered the station. "So what do you think?"

Benny walked around to the front of his desk, stopped in front of his sister and stared down at her. "I think Mom's gonna have an *aneurysm*. You... You told us you'd quit the police academy, not that you'd signed up to be a Judge! What was all that about working in a hardware store?"

"Cover story. We're not encouraged to talk about it, even with family." She shrugged. "Lot of people are still very hostile to the idea of Judges."

"Can you *blame* them?" He shook his head slowly as he looked her up and down. "Body armour. It's a bad sign when cops need body armour. And you don't have a body-camera!"

"What would I need one for? I don't answer to anyone. Look, Benny, more than everyone else—even more than *Dad*—you were always telling me that I should go into law enforcement."

"Yeah, but I meant be a *cop*. That was before there were Judges! I mean, Judges like you. I thought you and me and Stav could be like a team, working the same beat, watch each other's backs. That's what Dad always wanted for us. Not... *this*." He took a step back and again looked her up and down. "Not this, CJ. He'd have *hated* Fargo's Footsoldiers and everything they represent."

A voice behind CJ said, "He's not alone in that."

She'd known that he was there. Unlike Benny, Charlotte-Jane actually *had* been trained to be aware of what was around her at all times, and she was good at it. It was one of the reasons Judge Deacon had selected her for his team.

Her oldest brother, Sergeant Stavros Leandros, had entered the room right after Benny had walked around to the front of his desk. Stav had been watching her from the doorway, and CJ had in turn been watching his reflection in her helmet's visor. On her way into the police station, she'd seen his car parked in the lot outside, and as sergeant he would have already been informed that a Judge had been seen riding through town.

He shook his head slowly. "If I'd known you were going to do this, I'd have stopped it."

"How? It's my life, my decision."

Stavros nodded towards his office. "Let's talk. Right now." To Benny, he said, "Not you. Get that report done and go home. You're back on at oh-nine-hundred."

As Stavros stomped away, Benny said, "Better do what he says, CJ. You know what he's like when he's under pressure. Until yesterday we had half the town without power because the Settlers knocked out the grid again, and we've got like ten guys down with the flu. So..." Benny shrugged. "I figure the last thing he needs is a bunch of Judges showing up and throwing their weight around."

He paused in the middle of dragging his chair back to his desk. "That's *not* what's happening, is it? Tell me that you're here on your own and you just came back 'cause it's my birthday and you wanted to surprise me."

"I came *early* because it's your birthday. There are six of us, working under Senior Judge Francesco Deacon. The others will be arriving tomorrow."

Benny dropped into his chair. "Oh, Stav is not going to like that. And the *captain* is gonna have a *fit*."

CJ Leandros smiled and shrugged at the same time. "Happy birthday, Benny. I'll see you tomorrow back at Mom's, yeah?

17

And don't tell her I'm here—I want to surprise her."

"I won't say a word... You know, I can't decide whether she's gonna be madder that you became a Judge or that you cut your hair. You always had great hair. Everyone said so."

She was already backing away from his desk. "Judges can't have long hair. Regs."

She recognised some of the other officers and staff—there were a few she'd known her entire life—but right now they were pulling off that awkward trick of staring at her without looking her in the eye.

From the day she'd been hand-picked from the police academy, she'd known that this was going to happen. Ordinary cops didn't like the new Department of Justice, and not just because it signalled the end of their careers.

As she passed the open doorway to Stavros's office, he yelled, "CJ! Get in here!"

She stopped, and looked in through the doorway to see her brother standing next to Captain Virginia Witcombe, a cold-looking fifty-year-old woman with grey hair so tightly pulled back that CJ was surprised she could still blink.

"So," Captain Witcombe said. "Welcome home, Charlotte-Jane." CJ had the impression the captain was just barely keeping a lid on her emotions.

"Thank you, Captain. It's nice to be back. I honestly never expected to be posted here."

Stavros said, "Yeah, *about* that. So out of the blue this afternoon we get an official e-mail telling us six Judges have been assigned to St. Christopher. We've got forty-three beat cops to manage twenty-eight thousand people, and now we're babysitting half a dozen Judges too? And my own *sister* turns out to be one of them? Hell with that."

"Yeah... I don't like this either," Captain Witcombe said. "Not one bit. You people want to make a difference, you should set up station in one of those towns in the Midwest that're being overrun by gangs. Not here. It's bad enough that I've got to put up with Judges at home in Colton, but

I've worked too long and too damn hard to get where I am to throw it all away now. St. Christopher might not be the picture-postcard small town, but it's a damn sight better than most, and I'm not going to stand by and watch while you Judges clear the path for the handcart this country is going to Hell in. You get what I'm saying?"

"You think that the Judges are a symptom of the problems, not the cure. I understand that, Captain, but I don't agree."

Stavros nodded. "Well, *I* agree with the captain. You remember what Dad always said, CJ. I remember Pappous saying it too, before you were even born. The single most important right any American citizen has is due process. The right to unbiased judgement when accused. You Judges have taken that right and flushed it down the crapper." Stavros looked away from her, shaking his head. "It's unconstitutional."

Captain Witcombe said, "No, it's not, Sergeant Leandros. Not since Eustace Fargo got the constitution *changed*."

CJ said, "Captain, when you spoke at my dad's funeral, you said that we need tougher laws to clamp down on drunk-drivers so that sort of thing would never happen again. Afterwards, at the reception, I found you crying in the corridor, and your husband... Harvey, right? He was trying to console you. But you didn't want that. You didn't want to be consoled, and you were furious with him because you said he was trying to pretend it had never happened. Then you saw me, and you took my hands and told me that it wasn't fair, that my dad was a great man, and to have his life snatched away by some drunken loser was the worst possible crime. You remember that, don't you?"

"Yes, I do. And that's not all I remember." The captain stepped closer to CJ, arms folded. "I remember an incident about a year earlier. You were fifteen years old, and I caught you and Tenna LeFevour stealing beer from the One-Stop."

Stavros said, "What?" but both CJ and Witcombe ignored him.

The captain continued, "And now you're a Judge. I heard you all had to be squeaky-clean. Can't see how that's possible if you were a shoplifter."

"I wasn't charged," CJ said. "Remember? Dad asked you to take care of it."

Witcombe pursed her lips. "Hmm. So if I hadn't done that, maybe we wouldn't be having this conversation now."

"Possibly not. But you broke the law when you persuaded the store's owner to drop the charges. That's a bad mark on *your* record sheet, Captain, not mine."

Captain Virginia Witcombe remained perfectly still, and her voice was almost a whisper as she said, "You don't talk to me like that. I don't care who your father was or what happened to him. You *never* talk to me like that. Sergeant? Throw this smart-ass little *punk* out of my station in the next ten seconds or someone will have to arrest me for assaulting a Judge."

Stavros took a step towards CJ. "Captain's right. Get out, CJ. You and your new friends are not welcome in this town. The system we've got might not be perfect, but it's fair and it *works*."

CJ stood her ground. "Recorded crime in St. Christopher is up one hundred and sixty per cent from five years ago. In the same period, conviction rates have dropped twenty-nine per cent." She sighed. "Stav, I drove by Mom's place on the way into town. You know what I saw? Bars on the windows. They weren't there when I left two years ago. Four houses down the street, the Johnstone place? Used to be a nice house. Now it's just a pile of rubble and burnt timber."

Stavros began, "That's not—"

"I'm not done. Six weeks ago Cain Bluett stabbed Kirby Decosta twice in the chest on Main Street. Three sober, reliable eyewitnesses, plus CCTV footage from two angles. Where's Cain Bluett right now? Drinking in Whelan's bar. Why? Because he's rich enough to hire the slickest law firm in the county, and his family has the political strength to bury the case. Dad might not have approved of Judges, but you *know* the drunk that ran him over was awaiting trial for DUI at the time, and wasn't in jail because of overcrowding.

"You want me to go on? No, you don't, because you both know that the system is *not* fair, and that it *doesn't* work." CJ turned from her brother to Captain Witcombe. "Judge Deacon and the others will be here early tomorrow morning. During this period of transition, we will work alongside you and your officers, but Judge Deacon has seniority. His word is final."

Stavros looked away in disgust. "Jesus, CJ! Don't—"

"Judge Leandros."

"What?"

"Judge Leandros. Or just 'Judge,' if that's simpler. That's how you'll address me, Sergeant."

"Right. And does that apply when you're off-duty? Because I can think of a few other names that might apply."

CJ took a step back towards the door. "We're never off-duty. Remember that."

Captain Witcombe glanced at Stavros. "Looks like your baby sister outranks you, Sergeant."

"Matter of fact, I outrank *both* of you," CJ said.

JUDGE FRANCESCO DEACON slowed his Lawranger and pulled in towards the sidewalk on Main Street. The four Judges following pulled in behind him.

Deacon climbed off the bulky motorcycle and trudged back through the refrozen slush, glad of his helmet's auto-tint visor that cut off most of the glare from the morning sun. As he passed his fellow Judges, he held out his left hand, palm down.

Judge Lela Rowain asked, "Sir...?"

"Stay put, Rowain. They're cops."

Judge Kurzweil said, "Cop *car*. Doesn't mean there's real cops inside it, sir."

Deacon ignored that. In the academy, Kurzweil had always been a touch paranoid about police officers and lawyers. She'd always believed that they were going to cause the Judges more trouble than the citizens would.

The police car had signalled them to pull over when they'd turned onto Main Street. Ordinarily, Deacon would have ignored it, but this was their first day in St. Christopher. Ruffled feathers weren't conducive to a smooth transition.

As Deacon passed Hayden Santana, the last Judge in line, the police car's door opened and a fifty-year-old woman climbed out. She stepped towards him, breath misting as she shrugged herself into a padded jacket and zipped it up. "Cold one. Again."

"We were on the way to see you, Captain Witcombe."

"You know who I am?"

"I've been briefed." Deacon extended his hand to her. "Francesco Deacon."

As she shook his hand, she asked, "So is that Frank, or Fran? Or...?"

"'Judge Deacon' is fine." He looked around.

A couple of locals had stopped to stare at the Judges. They were passed by a teenaged boy dragging a large gasoline canister on a battered sled. The teenager glanced at the locals, then across the street to see what had snagged their attention. He said, "Oh, great. Judges." He spotted Deacon glaring at him, forced a smile and added, "I mean, 'Oh, great! Judges!'" before turning away and increasing his pace.

On the street, an old red pickup truck was crawling past, its white-bearded driver pointedly staring straight ahead and very definitely not looking at either the police captain or the Judges.

"Suspicious," Deacon said, nodding towards the pickup. "You want to pull him over, Captain, or should I?"

Captain Witcombe stepped closer to Deacon. "Leave him be. That's not guilt on his face. He's in shock. His name's Henderson Rotzler, seventy-one, lives on the west edge of town. Loudmouth when he's drunk, but aside from that he's all right. And he's the reason I've stopped you...

"Rotzler's just brought his dogs to his brother's place, now he's heading back home. I'm going to meet him there, and I expect you'll want to, too."

Deacon turned back to face the captain. "So what's happened?"

Witcombe hesitated. "Way I understand things, you're here to work *with* us, yeah? You Judges are gonna replace the entire judicial system, but that can't happen overnight, because there just aren't enough of you. So for now, you work alongside us ordinary cops and lawyers. Tell me I'm right."

Deacon nodded. "That's right." Before the team had left Boston, Judge Fargo had called him in. *"Go easy on them,"* he'd said. *"Let them have their last moments in the sun before the Justice Department takes everything away from them."* Deacon had fully intended to comply with that suggestion, but now, with the captain looking haggard and more than a little worried, diplomacy seemed like a luxury. He told her, "Do us both a favour and skip to the end."

Captain Witcombe slowly shook her head. "It's not that simple, Judge. I spent a few hours last night reading through the new directives. I was hoping to find something that tells me you're not allowed to do anything until I sign you in, something like that."

"We're Judges," Deacon said. "We're *already* signed in. Doesn't matter where we are—we've already got all the authority and approval we need. So get to the point, Captain."

She glanced behind her, towards the back of the red pickup truck, then said, "Rotzler's dogs woke him up last night. He said they went crazy, barking like there was an intruder. He went to check it out... There was a body in the back yard of his home. Someone had dumped her over the wall. Female, mid-twenties. Stripped naked. Shot at least once, in the head. According to Rotzler, she was still warm when he found her."

Deacon stared at the captain for a moment, unmoving, and suppressed a shiver that he knew wasn't down to the cold.

Witcombe continued, "Judge Deacon, we haven't formally identified the deceased, but we have every reason to believe that she is Charlotte-Jane Leandros."

CHAPTER ONE

JUDGE HAYDEN SANTANA had made three strides towards the main entrance to St. Christopher's Police Station when he felt Deacon's hand on his shoulder.

"What did I say back on Main Street, Santana?"

Santana turned back towards the senior Judge. "I was just gonna—" He cut himself off. It was a waste of time trying to get anything past Judge Deacon. The man was like a human lie detector. "You said not to talk to anyone until you briefed us. Sir, I was just gonna test the water. You know. See how they're reacting in there."

"You'll stay put and listen." Deacon turned to the others one by one. "Kurzweil and I will go check the crime scene. Even if it *is* Judge Leandros, we'll treat this as any other suspected homicide until we know otherwise. Understood?"

Santana said, "Got it. But sir... CJ's *brothers* work here. They're cops."

"I know that," Deacon said. After a second's hesitation, he added, "That brings up an important point. You will refer to her as *Judge* Leandros at all times when discussing the case with anyone outside of this group. Reinforce the idea that the murder of a Judge is a capital offence. And you'll refer to each other as 'Judge,' too. The citizens need to see us as separate from them. We're not cops who become citizens again at the end of patrol. We're Judges, all day, every day." He turned to Lela Rowain. "You, Santana and Boyd are down for the first patrol. Plan was that you'd be riding shotgun with beat cops for the first few days until you knew the layout of the town. That might have changed after what happened, but if not, go with it. And I expect you to use your own common sense. You with us on that, Boyd?"

Judge Xavier Boyd said, "Sir, yes, sir."

Deacon continued, "Judge Leandros's brothers have been relieved of duty. They're at the hospital's morgue right now... Kurzweil and I will deal with them. But a lot of the other cops in there knew Judge Leandros all of her life, so they're going to be pissed and looking for blood."

Santana couldn't help himself. He blurted, "Like we're *not?*" He withstood Deacon's glare long enough to add, "Just saying that we all trained alongside CJ twenty-four-seven for the past two years. We've got a right to be angry too."

Deacon said, "No. You don't. You're a *Judge*, Santana. The law comes first, above any and all other considerations. We are the physical embodiment of the law. We do not weaken, we do not compromise, we do not show bias. And we do not allow our emotions to guide us." He stepped closer to Santana. "Tell me I didn't make a mistake picking you for this team."

Santana found his mouth had gone dry, and he desperately wanted to swallow. "You did not, sir. I understand my duties."

Deacon regarded him for a moment, then stepped back. "I hope you do, Judge Santana. Kurzweil, with me. Mercy South Hospital is eight blocks west. Rest of you, get to work. And step *lightly*, you hear? Regardless of what these people think of Judges, they lost someone they knew."

Santana watched Deacon and Kurzweil steer their Lawrangers into the early-morning traffic, then turned to Boyd. "You okay?"

The younger Judge nodded. "Yeah. We're gonna find who did this... Jesus, they *stripped* her." He glanced back towards the

26

police station: several officers were at the windows, watching them. Boyd beckoned both Santana and Rowain closer, then added, "Captain Witcombe didn't say anything about a sexual assault, so it seems to me that stripping her could mean that the killer wanted to hide that she was a Judge. Or wanted to *deny* that she was a Judge. You get what I'm saying?"

Rowain said, "That's how a little kid might deal with something they didn't like: out of sight, out of mind."

"Thought of that," Santana said. "A kid, or an adult with perspective issues. But that's the big question. Was CJ targetted *because* she was a Judge? You know what these small towns can be like. Riddled with corruption. They find out that Judges are coming and they..." He stopped. "Aw crap. It's *my* fault. Well, kinda."

Rowain asked, "What do you mean?"

"*I'm* the one who suggested to CJ that she come early. Because this is her home town and her mom still lives here, plus yesterday was her brother's birthday. I told her she should come home a day early and catch up with them." Santana looked from Rowain to Boyd. "It's a damn sight easier to take down a single Judge than a whole squad. If she hadn't been alone..."

"That's hardly your fault, Hayden," Rowain said. "And speculation without evidence won't help anyone. Let's get inside."

Boyd said, "Right." He straightened up, pulled off his helmet long enough to run his gloved hands over his closely-shaved head, then replaced it. "Lela, you take point."

Santana followed Rowain and Boyd into the building.

Inside, in the warm but slightly scruffy black-and-white-tiled public lobby, a lone desk sergeant glowered at them. He was a short man, with white thinning hair. Santana guessed he was maybe sixty years old. *Step lightly*, he reminded himself.

The desk sergeant said, "Seen you there, out front. Synchronising your stories, yeah? Making sure you're all on the same page, I'm guessing. So it's true, then? Sergeant Leandros's little girl is dead?"

Judge Rowain said, "I thought Sergeant Leandros was her brother?"

"No, I mean the *original* Sarge, her father. Tobias. A good man, until that S.O.B. Farrell Silberman figured he was okay to drive after eight beers. I swear, if Silberman wasn't locked up in county right now... Well, let's just say that there's what's right, and there what's *right*, you know what I mean?"

Rowain said, "We do know what you mean. And that sounds like a threat against a prisoner."

The man glowered. "Yeah, there's a *reason* it sounds like a threat."

Judge Boyd said, "Given the heightened emotional state of this situation, Judge Rowain, I recommend we let that drop for now."

Rowain said, "Agreed." She stepped closer to the desk. "I'm told that Captain Witcombe and the current Sergeant Leandros are unavailable. Who's in charge?"

"Right now, that'd be me." The man consulted a sheet of paper in front of him. "So. Six of you. Well, five now. Really is a shame about Leandros. She was a good kid. I swear, whoever did it is gonna—" He cut himself off. "Says here you don't need an office as such, but you'll need a room big enough for three bunks. We can do that." He leaned forward a little and looked at the floor at their feet. "No bags? Rest of your personal stuff coming later?"

"We have no other personal stuff," Rowain said.

"Is that so? Well, good for you, casting away the material things... So, you're Lela Rowain, Hayden Santana and Xavier Boyd... Heh." He grinned at Boyd. "Your folks had a sense of humour, huh?" He looked at the list again. "Not as much as your *friend's* folks, I guess... Unity Kurzweil. Who the hell calls their kid 'Unity'? Whatever. You all been assigned patrol partners for the week." He used the chewed end of a ballpoint pen to point towards a wall lined with mismatched plastic chairs. "You're early; your patrol buddies ain't ready for you yet. Take a seat."

* * *

NIÑO AUKINS SLOWED as he approached Mister Romley from behind. Any fool knew that you didn't surprise Mister Romley with bad news.

Romley was average height and slender-framed, with pale, lightly-freckled skin and hair so blonde it was almost transparent. Almost everything else about him was a mystery to Niño, who had known him for twenty years and still wasn't entirely sure of the man's first name. He was aware that he *ought* to know it—it was either Irwin or Irving, maybe, or Ivan—but now too much time had passed, and Niño didn't have the guts to ask him. So he was always Mister Romley.

Niño was fifty-four now, and had one eye on retirement. He was slowly building up what his grandmother had always called "a nice little nest egg," but—unlike Grandma—Niño had no intention of dying before he had a chance to spend it. He kept himself healthy and in shape. He never ate processed foods or anything grown with chemical fertilizers. Even the heroin with which he regularly injected himself was organically sourced, or so his dealer claimed.

Deep down, he knew that the heroin would probably kill him eventually, of course, but if it did, he hoped it was before Mister Romley found out he was using.

Romley was the boss, plain and simple. The rest of the hierarchy of his organisation was deliberately confusing, even to Niño; and he was—he was almost certain—second in command under Romley himself. Everyone knew who was one step above them and one step below them, but beyond that it was anyone's guess. Just as it should be: you can't rat on someone if you're not even sure that they work for the same organisation as you.

Niño had Rafe Carfey, Shiraz Castro and Wan Gaimaro working directly under him. They were solid guys, dependable. In college, a visiting lecturer had told Niño's Business Management class that, *"It's vital to hire people who will tell you why they* won't *be able to do something, not why they* weren't *able to do it."* Some of Niño's friends had been baffled by that, but Niño had understood it, and remembered it, and he believed that was why he was doing a good job.

Right now, Mister Romley was standing on a gantry in the factory looking down at the manufacturing process. He had his hands thrust deep into his pockets as he peered over the edge with apparently casual curiosity. Almost directly below, a conveyor belt trundled endlessly as the workers placed carefully-measured scoops of grey powder into compression units that pressed the powder into tablet form, then inserted the tablets into plastic bubble packs, glued the professional-looking foil backing into place, and placed the packs into small pre-printed cartons. To a casual observer, the cartons looked identical to a popular brand of diarrhoea medicine, *Impasse.*

The final stage, before the cartons were packed into cardboard boxes ready for shipping, was hand-stamping each with a use-by date that was already three years old. That way if one of the drivers was caught carrying a shipment of boxes, he could claim that they were out of date tablets that were recently found in an abandoned warehouse, and he was taking them to be incinerated. After all, who would counterfeit out of date diarrhoea medicine?

Niño cleared his throat. "Mister Romley?"

"What is it?"

"Could be bad news. Not good, that's for certain."

Romley turned around to face Niño, and beckoned him closer. "I'm not the sort of person to shoot the messenger, Niño."

Yes, you are, Niño thought. "Of course not, sir... But... There are Judges in town. And one of them was killed last night. They're going to tear the town apart until they find the killer."

Romley nodded. "I'm aware of that."

"I'm thinking we need to, you know, do something about it. Move the merchandise. Shut down for a few days, maybe."

"Perhaps. Put a watch on them for now, Niño. If it looks like they're going to be trouble, we can deal with them. We've already seen that Judges can die just like any other cop."

CHAPTER TWO

LESS THAN FOUR minutes after they'd entered the station, the desk sergeant called over to the Judges. "Yo, Santana?"

"*Judge* Santana."

"Whatever. You're up." He gestured towards a set of doors behind him. "You're with Chaplin. You'll find him through the doors, first left, then third door on the right. Unless he's in the john. Rowain and Boyd, your partners are on watch at the crime scene—they'll be back here in about twenty."

Santana nodded to his colleagues and pushed open the double-doors. He was hit with the familiar smell of scorched coffee and stale sweat, common to pretty much every police station he'd ever visited.

A young female officer glared at him as he passed, and muttered something sharp under her breath. He resisted the temptation to stop and reprimand her; Deacon had made it clear that the transition was to be as seamless as possible. *"You don't throw rocks in your own path,"* he'd said.

A week ago, as the cadets in Boston Academy prepared for their final assessments, Chief Judge Fargo himself had paid them a visit. Santana hadn't met him before, but he'd known what to expect. A tall man in his early thirties, broad-shouldered but with a wiry build, and a look in his eye that very clearly conveyed the message, 'We are not here to have fun.'

"Our first duty is to the citizens," Fargo had told them. *"Their current system is strangling them in red tape. The simplest cases are taking years to come to trial. Everywhere we turn, we see lawyers becoming rich on the sweat of the ordinary people. Cities setting arrest quotas, which leads to cops targeting minorities and the poor because they believe that's the quickest way to get their numbers up. We see major corporations crushing their opponents by bribing officials to twist the laws in their favour.*

"But no more. That all ends with this current generation. We will be the sword that frees the people from the Gordian knot of ineptitude, bureaucracy and corruption. Yes, we will be ruthless, and uncompromising, and at times merciless, because that is what's necessary. The gentle touch does not work."

After Fargo's lecture, Judge Deacon had told his own team, *"We are the only viable solution. The alternative is anarchy. The citizens won't understand that. They'll hate us, and fear us; they'll curse our names and they'll plot against us. They'll lie and cheat and accuse us of being ruthless monsters. And I can live with that because this isn't about our feelings, or how cosy the citizens are. It's about keeping them alive."*

Santana reached the third door on the right, opened it and strode in. It was the station's canteen; two uniformed officers—the only occupants—sat at one of the small round tables, a plate covered in pastry crumbs in front of them and steaming coffee mugs in their hands.

The officer on the left—female, average height, stocky build, mid-fifties, wearing glasses and a very neatly-pressed uniform—passed her male colleague a five-dollar bill. "Good call."

The male officer grinned up at Santana as he stuffed the bill into his shirt pocket. "I bet her that you'd walk in without even knocking. That's why we closed the door." His chair scraped across the floor as he stood up, hand extended. "Roderick Chaplin. Everyone calls me Roddy. I'm told that you're with me today." Chaplin was as tall as Santana, but with a heavier build. He clearly spent a lot of time in the gym.

Santana hesitated before shaking the officer's hand. Didn't they understand that this was the first step in their enforced early retirement? He shook Chaplin's hand anyway. "Hayden Santana."

The female officer remained seated. "Sophia Gress." She tilted her head a little to the left as she peered at Santana's face. "Now, surname like Santana, I'm thinkin' Latin America, but your hair's too light and your skin's kinda pale and them eyes... Yeah, I figure you got some Chinese in the mix. Maybe Japanese or Korean, but somewhere from that side of the world, am I right? Sure I'm right. One of my tricks. Chaplin here's good at accents, but I can guess folks' ancestry from their faces."

"Sounds useful, if it's accurate," Santana said.

"Oh, it is. So we heard about the Sarge and Benny's sister, CJ. You knew her well?"

"We trained together," Santana said.

"Their old man was a sergeant here, too," Chaplin said. "Good fella. CJ was like family to most of us. Whoever did this is a *dead* man. Statement of fact. He just doesn't know it yet." He stared at Santana. "You Judges don't have a problem with that, do you?"

Santana returned the stare. "We don't do revenge. We'll find the perpetrator and punish them appropriately. As we will with anyone who interferes with the investigation."

Gress said, "Yeah, well, sometimes you've gotta make *exceptions*. Like when a kid you've known her whole life is gunned down in the street."

This is going to be a problem, Santana told himself. But this was not the time to reprimand the officers: flared tempers and sidearms were a dangerous mix. To Chaplin, he said, "Let's go."

Chaplin glanced at the clock on the wall. "We got, like, eleven minutes before we're on duty. Sit down, sit down, take a load off. You can tell us about yourself. How'd you get into being a Judge?"

Santana said, "Four weeks ago this town suffered a riot at the junction of Main Street and Elm. Report says that the citizens were protesting food shortages and rising prices. Property damage estimated at over a million dollars. Not counting the costs of sixty-four arrests and thirty-one injuries, including three officers."

Chaplin and Gress exchanged glances, then Gress said, "Yeah. We *remember*. We were there, in the thick of it."

Santana stepped back towards the door. "Justice has to be *seen* to be done. The citizens can't see justice being done if you're in here sitting on your butts waiting for the big hand to hit the twelve. Let's go, Chaplin."

Chaplin moved to follow Santana, but Gress reached out and grabbed the sleeve of his shirt and held him back. To Santana, she said, "We got a way of doing things here. And we got a *union*." She shrugged. "I'm just sayin'."

Santana leaned forward, placing his hands on the table as he pressed his face close to Gress's. "I get that you've got a way of doing things, Officer Gress, but that way is changing. There's no going back. Not now, not ever. Do you understand that?"

Gress seemed unexpectedly placid as she replied, "Yeah, sure. I get that. And I'm not fighting it, Judge. You can't push the avalanche back up the mountain, I know that. But *we're* not Judges. You're dealing with *people* here, people who've lost someone they care about. Family. Do *you* understand *that?*"

Santana straightened up, and nodded down at Gress. "Yes, I understand."

"Well, then. We're all going to get along just fine." Gress winked at Chaplin. "Guess you're hitting the streets a few minutes early today, Roddy."

"Yeah, looks that way." Chaplin pulled open the door. "Let's go, Judge. I'm driving."

As Chaplin led him through the station, Santana took note of the reactions of the other officers and staff. Two or three of them ignored him, but the rest watched in silence as he passed.

Judge Deacon had told them to expect some hostility, maybe even outright opposition, and the death of Judge Leandros was likely to magnify that. If she'd been as well-liked here as she had been at the academy, tempers would be flaring.

The cops would already have had mixed feelings about CJ becoming a Judge. Her return home in a position of authority over everyone—including the captain—would only have made things worse. And now this. Murdered on their own turf.

When Santana and his squad received news of their assignment to St. Christopher, Deacon had told them, *"Small-town cops have deep roots and long memories. Goes with the territory. They're already entrenched, and if we go in heavy-handed, they'll dig in deeper."*

A few months earlier, in Philadelphia, a cop in a town not much bigger than St. Christopher had put her gun to her head right in front of the assigned senior Judge. The last words before she pulled the trigger were, "This is not the America I signed up to protect."

In Utica, New York, the entire police force had gone on strike the day they were informed that three squadrons of Judges had been assigned to the city. The Judges had simply ignored the picket lines and gone to work.

Pro-Fargo politicians pointed to the clear decline in serious crimes in those cities and towns where the Judges had had time to settle in. Their rivals tried to drown them out with statistics showing a sharp rise in civil unrest in every Judge-run city. Justice Spender J. Gant—Santana's former would-be mentor and now one of Fargo's most visible and vocal opponents—had attempted to spark a furore by declaring that, *"The Judges are responsible for more crime-related deaths than the perps ever were."* Fargo's response had been, as always, to offhandedly dismiss anything to do with Gant, even when directly asked about him by White House-approved reporters.

A door at the rear of the station opened out onto a cracked-concrete yard stained with rust and oil. Chaplin slowed enough to allow Santana to fall into step beside him, then said, "This was our maintenance lot until about two years back. We'd a mechanic on duty at all times, kept the cars and bikes purring like a cat in front of the fire." He shrugged. "Cutbacks. Now we outsource the work to a garage three blocks over. They do a half-assed job at the best of times." He pointed ahead towards a line of three patrol cars. "I park on the back street here. Quicker than getting out of the front lot when the traffic's heavy. So, you guys just rolled into town, didn't you? You wanna get breakfast or something?"

"No. What's the worst part of town, Chaplin? The place you just don't want to go, even with backup?"

Chaplin pulled open the driver's-side door and then pointed off to the west. "Oh, that'd be the Crush. Nickname for the Croft estates. Place is the pits. It's like a magnet for squatters, illegals, junkies, gang-bangers... I swear, you can't *move* in that place without some scumbag trying to start a damn war. You breathe in too deeply, you could be inhaling anything from fresh sewage to methamphetamine dust. We get a call out to the Crush, odds are it's a turf war, so we make damn sure to drive slow. You get me? Get there *after* all the bangers have shot each other up. Gress always says we can clean up the Crush no problem, once we get hold of enough napalm. I'll tell you, if you Judges can make any sort of difference out there, I'll sign up myself."

"You're not qualified," Santana said. "Take me there."

Chaplin laughed. "Sure thing. Right after I slam my own nuts in the door for being so goddamn stupid."

Santana opened the passenger door. "That wasn't a joke, Chaplin. And it wasn't a request, either. It was an order."

CHAPTER THREE

BY THE TIME Deacon and Kurzweil arrived at the scene, the body had already been taken to the morgue, and Captain Witcombe had accompanied it.

Now, a woman wearing a too-large winter coat over a grey suit briefly glanced at Deacon, then pointed at the wall with her left woollen mitten and said, "Wall's two-point-four metres high at this point. Means two people to heft her body over it. At *least* two, maybe more."

Deacon could hear Judge Kurzweil talking to the police officers on the other side of the wall, and it sounded like they were grunting single-syllable answers at her. She wasn't going to like that.

The woman took a step back from the wall. "I'm Detective Morrow, by the way. St. Christopher's one and only plainclothes officer. So naturally the whole town knows who I am." She returned her attention to the wall. "Now, you're thinking that one real strong guy could do it, sure, but we've got to apply the rule of smaller and fewer jumps, right?"

"And what's that?"

"They don't teach you that in Judge School? Any unknown situation, the theory with the least amount of wild assumptions is most likely to be the right one. Like, in this case we could assume that the body was dropped from a copter, but then it would have suffered a lot of damage. So to get past that, we assume a large body of snow to cushion the fall. But that snow's not there now, and wouldn't have melted yet, so maybe we conjure up a bunch of guys with shovels to clear it away. But that can only happen if those guys are already on the ground waiting for the body to land. See? Now we're getting into wilder and wilder speculations. So if—"

Deacon held up a hand. "I got it. Thanks." He looked left and right along the narrow, snow-packed road that ran past the rear of Henderson Rotzler's home. It was heavily lined with Canadian Hemlock trees in both directions: their densely-packed foliage effectively blocked the view of any satellites directly overhead.

"Any CCTV coverage in this area?" Deacon asked.

The detective shook her head. "Nothing useful. Could be that some of the neighbours or farms have their own private cameras. Captain's got some of her people doing a door-to-door right now. This ain't our first rodeo, you know."

The voices from the other side of the wall were rising in volume. Detective Morrow shouted, "Hey, keep it down over there!"

A man's voice came back, "Sorry, Detective."

The Judge looked down and stamped the heel of his boot into the ground. "Solid... no recent tracks. What was last night's snowfall?"

"I'm told it was very light. You'd get more flakes in an empty cereal box." She hesitated for a second. "The body had been stripped naked, they tell you that? Post-mortem, too: there was no blood-splatter below the neckline. A lot of smears, yes, but no splatter. No fingerprints in the smear, no tell-tale bloody footprints in the area, no tyre tracks. Whoever did this had some idea of what they were doing. So how'd you get to be a Judge?"

"I was asked." Deacon walked in parallel to the wall until he was about four metres away from the point at which the body had been dumped, then hoisted himself up. The breeze-block wall had been constructed perhaps five years ago, judging by the mild erosion and the patterns of lichen and moss. Its unevenness and low-quality pointing, and the occasional chipped corner, suggested that it had been built by an amateur, possibly Rotzler himself.

On the far side of the wall, eight uniformed officers and Judge Kurzweil were looking up at him.

"What do you hope to see from up there?" one of the officers asked.

Kurzweil answered for Deacon: "Any traces of skin or blood on the wall that might correlate with post-mortem scratches on the body. Something like that could indicate whether the body was pushed over or thrown. That in turn might give us some idea of the size and strength of the perp."

Deacon examined the ground on the other side of the wall. The oversized yard was littered with decades of junk: discarded kitchen appliances, a pile of rusting four-metre-long girders, a dozen wooden sheds in various stages of disintegration, and several collections of rotting lumber half-buried under damp, sun-faded mattresses.

Even this high up, Deacon didn't have a clear line of sight to the house. If it hadn't been for Henderson Rotzler's dogs, the body could have remained hidden for weeks, maybe months.

Deacon said, "Kurzweil, we're done here. Meet me back on the main road, four minutes." He dropped down off the wall, landing lightly on his toes.

"Morrow, we're heading to the coroner. Preserve the scene as long as possible."

"I will, as a professional courtesy, but I don't work for you, Judge."

"You do if I say you do."

MERCY SOUTH HOSPITAL's mortuary room was marginally warmer than the weather had been outside. As he watched the town's coroner cut into Charlotte-Jane Leandros's body, Deacon pulled off his helmet, tucked it under one arm and stuffed his gloves into it.

Standing next to him, Unity Kurzweil shifted a little. She and Leandros hadn't known each other well—Kurzweil had been the last Judge to join the squad—but there'd been no rivalry between them. Deacon knew Kurzweil's discomfort at watching her former colleague being cut open was more to do with the past than the present. Back when she'd been a cop, Kurzweil had investigated a killer who'd specialised in pre-mortem autopsies. He would administer a paralysing agent that prevented his victims from moving or screaming, but allowed them to still feel everything that happened to them. That case—and the subsequent trial, in which the murderer came close to being acquitted on a technicality—was what persuaded Kurzweil to join the Justice Department.

She's going to have to toughen up, Deacon told himself. *Chances are we're all going to end up like that: horizontal and naked, with someone slicing us open as if the cause of death could be anything other than the very obvious bullet holes.*

The coroner, a stocky woman called Loretta Abramson whose entire face Deacon had yet to see, spoke constantly as she worked, her voice slightly muffled by the surgeon's mask. "Deceased is female, mid-twenties. One-seventy centimetres, sixty kilograms. Low body-fat, in apparent good health. Spectrograph's showing some old scars on both forearms... both thighs, both calves... hell, she's *covered* in scars." Abramson looked up at Deacon. "What, she spend the past couple years falling down the up escalator?"

"The training's intense," Deacon said. "You'll find similar scars on all of us."

"Right. Contusions over the sternum suggests two non-penetrating gunshot wounds. Enough to slow the victim down, but not powerful enough to pierce her armour. Then two more shots to the face, left cheek and centre forehead. Either would be fatal. Obviously, she was not wearing her helmet at the time. Absence of cartridge discharge residue on the exposed flesh suggests that the shooter was at least two metres away."

"Weapon?" Deacon asked.

Abramson said, "Possibly a semi-automatic but no way as yet to be sure. Head-shots were through-and-through, so we're not seeing any fragments, but my guess is we're looking at a thirty-eight calibre minimum." She glanced up at Deacon. "For the record, can you positively identify the victim, Judge?"

The victim's DNA test had already proven her to be Charlotte-Jane Leandros. This part of the process seemed so unnecessary, so archaic. Down the corridor, in the family support room, Leandros's mother, brothers, and sisters-in-law were waiting. None of them had wanted to see the youngest member of their family with such disfiguring wounds. Even Captain Witcombe had been reluctant to do it.

Beside him, Judge Kurzweil said, "It's her."

Abramson asked, "You're certain? Even with so much damage to her face, you're certain that this is your colleague?"

Kurzweil nodded. "Her hands. Everyone's hands are different... This is Judge Leandros."

"That good enough?" Deacon asked.

The coroner took a step back from the table, then pulled off her face-mask and cap, allowing the Judges to see her face for the first time. "I don't know..." She shrugged. "The law makes it very clear that that a visual confirmation of identity is required in the event of an unlawful death." She turned and reached for the phone. "I think we should bring in the family. Or maybe Captain Witcombe will—"

Deacon sidestepped into her path and put his hand on the phone's handset. "That won't be necessary, Doctor Abramson. From now on, DNA confirmation is sufficient to establish identity."

She gave him a weak smile. "You can't just rewrite the laws, Judge."

"Yes, we can," Deacon said. He looked back towards CJ's

body. "Give her the works. Full analysis. Check for traces of *Lycopodium obscurum* and *Flavoparmelia caperata*."

"That's... prince's pine moss and common greenshield lichen?"

"Correct. They were growing on the wall at the scene where she was found, and something recently disturbed them. If there are no traces on the body, then chances are they're on the perpetrator. You've got a particle harvester?"

Abramson almost laughed. "A harvester, on *our* budget? No. There's probably not much point. Her body's been scrubbed clean. A rush job, by the looks of things, but the chances of finding anything useful are pretty slim."

"I'll get you a harvester anyway."

"Judge, there's just me and two assistants here, and we're already overloaded. I'll need to check with the board of pathology to confirm—"

"Consider my word to be all the confirmation you need, Doctor."

"No, I need written approval from my superiors to authorise that level of overtime and release the necessary resources! You know how many laws I'd be breaking otherwise?"

"Sure I do. None." Deacon tapped the badge on his chest. "I'm a Judge. I *make* the law. I say you have the authority, then you have it. You tell your superiors that they can talk to me directly if they've got a problem. But you might remind them that questioning a Judge's decision would be skirting dangerously close to sedition."

The coroner glared at him for a second, lips tight and eyes narrow. "There's no going back, is there? This is how things are now. I commit a crime, you can sentence me on the spot. There's no jury, there's no process of appeals... But the reality is that no one is infallible. If a Judge makes a mistake, an innocent person gets punished and the real guilty party is off the hook *forever*. How is that fair, Judge Deacon?"

Deacon looked around the room, turning in a slow circle. "You've got... ten body-drawers here, Doctor. How many of them are currently occupied?"

"Eight."

"Right. I guarantee that within a year, the number of bodies per day you have to examine will be considerably less than half of what it is now."

Doctor Abramson nodded slowly. "That's an attractive idea, Judge. But *before* that happens, that number is going to spike, isn't it? I watch the news, I read the web. Judges move into a city and all Hell breaks loose. I heard that in some places they actually run out of body-bags."

"I won't lie to you, Doc," Deacon said. "You're going to be busy over the next couple of months. If you find anything that might point to the killer, you talk to me directly. Not to Captain Witcombe or any of Leandros's family or friends. To me." He nodded to Kurzweil. "Let's go."

"So what now?" the doctor asked. "What's your next step?"

Judge Kurzweil was already striding through the open doorway as she called back, "Now we hit the streets and find the killer."

Abramson fell into step beside Deacon as he headed towards the door. "But... there's more to it than that! There's paperwork, and departments that need to be informed, and you need to establish a chain of command and define the parameters of the investigation!"

"You've never actually seen Judges in action, have you, Abramson? It's a mistake to think of us as cops with different uniforms." He pulled on his gloves.

She stopped at the doorway. "But *you* were a cop before you retrained as a Judge, weren't you?"

"Sixteen years Military Police Corps. Hand-picked by Eustace Fargo to help train recruits into the Judge programme. I also have a first-class degree in interpretation of the law and a doctorate in criminal psychology. Trust me, I'm qualified."

"What about the rest of your squad?"

Deacon glanced back through the doorway at the cold, dead body of Judge Leandros. "They each have their own sets of skills. We *will* make a difference here in St. Christopher. You're a doctor, you've seen the inside of an ER. You understand that sometimes to save a patient's life you need to be ruthless and keep cutting, no matter how much that patient might be begging you to stop."

"And in that analogy, the patient is the town?"

"No. It's the whole damn country."

CHAPTER FOUR

JUDGE ROWAIN LOOKED up as an older uniformed officer approached her across the station's public lobby. The officer was female, maybe fifty-five years old. She had grey hair tied back in a bun, and half-moon glasses. The shine on the officer's shoes told Rowain that the woman had been driving a desk for a long time.

The officer offered Rowain a paper cup of coffee. "You might need this, honey. I put two sugars in. Hope that's enough."

"We don't drink coffee, and try to avoid processed sugar, but the gesture is appreciated."

The woman looked from Rowain to the coffee cup and back. "You don't drink *coffee*? None of you?"

"No. Caffeine is a stimulant. It's not actually prohibited— yet—but it's discouraged." She looked up at the name-badge on the woman's neatly-pressed uniform. "Officer Gress... You're going to tell me that the dead woman has been positively identified as Judge Leandros."

Gress nodded. "So you've heard."

"No, but you thought I was going to be in need of a comforting drink, which suggested that you had bad news to convey."

Gress sat down next to Rowain, and said, "I knew little

Charlotte-Jane most of her life. She was so sweet when she was a kid. But everyone knew she was going to be a cop, even then. Her father was sergeant here too, just like Stavros. Some days we'd come off patrol and Charlotte-Jane would be sitting behind his desk, colouring or doing her homework or whatever, and she'd greet all of us by name. We were all so proud of her when she joined the academy... and so disappointed when she quit." Gress stared down at the cup in her hands. "She never told anyone she'd signed up to be a Judge."

Rowain wasn't sure how to react. The Judges had been taught to expect hostility, even violence, from many of the officers they'd be replacing. No one had told them to prepare for sadness.

"Guess she wanted to surprise us."

"We were encouraged to avoid telling anyone, if possible," Rowain said. Not for the first time, she thought of her old friends from back home, and wondered how they were going to react. She knew that she might never find out: at the academy in the Department of Justice they were told that the wisest course of action would be to shed their past lives entirely. "You can never go home again," one of the tutors had been fond of telling them. Now, Rowain couldn't help wishing that for CJ Leandros it had been more than just a saying. *If she hadn't come home...*

Gress looked up at Rowain. "Lela, isn't it?"

"We prefer formality, Officer Gress. Judge Rowain is sufficient. We're not here to be friends."

"That much is obvious, honey. You've been sitting here like a thrift-store mannequin waiting for Officer Mangold to take you out on patrol. But folks here are either too busy, too upset about Charlotte-Jane, or too intimidated that you're a Judge to tell you that Mangold's pulling a double shift out at the crime scene. He's not coming in, Judge. You're on your own today."

Rowain stood up. "I see. Thank you, Officer Gress."

"I saw your photos on the captain's monitor, Judge. You

look like your boss. Same nose, same colour skin, same eyes. You related?"

"Judge Deacon is my first cousin."

"Ah. That how you landed the job?"

"There's no nepotism in the Justice Department. I got the job on my own merits."

Gress gave her a wide, tight-lipped smile. "We'll see, honey. I've been in this game a long time, and I know a thing or two about how it works. We all start out like you, stern and idealistic and uncompromising. But the streets have a way of grinding down the sharp edges, even in a small town like this. It looks peaceful out there right now, but come Saturday night when the bars start vomiting their patrons out onto the streets and the riots kick off because another factory's closing down, and the juvie gangs clash, and the nutcase survivalists out in the hills decide they're running low on supplies and they want to run another raid on the town, and a bunch of Trance-heads are going out of what's left of their minds because their dealer got stabbed in the eyes by a vigilante mob who then burned all his stash... Well, then you're going to find yourself cutting all sorts of corners just to keep your head on your shoulders."

Rowain nodded. "I've heard other officers say similar things. Experience lends wisdom, and wisdom tells you that you can tolerate a lot of the smaller injustices so long as it means stopping the big ones."

Gress sipped at the coffee. "Yeah, something like that. You're all 'coffee is an evil stimulant' right now, but a week or two of fourteen-hour days and you'll be mainlining the stuff like the rest of us. You'll see. The tallest towers are always the first to crumble." She got to her feet, drained the last of the coffee from the cup, then balled it up and tossed it into a waste basket four metres away. She winked at Rowain as she walked away. "Ten points! Still got it—no need to put us all in mothballs just yet, right? You watch your back out there, Judge. Just 'cause St. Christopher's a small town doesn't mean we don't have our share of crazies. It just means that they have fewer things to distract them from whatever it is they've a need to destroy."

Rowain put on her helmet and pulled on her gloves as she strode towards the doors. The plan had been for Officer Mangold to take her around the town—both to acclimatise her with the streets, and to allow the citizens to see the Judges working alongside the police—but now she'd be going solo. That suited her. She would be more comfortable on her Lawranger motorcycle than as a passenger in a car.

Outside, the crisp air stung her lungs and cheeks, and she pulled up the collar of her tunic a little. A full-face helmet would have been warmer and a lot safer, but Chief Judge Fargo had vetoed that idea from the start: *The citizens have got to see that we're people underneath the uniforms, not robots. It's bad enough that the anti-glare coating on the visor means they can't see our eyes, but I'm damned if I'm going to block out the rest of the face too.*

She climbed onto the bike, started it up and felt the familiar and comfortable pull as its almost silent engine surged, drawing her across the parking lot. She steered out onto the street, slipping in next to an old white Toyota driven by a nervous-looking man who was white-knuckling the steering wheel.

Rowain dropped back and flipped on the Lawranger's scanner, aimed it at the Toyota. It read the car's licence plate, displaying the car's details on her screen. If she'd had reason, she'd be able to view the car's entire history, from the moment it left the factory eleven years earlier, right up to its most recent stop for gasoline. If necessary, Rowain could request that the Justice Department's database supply her with the exact times, dates and locations of every single time the car passed in front of a public camera.

Instead, she ignored the Toyota, which turned left at the next junction. Sometimes the presence of a Judge just made people nervous—that didn't mean they had anything to hide.

She rode north along Main Street until she saw snow-covered

fields ahead of her, then turned right, heading east towards what had once been a thriving industrial park and was now a square kilometre of silent factories, derelict offices and empty warehouses. Officially, the park was abandoned; but when Rowain rode past, she spotted unmistakeable signs of occupation: woodsmoke in the air, tyre tracks and footprints in the snow leading through the gates.

She slowed her Lawranger and was about to curve back towards the gates when her radio clicked into life, the police station's channel. "All units... this is base. Got a report of a disturbance out at the mall. Anyone able to take it?"

Rowain flipped the switch on her helmet. "Judge Rowain here. Specify *which* mall, Dispatch."

"That's Mayor Caroleen Omaha Mall, Judge. We just call it 'the mall' because the one over on the east side is—"

"I'm two kilometres away from Omaha Mall—I'll take it. What's the nature of the disturbance?"

She heard some brief muttering, then, "Uh, no need, Judge. Don't think it's a big deal. One of our guys will deal with it."

"Who am I talking to?" Rowain asked.

"This is Officer Gardner Clarke at St. Christopher dispatch. Seriously, Judge. Don't waste your time with this one. It's nothing. It's just a disgruntled customer making threats. The rent-a-cops are taking care of it. No need for you to get involved."

"Recommendation acknowledged, Dispatch, but ignored: no crime is too small. I'm on my way."

"Aw, no, don't... Judge Rowain, that's going to cause more trouble than—"

"Not going to repeat myself, Officer Clarke."

After a nervous "Okay, then..." the line clicked off.

The Lawranger's on-screen map showed the large shopping mall on the edge of town. This time of the year, post-Christmas and with the schools still on vacation, it would be busy even this early in the day.

Traffic on the way into the mall was dense. Rowain weaved

her bike smoothly between the slow-moving cars and trucks, and steered into the parking lot.

From the outside, the mall looked like a giant billboard, six storeys tall and covered in screens. Every square metre was advertising a product, a service or the mall itself, with most of the adverts animated, a chaotic mix of flickering neon and plasma delivering high-speed images into the eyes and brains of potential consumers. Many of the screens were cracked, showing distorted, fractured images, and most of the lower screens were partially obscured by graffiti or large handmade posters for local bands, unspecified 'services,' anti-establishment groups or garage sales.

There were regulations controlling the size, intensity and subject matter of adverts in public spaces. This mall's displays contravened most of them: as Rowain approached the building, one of the larger screens switched to a commercial for Brink's Red-Brown Harnesses, Extra-Max. She had no idea what that was, but the advert showed a smug-faced juve driving a car on public roads at a speed far in excess of any reasonable speed limit. *That's a fine right there*, she noted. *Eighty thousand dollars minimum for showing an illegal activity in a positive light. Could be a lot more depending on how long the ad's been running and how many people are likely to have seen it.*

As she watched, one of the larger screens switched to a local TV news channel that right now was showing a dark, blurry photo of Judge Deacon riding along Main Street on his Lawranger. The on-screen caption read, *Judges in St. Christopher! Justice for All, or Death of Liberty?*

She parked her Lawranger in a 'police only' bay close to the main entrance, attracting the attention of a mall security guard.

He strode angrily towards her until he spotted that she was a Judge, then abruptly shifted his focus and pretended to be angry at something else behind her. He passed her muttering something about "Damn kids..."

Inside the mall many of the stores were completely empty or had their shutters closed and locked, and of those that were still open, more than half were selling either cell phones or shoes. The air was warm and dry, laced with artificial lavender and jasmine—a familiar concoction that many mall-operators believed would keep the citizens calm but still alert enough to spend money.

It was busy, but not overwhelmingly so. Rowain deduced that most of the citizens were in the middle-income bracket, judging by their apparent focus and the number of bags they were carrying. The impoverished might flock to a mall like this when they've got nothing else to do on a cold winter's day, but they didn't have the funds to actually buy very much.

Her presence was noted almost immediately. By now, the rumours would have spread throughout the entire town that St. Christopher was getting a consignment of Judges, so those who spotted her didn't seem surprised, only guilty.

On the edge of her vision Rowain noticed a man who'd been selling cubic balloons casually sidling away from her, his colourful wares bobbing and spinning above his head and giving away his position. Heading in the opposite direction, and with the same far-too-casual manner, was a woman wearing a smock with the message, *Lonely? I Give the Best Hugs! One minute for only $30!* printed across the back.

An older man who spotted the Judge immediately after he'd casually allowed his hotpop wrapper to fall to the floor made a big deal of pretending to notice that the wrapper was no longer in his hand and then turning around to look for it and 'finding' it again with an audible sigh of relief.

It was all pretty much as Francesco Deacon had told her when she'd first signed up to become a Judge: "*You will never in your life see more polite, cheerful, decent, honest, hard-working people than when you unexpectedly show up where the middle-class citizens gather. The poor will shower us with curses, threats, saliva or bricks—often all four at once—and the rich will usually just ignore us, but the middle-income folk are the ones who think we're too dumb to notice their sweat-patches and badly-concealed expressions of blind panic."*

Another mall security guard was resting against a pillar close to the escalators, and as she approached him, the man's expression of boredom turned into one of surprise, then fear. He was about twenty-two years old, built like a linebacker and sporting what Rowain had always thought of as a 'shadow beard': facial hair that only seems to properly grow on the underside of the chin. He was at least fifty centimetres taller than her, and probably three times her weight.

Beads of sweat broke out on his forehead as Rowain stopped in front of him. He dry-swallowed and said, "What—?" in a high-pitched squeak. He quickly cleared his throat and composed himself. "Uh, sorry. What can I do for you, Judge?"

"I'm told there's a disturbance."

"Right. Look, no one was really hurt. Guy comes here every couple of months doing the same thing. He's not right in the head, see, and he has to let off some steam. Smashes up a few mannequins and maybe a window or two, but then when he sobers up, he always pays for the damage. The guys are just going to talk to him, calm him down. The cops know about this. I don't know why they thought they oughta bring a Judge into it."

"Where's the perp now?"

The guard nodded towards the escalators, "Next floor up, keep on straight until you see the signs for Sorrell's Entertainment Store. You get to Holoway's Holograms, you've gone too far. But..."

Rowain was already on the escalator. She looked back towards him. "But what?"

"Don't kill him!"

Rowain turned back, aware that everyone around her was staring. *Is that really what they think of us? That we're indiscriminate state-approved killers?*

As she stepped off the escalator, a young father scooped up his children and carried them away.

Part of her knew that this wasn't right. In an ideal world, the citizens would not be afraid of the law. But that ideal world was a dream, no more substantial than fog. The day Deacon arrived at Rowain's apartment and told her that he'd submitted her name to the Justice Department, he'd said, *"Lela, this country is not going to heal itself. Someone has to stand up and say, 'I'll do it. I'll devote my life to justice, to helping those who can't help themselves.' I think you can do it, Lela. I've known you all your life, I know you've got what it takes. You get through the assessments and the training, there's a spot for you on my team."*

Nearby, a nervous man staring at Rowain collided with an artificial tree. He automatically snarled at the tree that it should look where the hell it was going, then realised a Judge was watching and immediately apologised to the tree.

Rowain quickened her pace. Ahead of her, a pair of women clutching onto each other were backing away from a store. Citizens all around were muttering and pointing.

The word "Gun!" reached Rowain's ears, but she was already running, drawing her handgun at the same time.

"Clear the way!" Rowain shouted.

The first gunshot rang out and a plate-glass window shattered.

CHAPTER FIVE

ON HIS FIRST day as a military police officer, Deacon's commanding officer had told him, *"The hardest part of the job is informing someone that a loved one has died."*

The following day, Deacon had had to do just that: a young corporal had died in a training accident and Deacon had been given the task of informing her parents. He'd had a lead weight in his guts on the drive to the parents' house; he considered quitting on the spot rather than tell them their daughter was never coming home.

He'd found the process a lot less unsettling than he'd been led to expect. He'd remained composed as he explained to the corporal's parents what had happened and expressed his condolences, and half an hour later drove back to the military base feeling lighter and calmer. It wasn't long before some of his fellow MPs were asking Deacon to deliver the bad news in their place. One of them told him, *"It's not just that you don't mind doing it, Deac. You've got that air of... I dunno... authority. They know you're not lying; they can sense that even though you're not bawling your eyes out, you do sympathise and understand."*

But he never enjoyed delivering the bad news. He still always had that feeling of lead in his stomach.

Stavros and Benjamin Leandros were waiting for him in a small side-room at the mortuary, along with their mother, Captain Witcombe and two other women. The door was open and Benny looked out as Deacon approached, then pushed himself to his feet and nudged Stavros's arm.

They already know, Deacon thought. *They know it's her in there, but they still had a tiny spark of hope. Now I have to snuff it out.*

He stopped in the doorway and focused his attention on their mother. He would have recognised her as CJ's mother even if he'd just passed her on the street, the resemblance was so strong. "Mrs Leandros, I'm Francesco Deacon, Charlotte-Jane's supervising Judge and senior officer. It is my sad duty to inform you that I have formally identified the body of the deceased as your daughter Charlotte-Jane."

Mrs Leandros sobbed, covering her face, and one of the other women present put her arm around her shoulders.

Benny dropped back into his chair, and Stavros glanced back at the other woman—Deacon presumed she was his wife—before stepping up to Deacon. "You're certain?"

Deacon nodded. "I am truly sorry for your loss. Charlotte-Jane had the makings of an exemplary Judge, and I was honoured to train and serve with her. She was a good friend and a resourceful, reliable, good-natured colleague."

Stavros backed away, shaking his head. "Stop, please." He closed his eyes and took several deep breaths, then turned and pushed past Deacon, out into the corridor. "I want to see her."

Deacon caught up with him, grabbed his arm. "That's not necessary, Sergeant. Trust me. You don't want that to be your last memory of her."

Stavros bit his lip to stop himself from trembling, then quietly said, "I'm going to find the son of a bitch who did this and—"

Deacon put his hand on Stavros's shoulder and squeezed just hard enough to focus his attention. "Sergeant Leandros... You cannot be involved in this investigation in any way. You know that. I understand that she was your sister, but this is out of your hands. *We* will conduct the investigation, and you will step aside and do nothing to hinder it. Do we have an understanding here?"

"We do. But... I'm just saying that a lot of people in this town—cops or otherwise—are not going to let this lie. They're going to want payback."

"And *I'm* just saying that your anger is understandable, but if you or your brother or anyone else goes off book, we will consider that to be interference with an investigation. We do not take something like that lightly. Am I making myself clear?"

Sergeant Leandros nodded. "Yeah." He hesitated, then, a little calmer, repeated, "Yeah."

Captain Witcombe emerged from the side-room and stopped next to them. "Judge, the department will give you any help you need to find Charlotte-Jane's killer, but we won't get in the way. You have my word on that."

"I hope so. Because those who go looking for blood are very likely to end up spilling their own."

HENDERSON ROTZLER SAT in the police station's interrogation room being watched by a cop who could have shaved with a facecloth. Rotzler had a paper cup of coffee in his hands. It was no longer warm, but he held onto it anyway. "How much longer?" he asked the officer.

The man shrugged. "No idea."

"I could just go. I'm not under arrest, am I? I found her in my yard, and I called it in. That doesn't make me a suspect, does it?"

"Not to us," the officer said. "But the Judges are running this show. Who the hell knows what *they're* thinking?"

Henderson Rotzler had dealt with the cops many times before; trivial matters, usually. His dogs could be noisy at times and some folks didn't like that. But there were no neighbours within two hundred metres, so if the girls did get loud enough to bother them, there really was something wrong. Like last night, that body dumped in his yard. No way any of the neighbours were going to complain about that. And if they did, then the cops would surely make them understand, even if they *were* mostly city-folk.

Nearly everyone was city-folk nowadays, of course. When he was a kid, St. Christopher had been barely a village. You got one bus a day out of the town. There was no highway, so it took you the best part of a day to get to Boston if you didn't want to fly. But now it was sometimes hard to say where one city ended and another began. They were all merging into one. Pretty soon, satellite photos of the Eastern Seaboard would be a single mass of grey, without any of the green you used to see. Rotzler had heard that there were people who lived on the southern half of Connecticut who were running a campaign to get the state merged into New York just so they could claim to be New Yorkers.

Later, Rotzler would tell his friends that he had been just about to get up and leave when the Judge showed up—"Damn fascists keeping me waiting all day when I'm there to do *them* a favour!"—but the truth was that he was afraid of the Judges. He read the right websites, subscribed to the right magazines. He knew what was coming down the line.

The Judge was big, black, dangerous-looking. Rotzler didn't care about that—some of his friends, sure, they'd never be able to look a black man in the eye without feeling like something had been taken from them, but Rotzler had no time for that attitude. You were either an asshole or you weren't. The colour of your skin made not one damn difference to that.

The Judge dismissed the cop and sat down opposite Rotzler. When the cop lingered a little—he looked like he didn't know whether he should be taking orders from the Judge—Rotzler told him, "What's he gonna do? Arrest me for bein' a witness?"

"I'm Judge Deacon, Mister Rotzler," the Judge said. "Let's get all the facts down, then you can go. Henderson James

Rotzler, born 1962. Retired farmer. You've still got the farm, though?"

Rotzler scratched at his beard, wondering where this was going and why it was relevant. "I still own it, if that's what you're asking. Eighty acres. Sounds a lot, but it ain't worth a tenth of what most people expect. So I rent it out and I live on the edge of town now, just me and the girls. I mean, my dogs. Had to bring them to my brother's place this morning in case they disturbed the crime scene. And they don't like being left alone too long, so we need to keep this short."

"Tell me everything about last night's discovery of the body, Mister Rotzler. You called 911 at 23:56 from your cell phone."

"Sounds about right, yeah. I was asleep and the girls woke me up. I've got six German Shepherds. Five years old, all from the same litter. They went crazy. They sleep in the house, and I'd locked up the dog-flap because it was so cold last night. Otherwise, they'd be comin' and goin' all damn night long, letting in the freezing air. So last night they couldn't get out so, yeah, they woke me up, barkin' up a storm like there's someone out there. So I get my gun—I got a licence, you can check—and I go out. Don't see anything at first, so I get Bertha on her chain, 'cause she's the biggest, and she leads me right to the body. The woman was face down, naked, right next to the back wall. Someone had dumped her over."

"Your property backs onto Brock Lane... Does it get a lot of traffic?"

"No. Maybe there's five cars a day, on a good day. So I figure, see, that whoever it was killed her was local. They knew about my dogs. Threw the body over the wall thinking that the dogs would eat her. Destroy any evidence."

"That's a possibility I've considered. If the dogs had been free, do you think they *would* have eaten the body?"

Rotzler shrugged. "I don't know for sure. If she'd been a *prowler*, then yeah, they'd have torn her apart. Guy tried to break in eighteen months back and he's now got permanent scars on his hands, face and neck. The captain will've told you that, right? I wasn't prosecuted, and my girls weren't blamed for it. Punk knew the risks he was taking. But I'm thinking that whoever dumped your friend figured that the dogs would get to her. If they had, well, I usually got no reason to visit that end of the yard. She'd have been long gone before I found any sign of her."

"Your statement says that the body was still warm when you reached it?"

"Yeah, a little. I didn't *touch* her, though—there was some snow coming down, and it was melting when it landed on her. That's how I knew it was warm."

"You a detective on the side?" Judge Deacon asked.

Rotzler stroked his beard as he stared at the Judge. "Now I'm under suspicion because I'm trying to help? Figures. Am I done here, or do you want to arrest me on a charge of guilt by reason of proximity?"

The Judge took a deep breath and exhaled slowly. "Mister Rotzler, you'd want to put a lid on that attitude or I'll find myself wondering whether you've got licences for your dogs and whether the internal revenue know exactly how much money your land takes in rent. Did you see or hear anything unusual yesterday? Any people or vehicles in the area that shouldn't be there?"

"No. I'd have said." He shifted a little in his chair. "I gotta get back. The girls don't like being locked up in my brother's place for too long. They get antsy. You don't want to be around them when they're like that."

"You can go. We might need to question you again. If you're going more than ten miles out of town over the next few days, let them know at the front desk."

Rotzler was already on his feet and moving towards the door. "About time."

He didn't know whether he was supposed to say goodbye to the Judge: no one knew the rules yet. A police officer, you nodded hello if you passed them on the street, or maybe gave them a little steering-wheel wave when they ushered you through a checkpoint. You could go up to a cop and ask him for directions.

But Judges... he'd heard stories. Elisa Komorowski had told him that her friend in Stamford had approached a Judge to ask him the way to the bus station, and he'd fined her fifty bucks for wasting a Judge's time. And supposedly a Judge was allowed to shoot into the crowd if they were chasing a suspect: stopping the suspect took priority over the public safety. And there was that thing about the guns that Rotzler had read about online: if a Judge found you in possession of an unregistered firearm the chances were high he'd shoot you with it—in the arm or the leg—as a sort of warning. *You want to play with weapons, you damn well better understand exactly what they can do*, sort of thing.

Rotzler wasn't sure about that one. It sounded like scaremongering. The magazines he subscribed to warned about that, too:

> *The Powers That Be know how to play the system because they* wrote *the system—they* are *the system. You see some toothless twitchy hayseed on the news ranting about how the Mafia-funded 'guvmint' is putting mind-controlling fluoride or whatever in jet-engine contrails because they're obeying the wishes of their overlords, the Inner Earth aliens, well, you're not going to believe him. But then later you see a respected guy in a suit on TV telling you that public unrest is higher in cities that commercial jets don't fly directly over, then you're going to think, 'Yeah, yeah, chemicals in the contrails, heard it before.' And you dismiss it as nonsense. That's how they get away with everything: the truth* is *out there, but it's buried under a million tons of herrings and tape, all of them red.*

In the corridor, Rotzler passed the cops' break-room and saw another Judge—a woman—standing with her back to the door, looking out the window. Closer to the door two uniformed cops were sitting together, silently watching her. He moved on: it didn't pay to stare at officers of the law for too long.

For the past two years, Rotzler's magazines and websites had been full of 'What to do if...' lists. If a cop stops you on suspicion, and you know you're innocent, clam up until your lawyer gets there. Anything you say can be twisted around to sound like an admission of guilt. But if a Judge stops you, you tell him exactly what he wants to hear. Don't sass him, don't resist, and for the love of God, do *not* try to run.

There'd been a feature on the Judges in one of the magazines that went into great detail on their training. They were taught advanced marksmanship and five varieties of unarmed combat. Supposedly if a candidate couldn't run ten kilometres wearing all the gear, then they were kicked out. They had to be able to hit a bullseye at fifty metres eight times out of ten.

It was said that if you grabbed a Judge off the street, tied him up, blindfolded him and dropped him anywhere in the world armed only with a knife, then within a week he'd been kicking in your front door and arresting you for kidnapping.

The first rule of dealing with Judges was, apparently, 'Be afraid.'

CHAPTER SIX

JUDGE HAYDEN SANTANA said, "All right. This looks about the worst place we've seen so far. Pull over."

In the driver's seat beside him, Officer Chaplin said, "Not a chance."

"That's an *order*."

"Don't care. This is *Prospect Avenue*. You don't stop on Prospect, not in a cop car. On Prospect, you look straight ahead and don't catch anybody's eye and you say a prayer to Saint Michael that the scumbags around here don't get too curious and decide to track you down later at your own apartment and ask you why you were snooping around the area. Because that *happens*, Judge. Happened to Sergeant Leandros about three years ago. Ask him yourself if you don't believe me. Open the glove compartment. Go on, open it."

Santana popped open the glove compartment, and among the detritus that threatened to spill out was a bundle of photographs of a small terrier.

"That's Buster. He's the lost dog I'm gonna pretend I'm looking for if anyone in the Crush ever approaches me when I don't have backup."

"Well, today you're *my* backup." Santana tossed the photos back into the glove compartment and slammed it shut. "Stop the damn car, Chaplin."

Reluctantly, the officer pulled the car in to the side of the street and slowed to stop. "We might be okay. It's not even ten o'clock yet. And it's cold. This is probably the safest time to be here. A few hours and the junkies will be out sniffing around for their dealers. Only people out at this time are—"

Santana opened the car door and climbed out. He turned in a slow circle, taking in as much as he could.

Prospect Avenue ran through the heart of the Croft estate. The road itself was formed of cracked, stained, eroded slabs of concrete that had been hastily and shoddily repaired many times over. Right now, most of it was covered with large patches of grey, grit-filled slush. The road was bordered on each side by knee-high banks of filthy snow, the fallout of a single, hasty pass by a snowplough a few days earlier.

Every house in sight had boarded-up windows and bullet holes in the walls, front yards dense with dying weeds and long-since-discarded kitchen appliances.

Inside the car, Chaplin leaned over towards the passenger side and called out, "Told you. This whole area is a damn toilet. Now you've seen it first-hand, I hope your curiosity is satisfied. Get back in the car and we'll go somewhere we can actually do some *good*, okay?"

Santana pulled his datapad from his tunic's inside pocket and activated it. It showed his current location, and a few taps on the screen overlaid the image with information from the Justice Department's 'Offendata' program. "That house down the street... Number 872. Listed as abandoned. Scheduled for demolition four times, each time the paperwork has mysteriously disappeared. It's a suspected TranceTrance distribution node. Maybe even manufacturing. Why's it not been raided?"

"We never had actual *proof*. An informant said that someone else told her some guys were making TT in there, but we put surveillance on it and nothing moved for a week, so we had to let it go. To get a warrant, we'd need probable cause. There was a time when we'd just, you know, make like we heard someone in distress inside, so we'd bust in to 'save' them. But the lieutenant-governor's been a real hardcase about that sort of thing these past couple of years."

"Right. Get out of the car, Chaplin. And draw your sidearm. We're going in."

"Yeah... that's not happening, Judge. I bust in there without actual proof of wrongdoing or some other valid reason, I'll lose my job *and* get sued. I don't get paid enough for that."

Santana crouched down and peered in at Chaplin. "You either come with me, or you stay the hell out of my way, Chaplin. What's it to be?"

"What do you think? Going in there without, like, *twelve* other guys in full body armour is suicide!"

"Then stay here and keep your head down until I call you."

"Santana, it's not just whoever's inside that you have to worry about—they're going to be watching this place."

"Who?"

Chaplin shrugged. "Hell if I know. Whoever's running the gang. Guys with a lot more guns than we have, and a lot less paperwork if they *use* them."

"Keep your eyes open. You see them coming for me, feel free to shoot them." Santana straightened up and pushed the car door closed.

Keeping close to the rotting fences and sparse hedges as he slowly made his way towards the run-down house, he unclipped his radio. "Boyd, this is Santana... You there?"

Judge Boyd sounded like he was on his Lawranger on the highway. "I'm here. What's up?"

"About to enter suspected Trance hive... Unknown situation. Two exits, front and back. Could do with someone other than my cop buddy watching one door while I take the other. I'm on Prospect."

"I'm fifteen minutes away and heading in the wrong direction. You wanna hold off?"

"No, shouldn't be a problem. Catch you later."

The gate to 872 Prospect Avenue looked to have been broken and repaired many times, most recently with parcel tape and cable-ties, apparently by someone either working with only one hand or largely disinterested in the job. The house was a late twentieth-century model, single-storey, fully detached. All three windows at the front had been inexpertly boarded over and decorated with several years' worth of graffiti, mould, bird-droppings and cobwebs. But this close Santana could see that the front door was grey-painted metal, and it had been installed a lot more recently than the boards on the windows.

Santana pulled out his gun and opened the gate by applying his boot to its rusting hinges. Its cable-ties and tape snapped and it crashed loudly to the ground, and a man's voice somewhere inside the house said, "The hell was *that?*"

The Judge tossed a golfball-sized stun grenade towards the foot of the door as he darted around to the side of the house. From somewhere inside, a metal bolt was shunted back, then another. Santana held the grenade's remote trigger in his left hand, thumb hovering over the button.

Door now open, the man's voice said, "I'm not seein' anyth—"

Santana hit the button as he broke into a sprint towards the back of the house. The report from the front door rippled throughout the house, shuddering the walls and rattling the windows, and was followed almost immediately by a woman inside shouting, "It's a raid—get out!"

Ahead of Santana the passage along the side of the house was blocked by an old garbage can and a two-metre-high wooden gate. He heard something crash and break inside the house as he leapt onto the garbage can. Heard the back door crash open as he vaulted the gate.

He landed in a crouch close to the back wall and shouted, "Halt!" at the two barely-dressed young men desperately scrabbling barefoot across the rubble-strewn, snow-patched lawn.

They didn't halt—Santana hadn't expected them to. He opened fire, two shots, one in each man's left thigh. Before they'd even hit the ground Santana was on his feet, spinning, aiming at the back door.

A red-haired woman in stained pyjamas stood in the doorway, staring at him, hands clasped to her face. "Oh, thank god! They... They *took* me. Kept me locked up here!"

"On your knees!" Santana yelled, striding towards her with his gun aimed steadily at her face. "Right now! On your knees, hands behind your head!"

"No, you don't understand," the red-haired woman said. "I'm not *with* them—I'm their hostage!"

Santana shot her in the leg, then ignored her screams as he reached in, grabbed her by the arm and dragged her out into the yard. "Anyone else in there?"

"You *son of a bitch!* You *shot* me!"

"Told you twice to get on your knees. You didn't comply. Anyone else inside? Don't make me ask again."

"Just Gregor—he went to check out the noise out front!" The woman was sitting on the ground now, clutching her leg above the wound. "I told you I was a victim!"

Santana pulled a handful of steri-patches from his belt-pouch and tossed them to the woman. "Peel off the backing, slap them over the wound. One on each side. Do the same for your friends." He glanced back towards the two men and said, "Don't move!"

The door opened into the house's kitchen. It was dark, and stank of sweat, faeces, mildew, stale beer and the sickeningly-sweet tang of the raspberry-flavoured additive used to make TranceTrance a little more palatable for its users. The drug was an addictive and highly unstable substance that gave the user a three-hour high while suppressing many of their higher brain functions, rendering them highly credulous and unable to distinguish truth from lies. In recent months, dealers had taken to using TranceTrance in muggings: hit the target with an aerosol can modified to spray a powdered version, wait for the effect to kick in, then simply order the target to reveal their ATM number.

Holding his breath, Santana felt his boot sticking to the grimy floor as he kicked his way through a layer of detritus: old pizza boxes, rusting baked-bean tins, broken beer bottles and crushed cans, used adult-sized diapers and split garbage bags that had vomited their contents across the floor.

The doorway from the kitchen to the hall was missing a door. Santana stepped through and found a large, almost-naked man—presumably Gregor—lying on his back among the debris, moaning softly. There was a large kitchen knife tucked into the waistband of his underwear, and a Heckler & Koch P30 on the ground beside him.

The Judge grabbed the gun and the knife, then slapped a pair of cuffs on Gregor's wrists before quickly checking the other rooms. There was no one else, unless they were hiding inside one of the piles of garbage, which wouldn't have greatly surprised him. There was no TranceTrance-making equipment either, but there was a suspiciously large pile of cartons of the diarrhoea medicine Impasse.

He returned to the hallway, grabbed Gregor's wrists and dragged him back through the house, the process made a little smoother by something indeterminable but greasy smeared across the hall floor.

When he reached the kitchen, he briefly gave some consideration to Gregor's bare skin and the broken glass on the floor, but then decided that it had been the man's choice to live in such conditions.

Gregor was starting to regain consciousness when Santana dropped him on the ground next to the woman. He unclipped his radio and raised it to his helmet. "Dispatch, this is Judge Santana."

After a moment, a man's voice replied, "Okay... This is Officer Clarke. What can I do for you, Judge?"

"Catch-wagon and paramedics required at 872 Prospect Avenue. Four wounded perps, none critical. Minimum four years apiece for possession with intent to supply. Expect all sentences to be revised upwards once I determine what else they're guilty of." He strode across the yard to the two wounded men. One of them had landed face-first and was now lying on his side, moaning and clutching his blood-spattered nose. The other was slowly trying to crawl away, his wounded leg dragging uselessly behind him.

Officer Clarke said, "Uh, Judge, I know for a *fact* that the captain didn't authorise any action in that part of town. I mean, she's still out with the Leandros family, so..."

"I don't *need* her authorisation." Santana tossed a pair of cuffs to the ground beside the first man, then stared at the other until he glanced back, saw the Judge watching him, and stopped crawling. Santana threw a second set of cuffs towards him.

"Acknowledged, Judge. Backup and paramedics on the way to you. ETA five minutes."

"No backup required. Just a team to lock down this location, seize the evidence and treat the prisoners' wounds." He switched channels. "Chaplin, you still there?"

"I'm here, Judge."

"Location's secure. Pull the car up out front and make sure it's visible. We want anyone coming to hesitate before they rush in. Then come inside." Santana put away his radio as he looked down at the first man. "Cuffs go on your wrists. Do it."

Trembling, the young man picked up the cuffs with his blood-slicked fingers, dropped them, then scrambled to pick them up again. "I'm doin' it, I'm doin' it!"

"You or your friend armed?"

"No! No, I swear!"

"Because if I find out that you *are* armed, your sentence will be considerably shortened."

"I got a pocketknife!" the second man blurted, awkwardly fishing it out of his pocket. "But it's not a weapon—it's a tool!" He threw the knife off to the side.

Santana crouched down next to the first man and checked the cuffs. "Name and address."

"Honey Buccio. I live here, mosta the time. I mean, I'm really *Henry* Buccio, but everyone calls me 'Honey' because I sell the best... um..." His eyes grew wider. "I don't know why. They just do."

"And who's your pal over there?"

The second man shouted, "Don't tell him *nothin'*, Honey!" When Santana glanced in his direction, he added, "You too, Carmel! And I want my damn lawyer before I say another word."

Santana straightened up, looked from one man to the other, then walked back to the woman. "Interesting. Your friend here has just confirmed that you're not a hostage. I told dispatch that you're all getting four years minimum. But I'm a Judge: sentence is at my discretion. So that four years is a starting point. Rough guess, I'd say there's at least a thousand doses of TranceTrance in that house, disguised as Impasse pills. Divided by the four of you, that's two hundred and fifty doses each. Call it one month per dose. What's two hundred and fifty months come to in years? Any of you still got the capacity to do the math?"

Gregor, the man lying next to the woman, said, "Twenty-one years, almost."

"So you're back with us, Gregor. Yes, twenty years and ten months. Or... maybe one of you will tell me where I can find your boss. You know, next person up on the chain of command? Information like that, I might be inclined to *not* divide the TranceTrance doses evenly among you."

Honey Buccio said, "Wait, *what?*"

The woman—Carmel—snarled at him, "He means that whoever rolls on the boss gets a reduced sentence, and the others get their sentences increased." She looked up at Judge Santana. "He's kinda slow. Dropped on his head one time too many as a kid." Then she shrugged. "Or maybe it was one time too few. What do I have to do to just get off with a warning?"

"Go back in time and take a different path." Santana glanced towards the back door, where Chaplin was standing with his gun by his side. "Chaplin, what's the capacity of the town's jail?"

"Twelve. Fifteen at a push," Chaplin called back. "Got three in there at the moment, I think. But it's not a proper prison, just for holding."

"You recognise any of these creeps?"

He stepped out into the yard and pointed to the two men who had run. "Those two, they're in the system. Abusive childhoods and broken homes. Judge, we've been down this road before. We lock them up, their lawyer comes in making a big stink about how we've violated their rights. Doesn't matter if we found a room fulla dead baby *angels* in there, the arrest is invalidated and therefore we can't tie them to anything. Seventy-two hours max, they're back on the streets."

Santana looked from Chaplin back to the woman, and said, "It looks like you and I are the only two here who understand what's going on. You want to tell them, or should I?"

The woman rolled onto her side, then awkwardly sat up. To Chaplin, she said, "The arrest'll stick. He's a Judge. We don't get a lawyer. Our rights weren't violated, because *he* decides what rights we have. That's the whole point of Judges." She glared up at Santana. "Your cop friend here fires his gun even in self-defence, he spends the next week doing paperwork and then a month in therapy. *You* could execute everyone in this neighbourhood and there's not a damn thing anyone can do about it."

Santana nodded. "Exactly. Judges don't obey the law. The law obeys the Judges."

CHAPTER SEVEN

"ONE OF THE Judges got the house on Prospect," Niño Aukins told Mister Romley. "Arrested all four of our people there. Minor wounds only. And they're talking."

Romley's voice on the phone sounded calm. "How did the Judge find them? Someone else talk?"

"I don't think so," Niño said. "We couldn't track them too closely. Well, you know what it's like out there, all them wide streets. That's why we had the place there, to make it harder for the cops to tail us without us seeing them. But near as we can figure, the Judge—Santana, his name is—just picked the house pretty much at random. See, they can just enter a house for no reason and—"

"They don't need probable cause," Romley said. "I know that. What did they get?"

"All of our product destined for the north. That's thirteen hundred units. Twenty-five bucks a pop, that's thirty-two grand."

"I do know how to multiply, Niño. Where are you at the moment?"

Niño looked around the small diner. It was almost empty, with only one other customer tucked away in the opposite corner. He liked this place, but not enough to die in it. And he certainly didn't want Mister Romley's people shooting the place up as a warning. But you didn't lie to Mister Romley. If Mister Romley thought you were lying to him, he went very quiet and still, so still that you could almost imagine the air itself thinking, *Aw crap. Bad stuff is going to happen.* Niño took a breath to steady his nerves, then said, "I'm at Florentino's, Mister Romley."

"Order me a peppermint tea, would you? I'm about three minutes away. I think we need to talk strategy."

"Sure, yeah," Niño said. "See you in a few minutes." He ended the call and stared at the cell phone.

He's coming here. In public, in daylight. That means he's... what does it mean? That I'm safe? If he's planning to sacrifice me to the Judges, then he's not going to incriminate himself by being seen with me in public. That's got to be it. Sure. If he wanted me dead, I'd be dead already.

Niño lifted his head and glanced towards the counter. "Norma? Can I get a peppermint tea?"

The waitress looked at him as though he had just ordered a carriage-clock on toast. "What?"

"Peppermint tea. You've got peppermint tea, right?"

She chewed thoughtfully on her gum. "Yeah, we *got* it. Can't remember the last time anyone *ordered* it, though. You never have. You sure that's what you want?"

Niño almost told her that no, what he really wanted was to slink back home and take another hit. He didn't normally shoot up twice in the day, but this morning's shot was wearing off. He could feel himself starting to fray at the edges, and the real world was beginning to creep in. Heroin was his force field, his cosy, invisible bubble that no one else even knew existed. But it didn't last forever, and without it he felt exposed and uncertain. It was a harsh world filled with sharp edges and strident noises and people with grubby hands and lines of moist, dark crud under their chipped fingernails, and when they parted their too-wet lips to smile, you could see broken brown-and-black teeth for a second before their garlic breath washed over you and forced you to flinch and turn away. Every surface was cracked, or stained, or sticky. There was dust accumulating in the corners, and cobwebs in the shadows, and spiders on the edge of your vision and other things, too, that scuttled away a moment before you looked at them.

And there were memories, dark memories that just wouldn't stay hidden, and they were starting to bump up against the edges of his consciousness like bloated bodies rising through the mire and breaking the surface, moonlight glistening on their scarred, seeping backs, slashed with knife wounds that parted like mouths on the edge of a scream, and their words were blood and betrayal and death and decay—

Niño realised what he was doing and sat bolt upright. *Not now! Keep it together!* He took several deep breaths: in-out, in-out, in-out. *Stay focussed—if he sees you coming apart he's going to figure it out. If he does that, you're dead.*

"You all right, Niño?" Norma asked.

He forced a smile. "Sure, yeah. Sorry. Accidentally bit my tongue."

"Oh, *yeah*. There's nothing worse, right?"

"Absolutely," Niño said, still smiling. "Nothing worse than that."

CHAPTER EIGHT

Judge Rowain's footsteps echoed through Mayor Caroleen Omaha Mall as she approached the store where the gunman had taken hostages.

At least four of them, she figured. The mall's security people had told her they didn't know how to feed the store's CCTV footage to the local police server, so as yet she had no view of the store's interior.

A voice from the store—male, scared—yelled, "That's close enough!"

Rowain took one more step, then stopped. Three metres in front of her and slightly to her left, an eight-year-old boy was huddled behind a large concrete planter. He'd be safe there, Rowain was certain—even if the perp was using armour-piercing rounds, the walls of the planter were six centimetres thick, and there was a tonne of compacted dirt and sand keeping the palm-tree upright. But this was an opportunity, maybe.

She took another step, staring at the shopfront, keeping her hands well clear of her gun. "We've got a problem here," she called back.

"Damn right, we do! I said that's close enough! I swear on all the saints, pig—one more goddamn step and I'll open fire on these people!"

"I get you. I'm not coming any closer until you say it's okay." Rowain could see nothing but darkness inside the store: the perp had ordered someone to shut off the lights.

She'd stopped a mall security guard who was running away from the scene and forced him to tell her what was happening. From him, and a couple of the less-terrified witnesses, Rowain had learned that the perp had entered the electronics store to complain about a purchase, the transaction hadn't gone as well as he'd hoped, and he'd produced a gun.

Rowain had counted five shots, all from a revolver, but there was no way to know how many guns the man had brought with him. One of the witnesses had reported that at least one staff member—a man—had been shot: *"I hightailed it outta there minute I saw the gun, but I looked back when I heard the first shot—the one that took out the window—and then I saw him shoot the guy."*

The gunman was described as male, Caucasian, slender build, about thirty years old, red hair and beard. He'd entered the electronics store wielding a baseball bat and complaining loudly about being ripped off. The mall's security guards had shown up to take him away, and on the way to their office he had produced the revolver: *"He never had a* gun *with him before,"* Rowain was told. *"Coupla times a year he does something like this, but this is the first time he came* armed.*"*

She shouted into the store, "Look... I need you to hold fire for a second. I've got to come a little closer. Just as far as that planter. Can you see that? I'm pointing to it. There's a kid right behind it. You open fire, you might hit him. Now, whatever you've got going on, I'm sure you don't want to shoot a little kid. You don't want to be *that* guy, do you? You shoot a kid, then no matter how valid your grievance is, the public are going to hate you."

Rowain counted while she waited for a response.

At twelve seconds, the gunman said, "All right. Move slow. Get the kid out of there. You try anything and all these people die. Understood?"

"How many?"

"What?"

"How many people do you have in there?" Rowain asked. *Twelve seconds while he considered his options. He's not entirely over the edge yet.*

"What the hell difference does that make? One, a hundred... your job is to preserve life at all costs!"

"I've *got* to ask stuff like that," Rowain called, carefully walking towards the young boy. "It's in the regs. Sometimes situations like this are resolved peacefully, but only if there's a dialogue going on. You understand that, right?" She stopped in front of the wide-eyed boy, and looked down at him. "You okay?"

The boy nodded eagerly. "Are they gonna kill us?"

"Doubt it. I'm going to pick you up and carry you away, all right?"

"I can walk."

"I know. But my armour is bulletproof; if I carry you with my back to him, then you'll be protected." She turned again towards the darkened store and called, "We're ready. *You* ready?"

"Just do it!" the perp called back.

Rowain crouched down in front of the boy and scooped him up in her arms. As she straightened up, she turned around so that her back was to the store.

She was certain that the gunman wouldn't willingly open fire on her while she was holding the boy, but mistakes happen in situations like this, and those mistakes are often followed by an exchange of lead. Besides, it was important that anyone watching saw a Judge putting an innocent person's life ahead of her own.

As she carefully walked away from the planter, she watched her own reflection in the window of the store opposite—and the reflection of the darkened store. Still no sign of movement. "We're almost there," she told the boy. "You here with your folks?"

"My mom." He pointed off to the side, where a large group of citizens were huddled. "She's over there."

"Okay. I'm setting you down now." She lowered the boy to the ground and said, "Walk to your mom. Don't run. Just walk nice and steady. Keep your eyes on her, got that? Now go."

She watched as the boy calmly walked towards his mother, but—as she'd expected—he spent most of the journey staring back at the store.

Rowain walked back towards the electronics store and managed to get past the planter before the gunman inside ordered her to stop. Her boots crunched loudly on the broken window glass as she replied, "Sorry, what?"

"That's close *enough!* I swear, you're treating me like I'm some kinda moron and that pisses me off! Now I got five people in here who're gonna be chatting with Saint Peter pretty damn soon if you don't start showing some respect!"

Five hostages, Rowain thought. *Still no way to determine exactly where he is. Two religious references so far... that could just be coincidence.*

Through the darkness she could see vague silhouettes. All of the store's TV screens had been turned off, but not powered down: most of them had small red or green standby lights, and as she watched, a line of them vanished and reappeared in sequence: someone passing in front of them. She resisted the urge to use her flashlight—the gunman would not react well to that.

"So what do you want?" Rowain asked. "What's this about? What can I do to end this without anyone else getting hurt?"

"I'll *tell* you what it's about!" the gunman yelled. "It's about the big corporations trying to rip off the little guy! Not this time, sister! This time, they're gonna answer for it!"

"What did they do?"

"Sold me a TV last month, now it's broke and they won't honour the warranty!"

Another man's voice called out, "He threw a beer bottle at

the TV because he was pissed that the Chandra decided not to join up with Drake's army on *Priestess of Arax*!"

The gunman yelled, "Shut the hell up, Mulcahey!"

"Now he thinks we should replace the TV for him!"

Rowain took a step closer towards the door. "What's that TV cost?"

Mulcahey replied, "Seven ninety-nine."

"Eight hundred dollars?" Rowain asked. "That's all? The lives of all five human beings are worth eight hundred dollars to you? Well, seems to me a TV should be able to stand up to a beer bottle being thrown at it, so that means *you* sold him faulty equipment. Just give the man his new TV and we can all go home early."

"No, but—"

"That's an *order*," Rowain snarled, as she passed through the doorway. "I'm a Judge. You do what I say, Mulcahey. You can send a bill to the Justice Department, see if that does you any good, but in the meantime you'll stop being a dick and you'll either refund this man his eight hundred dollars or give him a new TV. Unless you want three years for obstruction of justice. Your choice."

The gunman's voice said, "See? You heard her."

Rowain yelled, "And someone turn on the damn lights so I can see who I'm talking to!"

The lights overhead flickered on. Rowain had already determined where the gunman was standing from the sound of his voice. Now, she was three metres directly in front of him with her gun pointed directly at his chest.

As the witnesses had described, he was thin, about thirty, red hair and beard. He was crouched behind a large display cabinet with three hostages behind him, and two more off to the side, one of them—a man—clutching his stomach. The gunman was pointing an old Smith and Wesson revolver at the floor. There was a baseball bat on the ground next to him.

"Drop the gun!" Rowain said. "You will *not* get a second warning!"

The gunman glanced briefly at the hostages, then back to the Judge. The gun in his trembling hand was slowly rising, swinging towards her. "But, no, you *said* they were in the wrong! We had a deal! They've gotta—"

Rowain pulled the trigger and the gunman toppled back into the three hostages behind him, a large hole in his chest.

She put away her gun and unclipped her radio from her belt. "Dispatch, this is Judge Rowain. Paramedics and a coroner required, Sorrell's Entertainment Store, Mayor Caroleen Omaha Mall. Send a clean-up crew, too." She crouched next to the wounded hostage and checked him over. He was conscious, though drenched in sweat. His breathing was steady but shallow, and he'd lost about half a litre of blood. She took a steri-patch from the med-pouch on her belt, peeled off the backing, and pressed it against the man's wound. "Keep steady pressure on it. Not too much. Paramedics are on the way."

One of the store's staff members—his name-badge identified him as Mulcahey, the man who'd spoken earlier—fell backwards as he tried to scramble away from Rowain. "Oh, my god... You... you just *executed* him!"

"I told him to drop the gun. Also told him there wouldn't be a second warning."

Mulcahey shook his head. "You could have wounded him instead—that was murder!"

One of the woman who'd been behind the gunman squirmed out from under him, her legs covered in his blood. "No, she did the right thing. He would have killed us!"

Rowain picked up the dead man's blood-spattered gun and baseball bat. She unloaded the gun and clipped it to her belt.

"No, he wouldn't," Mulcahey said. "He fired five times, and that's a *revolver*. See? He only had one round left."

"There was no way she could know he didn't have another gun," the woman said. She approached Rowain, her hand extended. "You saved our lives."

Rowain nodded an acknowledgement, but ignored the woman's hand. She turned towards the doorway, where two of the mall's security guards—the shadow-bearded man she'd met when she'd arrived, and a slender woman—were cautiously peering in, Tasers in hands. With the baseball bat over her shoulder, Rowain beckoned them closer, and said, "I was told that you people were taking him into custody: I want to know how he got away from you, and why he had a gun. And lock this place down until the police show up."

The female security guard said, "Yeah... Well, I don't recognise your authority. I didn't vote for President Gurney and I sure as hell don't agree with him giving your boss Fargo complete control of the country's law enforcement. So you'll understand when I tell you to go and take a flying—"

"Drop the Taser," Rowain said. "Won't tell you a second time."

The woman's colleague started to back away. "Do it, Hazel! Didn't you just see what happened in there?"

Her eyes narrowed. Still holding onto the Taser, she said, "Yeah? She wants my Taser, she's gonna have to pry it from my cold, dead ha—"

Rowain swung the baseball bat, slamming it hard into the woman's forearm. Bones cracked and the Taser dropped to the floor.

The woman staggered back, face pale as she cradled her arm. "You goddamn—!"

"Threatening a Judge," Rowain said. "But it's my first day, so I'll let you off with a warning." She turned to the woman's colleague. "I take it *you* have no problem recognising my authority?"

The bearded man threw his Taser to the ground and backed away, arms raised. "Oh, yeah. No problem. You're the boss."

Rowain sighed and rolled her eyes. "Pick up your weapon. *You're* not in trouble."

As the man nervously and awkwardly reached for the Taser, Rowain became aware of a dozen faces peering in at them, citizens curious enough about the Judges to risk coming closer. Many of them were holding up cell phones, and Rowain knew that within the hour pretty much everyone in the town of St. Christopher would have seen her break the rent-a-cop's arm.

Not the first impression she'd wanted to make.

CHAPTER NINE

In the back yard of the house on Prospect Avenue, Carmel, Gregor, Honey Buccio and the fourth perp—Santana still didn't know his name; but then he hadn't asked—were competing to see which of them could spill the most beans about their employers.

Honey insisted that TranceTrance was manufactured up north, somewhere in Massachusetts. Gregor was sure it was in Southbridge, and the fourth perp was certain that the manufacturers had a farm much further north, probably in Spencer.

Officer Chaplin said, "Over state lines. Makes it a federal case. We've got to get the DEA involved." He looked relieved.

"We don't," Santana said. "The rules have changed."

"Right. So... What, we're going after them? Because *you* might be allowed to go outside the state without permission, but we're not. I'd get fired for sure."

"We're not going north."

"So what are we doing?"

"This place is just a distribution node, but the packages inside are very fresh. The glue's still tacky on some of the boxes. That tells me the manufacturers are here in St. Christopher. Exactly where is going to be hard to pin down. These creeps... at their level they get told different stories to make it hard to track down the real bosses."

Honey Buccio said, "That's not true! I'm right about where they make it—I was there!"

Santana shrugged. "No, you weren't. You're looking *up* at the lowest rung on the ladder, Buccio. But maybe you'll give me the name of your distributor and—if you're right—I'll take... a year off your sentence."

"Make if ten years."

"Eleven months. Want to keep haggling?"

Then the woman, Carmel, said, "Judge... You let me go without charge and I'll give you everything. *Everything*, you get me? See, I've been keeping a journal. I've got full details on all the names, dates, locations and products for the past four years and five months. I know who's manufacturing and who's behind them. Big names. Important people. Names you'll maybe recognise. Every customer, every dealer..." She glanced at Officer Chaplin. "Every *cop* who has a price for looking the other way. And *their* bosses who take a cut of that."

Santana ignored Chaplin's protests, remembering something Judge Deacon had told him in the early days of their training: *"The biggest enemy we're going to face won't be the thugs on the streets. It'll be the establishment. The cops, the lawyers, the politicians, the judges. A lot of them are very comfortable right now and we're going to screw up their lives in a big way. They're the ones we have to worry about."*

Chief Judge Fargo had said the same thing a week ago, as Santana and the other cadets at the Boston Academy prepared for their final assessments. *"It'd be nice to think that all cops are law-abiding, but that's a fool's game. There are bad cops— there will be bad Judges, too; we'll deal with that later—and even the good ones are going to resent us. That's to be expected. Don't punish them for that. A little... latitude will go a long way. But be sure you know where to draw the line. If a cop's going easy on the local juves because he believes a soft touch is better than a heavy hand, then he's wrong, but that doesn't make him corrupt. But if he's getting something in return for looking the other way, you come down on him hard. You hit him like a ton of bricks and you keep damn hitting him until he and everyone else around him knows the score."*

Justice Spender J. Gant had made almost the same arguments. The two men were united in the belief that the current regime must change, but almost diametrically opposed as to what should replace it.

Santana had only met Gant a couple of times, back when Santana was a lawyer specialising in personal injury claims and Gant had still been a travelling judge on a local circuit, visiting small towns for one day every couple of weeks to deal with small claims and local matters.

HAYDEN SANTANA'S CLIENT was Edmond Jarrell, a waste of carbon he'd known since they were in middle school. Jarrell was making a claim against a local barbershop. The barber, Sylvester Mousseau, had allegedly sneezed while using an electric razor to trim Jarrell's neck-hair; his arm had jerked and the razor skidded up the back of Jarrell's head and given him what Santana had referred to as a "reverse mohawk."

Santana's letter to Mousseau's solicitors stated, *My client had been having his hair trimmed in anticipation of a job interview the following day. The unwarranted and careless actions of your client caused such mutilation to my client's appearance that he had no choice but to cancel the interview. Consequently, that job was awarded to another party.*

Santana was pretty certain that Jarrell could get a decent settlement. Punitive damages seemed unlikely, especially given that the two eyewitnesses were on the defendant's side: they were going to testify that the barber had not sneezed, and in fact Jarrell had deliberately jerked his head backwards against the razor. Jarrell was known for trying to scam his way out of paying for services, and it was clear to everyone that he'd hoped to get a slight nick from the razor and then complain long enough that the barber would just let him go without charge. Maybe even throw in a free comb. But the deep, straight-edged furrow in the back of Jarrell's head looked like a gift from the gods.

"We can win this," Santana told him. "But you've gotta play it right, Edmond. Get me? No getting drunk over the next few days and bragging about the money you've got coming. You're a *wounded man*, yeah? You had a chance for that big interview— yeah, I *know* there wasn't really an interview, I'll fix that for you—and it was snatched away from you by the barber's carelessness. Now, it's just a pity he doesn't drink. If he'd been drinking on the job, or even just drinking the night before, then maybe we could be looking at reckless endangerment and that's where the big bucks are. As it is, I reckon we're looking at somewhere about fifteen or sixteen grand. We're going to ask for fifty, but we'll never get that. My fee is two thousand dollars or forty-five per cent, whichever is larger. Now, just to be clear, that means that if you only get two grand, *all* of that goes to your lawyer, do you understand that?"

"Sure, yeah," Jarrell said.

"Edmond, it also means that if you're awarded two thousand and one dollars, you only get one dollar."

"Yeah, I *get* it, Hayden. I'm not a moron."

Santana leaned back in his chair, and looked at his client for a second. Back in middle school, Jarrell and Santana had moved in different circles. Hayden Santana had been top of his class in pretty much everything, while Jarrell had hovered around the middle, never showing any real interest or potential in anything other than not being in school. "Ed... Sorry to stick with this like a dumb dog who won't let go of the tennis ball, but you do know that I don't win every case, right? No lawyer does. We might not win this one."

"I know that."

"Okay. So, bearing in mind all that I've said so far about my fee, I need you to tell me what happens if we lose, or if the judge throws out the case."

"We get nothing."

"Hmm..." Santana said. "Not *quite*. My fee is...?"

"Two grand. Yeah, but, y'know, I don't *have* two grand, so..." Edmond Jarrell shrugged. "Can't pay you what I don't have, Hayden, can I?"

"You'll still owe me. Ed, we've known each other a long time, so I'm not going to hunt you down or anything like that. I'd be happy for you to pay me twenty-five bucks a week until we're clear, but it won't come to that if you keep your mouth shut and play the victim right."

Hayden Santana had known, from his first semester in law school, that he was never going to be a great lawyer. He knew the law—knew it better than most—but he didn't have the tenacity or the interest to spend days at a time arguing tiny points of law with people in slick suits who didn't care any more for their clients than Santana did for his.

He'd worked out the figures, once: he won about three out of every seven cases. He had learned very early in his career to keep quiet about the losses and shout from the rooftops about the wins. Now, Santana had thirty-two losing clients paying him back twenty-five dollars every week, and most of them were thankful to him for being so understanding. He was coasting, he knew, but that was fine. He'd worked long enough and hard enough to get here. He deserved to be able to kick back for a while.

And then Edmond Jarrell's case reached the courtroom, and Justice Spender J. Gant was assigned.

Santana thought it was going pretty well, right up to the moment Gant cut across the defence lawyer's questioning of one of his witnesses.

"I've heard enough," Gant said. "Seriously. We're done here. The court finds in favour of the defendant."

Santana began, "What—" but Gant wasn't done.

"Mister Jarrell, it's clear to me that you're a greedy, lazy, unscrupulous man in search of a handout at someone else's expense."

Santana jumped to his feet shouting, "Objection! My client is not on trial here, and such comments are inflammatory, derogatory and—"

"You want to know what's wrong with America, Mister Santana?" Gant glared at him. "*You* are. You, your client and people like you. You *know* that this man is lying, and you're helping him do so. If you'd had even an *ounce* of decency, you'd have instructed him to abandon the lawsuit and pray that the defendant didn't counter-sue. But you're just as greedy as he is. This country is overrun with cancerous, opportunistic scum like you getting a free ride on the letter of the law while pissing on its spirit. Your kind are bleeding this country dry, growing rich on the misery of others when in many cases it would cost you *nothing* to alleviate that misery. What does that make you, Santana?"

Fists clenched to stop his hands from shaking, Santana said, "Judge Gant... all of this is on record. As a lawyer I feel obliged to advise you to desist. These are actionable words."

"I know the law, Santana, trust me. And yes, I know that I could be reprimanded or even disbarred... but I've had enough." He tossed the file containing his notes on the case into the air. "This is garbage. A mockery of the intent of the law. People like you and your client have turned the American legal system into a goddamn nightmare. Someone gets hit by a car, the driver's uninsured because she can't afford insurance, the victim sues her but if she can't afford insurance, she damn well can't afford the settlement, so she goes bankrupt, the victim can't pay his hospital bill so *he* goes bankrupt, and the hospital raises its prices to cover its losses, and everyone loses. Everyone but the lawyers." Gant pointed to Jarrell. "You. Did you deliberately push your head against the razor in order to avoid paying the barber the fifteen dollars your haircut should have cost? Simple question, Mister Jarrell. Yes or no. Be a goddamn *grown-up* and tell the truth."

Jarrell nodded, unable to look anyone in the eye, and at the moment Hayden Santana knew that this would be his last day as a lawyer.

But Gant still wasn't done. "In case some of you haven't heard, last month, in Washington, Eustace Fargo announced that the president has given the go-ahead to his plan for a new taskforce. It's... a tragedy. Fargo's plan goes against everything our forefathers fought to build. People like *you* brought us to this point, Mister Santana. You've treated the pockets of the poor like your own personal piggy bank. You've committed unconscionable acts, not because they were right, but because they were *legal*, and you are apparently ignorant of—or indifferent to—the distinction. Fargo's Judges will roll over this country with an iron fist and I've no doubt that eventually they *will* bring about a form of peace, but at what cost, Mister Santana? At what cost?"

Santana shook his head. "Your honour, I don't—"

"Liberty. That's the price of justice, and in Fargo's eyes it's a good deal. But not in *my* eyes. I intend to fight him on this, to prove that the old way can and will work... but *that* can only happen, Santana, if lawyers like you start working for the people instead of for yourselves. It's an idealistic notion, you might argue, but the alternative is the jackboot."

Santana spent that night at home, alone, ignoring the phone calls from colleagues and reporters and everyone who wanted to know whether he was going to officially report Spender J. Gant for his behaviour.

He was up and dressed again before dawn. He walked across town to the small boarding house where Gant was staying, and found the judge at breakfast.

"Hayden Santana. You look like you slept about as well as I did," Gant said, peering at him over the rim of a coffee cup. "I don't regret a word. I was right, and you know it."

"You're *mostly* right, Judge Gant, I'll give you that. You're—what—forty-three? Young for a judge, but not old enough to have accumulated a nice retirement package. You could lose everything."

"What kind of a judge would I be if I was living in fear? I told you yesterday that we should be working for the *people*, Santana. Not for ourselves, like you do, or for the state, like Eustace Fargo and his brown-nosers. Without the support of the people we are nothing but dictators. This country is falling apart—anyone can see that. The hyperactive, omnipresent, liberal media has turned the cops into cowards too scared to even chase after a crook, in case he sues them for violating his running-away rights, or whatever. We've got lawyers like you only interested in lining their pockets while claiming to uphold the law. Well, there's a canyon between the law and justice, and we're all trapped in it. Every single one of us. Anyone tries to climb out of that canyon and stand on the higher ground, there's a hundred jerks like you who'll drag them back in."

Santana nodded slowly. "You done? Because I just came over here to tell you I'm quitting. You're right, in some ways. But America's problems won't go away just because we all decide to play nice. We've got to play *hard* first. We beat the problems into submission, and *then* we get to be the nice guys."

Gant sighed. "Santana... You're not getting it. If I'm to oppose Fargo, I'm going to need people like you on my side. I thought I was getting through to you, but you sound like *him*."

"That's what I was aiming for. I'm going to sign up with the Justice Department. I know the law, I can fire a gun, I keep myself in shape. I can do it."

Gant lowered his coffee cup and pushed his chair back. "I'll say this, then, and no more. You've got a spark in you, Santana. I can see it. With the right guidance, you could be leading the team I need to take down Fargo once and for all. You side with him, he'll snuff out that spark and turn you into just another mindless storm trooper. Think on this from time to time, will you, while you're out there trampling on people's rights? Give it a moment's consideration and understand that you're not saving anyone by becoming a Judge. You're just pushing us deeper into the pit." He turned and walked away.

Santana called after him, "I thought you said it was a canyon."

Without turning back, Gant said, "I'd tell you to go to Hell, Santana, but we're all already there."

CHAPTER TEN

"SHE DIDN'T EVEN make it back here," Sergeant Stavros Leandros said to Judge Deacon.

Deacon was standing in what had once been Charlotte-Jane's bedroom. Now it was piled high with cardboard boxes and plastic crates. A single mattress was propped up next to the window, leaving just about enough space on the floor to lay it down.

The sergeant was standing in the doorway, watching the Judge. "When she left for Boston, she told Mom that she could do what she liked with her room." He shrugged. "CJ's like me in that regard. We're not sentimental about stuff. Ask my wife: a month after we tied the knot, she gave me hell when she caught me throwing out the wedding cards. Benny, now, he's the sentimental one. Mom talked about redecorating *his* room—this was about four years ago—and Benny went nuts. Sulked for weeks. He moved out nine years ago."

Deacon turned on the spot. No posters that he could see, no cute ornaments hanging from the ceiling or stickers on the back of the door. "Where's all her stuff?"

"She gave most of it away before she left. Like I said, she wasn't that kind of person. Didn't hang onto things. Judge, what did you expect to find in here?"

"Nothing. But your mother and brother are still in shock and it's important for them to believe that something is being done." Deacon regarded Stavros for a moment. "*You* don't seem to be in shock. Your only sister has been murdered. I'd expect more of a reaction."

"I know... This is how I am. Ask anyone. It'll hit me later. A few days, maybe. Same thing happened when Dad was killed. I'll do what needs to be done and *then* I'll grieve. I'm not going to go to pieces; it's not going to help anyone."

"Pragmatic," Deacon said. "So, where would you start?"

The bedroom door was pushed open, and Detective Morrow entered. "Start right here in town. Sorry, I've been listening."

Stavros said, "There was no one in town who had a problem with CJ. Not that I know of. All her life, she mostly did her own thing. A few friends, no one too close."

"Boyfriends?" Morrow asked.

"Same thing. I don't know, maybe it was *their* decision not to get close to her. That can happen when you've got three cops in your immediate family and five more among the aunts, uncles and cousins." To Deacon, he added, "I guess you know that, too, right?"

Morrow raised an eyebrow. "You've got family on the force, Judge?"

"One of the others is his cousin," Stavros said.

"This is not about me," Deacon said, "but I acknowledge that you're letting me know you checked me out." He looked around the room once more. "Sergeant, we have almost nothing to go on here. No trace of DNA on her body, no murder weapon, no scene of death, no witnesses, and apparently no motive other than that she was a Judge. And even *that's* not much more than an assumption."

The detective asked, "Anything on the satellite feeds?"

"The trees at the scene obscure any overhead visuals. I've requested data from further satellites that might have picked up something on the periphery. Should be coming through in the next couple of hours, but I'm not pinning too many hopes on that." Deacon peered behind a pile of boxes, more out of habit than anything else. "Sergeant Leandros, your sister left your office a little after twenty-one-hundred last night, and three hours later her body was discovered by Henderson Rotzler. So what time was she taken? What did she do before that?"

"None of her friends knew she was coming home. She couldn't tell anyone—she wanted it to be a surprise for Benny's birthday, and she didn't trust them to keep their lips sealed. She didn't even tell *Mom,* just in case something happened, like she got reassigned at the last minute." His eyes narrowed as he peered at the Judge. "You knew she hadn't told us, didn't you?"

"I did. When I was assigned to St. Christopher, I already knew that Leandros had grown up here, but that's not why I chose her for the team. I chose her because she was one of the best. She complemented the team well."

Morrow said, "And now she's dead. Maybe now you're thinking that if you'd picked someone else, she'd still be alive? Because *I'm* sure as hell thinking that."

Deacon ignored that. "Sergeant, I'm told that she argued with you and Captain Witcombe before she left your office."

"What, so *we're* suspects now?"

Deacon stepped closer to him. "Sergeant, if you're genuinely surprised that you're a suspect, then you'd be too stupid to be in the police force in the first place, so don't play that role."

"I didn't do it, and you know that, Deacon. And neither did Virginia. I mean, Captain Witcombe." He pointed towards the window. "She and Harvey are like family. We grew up with them. They used to live right across the street, before Harvey got his fancy office job and they were able to afford the place in Colton. But there's nearly thirty thousand other people in this town and most of them don't want the Judges taking control. Any one of them could have done it. Maybe it was even one of your own, a supporter who figured that taking one of you out would be enough to prove that the Judges really *are* needed. You think of that?"

"Of course." Deacon pushed past Leandros and out into the hallway. "Stay here with your family, Sergeant. I'll liaise with Captain Witcombe and keep you posted on any progress. Detective? A word outside, please."

As he passed the doorway to the sitting room, Morrow and the sergeant behind him, Deacon glanced in and saw Mrs Leandros sitting with Benny. Both were pale and unmoving.

A smartly-dressed woman was sitting opposite them.

"That's Marisa Pellegrino," Sergeant Leandros said. "One of your lot. A grief counsellor."

The woman nodded towards Deacon, and raised her cell phone a few inches from her lap. He returned the nod, and kept going.

At the front door, Stavros said, "I don't care for the idea of Judges. I think it's twisted, and very dangerous, but I'm setting that aside for now. You find out who killed my sister, and make them pay."

Judge Deacon opened the door. "They'll get the appropriate punishment, Sergeant." He stepped out onto the snow-covered steps.

Morrow followed him out and pulled the door closed after her. "So what are your thoughts, Judge?"

"Give me a couple of seconds here." Deacon slowly looked around. A few neighbours were out, huddled in groups of three or four, and he figured they were keeping their distance but letting the Leandros family know they were there, just in case they were needed. He liked that. It reminded him of his neighbourhood back home in Queens, before the gangs scared everyone off the streets and behind locked doors.

The sun was a few degrees above the horizon in an almost cloudless blue sky, and the air was crisp. He could hear the constant rumble of traffic on the interstate several kilometres away. Somewhere nearby a bird chirped enthusiastically.

Life goes on, and the world keeps spinning, Deacon told himself, as he frequently did in situations like this.

It was almost noon. Twelve hours since the body of Judge Charlotte-Jane Leandros had been found, and devastating as that discovery was to her family, friends and colleagues, most of the world would never know or even care.

But somewhere out there, Deacon knew, one person certainly knew and cared. He would find that person, and it was going to take every ounce of Deacon's self-control not to bludgeon them to death with his fists.

"That's more than a couple of seconds," Detective Morrow said. "Judge... We're coming up empty here. Not one reported seeing your colleague after she left the station last night. The station's own CCTV shows her turning left out of the parking lot and that's it. We put out a call for dashboard camera footage from anyone driving through town last night. We've got fourteen responses so far, but there's nothing even remotely useful. Your bikes are tagged, right? I'm assuming that you traced her GPS signal?"

"It went offline four minutes after she left the station. That's not unusual in itself: even passing under a steel bridge can disrupt the signal. They're still ironing out the bugs in the system." He glanced back at the house once more. "Stay on it, Morrow. Keep me posted."

THE CALL FROM Marisa Pellegrino came through as Deacon was riding back through town towards the station.

"I see you're a counsellor today, Ms Pellegrino."

"*That's* where we are now, Francesco? Formalities?"

He suppressed a smile. "Right. You got my request for a particle harvester?"

"Delivered it to Doctor Abramson myself. I swear she almost giggled when she unpacked it. I've never seen anyone so excited to be able to gather up grit."

"Well, I hope it turns up something, because right now we're looking at dead ends. Anything on your side?"

"Nothing useful. Your Judge's mother had no idea she was even in town until her sons broke the news to her this morning. That can't have been easy."

"And what are *you* doing here? No, let me guess. Fargo heard what happened, sent you to watch us."

"To observe the case and help out where needed, yes. Francesco, he asked me to tell you not to expect a replacement for Leandros for a week at least. We're turning out the cadets as fast as we can, but we're still massively underfunded and, well, it's not a process that we want to skimp on. You understand that as much as anyone."

"I do. What sort of mood was he in when you spoke to him?"

"Someone murdered a Judge—what you *think?* He's put a gag on the big media outlets for now, but that won't stick for more than another hour, at most. And St. Christopher is close enough to both Boston and New York that the journalists will probably feel it's worth the trip. Nice juicy story like this... If the weather holds out, you're going to be swamped."

Deacon slowed his Lawranger as he neared a four-way junction. "I figured that. What sort of a distraction can you manufacture?"

"We've got a potential bomb scare scenario in Boston that should work well, but I don't want to squander that one unless we have no choice. You need to start making *progress,* Francesco. Justice—"

"Justice must be seen to be done. I know. I'll keep you posted."

NIÑO'S PHONE BUZZED in his jeans pocket; he had to lean way back in his seat to fish it out. He glanced at the screen and his heart sank. "It's Nodge. He says that the Judge who busted the house on Prospect is on his way out to the plant. Riding slow, making a lot of turns, but that's where he's heading."

Sitting opposite him, with his elbows on the table as he held a cup of peppermint tea to his lips, Mister Romley said, "I see."

"We should do something!"

"Not much we *can* do, right now," Romley said. "We don't have time to pull everyone out and hide the stock. And even if we did, an empty factory, clearly very recently used—the equipment still warm and free of dust? No, we let them have this one. The Judges can pat themselves on the back for the find, and then maybe they'll go bother someone else."

"That stock is worth *millions*, Mister Romley. You're going to just sit back and watch while the Judges cart it away?"

"What options do I have, Niño? We don't even have time to *destroy* the stock, never mind get it out. We let the Judges have it, then maybe there'll be a way we can take it back from them later."

"But... I've got my guys out there. I want to pull them out."

Romley shook his head.

Niño watched him for a moment, then braced himself and said, "Okay. I'm... I'm going to ask again, and I want you to know that I do respect your decision, but I have *reasons*. Is that all right?"

"Let's see where you go with this. Go ahead."

"My guys are Shiraz Castro and Rafe Carfey and Wan Gaimaro. You've seen them around the factory. You might not know their names, and they don't know who you are, but *I've* known them for years. I trust them like, well, as much as I hope you trust me. I can't throw them away. I mean, aside from the fact that they could give me up—though they *wouldn't*, I'm sure—we've invested a lot in them. We don't have to lose them. Pull them out and put someone else in their place."

Romley shook his head again. "No. The Judges will be able to tell. If they believe all they have is pawns, they'll widen their search. We'll throw them a couple bishops, placate them long enough for us to cover ourselves."

"Well, look, what if we can take the Judge out? I mean, I know *our* guys probably aren't up to it, but you've gotta know people who can do it."

Romley shrugged. "Same problem. Actually, no, worse. Killing a Judge is a bad move, and they've already lost one today. We're just going to have to sacrifice our people in the factory. All of them, including your friends. None of them can name me, and even if they could, they're not going to. They'd have to be insane, or suicidal. They know that. I don't recruit idiots."

Niño said, "Yeah, but you recruit junkies and Trance-heads," and immediately regretted it. "Sorry."

Romley closed his eyes and sipped at his peppermint tea. "You're right. It's not the dumb ones I need to worry about, it's those who think they can outsmart me." He opened his eyes again, and smiled. "You know, you should never be afraid to say what's on your mind. You're one of my most trusted people. I'm not going to have you executed just because you tell me something I don't like."

"I know that," Niño said, but didn't look Romley in the eye, because they both knew the other was lying.

"Who's our weakest link out of the Prospect crew and the factory, and everyone working closely with them? Who's most likely to make a deal with the Judges?"

Niño used his thumb to push crumbs around the table while he considered that, and tried not to think of his room at Lisbeth Harradine's boarding house. "Gregor is the weakest link. He *thinks* he runs Prospect, but he's only there because he's bigger and meaner-looking than anyone else. He doesn't even know you exist, and he thinks that I'm just an errand-boy; it probably wouldn't even occur to him to turn me in. Gregor answers to Rafe Carfey, and *he's*... Well, he can be pretty unstable under pressure, but I swear he's genetically incapable of talking to cops, *or* Judges. He comes from a pretty hardcore family. You know those psycho survivalists out in the mountains? His old man is their leader—Rafe's kinda their agent in the real world, I guess. Deals with stuff like mail and bank accounts and organises supplies and keeps the tax man away. No, I figure that *Carmel* is the one we need to worry about. She's smart. She's still a user, but she's careful about it. She knows what she's doing, when it's safe to use."

"What does she know about me?"

"Nothing, far as I know. She knows me, but only vaguely. I think I met her, like, three times. Never spoke to her for more than a minute each time. I don't think she knows who I really am. You know, in relation to you. Could be she thinks *I'm* the big boss, for all I know. But she's the sort who notices things, you get me? Like she's filing everything away in case it comes in useful some day."

Niño felt pleased with that answer for about ten seconds, then Mister Romley carefully set down his cup.

"I see. So... *You* are the only solid link between the factory and me. You've dug yourself an interesting hole, Niño. Now, give me a reason why I shouldn't have you removed from the equation to protect myself. Take your time. This is a big moment, after all, and I wouldn't want you to feel rushed."

Niño stared down at his hands. Hidden in his room in the boarding house was an old cigar box and in that box was everything he needed. *No! Focus!* He realised his palms were flat on the table, pressing down hard. He pulled them away and watched as the condensation outlines slowly faded. *Fingerprints*, he thought. *The whole damn* factory *is covered in my prints, and the cops have me on file.*

He briefly glanced up at Romley. *But he's at the factory a lot, so his prints are there too. Never wears gloves. So his prints are there and I could go to the Judges and offer him up in exchange for immunity.*

Unless...

Niño swallowed. He thought back to that morning, when he met Mister Romley at the factory, looking down at the workers. Romley had had his hands in his pockets. *Yeah, but... But he had to get out onto the gantry and the door... No, the door opens* out. *He could have pushed it with his shoulder. And when we were going back to the stairs, I held the door open for him.*

He tried to remember the last time he saw Romley actually touch something in the factory with his bare hands.

Aw, crap.

Aloud, Niño said, "I wouldn't betray you. I'm more scared of you than I am of the Judges. All *they* can do is lock me up."

Mister Romley nodded slowly, smiling. "Good answer. Consider yourself off the hook, for the moment. So what do you think we should do about Carmel?"

Niño realised his mouth had gone dry. He had never been so thirsty, and the urge to take a piss was almost overwhelming. That bothered him. *How can the human body have such an urgent need for liquid and be so desperate to get rid of it at the same time?* But a part of him knew it wasn't a drink that he needed. *One hit. That's all. Maybe I forgot this morning? That would explain it. I forgot and... No, I didn't forget. I never forget. Can't leave the house without my fix. But I'm not a junkie. I just need something to get me started, sometimes. I'm not like the scum you see slumped in the alleyways, frozen to death with one sleeve rolled back and a needle sticking out of her arm, and then another lowlife comes along and pulls the needle from the dead woman's arm and uses it himself in the hope that there's even the tiniest trace of a hit left, and that's bad and it was just one time and I was in the worst way possible oh god just get me through this day and I swear I'm done with this, with all of it—*

Niño grabbed his water glass and drained the last couple of drops. "The, uh, the cops have the entire crew in holding. There's no easy way to get to her. Unless you have someone on the inside?"

"Of course I do, but that's not a hand I want to play unless I have no other choice. Seems to me the Judges won't have had time to interrogate her yet."

"No, no, they won't. There's only five of them. Our people are keeping watch."

"Your hands are trembling, Niño."

He clasped his hands together, interlacing his fingers, and squeezed. "Sorry." He forced a smile. "I'm just worried. I've heard stories about the Judges."

"As have we all." Romley shrugged. "But a mind poisoned with worry is unlikely to be fertile ground for solutions."

Niño stared at him. "What? I mean, I'm... I don't follow you."

Romley slid out of the booth and stood up. "Worrying doesn't *help*, Niño. We need answers, not just lists of the things that might go wrong."

"Mister Romley, can I ask you one last time to reconsider my guys at the factory?"

"No. Don't ask me again, Niño. I'm already a tad upset that you didn't take my first answer."

"It's just that there's likely to be... fallout. You know? Serious repercussions."

"Enough," Romley said. "If the Judges get too close, we'll just distract them. You can do that, can't you? Have something ready, just in case?"

This was familiar territory, and Niño felt a little calmer, though not much. "A distraction. Yeah, sure, I can do that. I'll set things up. How big a distraction do you want?"

"Big as you can manage. Something spectacular, I think." Mister Romley smiled down at Niño. "How much do I owe you for the tea?"

"Uh, a buck eighty-five, I think. But it's on me."

"No, thank you, but I prefer to pay my own way." He winked as he pulled two dollar bills from his wallet. "I'm not comfortable being in anyone's debt."

CHAPTER ELEVEN

IT WAS CLEAR that Officer Chaplin had volunteered to accompany Santana to the abandoned industrial park solely because he'd never really seen a Judge in action.

Santana told Chaplin to stop a kilometre from the target location, and as the officer pulled the patrol car in to the side of the road, Santana said, "We go the rest of the way on foot. Chances are they know we're coming, but let's not advertise, just in case. You up to the walk, Chaplin?"

"Sure, yeah. And call me Roddy. Everyone does."

"I'm not everyone." Santana opened the car door, climbed out and began to walk along the tree-lined road.

Chaplin had to almost run to catch up with him. "Okay. So, if they *are* holed up in the park, then what? We still need probable cause to... we don't, do we?" He grinned. "I could get used to that. So we just bust in and start making arrests, right?"

Individual interrogation of the suspects at 872 Prospect Avenue had turned up two names: Isaac McGowan and Daryl Chin, allegedly responsible for distribution of TranceTrance and other controlled substances throughout the town.

The Judge asked, "You wearing any protection under that jacket?"

Chaplin thumped his chest. "Bulletproof vest. Not exactly regulation, but I put it on this morning when I heard you guys were coming. You think I'm going to need it?"

"Probably." Santana unclipped his radio. "Kurzweil, what's your ETA?"

"Eighty seconds. I've got a lock on you."

Chaplin said, "We cut across the field, we can get there quicker. It leads right up to the back of the place."

"It's open ground—no cover. They'd be able to pick us off before we got anywhere near them."

"Then we wait a few hours until it gets dark."

"You know the kind of people we're dealing with—they tend to be more active at night. So we hit them now, before they've had time to prepare." He turned back to see a Lawranger approaching.

Judge Unity Kurzweil pulled in ahead of them, and waited for them to catch up.

"Busy morning?" Santana asked, as they walked.

"Four fines for traffic violations, and a *lot* of people staring and whispering. Deacon told me that Boyd's investigating a group of survivalists who've been ram-raiding corner stores all over the county. When we're done here, we should back him up... So, what are we facing?"

"Unknown number of assailants, probably heavily armed. Almost certainly forewarned that we're on the way. In a location we're unfamiliar with."

Both Judges looked at Officer Chaplin for a moment, then Kurzweil said, "I recommend you hold back. This is not going to be a walk in the park."

"I can take care of myself," Chaplin said. "I'm not *entirely* useless."

"Jury's still out on that one."

CHAPLIN STAYED BEHIND the two Judges as they made their way through the industrial park, keeping to the shadows wherever possible. The knot that had formed in the pit of his stomach was tightening by the second, and his heart was now thumping so hard he could feel the artery in his neck actually straining against his collar.

In the lead, Kurzweil led them along a narrow alley between two factory buildings and stopped a metre before the corner. She leaned forward and briefly glanced around it. "I see it. Across the lot. Fifty-five, sixty metres away. Three men out front, at least. Two on foot, either side of the doorway, one in the white truck, passenger seat. No weapons on display."

"Access?" Santana asked.

"Metal shutters on the door, but they're up. Door itself is closed. Looks like standard reinforced glass. No windows that I can see."

Santana checked his datapad. "Warehouse 118A. Owned by Edenvere Incorporated. Last rented out to Sparkles McBacon—whatever the hell *that* is—two years ago. Lease expired after three months, renter chose not to renew. No reason given. Edenvere's been trying to sell the place ever since. No one's interested."

Chaplin said, "Not surprising. Anyone seriously considering renting warehouse space here is looking at repairing the roads first, and that's going to cost *millions*."

Kurzweil said, "Hayden, I'm thinking these creeps have no legal reason to be here. Suggest we ask them what they're doing."

"Agreed. If they *are* our distributors, by now they know we're coming. But they might not know you're here. Chaplin and I will confront them." Santana checked the datapad again. "Registered plans show a docking bay at the rear... that's your way in."

"On it." Kurzweil pushed past Chaplin and ran back the way they had come.

"Stay behind me," Santana told Chaplin. "Gun holstered, but be ready. Try not to look too interested in what's going on—we don't want them any edgier than they already are. They're expecting us, but they don't know what *we're* expecting."

"I have done this sort of thing before, Santana."

Santana gave him a fleeting smile. "Not like this. Just follow my lead."

The Judge stepped out from around the corner, and Chaplin followed, his heart still racing. Years ago, Gress had told him, *"The day you're* not *sweating about confronting a bunch of perps is the day the bullet with your name on it finally hits home."*

He glanced past the Judge towards the two men standing either side of the door. He didn't recognise either of them, nor did he know the man sitting in the truck's passenger seat.

All three of the men were on alert now, staring at the Judge as he approached.

The man to the left of the door looked to be about thirty years old. Pale-skinned with a gaunt face and a shaved head, wearing a short jacket, he was ticking all the 'white supremacist thug' boxes, except that his colleague on the other side of the doorway was darker-skinned. Hawaiian, maybe, Chaplin guessed.

The Hawaiian was taller, with an athlete's build. The man in the truck's passenger seat was Caucasian, maybe forty years old, a little overweight, and wearing thick-framed glasses. As Chaplin watched, he carefully folded his newspaper and put it away.

How's he going to do this? Chaplin wondered. If he'd been running this show himself, his take would be to have the place staked out first. Get a better picture of what's going on instead of rushing in blindly. He'd heard that Judges could be impetuous, but this seemed foolhardy to him.

The man in the truck was the one Chaplin was most concerned about. *Can't see his hands. Could have a gun there.*

When Santana was about fifteen metres away, the shaven-headed man took a step towards him, his left hand moving around towards his back. "Private property. What do you want?"

"Step aside and open up," Santana said. He hadn't yet slowed down.

The Hawaiian man moved in front of the door, arms folded.

"Move," Santana ordered.

The man smirked. "Yeah, like *that's* gonna—"

Still not slowing, Santana pulled out his gun and fired, the shot missing the Hawaiian man's head by less than a centimetre.

The man threw himself to the side, swearing and clutching his head.

Santana fired again, putting a round into the door's lock, then swung his gun around to aim it at the skinhead's face. "Drop the gun and back off."

The skinhead dropped the gun he'd pulled out of the waistband of his jeans and raised his hands, backing away. Santana kicked the side of the door with enough force to knock it out of its frame. He strode into the building, calling over his shoulder, "Subdue them and cuff them, Chaplin. They give you any trouble, you have my permission to use whatever force is necessary."

All four men outside—the three thugs and Chaplin himself—stood still for a moment, staring at Santana, then the skinhead moved to snatch up his gun.

Chaplin slammed the butt of his own gun into the skinhead's jaw, then aimed at the truck's passenger. "Get out, nice and slow! Hands where I can see them! I swear to *God*, you try anything and the rest of us are gonna learn what the inside of your head looks like!"

On the ground, the Hawaiian man pulled his hands away from his head and stared at them. "No blood... I thought he shot me! I thought he shot me in the head!"

Chaplin threw a pair of handcuffs at the man's feet. "Put them on, behind your back. Do it!"

The Hawaiian man snatched up the cuffs and fumbled with them. "I'm doing it!"

The truck's passenger was out now, moving slowly, hands raised. "Look, I don't know what you think is going on here—"

"Shut up," Chaplin ordered. "On your knees." He quickly glanced at the skinhead, who was lying on his side, holding his jaw. "You too. Don't make me ask again."

Chaplin gripped the gun tighter to keep his arm from trembling. This was a rush like he hadn't felt since his first day on duty. Past few years, a cop practically had to beat a suspect to the ground before the suspect complied, but these men—who looked like they had considerable experience—were obeying his every word.

It was the Judge, of course. The Judges were still an unknown variable. The perps hadn't yet learned the boundaries. They knew that the Judges were empowered to carry out on-the-spot executions, and a few of them had maybe even witnessed that in action. So they were playing it safe. Chaplin had occasionally thought about signing up with Fargo's new Justice Department. In time, it was said, the department would be training Judges from childhood, but that would take years, and they needed Judges on the streets a lot sooner. It wasn't like they could grow Judges in vats: they needed experienced cops and lawyers to sign up.

I could do it, Chaplin thought. *Two years on the retraining program, and they pay you for doing it; even if I flunk out, I'll have all that extra training. That's gotta look good on my record. And Santana wasn't even a cop when he joined the academy. If he can do it, so can I.*

"I want names," Chaplin said. He aimed his gun at the skinhead. "You."

"Lawyer."

Chaplin smirked. "Not any more." He quickly gave the man a one-handed pat-down, finding a thick leather wallet in an inside jacket pocket. He flipped the wallet open and examined the drivers' licence. "Isaac McGowan. You're on our list."

A fresh burst of gunfire echoed throughout the warehouse and the man with the glasses muttered, "Aw, *crap*." Louder, he said, "Hey, you, Officer Dibble? Make you a deal, okay? Odds are your friend in there is getting shot to hell right now. When our people are done with him, they'll come for you. So here's the offer. You let us go right now, and you get to walk away. No repercussions. What do you say?"

"I say no deal. But keep talking if you want to incriminate yourselves even further."

An explosion inside the warehouse shook the entire structure and caused the concrete underfoot to tremble.

The Hawaiian man said, "Figure that was the *condenser*." He glared up at Chaplin. "That costs about three hundred kay. Man, you got any idea how much money we're looking at here? We could set you up for *life*, and it wouldn't make a dent in our profits. Seriously."

The man with the glasses shook his head. "No, screw that. We're not *buying* our way out of this! You, Officer Dibble, are a *dead* man. You got a mom? She's dead. Sisters and brothers? All dead. Kids? Dead. Wife? Dead, but only after watching her kids get their eyes gouged out and their throats cut."

Another explosion rocked the building, and the man pushed himself to his feet, arms still cuffed behind his back. He snarled at Chaplin. "We will destroy everything you care about. *Everything*. And the survivors, the few people you know who we've not managed to find, well, they're gonna know that *you're* behind it. All you had to do was walk away." He took a step towards Chaplin. "That's all you have to do, man. Walk. You can tell your Judge buddy that we overpowered you, or one of us ran and you chased us, then you got ambushed. Whatever you like. You do that little thing, and your family and friends get to keep living their sweet little lives and they're none the wiser."

Chaplin gritted his teeth. "Not a chance. Get back down on your knees!"

"Or what? You're gonna shoot me? No, what you've got here, Officer Asshole, is the *illusion* of control. The Judge has the power, you're just his sidekick. So tell me... you ever *seen* someone get their eyes gouged out? No? I have. That sort of thing stays with you, man. I saw it once and I'm still having nightmares about it. So imagine that happening to your wife and kids, if you've got any. If you haven't, imagine it happening to your girlfriend, or boyfriend, or whatever. Now imagine it happening slowly. *Real* slowly. Their heads are clamped down so they can't move, and their eyelids are taped back, and then one of our guys comes at them very slowly, with, say, a fork, or a pencil. Left eye first. And everyone else on the list is there too, watching. They get to see what's gonna be happening to them real soon." He slowly looked Chaplin up and down, and sneered, "You *want* that to happen, Mister Hero? Mister Good-Guy who thinks he's doing the world a favour?"

Chaplin inhaled deeply, held it for a second, then let it out slowly. "I said, get back down on your knees. I won't tell you again."

The man with the glasses grinned. "The offer ends the moment the shooting inside stops, little piggy. And believe me, this offer is weighted very heavily in your favour, I figure. Your one Judge against all our guys inside? When they kill him— and they *will*—they'll come out here and that's it for you. Your own mother won't even be able to recognise you when they're done."

"Enough," Chaplin said. He aimed the gun directly at the man's forehead. "Two things. First, he's not the only Judge in there. Second, I ordered you to get back down on your knees. Now do it!"

The man raised his eyes. "And you said you weren't going to tell me again. You're *weak*, pig. You don't have—"

Chaplin squeezed the trigger. The gun boomed in his hand and the man with the glasses toppled backwards, showering his colleagues with blood.

Chaplin looked from the Hawaiian to the skinhead and back. "Either of you two assholes want to try your luck?"

The skinhead, McGowan, turned to the side and retched. A thin stream of bile splashed onto the ground, then he raised his head and stared at Chaplin. "Oh, Jesus... You killed him!"

The Hawaiian said, "That's it. You just shot a handcuffed

prisoner in the *face*. No way you can spin this so that it doesn't look like an execution. You're *finished* now, man."

Chaplin swung the gun towards the Hawaiian. "Are you so stupid that you can't learn from what just happened? Shut the hell up or the next one's for you!"

A voice off to the side yelled, "Chaplin! Lower your weapon!"

Chaplin turned towards the side of the warehouse to see Judge Santana slowly walking towards him, his gun raised and aimed at him.

"Drop it, Chaplin! Right now!"

"Judge, I was—"

The last thing Officer Roderick Chaplin saw was the muzzle-flare from Judge Santana's gun.

CHAPTER TWELVE

FROM TWO BLOCKS away, Judge Lela Rowain saw the crowd gathered outside St. Christopher's police station. She'd already passed two parked news trucks and a lot of cars with out-of-state licence plates. She'd expected this from the moment they'd learned that CJ had been killed.

One of the reporters spotted her coming and darted out into the street, brandishing his microphone. The man skidded on a patch of ice and landed on his side.

Rowain carefully steered around him as the other reporters made their way towards her. She stopped the Lawranger at the side of the road and climbed off.

Another male reporter shoved a minicam in her face. "Portman Fullerton, BiggestEverNews dot com. Judge, what can you tell us about the brutal murder of your colleague, local girl Charlotte-Jane Leandros?" He was walking backwards, awkwardly, so as not to get *too* close to her as she made her way towards the station.

A female reporter nudged Fullerton aside, "Judge Rowain, isn't it? We've just heard that you shot and killed a suspect in Sorrell's Entertainment—the home of entertainment at super low, low prices—over in the Omaha Mall. Can you comment on that?"

A third reporter, a man walking alongside Rowain said, "Look this way for the camera, please. Nice big smile. Let the viewers at home see the *pretty* side of the Law, right?"

Rowain couldn't help but be impressed that the reporters weren't actually slowing her down. They were keeping pace with her and jostling each other, but not actually coming within a metre of any part of her body.

At the entrance to the station's parking lot, the huddle of reporters in front of Rowain dissolved as they darted to the sides. Clearly, they'd been ordered not to set foot on the property.

They continued to shout questions at her, until the station's doors opened and a man she didn't recognise strode out to meet her, followed by two burly men in suits with telltale bulges under their jackets: personal security guards. The reporters started addressing him instead: "Lieutenant Governor Schubert! Does the murder of Judge Leandros mean more Judges will be assigned here? What does that do to the law enforcement budget, Mister Schubert?"

The man stopped in front of Rowain and jerked his thumb over his shoulder. "Captain Witcombe wants you inside. Right now. Her office."

"You are?"

"As you've just heard from the jackals with the cameras, I'm Lieutenant Governor Marius Schubert, *that's* who the hell I am. Inside, Rowain. Now."

He marched alongside her towards the doors. "You are in so much trouble. I knew something like this was going to happen. Told Fargo himself this was a mistake. Should have stuck to the bigger cities first, but he insisted that even tiny little burgs like this place needed to see Judges in action."

Rowain glanced back to see that the security guards were following.

"Six of you here only half a day and already one of you is dead, one of you has shot one of our finest officers, and *you've* executed one civilian and maimed another." Schubert pulled open the doors and Rowain slid past him. "Well, your boss is in there now getting the riot act read to him by Captain Witcombe and you're next, Rowain!"

In the public lobby, four uniformed officers were gathered at the front desk, talking to the desk sergeant. They fell silent as they watched Rowain cross the lobby.

The Lieutenant Governor kept pace with Rowain along the corridor. "Knew this was a mistake. Shoulda just been two of you to start, observing at first. But that little stunt your people pulled out at the warehouse has lit a damn fuse. You ever seen a full-scale riot, Rowain? Because *we* have. We get one somewhere in this state nearly every damn weekend. But the next one's not gonna wait for Friday night. It's ready to kick off right *now* and those media vultures out there are advertising the damn thing."

The door to the Captain's office was open. Rowain could see Captain Witcombe inside, standing behind her desk. On the opposite side of the desk were Judge Deacon and a woman wearing a grey suit. Deacon nodded towards Rowain, but she couldn't read the expression on his face.

In the doorway she hesitated for a second, and that was when Lieutenant Governor Schubert put his hand on her shoulder and shoved her forward. "Get inside!"

Rowain spun, jamming her elbow into Schubert's chin. The blow staggered him. He stumbled backwards, cracking his head against the opposite wall.

His guards immediately reached for their guns, but Rowain's weapon was already in her hand. They backed off, one of them saying, "Woah, hey... Just a misunderstanding."

Deacon leaned out through the doorway and calmly said, "Warned you to play it cool, Schubert. You asked for that."

Schubert ran the back of his hand across his mouth—it came away streaked with blood. "Split my damn lip..." To Captain Witcombe, he said, "Virginia, you're a witness. That was assault!"

Rowain said, "Put your hand on me again if you want more of the same."

121

The Lieutenant Governor glared at her as he entered the captain's office.

As Rowain followed him, Judge Deacon asked, "Remember what I told you this morning when we got here?"

She nodded. "You said to step lightly, sir."

"So your memory's not faulty. Just your interpretation of the word 'lightly.'" Deacon calmly pushed the door closed, in the faces of the Lieutenant Governor's two guards. "Rowain, you met Captain Witcombe this morning. And this is Detective Morrow."

Captain Witcombe began, "Rowain..." then corrected herself. "*Judge* Rowain. Hazel Pinheir, a private security guard at the Mayor Caroleen Omaha Mall, has accused you of an unprovoked attack on her person during which Ms Pinheir's right radius and ulna were both fractured. We've already heard from her solicitor, who has intimated that if satisfactory compensation is not offered by the end of the day, they will be pressing charges. Do you have anything to say to that?"

Rowain glanced at Judge Deacon, who shrugged. She turned back to the captain. "I'd like you to give me her solicitor's name and contact details, because that sounds like a threat of extortion to me. Two years."

The detective laughed at that, but stopped when Captain Witcombe glared at her.

To Rowain, Witcombe said, "Pinheir is going to sue you—and probably us as well—and she has a strong case. There are eleven witnesses willing to swear that you attacked her without cause."

"I warned her to drop her weapon. She refused. I disarmed her. Captain, I have a job to do and I'm not willing to explain and justify every action I make."

Schubert paused in the process of dabbing at his lip with a handkerchief. "You're gonna have to, because this cannot stand. This... judicial takeover. When Fargo comes to his senses—or when President Gurney comes to *his* and realises what a mistake he's made—then all this will end, and you

Judges will go back to begging for work as nightclub bouncers. Then *we're* the ones who will have to pick up the pieces. The ordinary taxpayers whose lives you've ruined. Rowain, if you have any damn sense, you'll get yourself the best lawyer you can afford."

Slowly Rowain turned to face Schubert. "You really don't understand, do you? Let me make it clear. I do *not* need a lawyer, because I am a Judge: I know the law better than almost anyone. Pinheir will not sue me, because I did nothing wrong or illegal. She has no case."

"Eleven witnesses, Rowain!" Schubert said. "*Eleven*. They can't all be lying! You need to talk to your union rep or whoever, because they are going to come down on you—on *all* of you—so hard that we're going to have to check your dental records to figure out who's who when this is all over."

Rowain sighed. "Judge Deacon?"

"Your show, Rowain," Deacon said.

Rowain said, "Lieutenant Governor, there is no going back, no reset button that's going to fix everything. The life that you know now is almost gone. There will be no more lawyers, or cops, or—in time—politicians. Just Judges. I do not need to worry about Pinheir making accusations against me. *She* needs to worry about making accusations against me. And I hope *you* understood that, because if I have to go through it with you again, I'll arrest you for wasting a Judge's time." To the captain, she said, "We're done here."

"No, we're not." Captain Witcombe said, "There's still the matter of Judge Santana. Officer Chaplin is in critical condition. If he dies... hell, even if he *doesn't* die. Chaplin's a good cop. He's popular. My people are going to close ranks against you. Nothing I can do to stop that."

Deacon said, "Judge Santana told me what happened. I have no reason not to believe him. Your officer shot an unarmed, handcuffed suspect in the head, point-blank. As far as I'm concerned, that's murder one." He stepped closer to Witcombe's desk and leaned on it, pushing his head close to the captain's. "You might recall that we've still got our own murder to investigate. For that, we're going to need the continued support of your department. If your people refuse to do their jobs, or in any way hinder our investigation, or if I find that they're openly hostile to Judge Santana, I will consider that aiding and abetting the murderer. Are we on the same page, Captain?"

She nodded slowly. "Right now, we are."

"Good." Deacon turned to the Lieutenant Governor. "Judges Kurzweil and Santana arrested thirty-three perps at the TranceTrance factory. They're holding them and the merchandise in a nearby abandoned warehouse because this town doesn't have a prison or a secure enough evidence lock-up. Schubert, I called you here because four months ago the Justice Department sent you instructions to begin construction on a prison with a one-thousand-inmate capacity. You were given one year and told that weekly progress updates would be required. The Department has received precisely zero such updates. Instead, you appear to have assembled a task force dedicated to resisting the idea of a prison at every possible stage. What progress *have* you made?"

"I—"

"Not good enough," Deacon said. "I'll be recommending to the Chief Judge that you be made personally liable for the timely construction of the prison. You've squandered four months of your allotted twelve, Lieutenant Governor. Don't squander the rest unless you harbour a desire to be the prison's first occupant. In the meantime, you will authorise the deployment of fifty National Guard reservists to police our makeshift prison, and you will release appropriate funds from the state's budget to cover any and all refurbishment and reinforcement costs. Please understand that this is not a suggestion or a request, Mister Schubert. Nor is it to be considered the opening gambit in a negotiation. It is an *order*." He stepped back and glanced at Rowain. "*Now* we're done. Let's go. You too, Morrow."

He moved towards the door, but the Lieutenant Governor grabbed his arm. "No! Deacon, this is absolutely unaccept—"

"Take your hand off my arm and go do your job, Mister Schubert."

Schubert backed away, but he wasn't finished. "This won't stand, Deacon! I *warn* you, I have the president's ear!"

"And I have my mother's eyes, Lieutenant Governor. Right now, they're looking at a relic that can't comprehend that its time has passed."

CHAPTER THIRTEEN

JUDGE ROWAIN FOLLOWED as Judge Deacon and Detective Morrow
walked side by side through St. Christopher's police station.
Rowain ignored the dark stares and muttered comments of
the officers and staff, but as they neared the public lobby, she
became aware of raised voices, and recognised one of them.

"You deal with it, Lela," Deacon said, turning back to her.
"I need to check in with the coroner."

Rowain increased her pace and pushed open the double-
doors to the lobby. Judge Boyd was standing with his back to
the door, facing the same four uniformed officers she had seen
earlier, one of whom now had his hand on the gun at his hip.
More officers and staff were watching from the sides, clearly
not wanting to get involved but unwilling to miss whatever
was about to happen.

The four officers spotted Rowain approaching and one of
them said, "*Another* one. Damn place is *crawling* with Judges
now."

Judge Boyd said, "Seems these officers are upset with me
because of something Judge Santana did." He nodded towards
the officer holding his gun and said, "I was just about to arrest
Stenning here for the sinking of the *Titanic*. You know? *Quid
pro quo* kind of thing."

Stenning turned back to Boyd. "What? No, screw that. And screw *you*. Roddy Chaplin is fighting for his life out in Mercy South and you're cracking jokes. You Judges think you're better than us, admit it."

Rowain looked from one to the other. Boyd was about the same age as Stenning—mid-twenties—but the officer was taller and had a heavier build and a longer reach. He still didn't stand a chance if it came to a fist fight.

"Better than *all* cops?" Boyd said. "Not necessarily. But better than you? Yes. Chaplin's lucky he's got a life to fight for. The man whose head he perforated doesn't have that chance. Now you will stand down, Stenning, or I will consider this an act of aggression against a Judge."

The officer pulled his gun from its holster and handed it to one of his colleagues. "All right, tough guy. You want to see aggression? I'll goddamn *show* you aggression!"

Boyd said, "Seriously?" He looked at the other cops. "Did any of *you* hear me say I wanted to see aggression? No, because I did not. But that's what your friend heard. Now take him away before this turns messy and Stenning ends up in the hospital bed next to Chaplin's."

Stenning started towards the Judge but one of his colleagues grabbed his arms and held him back. "Let it go, man."

Rowain stepped in front of Boyd and looked up at him. "You know better. Walk away."

Boyd nodded, then turned, pushed open the lobby doors and marched out into the parking lot.

Stenning said, "Son of a bitch has to get a damn *woman* to fight his battles for him."

Someone nearby muttered, "Oh, he did *not* just say that!" and Rowain identified Detective Morrow, watching from the wall.

"Officer Stenning, this is how things are," Rowain said. "You can't change it. Soon there will be no more police officers, or staff. Just Judges. So I suggest that you—that *all* of you—make the most of the time you have left. Get the work done, keep your heads down, and concentrate on saving as much money as you can before you're all made redundant. Unless you want to retrain as Judges."

Stenning said, "Huh. Hell with *that*. Being a Judge is what got CJ Leandros killed."

Rowain might have let that one pass as just another of Stenning's comments, if one of the onlookers hadn't muttered, "God*damn* it, Stenning!" under their breath.

The voice had been too low and too indistinct for Rowain to tell exactly where it had come from, or even whether the speaker was male or female, but its tone was more than enough to trigger Rowain's radar. She turned slowly on the spot. "Who said that?"

Stenning began, "Who said what? I didn't—"

"Shut up. Someone said, 'Goddamn it, Stenning,' and I want to know who. Right now. No one leaves here until I know who said that."

Detective Morrow eased her way through the crowd and said, "Rowain, seriously, this is coming across like a *witch-hunt*. Let it go."

She ignored that. Most of the assembled onlookers shrugged as if to say they didn't know what she was talking about, but one of them—a man in a stained janitor's uniform, holding a mop—was very slowly and casually stepping to the left while he tried to maintain an expression of innocence.

Rowain didn't look directly at the janitor. She kept turning. "This is not a joke, or some psychological game. Trust me, I *know* about psychological games. I know that whoever said, 'Goddamn it, Stenning,' didn't mean to let it out." She glanced at the janitor now, and saw that he was looking at the woman he'd been sidling away from. "It was a slip. Because *they* know or suspect something about Judge Leandros's death, and they were afraid that Stenning was about to inadvertently give it away." Rowain stopped turning, and directly addressed the woman she was facing. "Isn't that right, Officer Gress?"

The grey-haired woman shrugged. "I don't know. Could be."

Rowain caught the tiny flicker of Gress's eyes to the right. *Checking someone else to see their reaction... Whatever this is, Gress isn't the only one who knows it.*

Standing next to her, Morrow said, "Judge, what are you accusing her of?"

"I haven't decided yet. Gress, you and I need to talk," Rowain said. "Right now." With a glance at Morrow, she added, "*Just* us."

JUDGE DEACON WAS halfway between the police station and the hospital when he spotted Doctor Abramson driving the opposite way. He swung the Lawranger around and overtook her, signalling for her to pull over.

When she pulled into the side of the road, Deacon stayed on his bike and rode back to her, stopping next to the driver's-side window.

"Just on my way to see you, Doc. What do you have for me?"

She rolled down the window a little more and handed him a sheaf of papers. "Not a lot. Judge Leandros's stomach contents show she hadn't eaten in about four hours. No unexplained puncture marks or other wounds. And your harvester crawled over every square millimetre of her body and came up empty, aside from the grit and dirt she picked up when she landed in Rotzler's yard. Sorry, Judge. There's nothing more I can do. Even with the harvester, the X-rays, the MRI and the spectrograph, we've come up empty-handed."

Deacon had been flipping through the pages as she spoke, and now he tucked them inside his tunic. "Got it. Thanks, Doctor. When can I expect your full report?"

She glared at him for a moment. "That *is* my full report, Judge. There's nothing more I can add to it."

"If you say so."

"I do. Goodbye, Judge Deacon."

"Keep your phone handy, Abramson—I might need to call you."

Deacon headed back towards the station, and on the way contacted Marisa Pellegrino. She'd been a friend of Eustace Fargo since their college days, and he'd introduced her to Deacon as the one person he could trust above all others. *"Marisa will be my eyes and ears out there among the new Judges. As far as most of them are concerned, she's an assistant, a data-gatherer. But she can be whatever we need her to be."*

Pellegrino was, Deacon reckoned, the smartest person he had ever met. As well as her considerable ability to blend into most situations and persuade even the most taciturn people to start spilling their secrets, she had a knack for slicing through problems to get to the core, and right now that was what he needed.

"We have nothing," Deacon told her. "No suspects, no evidence, no motives... just a body. I take it from the lack of communication that the satellite feeds were just as useless?"

Pellegrino said, "You take it correctly. I'm sorry, Francesco. The satellite coverage of Henderson Rotzler's property is too patchy to get anything useful. We do have some still images from around the time of his call to 911, but they're low-res and even our best people haven't been able to pull anything out of them. I've uploaded them to your account so you can see for yourself."

Deacon thanked her and ended the call.

Not for the first time, he was hit by a wave of doubt. The Judge system was not perfect. By its very nature it could never be perfect. Sometimes he wondered if maybe Spender Gant had actually been right when he'd said, *"You're talking about putting the entire country in thumbscrews until everyone agrees to calm the hell down! That's insanity in action!"*

Deacon sighed. *The people don't believe that they need us, and that's* why *they need us. They think that everything is ticking along smoothly because we don't let them see the truth, that this is a nation that grew too fast and squandered its resources and partied too hard, and now it's paying the price. The only available options are austerity or starvation, and even an idiot ought to be able to see that of those two options, there's only one you can recover from.*

"Could be days until the prison space is found," Judge Unity Kurzweil told Santana as they strolled around the commandeered warehouse. "Weather like this, *everything* slows to a crawl."

The prisoners were sitting on the ground, most of them wrapped in old blankets or torn strips of tarpaulin to keep out the cold, huddled together in groups of three and four.

Santana said, "Figure we can get another ninety in here, maybe a hundred at a push. But any more than that and we're looking at trouble."

As they passed a young female police officer standing guard inside the door, the officer asked, "So, what next?"

Santana stopped. "Meaning, Officer Palmer?"

"So, like, we've processed these prisoners, like you said. Names and addresses and everything. And they're nearly all verified. But..." She frowned. "Well, what happens to them now? Do they get a phone call, or what?"

Judge Kurzweil had continued walking, but now she stopped and turned back. "Who would they phone? Your fellow officers are informing their next of kin, if they haven't already done so. Who else would they call?"

Officer Palmer shrugged. "I don't know. I just... This seems so arbitrary. How do we know they're all guilty?"

Santana said, "They were inside the premises manufacturing prohibited substances. There's no *doubt* that they're guilty."

"Yeah, but... extenuating circumstances. You know. Some of them might have been *forced* to be there. That happens."

A nearby prisoner—male, in his early twenties—raised his

hand. "Me! *I* was forced! Guy said that if I didn't work for them, he'd break my legs! I want to see a lawyer!"

The man next to him called out, "I didn't know that TranceTrance was illegal, so you can't blame me for breaking the law! I have *kids*—you can't take me away from my kids for eighteen years when I didn't even do anything wrong!"

Santana glared at the second man and said, "You took a shot at us, numb-nuts!" He turned back to the officer. "Nice going. *Now* look what you've started." Santana unclipped his radio. "Dispatch, this is Judge Santana."

He waited. For a few seconds, nothing but static came back. "This is Officer Clarke. Go ahead, Judge."

"Dispatch, we're still waiting on the National Guard here. What's the delay?"

"Unknown, Judge. Cops and guardsmen tend to work together, you know? Could be that they're upset about you shooting Officer Chaplin."

Santana said, "You mean, *former* Officer Chaplin. What's your problem here, Clarke? You defending the actions of a trained police officer who put a round into the skull of a handcuffed prisoner?"

Clarke muttered something under his breath that to Santana sounded like, "Drokk it!" then, louder, added, "No, Judge. I'll pass on your instructions."

"My orders."

"Your orders. That's what I meant."

"Good. In the meantime, I want five more officers to back us up."

The line clicked off, and Santana put away his radio. To Palmer, standing beside him, he said, "That's a lesson for you, kid. Don't get on the wrong side of the Judges. One day, you're going to need us."

They stood side by side, watching the prisoners, and after a few minutes Santana asked, "Drokk it?"

Officer Palmer nodded. "Oh, yeah. Clarke's father was a pastor of some weird sect and he didn't allow swearwords at home, so in Clarke's family they all say that instead. Doesn't actually mean anything, but it *sounds* profane. I dated him for about a month when we were in high school, and Clarke took me to one of his dad's sermons. It was strange. In their church they're not allowed to use God's name."

"That's not uncommon. In the Jewish faith they tend to avoid using his name except when reciting prayers."

"I guess," Palmer said. "Clarke's family aren't Jewish, though. I'm not sure *what* they are, really, but they made up their own name for God so they won't accidentally use the word itself. They call themselves The First Church of Grud."

Santana said, "Makes sense from that point of view, I guess. I'm not religious."

"You don't believe in a greater power?"

"I do. I believe in the Law."

Officer Palmer said, "Yeah... I had a feeling you were going to say that."

CHAPTER FOURTEEN

NIÑO AUKINS HOISTED his backpack onto his shoulder as he walked towards the main entrance of Mercy South Hospital at a brisk pace, fast enough to keep ahead of the police officers who had arrived a few minutes ago, but not—he hoped—so fast that his speed would attract their attention.

His timing was fortunate: the two cops at the door were so distracted by the arrival of their colleagues that they barely glanced at him.

"You a reporter?" one of them asked, giving his fellow officers a nod.

"No, I'm sick."

"I find out you're a reporter, you *will* be. Go on."

Inside, he felt that he had legitimately earned the right to break into a sweat. This was madness. He hadn't wanted to come here, but Mister Romley had insisted. When Mister Romley insists, you comply or you say goodbye to the use of your elbows.

This would have been easier if Romley had given him more time.

Twenty minutes ago, Romley had told Niño what he had to do, and Niño had tried to gently persuade Mister Romley that it wasn't the best idea. Over the following minutes, Niño had graduated from gentle persuasion to pleading and actual crying, but Romley was stuck on the idea. The tears had been good: Niño's eyes were still red and his face was haggard—very useful when you want to pretend you're sick.

He knew the hospital well and was sure of where he was going, but in order to look more patient-like, he dutifully followed the line of red tape on the floor all the way to the orthopaedics unit, then the purple footprints led him through the X-ray building and to the day wards. Here, he ducked into the men's room and into one of the stalls, where he opened his backpack and removed an old T-shirt, his elasticated sweatpants and a pair of slippers.

A few minutes later, Niño made his way along one of the hospital's upper corridors until he found the geriatrics' ward. There, he purloined a wheeled drip-stand and a glucose bag from a sleeping patient.

On the next floor up, slightly hunched over and leaning on the drip-stand for support, Niño slowly shuffled towards the four cops on guard duty outside Officer Roderick Chaplin's room. The cops didn't know him, he was almost certain about that. He ought to be able to walk right past them; they wouldn't have any reason to think he was anything but another patient.

But he hadn't expected four of them. One would have been tricky enough, but four was impossible. Mister Romley had told him, "Niño, if that cop dies, the rest of them are either going to go to war with the Judges, or they'll walk out. Either way, that drastically reduces the security on the warehouse where they're holding the merchandise. That's our opportunity to go and take it back."

"And get our people out," Niño had said.

"Sure, whatever..." After a pause, Romley had said, "Actually, yes, that's perfect. We free our people and that's an even bigger distraction while they're rounding them up. So, Niño, your job is to find a way into Chaplin's room and unplug him from life support or tie a knot in his air hose or whatever it takes to sign him off forever."

Niño had tried to protest, claiming he'd never killed anyone before. That wasn't strictly true, of course, but he'd never deliberately *murdered* anyone. Not actually plotted to kill them and then carried it out. The nine people who had died at his hands were more victims of circumstance than victims of Niño. Especially the first three: they were just in the wrong place at the wrong time, an unfortunate synchronisation of their act of burglary and his commission of arson. And the next one, the old lady, should have believed him: when a carjacker points a gun at you, you have to accept that there's at least a *possibility* that the gun is loaded.

He realised that he couldn't recall the fifth person he'd killed and felt guilty about that for a moment, until he remembered where he was and figured that it was probably best to focus on the here and now.

Like the cops at the main entrance, the four outside Chaplin's room barely noticed him. Two of them had clearly arrived only recently—they were still stamping their feet and rubbing their hands together to get warm—and the other two were giving them a report on the situation. *If Romley had given me more time...*

"He's out of the woods now, doc said. The bullet missed anything major. But still, damn Judge could have killed him. He *tried* to kill him, I think. Didn't even give him a warning, is what I heard. Like, you put a man under pressure like that, then he snaps and shoots the perp, whose fault is it? Not Chaplin's. The Judges are gonna either kill us all, or force us out."

"Damn right. You know why, don't you? If we're dead or we quit, they don't have to pay us severance. That's what *I* figure."

Niño felt his sweat-slicked hand losing grip on the drip-stand and paused long enough to wipe his hand on his hip. He tried—and failed—not to think about the gun taped to the inside of his left thigh. *Four cops, eight rounds in the magazine. Two each, then I strangle Chaplin and... No, he's the priority, have to save a couple of rounds for him. One shot in each cop. That's not easy.*

No, wait, kill one cop and take his gun. That's a whole new clip. Use that one to fire at the other cops, then go for Chaplin. Then... then how do I get away?

Jesus, if I'd had more time, I could have gone home and taken another hit. Just a quick one. See me through.

"Keep movin'," one of the cops said, mostly out of reflex.

Niño didn't acknowledge him. He just reaffirmed his grip on the stand and resumed shuffling. *There's no way this can be done,* Niño told himself. *So that's it. I'm dead. Mister Romley is going to—*

An idea struck him so hard that he almost stopped again. *The Judges are not the cops. I could never turn Romley in because I didn't know who he had on his payroll; but it's different now. You can't bribe or threaten a Judge. They'd just shoot you right there and then. Romley has no power over the Judges. Which means he has no power over me.*

The idea was growing more attractive by the moment. Niño continued slowly shuffling down the corridor, and by the time he'd reached the elevator, he'd made up his mind.

"How THE HELL old *are* you, anyway?" Officer Gress asked.

"That's not relevant," Judge Rowain said. She pointed to the room's only other chair and said, "Sit."

"You're about twenty-six, right? I'm twice your age. I've been a cop since before you were even born. You don't give *me* orders. And you damn well don't interrogate me without my lawyer *and* my union rep present!"

Rowain knew that by now there'd be a cluster of other officers watching from the observation room, and more listening at the door, and no doubt there was someone telling Captain Witcombe what was happening, but she refused to let that distract her. "Gress, sit. Now. Or I'll charge you with refusing to comply with a Judge's order. That's a six-month sentence minimum."

Officer Sophia Gress pulled the chair away from the table and sat down, glaring at Judge Rowain. "Then let's get this crap done and we can both get on with our lives. But my union *will* hear about this, I promise you that."

"Out in the lobby, Officer Stenning said, 'Being a Judge is what got CJ Leandros killed.' Your reaction to that was to say, 'God*damn* it, Stenning!' What did you mean?"

Gress shrugged. "I just wanted Stenning to shut up. Guy's a good cop, but he talks too much."

"You're lying, Gress. Tell me what you really meant."

"Why don't you ask *him*? He's the one who said that about Leandros!"

"I'm asking you. Stenning believes Judge Leandros made herself a target by becoming a Judge. A lot of people think that way. But it's how *you* reacted to Stenning's comment that doesn't sit with me. What do you think he knows?"

Gress leaned forward and rested her arms on the table. "You can't force me to talk."

"Who killed Judge Charlotte-Jane Leandros?"

"I don't know. Everyone here *loved* that kid. We grew up with her. I've got a picture at home that she drew for me when she was six! I don't know *anything* about her death. Hell, you can damn well torture me if you want, but I can't tell you something I don't know."

"But you *suspect* something," Rowain said. "If someone wanted to send a message to the rest of us, then why pick local girl Leandros and not a stranger like me or Deacon or the others? Was it because she was alone? Or maybe it was personal. Someone had a problem with Leandros herself. One of her brothers, maybe. Stavros and CJ argued only a few hours before she died. He was upset that she joined the Justice Department. Was that it? They got into a fight and he killed her?"

Gress slowly shook her head. "I don't know anything about it. But Stavros would never kill CJ. Neither would Benny. They *adored* her. Even her becoming a Judge wouldn't get in the way of that."

Rowain sat back and watched Gress staring back her. *She suspects something... But she's not certain. That means her suspicions are about another cop, or someone else she feels she has a duty to protect. Maybe* that's *my angle here...*

"Officer Gress... Sophia. Let me put it as simply as I can. You don't tell me what you know, you're an accessory."

Gress snorted. "Hah, yeah! Good luck proving *that* in a court of law! You're never going—" She stopped, and dry-swallowed. "Oh, God. There *is* no court of law any more. I mean, there won't be, soon." She ran her hands over her face, and took a deep breath. "We... Judge, we deal with evidence. You understand that? Actual, physical evidence. Guy shoots his wife, ideally we'll have a gun and a body. If we have neither, then there's a chance that the guy will get off. It's not perfect, but it's fair. Because sometimes the guy *didn't* shoot his wife, sometimes it was someone else. We can't lock him up without actual proof, or near-as-damn-it circumstantial evidence that wouldn't crop up without a billion-to-one coincidence. Your way is to intimidate everyone until someone snaps and starts pointing fingers. That's not justice!"

"Just tell me what you know. What you *suspect*. Then let me decide whether it's worth pursuing."

"No. Go to hell, Judge. You can threaten me all you want, but I'm no rat."

Rowain nodded. That had been for the benefit of anyone listening, she realised. Gress wanted to talk, but didn't feel safe. *She's just admitted that she suspects a cop was involved.*

CHAPTER FIFTEEN

JUDGE FRANCESCO DEACON saw Captain Witcombe walking ahead of him along the hospital corridor and lengthened his stride to catch up with her.

She didn't seem surprised when he fell into step beside her, which suggested she'd known he was there.

"On the way to see Chaplin?" Deacon asked.

"This is a mess like I wouldn't have believed," Witcombe said. "Your Judge shot my officer without warning."

"Not according to Judge Kurzweil. Santana ordered Chaplin to drop his weapon and he didn't comply."

Witcombe threw him a quick glance. "We only have Kurzweil's word for that."

"Prisoners Isaac McGowan and Daryl Chin confirm that Chaplin was warned."

"Perps," Witcombe said. "You'll take their statement over Chaplin's?"

Deacon stepped to the side to allow an orderly to pass. "Right now, they rate higher on my credibility scale, because as far as we know, *they're* not murderers. Chaplin shot Rafe Carfey in the face at point-blank range. Carfey was handcuffed and in custody at the time. I understand your loyalty to your people, Witcombe, but that should not come at the expense of the truth. Regardless of Santana's actions, Chaplin unlawfully executed a prisoner."

They reached a stairwell and began to ascend, still walking side by side.

"Why are you here, Deacon? What do you want?"

"I came to talk to Chaplin."

"To get his side of the story?"

"No. Because Rafe Carfey is not the only person to have been shot in the face in the past twenty-four hours."

Witcombe stopped walking. "No. No way. Chaplin wouldn't... Is that what you think? That Roddy Chaplin, who's known Charlotte-Jane since before she could *crawl*... that he could have killed her? No. I don't accept that." She resumed walking, following Deacon up the stairs. They reached the landing, and Deacon held the door open for her.

"Chaplin's not like that," Witcombe continued. "It's not in his nature. He's very easy-going, rarely loses his temper. Trust me on that, Judge. Ask *anyone*."

Deacon followed her out into the corridor. "Anyone except Rafe Carfey." Ahead, he saw four officers standing outside a room with closed blinds. "I see you're advertising Chaplin's location."

"Standard procedure in a situation like this," Witcombe said. "Look, I'm not saying that I know for *certain* that Chaplin didn't kill CJ, but what's his motivation? There's nothing for him to gain."

As they passed a nervous-looking man leaning on a drip-stand for support, Deacon said, "You're his friend, Captain, and you're thinking like a defendant. You need to think like a prosecutor. Make the assumption that Chaplin did it, then prove that assumption."

"Is that what they teach you in Judge Academy? Guilty until proven innocent?"

"Everyone's guilty, Captain Witcombe. It's just a matter of determining *what* they're guilty of." Still walking, Deacon looked back the way they had come, then stopped. "Figured."

Witcombe asked, "What?" and then saw the patient with the drip-stand behind them.

"Judge... My name's Niño Aukins. I need to talk to you," the man said.

"You can start by telling me why you're masquerading as a patient," Deacon said. "You've got a glucose bag, but no cannula in your arm."

"God damn it, he's a reporter!" said Witcombe. She looked at the four officers and yelled, "Hoffman! Get this creep out of here!"

"He's no reporter," Deacon said, taking a step towards Aukins. "He's a junkie. High-functioning, I'd say, but look at his skin, at the tremor in his hands. At his eyes. He's a long-term user, habitual, and right now he's got a serious case of the sweats. He's in need of a fix. Am I right, Aukins?"

The man began to back away. "No, wait, you have to listen to me, Judge! I have information—I know the man you're after, and how to find him! All I want is protection until it's over, and then immunity from prosecution. You can do that, can't you? A cop promises that, he has to jump through all sort of legal hoops, but not Judges. Your word is the law."

"Tell me what you know, and then we'll talk about that."

"No, you promise me! You give me your *word* that I'll be safe!"

Captain Witcombe said, "It's a scam, Deacon. He'll say anything for a fix. He doesn't know jack. Hoffman, throw him out."

Deacon stepped in front of Officer Hoffman and said, "Aukins, how do you know who we're looking for?"

"I've worked for him. That's all I'm saying until you promise immunity!"

"Give me something to prove you're on the level," Deacon asked.

Niño shrugged. "I... I don't know. Sometimes there *is* no proof. Just trust me." His eyes flickered towards the cops. "But not here. It's not safe here."

* * *

"WE'RE A TEAM," Officer Gress told Judge Rowain. "We watch each other's backs. We *cover* each other." She paused. "You get what I'm saying?"

"I understand," Rowain said. They were standing at the police station's back gate, far from anyone who might be eavesdropping, watching the thin stream of mid-afternoon traffic. "What do you know?"

Gress bundled her coat around her, hugging herself. "I'm not going to say anything that'll incriminate someone. Judges have power."

"We do. That's the point of Judges."

"Yeah. You might want to think a little *deeper* about that, Judge Rowain." Gress sighed. "Judges have power. There are no doors closed to you that might be closed to, say, a police officer."

Rowain nodded. "This is true. And again, one of the reasons Judges are necessary. But tell me this, Officer Gress... Do you think that we're chosen to be Judges because we've been gifted limitless patience? Stop hinting and *tell* me or I'll charge you with hindering the progress of an investigation. You'll lose your job, your pension and at least two years' freedom."

"I don't know if there's a connection... But... I believe that Farrell Silberman is innocent. Don't get me wrong: he's one *nasty* son of a bitch, and he deserves to be where he is—no one else ever deserved anything more—but he was innocent of this." Gress looked away from the Judge. "Silberman's serving sixteen in county. But it wasn't him. The night it happened, Silberman was too drunk to even *find* his car, let alone drive it. *He* thinks he's guilty, but he can't remember it; and that's because it never happened. He was already awaiting trial for DUI, but we'd heard that his lawyer had found a pretty solid way to get the arrest overturned. So I was asked to swear that I'd seen Silberman driving north out of town at about midnight. Judge, I refused to do that. Not because of some sense of loyalty to the truth, but because I was off-duty. I was drinking in The Gilded Horn at midnight and there were twenty witnesses who could put me there. I knew the story would fall apart if I had to testify."

"Gress..."

"I'm just saying that *I* didn't do anything wrong. And that three years earlier, Farrell Silberman beat his own brother half to death, and no one could touch him because the brother was too scared to speak up. And he's done worse. *Much* worse. We've never been able to pin anything on him, so this was an opportunity to get rid of him and sort out a problem at the same time."

"What was the problem, Gress?"

The officer was shaking now, and Rowain could see years of anger and frustration and guilt boiling in her.

"I don't know for sure... But Farrell Silberman was charged with the death of Sergeant Tobias Leandros, and he didn't do it."

"Just tell me who asked you to help cover up Sergeant Leandros's death."

"Detective Morrow. On Captain Witcombe's behalf."

"Why do you think Morrow asked *you* if she knew you weren't on duty that night?"

"Because I helped the captain before. Helped her *husband,* I should say. Harvey's been caught driving under the influence three times in the past twenty years. And each time the captain asked us to make it go away. And that night... I don't know for sure, but—well, Harvey Witcombe went on the wagon around that time and he looked awful guilty at the sarge's funeral."

"I see." Rowain took a step back, and looked towards the police station. "Gress, my advice is that you take the afternoon off. Don't even go back inside. Just get in your car and drive. Don't go home. Go somewhere no one knows you. Just in case. And don't come back until you hear from me or one of the other Judges." Rowain unclipped her radio. "Francesco, come in. I mean, Judge Deacon."

*   *   *

Niño Aukins stood in the centre of the giant faded H painted on the roof. He briefly looked up into Judge Deacon's opaque visor, then looked away. "Hospital used to have a helicopter service, back in the day. When did everything turn to crud, Judge? The whole world has gone down the crapper and... and... I used to have a handle on things. I used to be in control of my own life. Or, I *felt* like I was in control, and maybe that's the same thing." He began to turn around on the spot. "You sure we can't be overheard up here?"

Deacon said, "There are no guarantees. What do you know, Aukins?"

Niño wrapped his bare arms tighter around his chest and wished he'd brought a sweater or a jacket. "Damn, I thought it was cold before. Up here?" He began to walk towards the western edge of the roof. "Cops have those listening devices, right? Those 'magic ear' things that can amplify sounds? Well, before I talk, I want to be sure that they're not—"

"Shut up a second," the Judge said, and Niño turned back to see him unclipping his radio. "Deacon. Go ahead, Rowain."

"But this is *important*," Niño said.

The Judge held up his index finger and gave Niño a look that said, 'Don't make me tell you again.'

Niño looked out over the city. The sun was low in the sky, reminding him how much he hated this time of the year. In a few weeks, sure, the days would start to lengthen and that sense of hope would return, the feeling that spring was within reach, bringing the promise of a long, warm summer. But right now, the air was sharp and freezing, the sky was dirty grey, and you were never sure whether the world was just asleep and would soon wake up again, or if it really was dead this time.

He was torn between rubbing his arms to keep warm and biting his nails. This was bad. *What were you thinking, you moron? He spotted immediately that you're a junkie, and you expect him to just* believe *you about Romley?*

Downstairs the police captain and the four officers were waiting, and they'd been right there when he told the Judge that he knew who he was looking for. *That was a mistake. Should have found a way to talk to him away from them!*

He still hadn't decided exactly what he was going to say about his employer when he wasn't certain where Romley lived or even what his first name was. The thought now occurred to him that if the Judge didn't believe him, and if one of the cops *was* on Romley's payroll—which was almost certain—then Niño was screwed.

Back away, Niño told himself. *While the Judge has his mind on other things, just back away slowly, and when you get to the stairs, run. And never look back.*

Romley's plan to get the cops and Judges fighting each other would never have worked anyway.

He's just going to have to accept his losses and move on.

And if one of those cops is working for him, and they tell Romley what I told the Judge, then I'll just say that it was a ruse, to distract them.

The Judge put away his radio, and looked in Niño's direction for a moment. "Aukins, you stay put."

"What? I'm *freezing* up here, man!"

"Not my problem. I come back and you're not here, you're in trouble." The Judge started heading for the stairs. "But not as much trouble as you'll be in if you've been lying to me. See, I can't yet figure out how you have anything to do with Judge Leandros's death, so you'd better have a damn good explanation."

Niño began to follow the Judge. "What? I don't—what the hell—"

Then Judge Deacon stopped.

Ahead of him, the doors to the stairwell opened. The police captain and three of her officers strode out.

The captain asked, "Everything okay up here, Judge?"

Niño knew that he should leave now, just skirt around them while they were all staring at each other and make a run for the stairs. But the expression on the Judge's face was enough to keep him interested. He had no idea what was coming next, but he sure didn't want to miss it.

Deacon stepped forward and said, "Captain Witcombe. There is no evidence."

Captain Witcombe said, "Excuse me?"

"Judge Leandros's body. The coroner used a particle harvester to check her entire body for foreign matter or DNA that might point to the killer. But there was *nothing*. Someone scrubbed Leandros's body before dumping it into Henderson Rotzler's yard."

"We already know that," the captain said, nodding. "But a lack of evidence doesn't get us anywhere."

"It proves that someone knew what evidence they needed to hide. Tell me about Judge Leandros's father, Captain. You served alongside him, didn't you?"

"I did. I knew him well." She moved to the side, still watching Deacon.

Niño looked from Deacon to the four police officers, all of whom were watching the Judge carefully. *They've already forgotten I'm here*, Niño told himself. *I should go now while I have the chance.*

He began to sidle towards the stairwell, but stopped when the Judge—who didn't even turn around—said, "Stay put, Aukins. I'm not done with you yet."

To the other officers, he said, "I want to see your hands. All of them. I see a hand straying towards a holster, my hand is going to move too. You don't want to test me on that." He turned to the captain again. "Captain Virginia Witcombe. You will answer these questions succinctly and in full. Did you order your people to cover up the death of Sergeant Tobias Leandros and manufacture evidence to point to Farrell Silberman?"

Through gritted teeth, Witcombe said, "I did not."

"Was your husband Harvey Witcombe in fact responsible for Sergeant Leandros's death?"

Witcombe kept moving, slowly but steadily, and the officers

moved with her. All of them kept their eyes on the Judge. "No."

The Judge now had his back to the stairs. *Can't he see what they're doing?* Niño wondered. *They're* herding *him!*

"Did you or someone acting under your orders kill Judge Charlotte-Jane Leandros to prevent her from investigating her father's death and uncovering evidence of your crimes?"

"No! You can't *do* this, Deacon—you can't just throw baseless accusations around!"

"Yes, I can." Deacon turned back towards Niño. "Aukins, can you corroborate any of this?"

Niño said, "Well, actually, no. Judge, I have zero clue what's going on."

"I can give you the protection you asked for."

"No, seriously, Judge. I did hear that a Judge was killed, but that's *not* what I wanted to talk to you about. Look, this has nothing to do with me, so I should go inside and—"

"Don't you move a damn *muscle!*" the captain snarled.

Niño froze.

A woman wearing a dark suit had emerged from the stairwell and was aiming a gun at the back of the Judge's neck.

CHAPTER SIXTEEN

DEACON WAS STILL looking towards Aukins, but it was clear from the junkie's expression and the tone in Captain Witcombe's voice what just happened.

Without turning around, he said, "I'm guessing that's Detective Morrow behind me. Witcombe... You've crossed a line. Until now you *might* have been able to find a way out of this. But now you're finished. All of you."

"No, *you're* finished," Morrow said. "Killed by a junkie who thought you were about to arrest him for his involvement in the TranceTrance operation."

Deacon slowly turned around, and his face was so close to Morrow's gun that he could smell it: machine-oil, mixed with the scent of her skin, and a trace of gunpowder that told him the gun had been fired in the past day. The three officers also had their guns drawn. "Five against one," Deacon said. "Bad odds."

"Shut up," Witcombe said, moving around to stand next to Morrow. "Damn you, Deacon. Damn *all* of you. Not even eight hours in my town and you've screwed up *everything*."

Still keeping the gun aimed at his face, Morrow took three steps back. "Hoffman, remember you always talked about retiring before you were fifty? You got your wish. The Judges are retiring all of us."

151

Deacon said, "Aukins... You might want to turn your back on these former police officers and start to move away, slowly."

"Turn my *back* on them? Are you insane? They're going to kill both of us!"

"Maybe. But we don't want to make it easy for them to cover it up. Explaining why they shot a suspect in the back is going to be tricky. Do it." He risked a quick glance back, and saw the junkie reluctantly turning around. To Witcombe, he said, "Even if you kill all of us, more Judges will come. You can't stop this. Drop your weapons right now and you get to live. That is the only offer I'm going to make, and the only warning. Do we have an understanding?"

Captain Witcombe said, "The junkie pulled out a gun, started shooting. We returned fire, but unfortunately Judge Deacon was caught in the crossfire. That sound feasible to you, Hoffman?"

Officer Hoffman said, "That's pretty much how I remember it, Judge."

"Morrow?"

"It's a tragedy. Honestly, Deacon, it really is. As a Judge, Leandros had the power to open every old case, and if she'd chosen to look into her father's death, she'd have spotted the holes. We couldn't let that happen. Locking Harvey up wouldn't have brought Sergeant Leandros back from the dead, and Farrell Silberman needed to be put away. Best of both worlds. If *you* hadn't assigned Charlotte-Jane to this town, none of this would have been necessary." Morrow paused, then added, "Actually, we can blame old man Rotzler, too. If he hadn't locked up his dogs last night, they'd have disposed of the body without alerting him. We would have had the time we needed to lay a trail showing Leandros had left town."

One of the other officers said, "Wait. If we're going to pretend that the junkie shot him, then where did the junkie get a gun? We have to be consistent about that."

Hoffman rolled his eyes. "For cryin' out loud, Turley, we can worry about that later! They—"

From behind Deacon something boomed, and Detective Morrow collapsed backwards.

Deacon threw himself to the side, pulling out his firearm. He hit the ground and fired, four shots.

He rolled to his feet, gun still aimed at the officers, but already knew that there was no need. Half of Morrow's head was gone, and Witcombe and her three officers were on the ground, clutching chest wounds.

Still watching them, Deacon said, "Aukins... that was you?"

"Yeah, Judge. I never really shot anyone before..."

"Well, it was a good shot for your first. Now, put your gun on the ground and come here." He unclipped his radio from his belt. "This is Deacon. Rowain, you almost here?"

"We're three minutes away from you, Judge."

"Contact Judge Vaughan in Colton, tell her to pick up Harvey Witcombe. Charges are driving under the influence, vehicular manslaughter and conspiracy to pervert the course of justice. Forty-five years." He put away his radio, and dropped a set of handcuffs at Captain Witcombe's feet. "I can see how bad your wound really is, Witcombe. Don't make out that it's worse. Put the cuffs on."

"This won't stick, Deacon! I *know* people. I can get this conviction overturned in a *day*."

"Is that so?" He glanced over his shoulder and beckoned Aukins closer, then handed him three more sets of handcuffs and a handful of steri-patches. "Cuff the others, Aukins, and tend to their wounds. Just peel the backing off the patch and press it down firmly."

Aukins tentatively approached the other police officers. "Oh, man... There's a *lot* of blood, Judge." He crouched next to Hoffman.

"Just be grateful that none of it is ours. So... what *was* it you wanted to talk to me about?"

"The TranceTrance factory. I work for the guy behind it. I can give him to you, in exchange for immunity. Uh, Judge? This one's still got his gun in his hand."

"I saw that. My bet is he's not going to use it; he'd rather be in prison than in pine... See? He's setting it down. So who's the boss?"

Aukins smiled. With all four of the officers now in handcuffs, he stood up and walked back to the Judge. "*You're* the boss, Judge."

"No, I mean, who is the man you've been working for?"

"Oh, right. I get immunity from prosecution? I mean, he has so many people in his pocket—or under his thumb—that I could never go to the cops, or even to a lawyer."

Deacon nodded as he put away his gun. "On the condition that your statements are full, frank and lead to a successful prosecution of a person that we deem to be a significant producer of illegal narcotics, yes. I promise that you will have full immunity."

"For this and all past crimes?"

Deacon realised the man was trembling again, this time more from relief than withdrawal. "Yes. And I can put you into a detox programme, help you break your habit. It's going to be tough, but it's usually effective."

"His name's Romley. I don't know his first name, or where he lives. But I know he's waiting for a call from me. He wanted me to kill the cop downstairs, Officer Chaplin. Make it look like he died from his wounds. Then the other cops would be so mad they'd go to war with you Judges, and he'd use that distraction to get his merchandise back. But you can trace his number, right? Find him and pick him up?"

"We can. Show me his number."

Aukins fished his cell phone from the pocket of his sweatpants, found Romley's number and held it out to the Judge. Deacon took it with his left hand, and with his right he closed a pair of cuffs over Aukins' wrist, then grabbed his other arm and did the same.

"Wait, what? You promised immunity!"

"I lied. You're involved in the manufacture and distribution of a controlled substance, plus you've just shot and killed an officer of the law."

Aukins started to back away. "No! No, that's not fair! I just saved your *life*, Deacon!"

"You did. Now save your own and accept your sentence. I promise that by the time the detox programme is done with you, you'll be clean." Deacon took out his own phone and dialled a number. The call was answered after a few seconds, then he said, "Marisa... Need you to trace a cell phone for me." He read out Romley's number, and said, "Soon as you can. Appreciate it."

"He's going to kill me," Aukins said. "He'll get someone to do it. Even if he's locked up, there'll be a way to get the word out and he'll find out it's me and then..." He almost screamed when he collided with someone behind him, and turned to see two more Judges glowering at him.

Deacon said, "Judge Boyd, take Niño Aukins here into custody. Possession of an unlicensed firearm, ten years. Discharging said firearm at an officer of the law with intent to kill or wound, twenty years. And two years in narcotic detox, to be served concurrently."

"But they were going to shoot me!" Aukins said. "I was just protecting myself!"

Deacon and Rowain watched as Boyd dragged Aukins away, then Rowain looked down at Captain Witcombe and the other officers. "There are paramedics on the way. I told them not to rush. You sentenced them yet?"

"Not yet," Deacon said. "I'm still adding up their crimes. At the very least, we're looking at a century of incarceration for Witcombe."

Rowain nodded. "Sounds about right."

Deacon walked towards the edge of the roof, looking west over the city, and Rowain followed him.

The sun was touching the horizon, but his visor cut out the glare. "Couple of minutes, I'll go talk to Leandros's family." His cell phone beeped, and he answered the call. "Got it, thanks, Marisa." As he was putting away his phone, he said to Rowain, "You're not done yet. Mister Aukins has given us his boss, creep named Romley. You'll need to pick him up. But before you go..."

Deacon pulled off his helmet, and looked down at Rowain. "So. First full day as a Judge. Any regrets?"

"Not yet." Lela Rowain also removed her helmet. "But... When I was three years old, you used to carry me everywhere. You basically took care of me for an entire summer, do you remember that? You'd take me to the park, and carry me on your shoulders. They're my earliest memories. Warm orange evenings in Cunningham Park, with me dripping ice cream on your head and you laughing as it ran down your forehead."

Deacon smiled. "I remember. I was seventeen, and all the girls in the neighbourhood thought you were adorable. I'm not ashamed to say that I used my baby cousin to get them to talk to me. I'm sure if I'd had a puppy, I'd have ignored you. What made you think of that?"

"I was just thinking... Those days are *gone*, Francesco. Maybe out here in the small towns, things will carry on as they were for a little while, but in the cities, no one goes to the park any more. No one walks to school because it's too dangerous. Back home, my mom won't go to the store on her own, even in the middle of the day."

"That's why they need *us*, Lela. The Judges will bring everything back into balance."

She shrugged. "I hope you're right."

After a moment, Deacon said, "Let's go find those paramedics, and then you go after Romley. We have a long night ahead of us."

He turned away, but Judge Lela Rowain lingered for another few moments, watching the sunset.

"Come on," Deacon said. "It's getting colder and darker by the second."

"Yeah. It is."

ABOUT THE AUTHOR

Irish Author **Michael Carroll** is a former chairperson of the Irish Science Fiction Association and has previously worked as a postman and a computer programmer/ systems analyst. A reader of *2000 AD* right from the very beginning, Michael is the creator of the acclaimed *Quantum Prophecy/Super Human* series of superhero novels for the young adult market.

His comic work includes *Judge Dredd* and *DeMarco, PI* for *2000 AD* and *Judge Dredd Megazine* (Rebellion), *Jennifer Blood* for Dynamite Entertainment and *Razorjack* for Titan Books.

www.michaelowencarroll.com.

LONE WOLF

GEORGE MANN

For Nick Kyme,
fellow investigator

OUTRAGE TODAY AT *the words of Governor Walter Adams,*
whose incendiary statement regarding Chief Judge Fargo and
his controversial Judges programme—which he likened to a
military coup—appears to have stirred a hornet's nest amongst
activists and concerned citizens throughout the State of New
York. As a small group of protestors took to the streets around
Central Park in support of the Governor's position, the new
Judges nevertheless continued to enforce the law all across the
city, appearing to work in concert with NYPD precincts to
bring criminals to justice.

Chief Judge Eustace Fargo was unavailable for comment,
but Governor Adams's statement has provoked a response
from the White House, with the Communications Secretary
claiming the President remains in 'full support' of the Judges
programme and the 'surety and protection it offers our
citizens.' "The streets," he went on, "have never felt so safe."

NYPD Commissioner Paul Donner appeared to echo the
President's sentiments: "There is no denying the impact of the
Judges. Arrests are up, unsolved cases are down. Homicides
are in decline. Provided the Judges continue to co-operate with
the NYPD, I believe they can be a force for good in our city."

Anti-Judge sentiment appears to be growing amongst local
citizens, however, many of whom feel emboldened by the
Governor's words. "What they represent is nothing short of

the erosion of liberty," said Josiah Mainwaring, an AI specialist who was down on the front line of the pickets this afternoon along with over a thousand other like-minded protestors. "Where's the burden of proof? The right to a fair trial? If one of these so-called 'Judges' doesn't like the look of you, you're done for, right? You could be staring down the barrel of a gun for nothing so much as looking at them the wrong way, and they don't have to answer to anyone. What makes them so special? It ain't right."

Referring there, of course, to the Judges' right to carry out sentencing on the spot for all observed crimes, including the lawful execution of any citizens deemed to have committed a capital offence.

The protests are expected to continue through into tomorrow, as more citizens join the gathered throng near Central Park to raise their placards against what they're calling 'the injustice of the Judges.'

In other news, citizens are advised that a fierce storm is raging over the Atlantic Ocean, and is expected to hit these shores within the next few days...

CHAPTER ONE

Thursday, September 14th 2034
10:21

BENEATH HER, THE Lawranger thrummed, its engine growling as she gunned it. Shop fronts passed in a blur of liquid neon, flickering across the front of her visor. She leaned into the wind, willing more speed from the machine.

To her left, Ramos was keeping time, weaving right and left through the beeping traffic, tyres screeching on the asphalt as he swung the heavy bike around a yellow taxicab. The driver slammed his brakes on, grinding to a halt as the two Judges shot by, and bellowed from his open window.

Up ahead, police sirens wailed shrilly, cutting through the roar of the cars. O'Shea could see dancing blue lights in the distance as three police cars sped through the sea of vehicles on 9th Avenue, leaving a trail of angry, displaced drivers in their wake. She'd only been on the job for a few weeks, but already O'Shea had come to realise this was the way of things, here in New York—the cops charge ahead, blind and ultimately powerless, leaving the Judges to clean up after them.

It couldn't last.

The call had come in a short while earlier—two NYPD detectives had managed to locate and corner the suspected serial killer Joseph Reece in the vicinity of Chelsea Market, on the corner of 9th and 16th. He'd resisted arrest—she'd expected nothing less—and half of Manhattan's finest were now descending on his location. If the detectives had called them in sooner, she and Ramos could have dealt with the situation quickly and cleanly, and none of this would have been necessary. But now the perp had got away, loose in the food halls, and the whole situation was spiralling out of control.

O'Shea shifted suddenly, hauling her bike over to avoid a pedestrian who had stepped unexpectedly from between two stationary cars. She dipped so low that her knee almost grazed the road, before heaving herself up again, sliding back into her seat and continuing her haphazard path through the mayhem. Behind her, the startled shopper dropped her bags into the road, loose oranges spilling out and tumbling into the storm drain.

"You should have booked her for jaywalking," said Ramos. His voice crackled and popped inside her helmet. She glanced across at him and he gave her a little salute, touching two fingers against the ridge of his helmet. He swung out wide to avoid another slow-moving car.

O'Shea grinned. "I suspect the fright of nearly being mowed down will be enough of a lesson for her."

"You're too soft," said Ramos. She could hear the amusement in his voice, but there was an edge to it too. "We're Judges now. We have to be seen to uphold the laws. All of them."

O'Shea dipped her head, twisted her accelerator and shot forward, pulling ahead down the road. They were closing on the police cars now.

He was right, of course—she had a job to do. Everything was changing. Give it a few years, and there'd be no need for the police, or the old judicial system. The Judges programme was the future, and she had to play her part in making it a success, despite all the naysayers and the protests, the detectives who wanted to keep her at arm's length. She had to rise above it all and be impeccable, a bastion of the law, an example to the people who would follow in her wake. At least, that's what Chief Judge Fargo had said on her last day at the academy.

The police cars were slowing. Others had already formed a roadblock, and a riot of taxicabs and civilian cars were being diverted down a side street, horns blaring in an angry cacophony. O'Shea pulled her bike to a stop by the sidewalk and hopped down, boots splashing in a dirty puddle. The rain had been sweeping across the island in persistent squalls for the past few days, and there was word that these intermittent downpours were just the vanguard of a massive storm that had been brewing over the Atlantic and now threatened to pummel the Eastern Seaboard. All across the city, people were buying in provisions and cancelling engagements, getting ready to batten down the hatches and lock themselves indoors for the duration of the storm. *All except the people here*, she thought wryly, scanning the faces of the slowly massing crowd. Didn't they have something better to do?

O'Shea checked her gun, and then fell in beside Ramos as they approached the cordon. Civilians parted like a wave before them. The people were still unsure of the Judges, and experience told her they typically responded in one of two ways—with righteous anger or sheer terror. So far, NYPD cops had proved no different.

Ramos approached a female officer who was leaning against one of the squad cars, a comms unit in one fist and her handgun in the other. Her hair was braided and tied back beneath her cap, her skin milky brown and smooth, flecked with a spray of freckles across her nose. She was young, like O'Shea: in her late twenties at most. She looked up as the Judges approached, and then, eyes widening, pushed herself slowly off the car.

"Sitrep?" said O'Shea.

The woman swallowed and licked her lips. "He's in there," she said, nodding towards the covered market building. "They've got him on the run."

"People are at their most dangerous when they're on the run," said Ramos. "Back them into a corner and they lash out like animals."

The woman nodded, but didn't add anything. O'Shea saw her swallow again, and then glance across at one of the other squad cars, where her eyes met those of a stocky male cop with close cropped blonde hair, his upper lip twisted by a thin, silvery scar. He looked away when he noticed O'Shea watching.

"Things are about to go south," said Ramos, eyeing the market building.

O'Shea turned to look. The noise was tremendous as squawking civilians tried to flee the food halls, only to be held in by a tightening noose of police officers with plastic riot shields. They'd been ordered to keep everyone inside until Reece had been taken into custody. An uncontrolled evacuation would provide too much cover. If the perp got out, he'd go to ground in the Chelsea slums.

Nevertheless, Ramos was right: the situation was about to boil over. If the terrified mob decided to take on the police...

O'Shea started forward, Ramos following in her wake.

"Wait! You can't..." started the police officer, but a glance from O'Shea was enough to silence her.

"Let me through," said O'Shea, as she approached the police perimeter.

"Are you mad? There'll tear you apart. *Look* at them." This from one of the male cops currently ducking behind his shield, feet planted firmly as if he expected the civilians to rush him at any moment. Sweat was beading on his brow. Beneath the brim of his helmet, his eyes were darting.

"They're *scared*, officer," said O'Shea. "Trapped in a building with a wanted man. A man who's growing more desperate with every second we waste out here." She glowered at him, though her visor obscured most of her expression. "I'm not mad, I simply wish to do my job and assist these people as quickly and efficiently as possible. What reason would they have to tear me apart?" She shoved her way through the perimeter, pushing the officer's shield to one side and walking directly for the nearest entrance to the market. Civilians looked up at her with a mix of awe and appalled fascination, before shuffling quickly out of the way. She ducked through the entrance, straight into a lobby area where more civilians were cowering in a huddle, clamouring for a chance to escape.

"We'll have you all out momentarily," said O'Shea, raising her voice above the babble. "Just keep out of the way and you won't get hurt."

She turned to seek out Ramos who was watching her from nearby, wearing a lopsided grin. She wished for a moment she could see his eyes. He was so damn inscrutable.

A quick scan of their surroundings told her the food court was empty. Even the stallholders had abandoned their wares; nuts, burritos, burgers, fine wines, gelato. The place was thick with the mingling scents of sizzling meats, spices and coffee, and smoke curled from a nearby hotplate, where now-indistinguishable vegetables had been reduced to smouldering black lumps. A box of noodles had been dropped on the wooden floorboards close by, spilling its contents like a nest of gelatinous worms. Overhead, the artificial lights were stark and bright, creating deep shadows along one wall of shop fronts. She heard mumbled voices in the other aisles, along with hurried footsteps—the police, she assumed, carrying out a sweep.

She felt a hand on her arm, and turned to see Ramos pointing. "Over there."

She followed his gaze. A male officer had appeared at the far end of the nearest row of shops, his arms extended before him, hands wrapped around the grip of his handgun. He was wiry and pale, and wore a short ginger beard. She watched as he entered one of the small shops through a glass door, re-emerged a moment later, glanced along the aisle and nodded at the two Judges. O'Shea took a step towards him, and then stopped as the man suddenly looked to his right. His gaze seemed to fix on the gelato stall opposite him.

"Hold it! Right there!" he barked.

A figure lurched forward from the shadows, slamming into the freestanding gelato counter and sending the whole thing toppling over. The officer was forced to lurch back to avoid a large plate of shattering glass. The figure from behind the counter—presumably Joseph Reece—took off at a run, and O'Shea realised he was dressed in an approximation of a Judge's uniform and helmet.

She raised her weapon, sighting along the barrel, but the man was too nimble and she wasn't able to get a bead. Cursing, she dropped her arms.

Ramos was already on the move, charging after the man, bellowing for any other police officers to converge on his position. Footsteps and raised voices erupted from all across the food court. The cop with the ginger beard had regained his footing and was also in pursuit.

O'Shea went left, ducking around the side of a pancake shop and into the next aisle of the food court. With Ramos coming up behind him, and the police swinging in from the sides, maybe there was a chance she could cut Reece off.

As she ran, thoughts tumbled through her mind. Why was Reece dressed as a Judge? What was he hoping to gain? He'd hardly be inconspicuous. In the current climate, wearing a Judge's uniform was just asking for trouble. Was it an attempted impersonation? Or was he trying to make a point? Either way, it wasn't going to look good, given the recent controversy and the protests.

She was running at full pelt now, her boots pounding the floorboards, her lungs burning. She barely noticed the gaudy signs of the shop fronts as she raced by, intent only on her goal—to bring this unnecessary mess to a swift, just conclusion.

Movement. She swung her weapon up as she ran, training it on the figure at the end of the aisle. Her finger twitched on the trigger, her aim wavering on the helmeted head of the perp... but at the last moment she pulled up and the shot went high, striking the brickwork on the far wall and causing dust and shattered brick fragments to rain down on the stall below. The concussive sound of the shot echoed loudly throughout the entire food hall.

Ramos—who'd made a dive for the floor as soon as he realised O'Shea had mistaken him for Reece—slowly got to his feet, dusting himself off. Once again, he fixed her with a wry smile. "You missed." Behind him, cops were still spluttering on the brick dust.

O'Shea studied her partner for a moment as he checked over his weapon. "You okay?"

Ramos nodded.

Somewhere close by, another weapon barked.

"Over here!"

The shout carried from the neighbouring aisle. The man's accent was thick, and local. Ramos looked at her for a moment, as if weighing up his next move, and then turned and ran. She followed behind, jogging now, still attempting to catch her breath.

Around the next corner, five officers stood in a semi circle around a coffee stall, weapons drawn, all looking down at the floor. Three of them—a woman and two men—wore the blue uniform of the NYPD, while the other two men wore jeans and shirts. Presumably the detectives who'd first cornered Reece in the market.

One of them—a guy with a shock of grey hair and startling blue eyes—glanced over his shoulder at their approach. "Oh, great," he muttered, making no attempt to disguise his disdain, "here comes the cavalry." Nevertheless, he stepped to one side to allow Ramos and O'Shea to join them.

Joseph Reece lay on the ground at the foot of the coffee stand, clutching his thigh, which—judging by the torn fabric and oozing blood—had taken a glancing shot from one of the detectives' weapons. Now that she got a closer look, it was immediately clear that Reece's costume was exactly that—a rough approximation of the uniform she was wearing, self-made, with shoulder pauldrons and a crudely fashioned badge.

Even his helmet was just a modified motorcycle helmet. He didn't appear to be carrying a weapon. He'd clearly been in hiding for some time, too—he stank of urine and excrement, and his trousers were dirty and looked damp.

He was a scrawny thing, thin, unkempt and jittery, and he was wailing pitifully as he pressed his fingers over the wound in his leg, attempting to staunch the blood flow.

"Joseph Reece?" said Ramos, his voice level.

Reece froze suddenly, and looked up at Ramos. He reached up and removed his helmet, revealing a gaunt, unshaven face, wide-eyed and pleading. "A Judge!" He jabbed a bloody finger up at Ramos. "Look at this! They shot me. That one, that policeman *there*." He indicated the second detective, a heavyset black man with a balding pate.

Ramos frowned. "Resisting arrest, impersonating a Judge... Murder."

Reece shook his head. "No, no, that's not right."

"So you deny killing Emilio Hernandez, Peter Sage and Eleanor Roberts?" This from the silver-haired detective, whose gun was still trained on Reece's chest.

"No, you've got it all wrong. We can clear this up. I've done nothing wrong. I killed them, yes, but I did it in the line of duty."

"The *line of duty?*" echoed O'Shea.

"Exactly!" said Reece. "I was just doing what was right. They were corrupt, wicked. They deserved to be punished. I heard what Fargo's been saying on the news, about how the Judges are necessary to uphold society, to ensure people are held to account. Well, that's all I've done. I saw that justice was done. I sentenced them to death."

"You sick bastard," muttered one of the uniformed cops.

"Get up," said the silver-haired detective. "You'll answer for this." He turned and glowered at O'Shea, and she knew that all he saw was the uniform, and everything it represented. They would get the blame for this. It would fan the flames of popular opinion. The Judges were going to be crucified.

Reece started to get to his feet. "You should be proud of me. A citizen, standing up for what's right." He leaned on the coffee bar, supporting his wounded leg, then turned to Ramos. "Following your example."

Ramos cleared his throat. "Joseph Reece. I find you guilty of the murders of Emilio Hernandez, Peter Sage and Eleanor Roberts. I sentence you to death."

Ramos's weapon barked, and Reece staggered back a step, his eyes wide. He looked down at the sudden fist-sized hole in his chest, made a wet sucking sound that might have been a laugh, and then toppled backwards, collapsing in a heap of limbs. Blood spread around him in a glossy pool.

O'Shea stared at Ramos in shock. Beside her, the bald detective was wiping blood spatter from his face with the crook of his arm. He looked furious. "Jesus Christ! We had him in custody. He didn't have a weapon. What gives you the right?"

"The law gives me the right," said Ramos. He holstered his gun and turned to leave.

"Oh, no," said the silver-haired detective. "You're going to have to explain this one to Flores yourselves."

Ramos looked as if he was about to round on the man.

"Of course," said O'Shea, carefully positioning herself between Ramos and the other man. "That man was dressed as a Judge. We'll need to assess all the evidence before briefing our superiors." She glanced at Ramos, who nodded his assent.

"All right," said the silver-haired detective. He turned to one of the uniformed men. "Carter, you and Shaw get those people out of here and help disperse the crowds. The last thing we need is another riot. The situation's bad enough already. Jackson—cover up that corpse and send for an ambulance." He glanced at O'Shea. "We'll see you and your partner back at the precinct, right?"

O'Shea nodded. "Right."

CHAPTER TWO

THE RAINWATER HAD finally stopped pouring down the back of his neck, but he could still hear it dripping, like some ominous clock, ticking away the remaining seconds of his life.

He drew a long, deep breath, and then choked, sputtering and shivering, his entire body wracking so that his bound wrists pulled on their restraints, stabbing at him where the skin had rubbed sore. He slumped, barely able to support his weight, but another flowering of pain at his wrists forced him to straighten his knees. He tried to lean back against the wall, but it curved away from him, taunting him with the unfulfilled promise of relief.

He spat a mouthful of sour phlegm into the water by his feet.

When had he last eaten? He wasn't even sure how long he'd been down here. It had grown periodically more and less cold and dark, but there was no real way of telling how long had passed. He felt hollow and weak, and the thought of food made his stomach clench. Nothing but rainwater had passed his lips since he'd been down here, and even that had made him vomit, at least the first couple of times.

He wondered how long it took to starve to death.

Above, he could hear the distant hiss of tyres on wet tarmac, the burr of engines, the chatter of the city. He'd shouted himself hoarse during the first few hours of his imprisonment, but the only response had been his own voice, echoing back at him along the empty tunnel. No one up there could hear him. No one was coming.

Weakly, he raised his head, looking up at the distant hole in the brick canopy above, but the light filtering through was meagre and washed out.

Just like me.

He clenched his jaw, forced himself to stop shivering. Then, slowly, he adjusted his position, careful not to lose his footing. The water level in the storm drain had risen, thanks to all the rain. It lapped at his ankles, spilling into his loafers, so that he could no longer feel his feet for the cold. He'd tried lifting them clear, positioning himself differently, but the wall was slick with algae and there was no ledge within reach— not without breaking his bound wrists, or at the very least, cutting off the circulation to his hands. Besides, he supposed it didn't really matter that much—he was going to die down here anyway, in the dirt and the slime, his blood washed away in the torrent of filth. That's what his captor had promised, and there was no reason not to believe him. The bloody gap where his front teeth had once been was testament to that. He probed the gums with the end of his tongue, wincing. The steel baton had taken six or seven teeth in all, and another was hanging loose. His lips were mashed, too, the scabs tearing open again with every movement. His jaw throbbed.

Something brushed past his leg, and he lurched back suddenly, kicking frantically until he launched whatever it was at the far wall in a shower of dirty water. It struck the bricks, squealed dully, and then sloped away, sliding back into the water and swimming off down the tunnel. It would be back, though. They all would. They were patient little bastards, and they'd come for him when he was too weak to fight them off. He'd probably sustain them for weeks.

He wondered when his captor would return. The man—he'd been dressed like one of the new Judges—hadn't been back for hours, maybe days. It was almost impossible to tell. His promise was still fresh, however, still ringing in the stagnant air: that the future held nothing but judgement and death.

CHAPTER THREE

"Hartigan, what the hell happened out there?"

The silver-haired detective offered Captain Flores a shrug as he strode into the precinct building flanked by uniformed cops, who swiftly dispersed under the thunderous expression on the captain's face. Flores had been waiting for them, and he didn't look happy. "You'd better ask *them*," said Hartigan, jerking his thumb at the two Judges walking in behind him. The other detective from the scene, Pennhouser, shook his head and scowled at Ramos.

"Judge Ramos?" Flores crossed the lobby to stand before them. He was a short man in his late fifties, with a muscular build and ink-black hair swept back from his face in a neatly oiled wave. His tone was disapproving, weary. O'Shea had met him briefly only once before, soon after being assigned to the area, and while not openly hostile towards the Judges like so many in the police force, he'd hardly been accommodating either. She had a sense that wasn't about to change.

Beside O'Shea, Ramos stiffened. "The perpetrator was sentenced on the scene, Captain Flores. The case is closed."

"Sentenced on the scene...?"

"He means he shot him," said Pennhouser. "Right there at the market. Never seen a damn thing like it. The perp was unarmed and in custody. Ramos here just took out his weapon and shot him dead."

Flores narrowed his eyes and looked up at Ramos, who appeared unmoved, his expression stony beneath his visor. "You shot him in cold blood?"

"I carried out his sentence," countered Ramos.

"In my book, son, that's called *murder*. No matter who he was, or what he'd done. He had the right to a fair trial."

"And that's exactly what he received," said Ramos.

"Goddammit, man! This isn't mediaeval times. We have due process. Evidence. You can't just execute someone in the street."

Ramos inhaled sharply, and O'Shea bristled, hopeful that her partner would be able to hold his temper in check. "Actually, Captain, I can." He let that hang for a moment, until the silence became awkward, tense. "Nor do I have to explain myself to you. You should be *thanking* me. I've saved the State a great deal of needless expense—fewer forms to fill in, no bloodsucking lawyers, no trial and custodial sentence, no endless interviews. Reece was clearly guilty; he admitted as much on the scene. He was *revelling* in it. His victims demanded justice, and I provided it, neat and efficient."

"You're a goddamn fool!" barked Flores, spittle flecking his lips. "Give a man a little power…" He trailed off, his face reddening as he tried to contain his ire. He'd been holding this in until now, O'Shea realised. "You're a liability," he said. "Both of you. You've come down here in your smart uniforms, with all your training and your bylaws and your high-and-mighty attitude, anxious to exercise your new powers, to be state-sanctioned killers. Well, I hope it was worth it."

O'Shea stepped forward. "Now hold on a minute, Captain. I understand that you're frustrated, that things have worked out a little differently to how you'd imagined, but Judge Ramos was carrying out his *duty*. You know why we're here, what laws we've been charged with upholding. You may not *like* what we represent, but the Judge programme is here to stay. We need to learn to work together—"

"*Together?*" Hartigan scoffed, cutting her off. "If we were working together, you would have allowed us to bring our *suspect* in for questioning. You would have helped us to do our jobs. We've got a shit storm brewing out there. You've seen the protests. Public opinion isn't going to go your way on this. And as soon as word gets out, half the goddamn city is going to descend on this precinct. So I hope you and Fargo are ready, because we're going to be too busy dealing with all the fallout to help."

Flores sighed, rubbing his hand over his face. He looked tired. "Hartigan's right, this isn't going to blow over. People are scared. They're scared of *you*. And that fear's going to turn into *anger*."

"We've taken a killer off the streets," said O'Shea. "We've made them safer."

"You don't get it, do you?" said Pennhouser, chiming in. "You being here, your presence in this city—it doesn't make people feel safe. It's put the fear of God into them. Now they don't just have to worry about getting mugged or robbed by criminals—they have to second-guess every action, every step, just in case a Judge is watching and takes exception. They're worried they'll get shot for dropping litter or crossing the street. And all the politicians—they're saying not to worry, that the Judge programme is working, that crime rates are already down, but every time one of you guys does this—"

"You think I give a damn about what people *think*?" said Ramos. "This isn't about me, and it isn't about them. It's about justice, about serving the law and doing what's necessary. You've had years to clean up these streets, and you've *failed*. How's that for a hard truth? The only reason the Judge programme exists is because the police couldn't hack it." A crowd had begun to gather around the edges of the lobby, officers emerging from their stations to listen in to the argument, their expressions sour. "If you're looking for someone to blame, you'd better start with the mirror."

Pennhouser edged forward, his fists clenching, but Hartigan placed a steadying hand on his shoulder. "Captain?" he said. "Maybe it's time we gave each other a little space. Pennhouser and I can get started on our report." He glanced at O'Shea, and his eyes suggested he was searching for an ally, rather than another fight.

"I think that's a good idea," she said. "We'll file our own report." She started to turn away.

"No," said Flores. "It's not as simple as that. You've still got a job to do. *All* of you."

"Captain?" said Hartigan. "As much as I hate to admit it, Ramos is right about one thing—there's no way Reece wasn't responsible for those murders. He was *proud* of it. He'd styled himself... well, he believed he was acting like a Judge, bringing justice to the people who'd wronged him. With Reece dead, there is no case."

Flores shook his head. His shoulders sagged. "I wish you were right. The call came in while you were down at the market. David Carrera's been reported missing."

"Carrera?" said Pennhouser. "Wasn't he on Reece's list of targets?"

"Yes," said Flores. "And given how Reece liked to restrain and torture his victims before death, there's a chance he's still out there somewhere, alive."

"Where?" said O'Shea.

"That's the problem," replied Flores. "We don't know."

"And with Reece dead, there's no way to ask him," added Hartigan. He shook his head. "All right, captain, so we have a manhunt on our hands. Where do we start?"

"We start by briefing these two," said Flores, indicating Ramos and O'Shea. "You wanna show this city you're more than just a gang of killers with uniforms and badges? You help us find Carrera."

Pennhouser was shaking his head. "Captain, you sure about this?"

"We do this together, and we do it quickly," said Flores. He looked at Ramos. "Well?"

A pause.

O'Shea had no idea which way this was going to go. Flores was playing a dangerous game if he expected Ramos to start taking orders from the NYPD.

After a moment, Ramos nodded. "All right, captain. Tell us what you need, and we'll lend our support." He glanced at O'Shea, and something silent passed between them. "But understand this—we're not part of your organisation, and we don't play by its rules. If faced with the same situation again, I wouldn't choose to act differently." He sounded stern, confident, but behind his back, O'Shea could see his left hand was trembling.

Flores gave a terse nod by way of reply.

Incredulous, Pennhouser lead them on to the incident room.

CHAPTER FOUR

"So far, we've been unable to ascertain where Reece has been holding his victims."

O'Shea's helmet rested on the battered, lacquered table next to her. She was pleased to be free of its weight, and she cricked her neck while she listened to Pennhouser running through the particulars of the case.

"What we do know is that they were each held for some time before Reece tired of them and killed them off, or they grew too weak and died. The forensic evidence suggests they were shackled by the wrists, and severely beaten with a baton or rod of some kind. Two of them had suffered broken ribs, and all of them had missing teeth. Post mortem, they were dumped in the Hudson river." Pennhouser sat back in his chair, grimacing. "Believe me, Ramos, I wanted this bastard dead just as much as you. I ain't arguing with the outcome, just the way you did it."

O'Shea glanced over at Ramos, sitting opposite her. He hadn't removed his helmet, and was sitting upright and rigid in his chair, hands on the table before him. He looked statuesque, unmoved. She wondered if this were simply his way of coping with what had happened—shutting everything down, focusing on the details of the case. They'd both been trained to deal with the aftermath of an execution, but she knew that when the time came for her to pull the trigger, she wouldn't take it lightly.

He cocked his head, but didn't otherwise respond.

"Leaving that aside," said Hartigan, "we've established that Reece was essentially seeking revenge upon the people he believed had ruined his life."

"How so?" said O'Shea.

Hartigan sighed. "Same old, same old. Progress pushing out the little guy. Up until last year, Reece worked for his brother's maintenance company. They had a contract with the city: keeping up repairs on everything from subway tunnels to storm drains, down in the Chelsea district. The area's been going backwards for years, as the up-and-comers started moving uptown and across to Brooklyn to the new developments."

"Nature abhors a vacuum," said Pennhouser, "and so does the city. Empty buildings have a way of filling up again."

"Slums," said Ramos.

"Let's just say I wouldn't let my daughter take a walk round there after dark," said Hartigan. "Anyways, Reece and his brother were making hay. A district falling into disrepair—there was work to be found, if you didn't mind rolling your sleeves up. That's until Carrera Enterprises moved in."

"As in, David Carrera, the missing man?" said O'Shea.

"The very same. Carrera put a bid in to regenerate the area. Level it all and start again. There was an outcry from conservationists, wanting to hold on to the city's legacy, but Carrera's bid got a green light. There was talk about backhanders, of course, but the paper trail was clean, and the deal was done. Carrera cancelled the Reece contract and moved his own people in." Hartigan tugged on his earlobe, a nervous tic O'Shea had already noted.

"So Reece went after Carrera," said Ramos. "But that sort of thing happens all the time, especially to contractors. And what about Reece's brother? Where does he come in?"

"I'm getting to that. At first, the brothers tried to get work elsewhere. They petitioned the local bodies to be assigned a different area, but I guess harsh words were exchanged about Carrera's regeneration project, and they were shut out. Blacklisted. Things went from bad to worse. You know how it is. Turns out Joseph Reece had previous for theft, and no one but his brother was prepared to give him the time of day."

"His brother had deeper issues too," said Pennhouser. "He was in debt up to his eyeballs. Couldn't make the payments. The company folded, and Reece—Carson Reece, the brother—was facing debtor's jail. Couldn't support his family any longer. So he threw himself into the Hudson."

"And *that* was the trigger that sent Joseph Reece after Carrera," said O'Shea.

"Exactly," confirmed Hartigan. "Or at least, that's our working assumption. Something flipped. He'd lost everything."

"Then what about the others? Emilio Hernandez, Peter Sage, Eleanor Roberts... Why them? Why not just go after Carrera right away?" Ramos leaned forward, resting his elbows on the table.

Pennhouser opened a brown paper file on the table before him, withdrew a sheet of paper and pushed it across the table to O'Shea. A photograph of a list, written in scratchy blue ink on a scrap of yellow legal paper. She recognised the names—the three victims, plus David Carrera, along with Governor Walter Adams.

"We retrieved that from Reece's apartment," said Pennhouser.

O'Shea passed it over to Ramos, who studied it silently from behind his visor.

"It's all the people involved in Carrera's bid," said Hartigan.

"Or at least, the ones Reece figured took backhanders to get the bid passed," added Pennhouser. "We've worked back through the victims, mapping their connections to the deal. No one seems to have done anything illegal... on paper, at least. But Reece clearly held them responsible."

"So Governor Adams was in Reece's sights too," said Ramos.

Hartigan nodded. "It seems likely. We think he was working his way through the list."

"Did Carrera know he was a target? And Adams, for that matter?" said O'Shea.

"Of course. But some people think they're invincible. We offered protection, but Carrera was having none of it, and Adams is so busy we've only been able to get in the same room as him once. We've been dealing mostly with his aide." Hartigan sniffed. "Still, I don't suppose it's an issue for Governor Adams now, is it? Imagine what he'd make of that? Couple of Judges doing him a favour." He grinned, and O'Shea offered him a weak smile. He was clearly trying to build bridges.

"All right, so Carrera was reported missing. We know our suspect is dead. How long's Carrera been gone?" said Ramos.

"Two days, according to this," said Pennhouser, glancing over the report in the file. "He hasn't been seen, and he's not answering his phone."

"I presume you've already tried tracking it?" ventured O'Shea.

"It's either dead or not connected to a network. Tech department can't pick anything up. Last time it pinged the network was just before he disappeared, somewhere close to his office," said Pennhouser.

"Then I guess we start at the office," said O'Shea, rising from her seat.

"I guess we do," said Hartigan.

CHAPTER FIVE

CARRERA'S OFFICE WAS a far cry from the tired, chaotic sprawl of the precinct building. Where the cops had grown into their space—cramming desks into every available corner, treading spilt coffee and food into the hardwearing carpets—Carrera's space had been *designed*.

The first thing O'Shea noticed was the view; one whole wall consisted of plate glass, with a view looking out over the hazy Manhattan skyline below. From up here, the surrounding skyscrapers looked like glassy protrusions, shards of sparkling light twisting out from the grey landscape below. Neon lights flickered in the distance—a recent trend to place the names of the immense new tenement buildings being erected in upper Manhattan on the sides of the buildings themselves. She supposed it helped, given that so many of them were being built to the same design. Soon, the street level would be nothing but a labyrinthine warren of narrow lanes and walkways between identical housing blocks. She noted the dark clouds gathering on the horizon. The storm was coming in, just as predicted.

She turned to regard the rest of the room. Diffuse light strips ran along the back wall, upon which the legend *CARRERA ENTERPRISES* had been emblazoned in foot-high steel letters. Beneath them, a woman stood behind a curved desk, looking nervously across at them and refusing to meet O'Shea's gaze.

The room was otherwise sparsely furnished, with a low wooden coffee table, surrounded by a pristine leather sofa and two matching armchairs. Three datapads rested on the table's surface, presumably to allow waiting visitors to browse. A wooden door—currently closed—led through into what she assumed was Carrera's personal office.

Everything about the place was designed to impress. It was impeccable, and expensive. Not a thing was out of place—aside from Carrera himself, of course.

Detective Pennhouser approached the woman at the desk, flashing his badge. He introduced himself. "This is my colleague, Detective Hartigan, and these"—he jabbed his thumb over his shoulder—"are the Judges assigned to Mr. Carrera's case."

O'Shea tried not to take it personally.

"We're here to ask you some questions about your employer," said Ramos, stepping around O'Shea so he was standing at the desk beside Pennhouser, who glowered at him but remained silent. "Tell me, what's your name?"

"E—El—Elizabeth," stammered the woman. "Elizabeth Soames. I'm Mr. Carrera's personal assistant."

"You're the person who reported him missing," said Ramos. It was a statement of fact, rather than a question.

The woman nodded.

"All right. I'm sure you've already explained this to the police, but I'd like to run through it again. When was the last time you saw Mr. Carrera?"

The woman cleared her throat and tucked a loose curl behind her ear. She was undeniably beautiful, but clearly nervous, pale and quiet; not at all the sort of person that O'Shea would imagine surviving for long in Carrera's world. Perhaps there was something O'Shea was missing. Or perhaps the woman was simply intimidated by the presence of two Judges. That was something she was still getting used to—the power inherent in her uniform. Ramos, in particular, had a manner that seemed to put people on the back foot, and he used it to great effect.

"Um, well... three days ago," said Soames. "Just before I locked up the office for the night. He left as usual. There was no sign that anything was wrong."

"Until the next day?" pressed Ramos.

"Yes, the following morning. At first, I didn't think too much of it. I mean—he's a busy man, always running about. I thought it was odd that he didn't show up for an appointment—"

"This was Tuesday, right?" interrupted Pennhouser. Inwardly, O'Shea groaned. She hoped the whole day wasn't going to be like this, with Pennhouser and Ramos constantly trying to one-up each other.

"Yes, that's right," said Soames. She had a kind of breathless quality to her voice, as if constantly struggling for air. "Tuesday. He had an appointment with Charles Rattinger, head of one of the building contractors he's engaged to help with redevelopment."

"But he didn't show?" said Ramos. "Was that typical of Mr. Carrera, to miss an appointment like that?"

"No, not at all," said Soames. She shook her head emphatically. "I tried to reach him on his personal cell phone, but he didn't answer. I presumed he'd been held up elsewhere, so I made his excuses to Mr. Rattinger and rearranged the appointment."

"And you didn't hear from Mr. Carrera at all?" said Pennhouser.

"No. He wasn't picking up my calls, and he didn't return to the office that day."

"So you called the station the following morning," said Pennhouser.

"Yes. By then I was starting to worry. It's so unlike him. He'd mentioned something about the police—about being on some sort of list—and so, after I'd tried him a few more times, I called the station to report it. Then I called ahead to cancel all of his appointments for the day."

Hartigan glanced at O'Shea. "We sent a patrol car to his apartment, but he wasn't there either. The bed hadn't been slept in."

"All right, Ms. Soames. Thank you. We're going to take a look in Mr. Carrera's office now," said Ramos.

The woman chewed her bottom lip for a moment, as if considering whether she should protest, but then nodded. "Of course. Just... You will find him, won't you?"

"We'll do our very best, ma'am," said O'Shea. She watched as Hartigan led the others through the door into Carrera's office, and then approached the desk. "Just one more question," she said. "What's your relationship with Mr. Carrera?"

The woman eyed her nervously. "I told you, I'm his personal assistant," she said. There was a tremor in her voice.

"Nothing more?" said O'Shea.

"That would be improper," said Soames.

O'Shea turned towards the door.

"He's a good man, you know," blurted Soames suddenly. O'Shea turned back to face her. "Kind. Considerate. I know he has a... reputation, but it's not true, not really. He's just been unlucky, that's all."

"What reputation would this be, Ms. Soames?" said O'Shea.

"You know, with women."

"There's no one significant in Mr. Carrera's life? No girlfriend, boyfriend?"

Soames shook her head. "No, no. No one like that. As I said, he hasn't been very lucky. Tends to meet the wrong girls."

"What do you mean by that, Ms. Soames? The wrong girls?"

"You know," said Soames. "They're always pretty enough, but they're only really attracted to his money and his influence. They see him as a step up, rather than a man."

O'Shea nodded. "All right. Thank you. We may have more questions once we're finished in there."

She crossed to the adjoining room. The tension was palpable. The office was even more sparsely furnished than the waiting area—just a single desk containing a large monitor and a keyboard, along with two chairs. There were no personal effects, no photographs, no scrawled notes. The only object of any real note was a large abstract canvas on the wall, filled with colourful shapes and splashes of paint. The original designers had probably placed it there when they'd first furnished the office.

Ramos was standing over the monitor, scrolling through a list of appointments. Pennhouser was peering over his shoulder, while Hartigan stood by the window, staring out over the city.

O'Shea noticed something flickering on the glass surface, and went to stand beside him. As she got closer, lines and shapes began to resolve into wireframes, describing towering structures; an overlay, she realised belatedly, of Carrera's planned remodelling of the Chelsea district. She stepped back, taking it all in. It was impressive, ambitious—everything she'd expected it to be. Where smaller, more characterful buildings now stood, immense tower blocks would rise, dominating the skyline for miles around. Walkways or roads criss-crossed the space between them, creating a new network of city streets, up amongst the canopy of the city. Here, the rich elites would migrate, lording it over all those below; a true upper class, intent only on growing fatter and richer, looking down upon those who failed to reach the heights.

It was obscene, and yet it was the story of the city, of America, of the world. It was an unstoppable tide now, the way of things. The rich would rise, and the poor would sink. She had no illusions. She'd grown up in a downtrodden district in Queens, amongst the alleyways and the gangs, the real people struggling to carve out a space for themselves, to live a meaningful existence in a world that barely noticed them. That was why she'd enrolled in the Judges programme in the first place: to protect people like that, and to prove to the world—and to herself—that everyone mattered. The rich were not above the law. No one was.

"I suppose it's impressive," muttered Hartigan, beside her. She glanced over, but his eyes were fixed on the city, and the coruscating overlay of Carrera's ambition. "If you like that sort of thing."

"Progress," said O'Shea.

"Progress?" echoed Hartigan. "I suppose you'd know all about that." There was no malice in his voice. Just weariness.

"We want the same things, you know. We're not what you think we are. We just want to uphold justice. To help people. To see that the law isn't impeded by red tape. We're here to cut through the bullshit."

Hartigan sighed again. "I know you mean well. I do. But you're rookies. Kids with guns. Look at what happened down there, at the market. Look at the mess it's made. Reece deserved to die, I don't dispute that. He was a foul human being, and he was guilty as hell. Every cop in this city has wanted to put a bullet in a perp, more than once in their life. When you see the sorts of things we've seen…" He trailed off, running a hand over his mouth and chin. "But lady, it just isn't that simple. I wish it was, I really do. But now this guy, Carrera, he's out there somewhere, maybe alive, maybe dead, and we've got no way of knowing. Where's the justice in that?"

O'Shea wanted to argue, wanted to tell him he was wrong, but the words wouldn't come. She stood in silence, staring out at the city, until the moment passed. She turned to Ramos, still standing over the computer. Behind him, Pennhouser was pacing.

"Find anything?" she called.

Ramos looked up, shook his head. "Not really. His schedule was full. There's no suggestion he was planning anything unusual."

"Pennhouser—have the PA run out a copy of that schedule. Let's see if we can trace his movements for the night he disappeared, fill in a few gaps. And see if she can give you the details for his car too. Let's run a trace." Hartigan didn't turn away from the window as he'd spoken. His eyes seemed to be transfixed by the gathering storm clouds. "We'd better work quickly. That storm's coming in hard."

Pennhouser turned and walked from the room without acknowledging the other man. Ramos looked up, visibly exhausted. "Come on," she said. "Let's take a look at Carrera's apartment." He nodded, coming around from the other side of the desk. "Detective?"

Hartigan half turned, glancing over his shoulder. "See you back at the precinct," he said.

IN MANHATTAN TODAY, *tensions continue to rise as civilians take to the streets in growing numbers, swelling the ranks of those protesting the controversial Judges programme. Many of them carry homemade placards bearing anti-Judge sentiments.*

In addition to the growing crowd near Central Park—now numbering in the tens of thousands—a second protest has formed in Union Square, and appears to be gathering momentum. There have been reports of similar movements in Brooklyn and Queens.

Many have come out in support of Governor Walter Adams, citing his statement from earlier this week, during which Adams made his position on the new programme undeniably clear: "All liberty will be lost. These so-called Judges are unconstitutional and must be removed."

Others have condemned Adams's words. Richard Paxon, Governor of Texas, said today that "the Judges have more than proved themselves," and that petty crimes and misdemeanours were at an all-time low, after just a few weeks. "Give me more of 'em," he said. "If Adams doesn't want them, I'll take 'em."

Adams himself has yet to respond to the wave of criticism, or to address the protestors who have rallied to his cause. As reports mount of violent activity and destruction to public property by protestors, the Governor is coming under pressure to make a statement.

More news as it arises.

Meanwhile, we have early reports that the notorious serial killer Joseph Reece was apprehended this morning in Chelsea Market, after NYPD detectives, working in tandem with Judges, were finally able to take him into custody. One civilian witness claims that Reece was seen to be wearing a self-styled Judge's uniform, leading to speculation that he was acting as a 'lone wolf,' a vigilante taking the law into his own hands.

Stay tuned for more on this breaking story.

In other news, the storm continues to roll in...

CHAPTER SIX

THE RAINS CAME not so much as a torrent, but as a drizzly veil, fine and mistlike, coating their visors as they rumbled through the slick streets on their Lawrangers. It was clear from the darkening skies that this was just the start of the storm—it would strike at full force soon enough, and there was every chance they'd have to take cover, abandoning the investigation while they awaited a break in the weather.

It would be far from ideal—there was every chance that Carrera was lying injured somewhere in the city, beaten, bruised, and tortured. The forensic reports showed that Reece had bound his previous victims by the wrists, and, judging by the severity of their injuries, even suspended them from the ceiling. It was imperative that they located Carrera in the next twenty-four hours. Otherwise it became increasingly likely that they'd be searching for a corpse.

O'Shea didn't know what to make of Carrera. The picture emerging wasn't particularly flattering: a businessman who'd used his political connections to leverage a regeneration contract at the expense of local workers, a man who—reading between the lines of his evidently smitten PA—was something of a serial womaniser. She wrinkled her nose in distaste. Nothing she'd seen so far suggested he was up to anything illegal, but it wouldn't surprise her. Nevertheless, she had to remember that he was the victim in all of this. Never mind his wealth, his flashy lifestyle; he was the man who'd been captured and possibly tortured... and that was assuming he wasn't already dead.

She wondered if the police were already searching the Hudson for his corpse. She considered calling Hartigan, but then decided to leave it until she saw him back at the precinct. She didn't want to stir the pot any more than they already had.

Ramos pulled to a stop and she followed suit, parking on the yellow lines and clambering off onto the sidewalk. Her uniform was dripping, although underneath she was still dry and warm.

They were standing in the shadow of one of the new tenement blocks she'd seen from Carerra's office window—an edifice of glass and steel, so tall that, even craning her neck, she couldn't see the top of it. Rain beaded on its slick, mirrored surface, and the stark neon sign—unreadable from this angle—cut through the gathering gloom like a knife.

Side by side they strode to the building's entrance. Uniformed guards stood by the sliding doors, eyeing them suspiciously. The doors remained shut.

"Can I help you?" said the guard on the left. He was a tall, muscular man, and his black uniform and cap lent him the appearance of a soldier. O'Shea could see the bulge of a firearm holstered under his left arm.

"We're here on Judge business," said O'Shea. "Investigating the disappearance of a resident, Mr. David Carrera. We require access to his apartment."

The guard hesitated for a moment, and then seemed to think better of it. He waved a finger at his colleague, who operated a control panel. The doors slid open with a pneumatic hiss.

Inside, the lobby was palatial, with a high ceiling supported by two rows of Corinthian columns, and a marble floor polished until O'Shea could see her face in it. There were no attendants or personnel. They crossed to a bank of elevators, their boots clacking on the hard floor.

"Seventieth floor," said O'Shea.

The elevator beeped in acknowledgement. She heard the whoosh of the car dropping down the shaft behind the ornate metal doors, and then, with a ping, the doors parted to allow them in.

"Even the elevators in this place are huge; this is as big as my apartment," mumbled Ramos, as the doors slid shut behind him. "Carrera must be raking it in."

O'Shea had to agree. Everything reeked of quality: the handrails, the gilt-edged mirrors, the top-of-the-range tech. It certainly beat the utilitarian stairwell in the Judges' quarters downtown.

"Ill-gotten gains?" ventured O'Shea.

Ramos shrugged. "Probably, but there's a fine line. Everything we've seen so far suggests Carrera has been operating within the law. Whether it's moral or not is none of our concern. Unless we see evidence of actual unlawful behaviour..." He trailed off, the implication clear. He, too, suspected Carrera was up to his neck in it, but they weren't there to investigate his financial history, and if there had been any unlawful dealings with the regeneration project, she was certain that all of those involved would have already buried their tracks.

They rode the elevator in silence for a moment.

"You doing okay?" said O'Shea.

"Why wouldn't I be?" replied Ramos gruffly.

O'Shea sighed. "You know, you did the right thing, whatever those detectives say. Whatever the protestors or the news reports say. You did what you'd been trained to do. You followed the law. I would have done the same thing."

Ramos glanced at her. The corner of his mouth twitched slightly. Not for the first time, she wished she could see his eyes. "You would?"

"Of course. None of this is down to you. Remember that. This is on Reece. He's the one who kidnapped Carrera in the first place." The elevator sighed to a halt, and the door opened. She stepped out into the hall.

"That costume he was wearing. Do you really think he thought he could be one of us? That that's what we do—kill indiscriminately? Seek revenge, rather than justice?" Ramos led the way along the hall to the correct door. There were only four apartments on the whole floor, and Carrera's appeared to occupy the entire southwest corner.

"I think he was blinded by grief and loss, and it broke him," said O'Shea. "He deserved his sentence, but he didn't deserve the suffering that came before it."

Ramos shook his head. "Don't start feeling sorry for him, O'Shea. Remember—the law is the law. He broke it."

O'Shea smiled sadly. "The law's the law," she repeated.

The apartment door was unlocked. Inside, two uniformed cops were sitting at a table. Their tablets were laid on the surface before them and they were playing some sort of game, bouncing a digital ball from one screen to the other. They looked up, startled, at the sound of the door opening, and one of the tablets bleeped.

O'Shea grinned. "Doing a fine job there, gentlemen," she said. "Don't let us stop you. We're only here to take a look around."

"Um… um… yes, sir," said one of the cops, a grey-haired man with a full beard and moustache. He started to rise, but his colleague waved him back into his seat.

"Give the Judges some room, Stan." He looked up at O'Shea, and then flicked his eyes to Ramos. "Just ask, if there's anything we can do for you. The boys from the precinct have already been down and given the place a once-over. Can't imagine you'll find anything."

O'Shea nodded. The apartment was like the rest of the building—spacious to the point of decadence, appointed with all the finest quality fittings, and with a view that rivalled the one in Carrera's office. And like his office, it lacked the personal touch. O'Shea had the distinct feeling that no one really *lived* there, so much as used it as a place to eat and sleep. She walked around, taking in the large TV on the living space wall, the automated coffee machine in the kitchen, the wardrobe filled with fine suits, all in grey. Somehow, it felt transitory, more like a hotel room than a home.

"For a rich guy, he doesn't have much of a thing for possessions, does he?" said Ramos.

"Something's certainly off," said O'Shea. "Nothing here's been touched. I mean, I can see that he's been staying here"— she'd spotted the basket of dirty laundry, the clean plates in the dishwasher—"but it looks like it's come right out of the catalogue. Nothing here gives us an insight into who David Carrera really is."

"Or more importantly, what's happened to him," said Ramos. "His diary was empty the night he disappeared. No dinner appointments, no late meetings, no social engagements."

"There's nothing to suggest Reece picked him up here," said O'Shea. "No signs of a struggle, no blood stains, not even an abandoned meal. And the guards would never have let Reece inside the building. His fake uniform wasn't *that* convincing."

"Precisely. So Reece must have picked him up somewhere else. The question remains: if Carrera didn't come home after leaving the office, where *did* he go?"

"Let's see if Hartigan and Pennhouser have been able to find anything in the schedule, or run a trace on his car," said O'Shea.

Ramos nodded. While he was clearly uncomfortable around the two detectives, he wasn't so stubborn that he wouldn't pool resources with them to resolve the case. He was a man driven first and foremost by duty.

"See, I told you there was nothing to find here," said the cop who'd spoken earlier, and had remained seated at the table throughout the Judges' visit.

"Well, you keep on guarding that nothing," said Ramos, "and make sure you get straight onto the precinct if Carrera or anybody else shows up."

The cop pulled a sour expression, and watched as the two Judges made for the door.

CHAPTER SEVEN

IT WAS RAINING again.

He'd come around to the sensation of water pattering against his face. For a moment, he'd forgotten where he was, but then he'd surfaced through the delirium, pushing his way up through the darkness and dizziness, and it had all come back to him in a sudden, gut-wrenching rush: the pain, the horror, the hopelessness.

He opened his mouth and allowed some of the dirty rainwater to trickle down the back of his throat. The water in the storm drain was up to his calves now, and he didn't have the energy to try to drag himself up any more. His feet were completely numb, and his damaged wrists were bearing all of his weight. The pain had become so complete, so ubiquitous, that it was now a comfort, and he could no longer remember what it was like not to feel it. That pain, that sharp, raw pain, was the only thing that told him he was still alive.

He tried calling out again, trying to raise his voice enough to be heard, but even that was betraying him now, and all that came out was a pathetic sob.

He knew he was dead. His captor wasn't coming back. All that was left was the water and the rats. He cursed his body for hanging on so long. Anything now would be relief. All he wanted was for it all to stop. He almost wished the man *would* return, and see through his dreadful promise. At least it would be over.

He wondered what he'd done to deserve this. Oh, there'd been plenty of backhanders and under-the-table deals, but they were all just part of the game, weren't they? That's how it worked, that's what kept the world turning. Sometimes you had to grease the wheels. He'd only done what was necessary, and even then, it was always for the greater good. He honestly believed that. He'd helped people all his life, and now this was his reward. An inglorious death, chained up in a storm drain amongst the shit and the rats, just like all the other detritus. This was the thanks he got.

He laughed, but stopped when the pain erupted right down the left-hand side of his body. He wondered what would get him first: the rising water or the rats. He hoped for the former. At least that way, he wouldn't know when the filthy critters started eating him.

A car passed overhead, displacing a puddle of standing water that sloshed down through the drain in a wave, crashing over the back of his dangling head. He willed the storm on, as if his swirling anger and his desperation were fuel, driving it deeper into the city, urging the rain to keep falling. All he could think about now was the water, and how it would consume him. Then, finally, he might be able to rest.

CHAPTER EIGHT

THE STORM WAS beginning to show its teeth. Thunder rumbled over the city like the murmurings of an angry god, causing the tower blocks to tremble. The rain had become a relentless curtain across the world. It drummed on O'Shea's helmet, drowning out the roar of her bike.

At least the streets were empty, she reflected—aside from the constant stream of yellow cabs which hissed through the streets in herds, ferrying their charges back to the safety of their homes. Most people seemed to be heeding the warnings, retreating from the storm before its true temper could be felt.

Nonetheless, she'd heard on the comm that the protests were ongoing, and that the protestors close to Central Park were erecting temporary shelters to see out the storm. People were going to get hurt. If something wasn't done soon to placate them, either the elements or the inevitable riots were going to lead to civilian deaths, and that would only make matters worse. The news stations were already pinning Joseph Reece's murders on the Judges, suggesting that since Reece had been inspired by the Judges, the blood of his victims was on Fargo's hands. All nonsense, but it was fuel for the poisoned rhetoric of men like Walter Adams, who claimed to have the best interests of the public at heart, but only truly cared about their own careers.

Still, all she could do was her job. It didn't matter if people wanted her protection or not—it was her responsibility to provide it, regardless.

She swung the bike around the corner of 32nd Street, sending a plume of rainwater up over the sidewalk. She could barely see for the rain. Another few blocks and they'd be back at the precinct, where she could dry off and see if Hartigan or Pennhouser had anything new to report.

Just as she leaned in her seat to swing the bike around another corner, the comm crackled loudly in her ear. "Judge O'Shea?"

"Speaking."

"Hartigan here."

"Detective. We're just heading back to the precinct now. We'll be with you in ten."

"That's why I'm calling. Pennhouser and I are heading over to Reece's place. The tech guys are still working on tracing Carrera's cell, but the schedule has thrown up a dead end. Oh, and we've located his car."

"At Reece's?" said O'Shea.

"Nothing so clear-cut. He'd left it parked in the street close to his office, but when he didn't return, the meter ran out and it was towed. We've had it picked up from the pound, but it's another dead end—the onboard computer says it hasn't been started since the morning before he disappeared."

"Damn," said O'Shea.

"Find anything useful at Carrera's place?"

"No, which is telling in itself. It doesn't look likely that he returned there after work," said O'Shea.

"We came to the same conclusion," said Hartigan. "Reece must have grabbed him off the street, before he made it back to his car. We've got uniform knocking on doors in the vicinity, just in case anyone saw anything."

O'Shea wiped rainwater from her lower face with the back of her glove. "All right, send through Reece's address, we'll meet you there."

"Already done." The comm clicked off.

O'Shea's nav system beeped, and she thumbed the new destination that popped up. She glanced at Ramos, but he was already turning his bike around. She turned at the end of the street and followed behind.

REECE'S APARTMENT WAS a far cry from the glamour of Carrera's place. From the outside the building looked near-derelict, with scores of boarded windows, graffiti tags and streaks of pigeon droppings scarring what might have once been a presentable apartment block. The weather didn't help, the rainwater turning the grey stone a slick, dreary black and the storm clouds dulling everything, so that the atmosphere around the place felt bleak and desolate.

Inside was no improvement. The stench in the lobby was vile, reminiscent of stale, rotten food and worse. The elevator was out of order, and the stairwell was crowded with the detritus of drug use. Unconsciously, O'Shea found herself reaching for her weapon as she climbed.

She could hear the sounds of a TV blaring from inside one of the apartments, along with the voices of a man and a woman, raised in argument. Empty cardboard boxes had been piled up against one apartment door, and another was hanging open, the upper hinge broken, the door panel cracked where someone had kicked their way in.

O'Shea's first question was why the police hadn't done anything about the place. There were numerous violations on display, and the landlord was clearly culpable for many of them. She made a mental note to report the situation later. Maybe she would return with Ramos once the Carrera matter was put to bed, see if she couldn't help clear the place up a bit, bring the law to bear.

That was one of the first things she'd learned at the academy: a Judge didn't wait for lawbreakers to be reported—they got out there and worked the streets, weeding out the trouble at its roots. For too long the police had relied upon citizens to report the lawbreakers in their midst. But what if those citizens were too scared, or intimidated, or just didn't care? It was all too reactive. The Judges would change all of that. They would look for trouble; they'd step in and take decisive action, right there on the spot. They'd change the way that law enforcement worked, and places like this would be shut down before they'd had chance to fester.

They reached the landing on the third floor. Garbage had collected in the passageway here, and at least three of the apartments appeared to be totally abandoned, the doors boarded up and chained to prevent squatters from taking up residence. Reece really had lived in the worst kind of circumstances. O'Shea wondered if he'd always lived like this, or he'd been reduced to this after Carrera's takeover of the district and the gradual collapse of his family business.

The door to Reece's apartment was open, and familiar voices echoed from inside. She walked straight in, holstering her gun on her hip. Hartigan, Pennhouser and two uniformed officers—both women—were standing in what she supposed counted as Reece's living room.

The apartment was cramped; little more than a single room, with a small bedchamber and even smaller washroom and toilet off of it. The kitchen was a row of cupboards, a work surface and a microwave. A compact refrigerator sat humming in one corner. The living space was a mess: food wrappers, dirty clothes, used plates and bowls strewn haphazardly on the floor, sofa and coffee table. The TV was mounted on the wall and looked ancient. The smell of rotting waste was near unbearable; it reminded her of the state of Reece himself when they'd cornered him, steeped in his own effluvia.

"How could someone live like this?" said O'Shea, and Hartigan turned around. He'd been deep in conversation with the uniformed officers, briefing them to carry out another full search.

"Less of an apartment and more of a hole," said Pennhouser.

"He was treading water," said Ramos. "O'Shea's right. No one chooses to live like this. I don't think he really *was* living. He must have seen this place as something temporary, a bolt-hole, somewhere to sleep and eat while he figured out his plans."

Hartigan nodded thoughtfully. "That makes sense. He'd lost everything. All he could focus on was revenge, on remaking himself in the image of a Judge. Nothing else mattered." His eyes flicked from Ramos to O'Shea, as if expecting them to challenge him. They didn't.

"Through here," said Pennhouser. He led them through into the bedroom, and pointed to a heap of clothes on the bed. There was a dark blue boiler suit, modified to vaguely resemble the Judges uniform. Beside it were clippings from magazines and newspapers, publicity shots of Judges being sworn in by Chief Fargo. Some had been drawn on in red ink, where Reece had presumably been highlighting areas of the uniform he was attempting to recreate. "We found these in the bottom of the wardrobe, beneath a false panel. Early attempts to fashion his own uniform."

O'Shea crossed to the bed and picked up the boiler suit. She peered at the stitches, the additional pockets, his handmade badge. It was an impressive approximation. Not that it would fool anyone, at least not for long, but he'd clearly put work into it. "Where did he get the tools to make this badge?" she said.

Hartigan looked thoughtful. "We've not found anything here in the apartment. Not even a sewing kit."

"He was clearly competent. You said he was a repair man?"

Pennhouser nodded. "Maintenance."

"So he had the ability," said O'Shea. "Did his brother have a workshop?"

"Yes, but it was shut down when they were forced into bankruptcy. All the assets were seized," said Hartigan.

"So he either made this before, or—" She'd been turning the boiler suit over in her hands, and something had clinked in one of the pockets. She popped the stud and felt inside: a small bunch of keys, looped on a brightly coloured fob that read *BAKER'S*. She held them up for the others to see.

"Baker's... That's the self-storage place down in the Battery," said Ramos.

"So Reece had a lock-up," said Hartigan. "Maybe that's where he carried out the work."

"Or maybe that's where he was holding his prisoners," said Ramos.

Hartigan's eyes widened. "Come on," he said. "*Now*."

MORE ON TODAY'S *top story, the apprehension of the serial killer Joseph Reece.*

New reports coming in from witnesses who were at the scene suggest that Reece, dubbed the 'Lone Wolf Judge,' was in fact killed on the scene during a shoot-out with officers of the Justice department. It's not yet clear whether Reece was shot resisting arrest, or whether the Judge was exercising their controversial right to execute felons at the point of arrest. We've reached out to the Justice Department, which has so far refused to comment.

Perhaps surprisingly, Governor Walter Adams is also yet to issue a statement regarding the matter. Many expect Adams to speak out against the shooting, arguing that any 'on the spot' execution represents a failure of due process, but so far he has not responded to calls. His aide said that: "Governor Adams is taking a much needed rest and will return to public duties shortly."

Whilst Adams's detractors claim that he is hiding in the wake of the protests carried out in his name, his supporters continue to rally under the 'anti-Judge' banner, despite the storm that is now ravaging the city.

It doesn't appear as if the storm, or the controversy, are going to blow over any time soon...

CHAPTER NINE

"THIS ONE," SAID the crotchety old man at the storage site. He banged the side of it with his stick, raising a deep, metallic booming. His face wrinkled in distaste. "I'll be up at the office if you have any more questions."

O'Shea watched as he waddled off, back stooped, white hair wild and untamed. She fished the keys from her pocket.

Behind her, Ramos, Pennhouser and Hartigan watched eagerly as she tested the first of the keys in the padlock, which opened with a well-oiled *click*.

The facility wasn't exactly state of the art—ancient metal shipping containers stacked inside a crumbling old warehouse, close to the docks. Long superseded by more up-to-date sites, the warehouse was rickety and barely watertight; ribbons of rainwater spattered on the ground nearby, worming their way in through holes in the corrugated iron roof.

O'Shea supposed the place was within Reece's meagre financial means, and it was the sort of place that didn't ask too many questions. She wondered what some of the other containers held. There were at least fifty of them, and most appeared to be in use. It wouldn't surprise her to discover all manner of dubious stock being stored here, ready to be peddled on the streets of New York. She made another mental note to follow it up... when she had the time.

Now, though, she had more pressing concerns. Could this rusty old container be the answer they'd been looking for? Was Ramos right? Could Carrera be trussed up inside?

Pennhouser had put a call through to the precinct, and there was an ambulance waiting on standby. They'd questioned the old man on arrival—evidently the day clerk, who switched out for armed guards of an evening—but if he knew anything, he wasn't saying. No mysterious comings and goings, no unusual sounds, nothing but a few good words to say about Reece, who paid his bills on time and never caused any fuss. It all seemed a little too good to be true. They'd have to return to speak to the night guards, of course, and to have someone go through the CCTV footage, but what really mattered were the contents of the container.

O'Shea slipped the padlock free and tossed it on the floor, then motioned for the others to step back as she dragged the steel panel open with a metallic creak.

Dust swirled in the darkness, and the musty odour of oil and grease pervaded. A cord dangled just inside the opening, and O'Shea grabbed for it and thumbed the switch. A light blinked on, stark and bright: a bare bulb, hanging loose on the other end of the cord, attached to the ceiling of the old container.

Ramos was beside her, peering into the cluttered confines of the small room. There was no sign of any prisoner. Just a makeshift workshop, filled with a few scrappy workbenches and racks of what she presumed to be stolen tools, rescued from Reece's brother's operation before the creditors moved in to claim it all.

"Shit!" barked Hartigan from behind her, banging his fist against the side of the container.

Ramos, though, had pushed past her and was rummaging through the junk spread out on the workbenches. He held up a sheet of twisted metal plating, similar to the fake badge they'd found at Reece's apartment. "This is definitely where Reece was making his equipment." He dropped the metal shard and picked up an iron rod, weighing it in his fist. "And didn't the forensic reports say that the previous victims had been violently beaten? This gives us an indication of the implements he was using, and where he got them from."

Pennhouser was studying the far wall. "This all relates to his old job. He must have had this place for years. Look"—he indicated the faded charts stuck to the bare metal—"maps of the maintenance tunnels beneath Chelsea, repair logs, lists of junction boxes... none of this is relevant, not really. It's just a workshop where he kept his tools. So we know where he made his little dressing up costume, and maybe some of his torture implements; it still doesn't tell us anything about where we might find Carrera. We're not looking for evidence. We're looking for leads."

"So it's another dead end," said Hartigan. "This day just keeps getting better." He shook his head, his shoulders dropping. They were running out of options, and worse, time. If they didn't get to Carrera soon...

O'Shea's comm trilled. She glanced at Ramos, who was frowning at his own device. Both of them receiving a call from Justice Department?

O'Shea thumbed the receiver. "O'Shea here." She heard Ramos mumbling something into his own receiver.

"Judge O'Shea. Judge Ramos. I have Marisa Pellegrino on the line for a conference call. Please hold."

O'Shea's eyes widened behind her visor. *Pellegrino* was taking a personal interest in the Carrera case? Unless the call had something to do with Reece's execution? Surely that would have been a matter for Ramos alone?

She felt a hand on her shoulder, and looked up as Ramos motioned for them to step outside into the warehouse proper, leaving the two detectives muttering to themselves in Reece's makeshift workshop.

The comm crackled. A woman cleared her throat. O'Shea studied the screen, watching as Pellegrino's face slowly resolved. She was sitting behind a desk. Her expression looked severe—but then she often did. "Judge O'Shea. Judge Ramos. I trust your investigation is progressing smoothly." It was a statement, not a question, but O'Shea felt the need to answer regardless.

"Um, yes, ma'am," said O'Shea. "The local police have been very co-operative."

"Indeed?" said Pellegrino. "I've read Judge Ramos's report…" She let that hang for a moment, and O'Shea felt her cheeks flush.

"How can we be of assistance, ma'am?" said Ramos.

Pellegrino sighed. "As you're no doubt aware, the Governor of New York has been kicking up something of a stink, and I'm concerned the protests are getting out of hand, especially with this storm blowing in. While the protests are legal, I'm anxious to defuse the situation before we have to shut them down. You can imagine the outcry if we're left with no other option but to start making arrests…"

"Yes, ma'am," said Ramos.

"I want you to pay a visit to Governor Adams, explain the situation. He needs to climb down from his pulpit and rescind his statement before anyone gets hurt."

"With respect, ma'am—wouldn't a call from the Chief Judge carry more weight?" ventured O'Shea.

"The governor is refusing his calls," said Pellegrino, frustration evident in her tone. "So we're left with no other choice. I know you've only been there for a few weeks, O'Shea, but you know these people. You've worked those streets. See if you can help him see reason. It's in everyone's best interests that he publically calls for the protests to end. I want the crowds disbanded before the full force of the storm hits this evening."

"Yes, ma'am," said Ramos.

"Pellegrino out." The line went dead.

Ramos exhaled slowly, the breath whistling through his teeth. "Well," he said. "We have our orders."

"Orders are one thing," said O'Shea, "but do you really

think the governor is going to listen to us? We represent everything he hates."

Ramos shrugged. "We have our orders," he repeated, although she could hear the resignation in his voice. They started off towards the warehouse entrance.

"Hey," called a voice from behind them. O'Shea turned to see Hartigan hurrying after them. "What's going on? Where are you going?"

"We need to talk to Governor Adams," said O'Shea, trying hard to keep the dismay from her voice. "We have orders to put a stop to the civilian protests before the storm hits."

Hartigan sighed. "What about Carrera?"

O'Shea had been wondering the same. "We won't be long," she said optimistically. "Once the governor agrees to speak out against the unrest, we'll be back to continue the search."

"We'll be waiting a bloody long time, then," said Pennhouser, emerging from the container. "Come on, Hartigan. I knew we couldn't rely on these rookies."

Hartigan looked as if he was about to reply, but then sighed, shook his head, and hurried off after his partner.

CHAPTER TEN

THE PROTESTS, IT seemed, were no longer confined to the two large gatherings being reported on the news channels. Outside Governor Adams's New York City office at 633 Third Avenue, a knot of protestors had gathered, waving their colourful placards about in the driving wind and rain, faces peeking out from the hoods of plastic anoraks. Their first reaction upon seeing Ramos and O'Shea pull up on their Lawrangers was awestruck silence—as if their angry bellowing had somehow summoned these terrifying avatars into being, and now Ramos and O'Shea were about to unleash Fargo's wrath.

When it became clear that the two Judges had no interest whatsoever in the small gang of protestors, they suddenly became emboldened, finding their voices in time to hurl vile abuse as O'Shea crossed the sidewalk towards the tall, glass-fronted building.

A gust of wind brought a shower of raindrops in with O'Shea as she opened the door and ducked inside. The weather was growing more and more inhospitable by the hour. By nightfall, people would be confined to their homes—not through curfew, but simply because it would be too impractical and too dangerous to be outside.

O'Shea crossed to the reception desk. The young black

woman sitting behind it looked up at her in surprise. "Can I help you?" she said.

"We're here to see Governor Adams," said Ramos, beside her.

"Do you have an appointment?" said the woman, turning to the workstation next to her.

"No, but we're here on official Justice Department business. The governor will want to see us," said Ramos.

"Are you sure he's even in the office today? He's usually in the Capitol Building in Albany."

"Thought we'd try here before trekking cross-country."

The woman consulted her screen. "I'm afraid the governor isn't seeing anyone today. If you'd like to make an appointment, I can put you through to his assist—"

"As I said," growled Ramos, leaning over the desk so that the water droplets from his chin dripped onto the woman's workstation, "we're here on official business."

The woman leaned back in her chair, looking petrified.

"What my colleague means to say," said O'Shea, "is could you point us on our way to Governor Adams's office?"

The woman gave a brief, jerking nod. "Thirty-eighth floor," she said.

"Thank you," said Ramos, straightening up and pushing himself away from the desk.

WHILE WALTER ADAMS clearly moved in the same circles as David Carrera—his name had been below Carrera's on Reece's list—his state-appointed office was somewhat less impressive.

There was no grand view—unless you counted a window looking straight out at the side of an adjacent building—and everything was just a little shabby, as if they hadn't been replaced for some time. O'Shea got the impression that if she were to lift one of the pictures away from the wall, there would be a stain on the wallpaper. The carpet was worn, the chairs mismatched, and the photograph of Adams on the wall particularly disconcerting. She felt as if the picture were staring down at her in judgement, its blue eyes boring holes, questioning her very existence. Which was ridiculous, she knew, and a symptom of listening to too many newsreaders and pundits. She wasn't at all looking forward to meeting him.

A Latino man was sitting behind a low desk, his back to the wall, his fingers dancing over the surface of his desk where a holographic keyboard was being projected. It resembled an old-fashioned typewriter, and he'd even gone as far as changing the settings to recreate the *click-clack* of the keys, which was both annoying and, as far as O'Shea was concerned, a needless affectation. He continued typing for a moment as the two Judges approached, and then, evidently reaching the end of a sentence, looked up at them from behind the thick-rimmed glasses perched on the end of his nose. He had long, black eyelashes, O'Shea noticed.

"Now, isn't this a turn-up?" he said with a wry smile.

"We're here to speak with Governor Adams," said Ramos, his voice neutral.

"Oh, I bet you are," said the man. "He won't be intimidated by you, you know."

"We're not here to intimidate him," said O'Shea, purposefully removing her helmet. She shook out her auburn hair. "We're here to have a conversation. Eustace Fargo has asked us to speak to him on behalf of the Justice Department."

"That's just because the governor keeps refusing Fargo's calls," said the man. He smiled placatingly. "Look, what can I say? The governor isn't interested in any deals with the Justice Department, unless it involves their immediate withdrawal from New York State."

"That's something he'll have to take up with Chief Judge Fargo," said Ramos, "if he ever deigns to accept the call."

The man laughed. "Look, I'm only an assistant. There's nothing I can do."

"Your name?" said O'Shea.

"Parks. Richard Parks."

"Look, Mr. Parks. We don't bear a grudge against the governor for the stance he's taken on the Judge programme." Ramos gave a snort, but O'Shea ignored it. "We understand he's doing his job. But we *all* have a problem, and we need to find a way to deal with it together. Those protests out there— people are going to get hurt. You must see that. People are getting carried away, getting angry, refusing to take shelter. And with the storm coming in…" She tried to look as reasonable as possible. "We're here to ask for the governor's help. He needs to speak to his people, to help them understand that they're putting themselves in danger."

Parks nodded. "V-ry laudable," he said. "And most convenient for you. An end to the protests... Wouldn't that just suit Fargo perfectly? Everything quietly brushed under the carpet. Well, I don't need the governor here to tell you that's not going to happen."

"Is he in there?" said Ramos, pointing at a wood panelled door on the far wall.

Parks stood, pushing back his chair. "I can't let you go in there."

"I don't see that you have much choice in the matter," said Ramos. He crossed to the door and flung it open, striding through into the other room.

O'Shea glanced at Parks, fixing him with a gaze that made it abundantly clear that he'd brought that upon himself. She started after Ramos, only to see him emerge from the doorway again a moment later. His jaw was clenched. "He's not there," he said.

"Governor Adams has taken a few days' leave," said Parks. "All the attention was getting a little much for him, so he decided to clear his diary for a while and wait until it's all blown over."

"That's precisely the point," growled Ramos. "It's all going to blow *over*. That storm isn't going to wait for anyone, and it's not going to make an exception for your protestors, not matter how righteous they think they are."

"How can we reach him?" said O'Shea.

"That's just it," said Parks. "You can't. He's cut himself off. His cell wouldn't stop buzzing. All those reporters, trying to provoke another statement. So he's taken a few days upstate to consider his options."

"He's run away, more like," said Ramos. "The coward. He's stirred up a hornet's nest of trouble and then run, leaving everyone else to deal with the aftermath."

At least, O'Shea considered, with Reece dead they didn't have to worry about *him* going missing too.

Parks shrugged. "Politicians," he said, as if that explained everything. He glanced at O'Shea, before sitting back at his desk and resuming his typing. "I'll be certain to let him know you called."

CHAPTER ELEVEN

"Look, I know we're asking a lot, but there's only two of us. Technically, we could *order* you to do it, but I don't think either of us wants to go down that path."

"Oh, now you're *really* helping your case," said Hartigan. He rubbed the back of his neck. "Look, I'll have a word with the captain, but I can't say he'll be happy about it. I can't say *I'm* happy about it. We didn't create this mess, and we certainly don't deserve to be doing the heavy lifting to haul your asses out of the fire. We're no closer to finding Carrera, and that storm's getting worse by the second."

"I know, I know," said O'Shea. "Once we get this squared away, we can get back to helping you locate him."

"All right. Give me a minute," said Hartigan. He sighed, crossed the room, rapped on the captain's office door, and slipped inside. Pennhouser perched on the edge of his desk, his glower speaking volumes.

They'd come back to the precinct directly from Governor Adams's office. With narrowing options, and a clear order to have the protests disbanded by that evening, she and Ramos had decided that their only option was to utilise the police. They needed numbers, and people that the civilians would trust. They'd considered reporting back to Pellegrino—after all, she probably wasn't really expecting them to succeed with Adams where Fargo had already failed—but that felt too much like admitting defeat. Better, surely, that they find an alternative solution.

Ramos was still raging after their encounter with Parks, and was all for heading directly into Captain Flores's office and giving him a direct order. O'Shea, however, had advised a different approach, working through Hartigan, who she'd felt was becoming something of an ally amongst the otherwise hostile police force. It was better, she argued, that Flores reluctantly agreed to help on behalf of the citizens they were sworn to protect, rather than being forced into it by an order he didn't want and didn't respect. Reluctantly, Ramos had agreed, suggesting that if her plan failed, they could still fall back on a direct order.

Around them, the chatter of the station was a constant background hum. Uniformed cops buzzed back and forth, ferrying information. Detectives came and went, checking in for updates before heading back out into the growing storm. While Hartigan and Pennhouser were heading up the Carrera investigation, many of the others had rallied to help, and units all across the city were on high alert for any sightings or reports that might help to break the deadlock.

O'Shea glanced at Pennhouser. "Any word on the cell phone trace?"

Pennhouser pursed his lips. For a moment, she thought he was going to ignore her, then he slowly shook his head. "Nothing. Unless someone turns it on, we're not going to be able to narrow it down."

"No GPS tracer?"

"No. Apparently, Carrera didn't like his PA to have too much of an idea of what he was up to."

That was it, then. They were out of leads. Carrera could be anywhere, and there was no way of even narrowing it down. He might not even be in the city any more.

Flores's door opened and O'Shea looked up. The captain

made a beeline for her, Hartigan trailing in his wake. Both of them looking sour.

"So, you've come asking for my help," said Flores. "Now isn't *that* a turn-up." Beside her, Ramos straightened.

"I think it's in the best interest of the citizens that the protests are broken up calmly and safely, don't you?" she said, trying to remain diplomatic. "Before the storm creates even more of a problem."

Flores shrugged. "I don't suppose I can argue with that. We'll handle it. And you can tell your Chief Fargo that's what happened too."

"Of course," said O'Shea. "We'll help, of course—"

"No," said Flores emphatically. "That I won't abide. The police will handle this, Judge O'Shea. The first sight of a Judge and those protestors will get difficult. I won't put people at risk. I've seen the photographs from Chelsea Market; I know what one of those weapons can do. And how willing you are to deploy them."

O'Shea bit her tongue, hoping Ramos would do the same. "All right," she said. "We'll stay out of your way, and continue with the Carrera situation."

"You do that," said Flores. He nodded at Pennhouser. "You and Hartigan are with me." He turned his back on the Judges and walked away.

CHAPTER TWELVE

HE JERKED AWAKE again.

Slowly, he became aware of a low, keening sound, like the moaning of an animal in torment, before realising that the noise was emanating from his own throat. He silenced himself abruptly, feeling suddenly embarrassed—which, when he considered it, was ridiculous.

Around him, he could hear only the thrumming of the rain in the street above, and the ominous sloshing of water all around him.

He had no idea how long he'd been out this time, but it must have been some hours—the water level had risen, now swirling around his waist. He drew a breath and shivered. His teeth were chattering, mouth hurting where his torn lips had healed, and split again, spilling warm blood down his chin.

The rats would return soon, attracted by the stink of blood. Their hungry mouths would begin to nibble and he'd barely feel it, so numbed his lower body had become from the cold.

He was close to death now; could feel it hovering over him, like a chill spectre, waiting to embrace him. He imagined a human skeleton with a broad, grinning visage, arms outstretched and welcoming, promising warmth and comfort and shelter from the pain. He wished it would get a move on. He was ready now.

He felt pathetic, drained of all vitality. He'd long ago lost the will to fight. He could hardly believe that this was what his life had come to—that he'd fallen so low, that his world had been reduced to the tunnel, the water, the pain.

He'd prided himself on being a powerful man—the sort of person who could get things done, who commanded respect. The kind of man people looked up to. Now, his true nature had been exposed, revealing the imposter who had always lurked within. Here, in the tunnel, all his money and influence counted for nothing. In the tunnel, he was just like anyone else, just as scared, just as useless.

And then the thought came like a flicker in the darkness: maybe he even *deserved* what was happening to him. He'd hardly lived a life of charity, if he were honest with himself. He'd coveted power, screwed people over on his way up the ladder, accumulated wealth while those around him suffered. Was this God's way of declaring his disapproval, of showing him the error of his ways? Perhaps this was payment for a life lived in error. Perhaps this was what became of men like him.

He realised he was getting delirious. He had a keen sense of it, as if he'd somehow managed to step outside of his body and peer down on the half-dead wretch chained to the tunnel wall, could see the mad glimmer in his own eyes, the willingness to fracture, to give in. Yet there was nothing he could do to hold that creeping madness in abeyance. It wanted out. It wanted to assume command, to help him to forget the pain and suffering, to forgo reason. It promised salvation and relief. It promised to hasten the end. And so he closed his eyes and he allowed it in.

There was little time left. The rhythmic dripping of the rainwater continued to count away the remaining seconds of his life. He took some comfort in that. At least he wouldn't feel so alone as he slipped into oblivion.

CHAPTER THIRTEEN

O'SHEA SAT BENEATH the awning and watched the rainwater bouncing off the sidewalk. The fat droplets struck with such force that they leapt back into the air, as if somehow attempting to resist their fate, refusing to mingle with the others of their kind to sluice away into the drains. There was probably a metaphor in that, but if so, she wasn't clever enough to see it.

She considered this as she took a bite of her burrito, spilling salsa down her chin. She wiped at it with a serviette from the dispenser on the table. Things weren't going exactly as planned.

Beside her, Ramos leaned back in the plastic chair, harbouring thoughts of his own. Probably about the quality of the burrito, she decided. She watched, as he seemed to study the food closely before taking another bite, forehead wrinkled in concentration. His helmet rested on the chair beside him.

The stall was one of the few remaining open in the city—a relentless entrepreneur in a relentless downpour. They'd left their bikes by the side of the road and were sitting beneath the red plastic sheeting the stall's owner had erected in front of his van. The food smelled better than it tasted, but it was something, and presented a welcome pause in what had otherwise been a difficult day. Not that there was any chance of it stopping soon. With Carrera still missing and the protests still raging, she and Ramos would be forced to work through the night. No matter what the regulations said, it was a matter of professional pride—they would find Carrera, and prove that Ramos had been right to pull the trigger back there in the market; even if she still wasn't entirely sure herself.

She took another bite of her burrito.

The comm was crackling with the constant cross chatter of the police officers involved in breaking up the protests near Central Park. People were not going willingly, but so far they seemed to be avoiding arrests, appealing to people's sense of self-preservation and warning them to get out of the storm. It was only a temporary reprieve, and with Governor Adams refusing to climb down from his position, O'Shea figured the protestors would be back just as soon as the storm had blown over. This wasn't something she or Ramos could control. She didn't even know if Chief Fargo himself would be able to turn things around.

She believed in the Judges programme, of course she did; but there was so much ill feeling out there. She understood the animosity of the police—the Judges were the future of law enforcement, and within a few years they'd replace the police force entirely—but surely the civilians could see the benefit? The increased efficiency, the ability to act on the spot, the protection offered by the law and the ability of those on the ground to enforce it. Regular, law-abiding citizens had nothing to fear. Yet Adams saw only the threat to freedom.

It was a self-serving political move, she knew. Adams had close ties to the police commissioner, and was leveraging the situation to gain support—support that had otherwise been on the wane. It was a dirty, cynical trick, and ultimately short-sighted: the Judges were there to stay, the President had signed off on their deployment, and history would not be in Adams's favour. The change was coming, whether he or anyone else liked it or not.

"Hang on, did you hear that?" said Ramos, suddenly shifting in his seat, tossing his half-eaten burrito onto the tabletop.

"Hear what?"

"The comm," said Ramos. "Something's going on."

O'Shea threw what was left of her own burrito down and reached for her helmet, tucking her hair back as she slid it over her head. The comm was alive with the buzz of voices.

Shhhszzt. "All units. I repeat, officer down at Central Park. Perp is escaping in a red Chevrolet down Fifth Avenue. Squad cars in pursuit." *Shhhszzt.*

O'Shea looked to Ramos. "Oh, shit."

Ramos was already out of his seat and running for his bike. He practically vaulted into his seat, gunning the engine. O'Shea was only seconds behind him.

He glanced over at her.

"Go!" she bellowed. His exhaust belched steam and he was off into the driving rain, tyres raising a fine mist of spray in his wake.

O'Shea fumbled for a moment, and then her bike roared to life, and she was off in pursuit, the beam of her headlamp stabbing through the gloomy veil before her, all thoughts of Adams and Fargo and the Judge programme gone.

SHE HEARD THE wail of sirens before she caught sight of the blue flashing lights. It was difficult to make out anything in the storm—the wind had picked up and was blowing rain across the avenue in vast, driving sheets, smearing her visor. The entire pursuit took on a dreamlike quality, as if she were somehow delving deeper and deeper into some strange realm, a place that echoed the streets of the city she was coming to know so well, but lacked its finer details, the things that made it real.

The streets were largely empty, save for the crowds still dispersing from the Central Park area, along with the swarms of cops, ambulances and police vehicles converging on the scene.

O'Shea didn't stop to hear the finer details of the shooting; that could wait. Instead, she and Ramos charged past, driving by instinct, weaving amongst the parked cars and hurtling down Fifth Avenue in pursuit of the shooter.

Up ahead, the red Chevrolet was nothing but a smear of colour, trailing lights. She watched as it skidded sideways, disappearing for a heartbeat behind a curtain of spray, before the engine revved noisily and the vehicle shot down a cross street. Two of the cop cars overshot the junction, too fast to turn without flipping on the wet road. Another two made it, following the Chevrolet in single file, sirens wailing. The sound echoed off the immense buildings, reflected back into the city like an endless scream.

The road surface was slick with water, and more than once O'Shea had to shift her weight to avoid aquaplaning as she shot along the street behind the cop cars, searching for any opportunity to get by. The side streets were too narrow, and lined with parked cars, and she felt her frustration building as she leaned on the handlebars, willing the cop cars to get out of her way. The Lawrangers were faster and more manoeuvrable; if she and Ramos could get ahead of the perp, they could box him in, leave him nowhere to go.

Up ahead, the Chevrolet shot across a junction, ignoring a bank of red lights overhead. She made a mental note to add that to the list of crimes she was going to charge the shooter with when they caught up with him.

"Go right," said Ramos, his voice loud in her ear.

She nodded as he peeled left, leaving the cop cars to trail behind the Chevrolet. He was going for a pincer movement, O'Shea realised—trying to get ahead of the perp before the next junction and cut him off.

She revved her engine, forcing the bike into the wind and rain, leaving the flickering lights of the chase behind her. She saw a turning up ahead and dropped, pulling the bike around, practically hanging off the seat as she forced the vehicle into a turn. The engine growled but the machine obeyed, dipping low before coming up again as she straightened, dropping back into the seat.

A taxicab sat in the middle of the road ahead of her, hazards lights blinking, blocking her way. O'Shea looked to either side and, without slowing, bounced the bike up onto the sidewalk and around the cab, sending sheets of water into the air as she thundered back down onto the road on the other side.

The road ended in another junction, opening out onto an avenue. She'd lost track of exactly where they were, but it mattered little; she could hear the sirens wailing behind her. She'd managed to get out in front. She swung left, joining the avenue just as the Chevrolet burst from the side street in a long, skidding turn and shot off along the avenue, heading downtown. Thumbing the throttle, she pulled in alongside it, trying to match its speed. Ramos swung in on its other flank, running in parallel.

"Front tyres!" called Ramos.

This was a manoeuvre they'd practised time and again at the academy: two flanking Judges simultaneously taking out a vehicle's front tyres to slow it down. She yanked her weapon from its holster, holding the bike steady with one hand.

"On three," said Ramos. "One, two..."

Their shots came in a staggered *crack,* followed by a tremendous *bang* as both front tyres exploded on the Chevrolet. The metal wheels caught the asphalt, and even in the heavy downpour, drew searing yellow sparks as the driver fought to retain control.

Something was wrong. The driver—O'Shea presumed them inexperienced at this sort of high-speed pursuit—couldn't control the careening car. She pulled back, giving the vehicle room as it shot across the avenue, raising parallel lines of sparks as it went.

She heard someone scream, and looked up to see a group of protestors on the sidewalk, still carrying sodden placards, transfixed by the oncoming Chevrolet, which was hurtling towards them at unstoppable speed. They were about to be crushed against the wall of a coffee shop.

She heard Ramos grunt, and watched as he threw his bike into a low skid and leapt from the seat, launching its bulk at the Chevrolet as he smacked into the concrete sidewalk and rolled.

The bike struck the nose of the car with a metallic *thunk*, crumpling the left side of the hood and starting it spinning as it slid towards the sidewalk. It struck the kerb ten feet from the civilians, pitching onto its side and coming to rest, engine still sputtering, wheels still spinning.

O'Shea started towards Ramos, and then remembered her training and instead made for the Chevrolet. Behind her, the two remaining cop cars were just coming to a stop in the road.

She ran through the rain, weapon gripped tightly in her fist. Her mouth felt dry. The civilians were still screaming, backing away from the overturned car. She paid them little heed as she circled around it, raising her weapon.

She could see that the driver's side door was buckled shut. Further around, the windscreen was spiderwebbed with cracks from the impact, and the driver—the cop-shooter—was trying frantically to kick it out.

O'Shea waited, rain pattering her visor, until he'd finished kicking out the shards of glass. He hadn't even noticed her standing there as he pitched himself forward, trying to wriggle out through the opening he'd created. He really was making it all too easy.

Keeping her weapon levelled, she strode forward and grabbed the man by the back of his collar, dragging him out through the shattered windscreen. He thrashed and screamed as a jagged fragment of glass bit into his thigh, but she ignored his squeals as she dragged him clear of the wreckage and tossed him into a puddle in the gutter. He looked up at her, terror in his eyes. He was a thin man in his thirties, with pale skin, a single strip of dyed red hair down the centre of his shaven head, and a morass of tattoos down his left arm. He was bleeding from a gash above his right eye, and the blood was running down his face in the rain, dripping onto his white shirt, stark and red.

She raised her weapon, so that its muzzle was only inches from his face. "Don't move."

Behind her, the uniformed cops were forming a semicircle. She risked a quick glance over her shoulder. They were covering the perp with their weapons, too, using their car doors for cover. All save for their sergeant—a tall black woman with startling green eyes—who was coming over to join her.

"Sergeant," said O'Shea, as the woman stepped up beside her. She was carrying a handgun.

"Judge." She looked at O'Shea expectantly.

She's waiting for me to kill him, realised O'Shea. She's heard about what Ramos did at Chelsea Market, and she thinks I'm going to do the same now.

Her finger brushed the trigger. Maybe she should? After all, none of the cops would blame her. He was a cop killer. He'd shot one of them—or so she'd been led to believe. She had no proof, not yet. And besides, she'd seen what could happen if she jumped to a hasty decision. What if this man knew something useful? He might be part of an organised gang. He might have insight into some of the other protestors. She'd heard stories about gangs like that, infiltrating peaceful rallies, trying to turn them into riots.

She nodded towards the kneeling man. "He's all yours, sergeant. Let's cuff him and get him back to the precinct."

The woman looked surprised. "All right," she said after a moment. She waved two of her officers forward. "You heard the lady—get that filthy POS in cuffs."

"Yes, ma'am."

O'Shea nodded to the sergeant and backed away, searching the street for Ramos. After the fall he'd had, he'd probably need time in the infirmary. She'd expected to find him close to where he'd gone down, perhaps being attended by one of the cops or ambulance crew still arriving on the scene, lighting the whole place up with their stuttering lights. Instead, she found him hauling his Lawranger out from under the wreckage of the Chevrolet. There were several long scratches down the paintwork, but otherwise—surprisingly—it appeared to have survived the collision intact. As had Ramos.

"Built to last," he said with a grin.

"You or the bike?"

"Both," he said, laughing.

"What you did back there..." said O'Shea. "Saving those people."

"I did my job," said Ramos. "We're here to protect people. As *you* keep reminding us."

O'Shea nodded. "I didn't shoot him," she said.

"I saw."

"I figured..."

"Yeah, I know." He stepped forward, put a hand on her shoulder. "Let's get back to the precinct, and see what sort of mess is waiting for us there, eh?"

O'Shea shrugged. "Out of the frying pan..."

CHAPTER FOURTEEN

THE PRECINCT WAS in a state of utter chaos with officers swarming left, right and centre, voices raised in a tumult of bitter recriminations. O'Shea could understand that: they'd lost one of their own. What was meant to be the peaceful dispersal of a civilian protest had turned violent, and now they were looking for an outlet for their emotion. They were looking for someone to blame.

They found it when O'Shea and Ramos walked into the lobby. A wave of deathly silence passed over the gathered throng. Uniforms plainclothes alike turned to look at them, then looked away again, revulsion on their faces. She could feel the animosity, the prickle of eyes on her; her cheeks reddening.

By now they must have heard about what Ramos had done, how the two of them had apprehended the killer and handed him over to the sergeant. The lives Ramos had saved. None of that mattered. The rallies had only started in the wake of the Judges' arrival, and—no matter that Governor Adams had been the one to incite them—she and Ramos had been the ones charged to put an end to them. And now a police officer was dead. Of course they were blaming the Judges.

O'Shea was grateful for her helmet. She didn't have to let them see how they got to her. She walked past them, Ramos at her side, dripping rainwater all over the worn carpet tiles as she made a beeline directly for Captain Flores's office.

He was standing by the window with his back to them as they entered. His shoulders were hunched; she guessed his hands were bunched into fists. There was a tension in the room—Flores clearly blamed them for what had happened too.

"Captain Flores," said Ramos. "We've apprehended the shooter. One of your sergeants has him in custody now. We... thought you'd want to carry out a full interrogation."

"Oh, so now you *don't* shoot criminals on the spot? Is *that* it?" said Flores, turning around to face them. He was trembling with barely contained rage. "I suppose it suited you to let this one live, now that Hartigan's down there in the morgue?"

"Hartigan!" said O'Shea. "He's the one who was shot?"

"You didn't know?" snarled Flores. He shook his head. "He'd been with this force since leaving school. He was a good detective, and a good man."

"He was," said O'Shea.

"He defended you, you know?" said Flores. His tone was incredulous. "When the others were complaining about being forced to tidy up your mess. He told them you were a good officer, that you would have made a good cop." He stared at her for a moment, and then glanced at Ramos, making it clear what he thought of the other Judge. "And now he's dead."

"I'm sorry," said O'Shea.

"Not as sorry as I am," said Flores. "We've lost one of our best. And for what? A bloody protest rally?" He turned away again, hanging his head.

"I'm sorry for your loss," said Ramos, "but we still have a missing person to find. I presume no more leads have come to light?" His tone was respectful, but firm.

Flores swung around, glowered at him. "Ask Pennhouser. See where *that* gets you." He paused. "We don't need your kind here. We were doing perfectly well until you showed up. Dead suspects, missing victims, and now a dead cop. I hope you and your Chief Fargo are happy." The words dripped venom.

"I'm sorry you feel that way," said Ramos, "but the law has no time for sentiment or recrimination, and neither do I." He turned and strode from the office.

Flores stared after him, then turned to O'Shea. "Your partner sure has a way with people."

"Doesn't he just?" she said.

SHE FOUND RAMOS by Hartigan's desk, surrounded by officers. Pennhouser was hurling abuse at him, blaming Ramos for his partner's death. It was unjust, but the only thing she could do about it was to prove them wrong through actions. Words were what had started this—the rhetoric of a desperate governor trying to cling on to power—but action was what would end it. They needed to finish the job and find Carrera.

Ramos stood passively, allowing the words to wash over him, but O'Shea didn't think for a minute he was unmoved by the tirade, or by what had happened. Hartigan was hardly a friend—he'd barely tolerated them—but they had come to a kind of easy understanding with him, an alliance of sorts, based on a shared goal.

Now, with Hartigan gone, that alliance was falling apart. Pennhouser had liked them, and while she still refused to blame him for it, his grief and his need to blame someone had blinded him to the urgency of their task.

Regardless of what had happened, they still had to find Carrera.

O'Shea pushed her way through the circle of gathered detectives until she was standing beside Ramos. "I'm sorry for your loss," she said, "but Judge Ramos is right. We still have a job to do. There's a man out there, and we need to find him."

Pennhouser stopped, muttering something beneath his breath, and the crowd slowly dispersed.

"Any developments?" she asked Pennhouser, as he dropped heavily into his chair. He looked tired.

He glanced up, his expression narrowing. "I thought *you*

were supposed to be looking for leads while *we* dealt with your other mess?"

"Just answer the bloody question, Pennhouser," she snapped.

He maintained his glower for a moment, and then relented with a sigh. "Just this." He picked up a brown paper file from his desk and flung it across at them. It landed on Hartigan's desk, printouts spilling out across the mess.

"And this is?"

"Reece's autopsy report," said Pennhouser. "Surprise, surprise—cause of death was a shot to the chest." He glared at Ramos, who studiously ignored him.

She picked up the file, shuffling the papers back into place. The first page was a short summary, highlighting cause of death, along with the contents of Reece's stomach, a chemical breakdown showing he'd recently used black market antidepressants and a list of medical conditions, foremost amongst them his state of malnutrition. Having seen the state of his apartment, none of this surprised her. The man had been scraping an existence from nothing and he'd evidently been sourcing cheap bootleg drugs, attempting to self-medicate. She wondered if they might have played a role in his final mental state.

She flicked through the pages, leafing past several grisly photographs of the man's corpse. Each of them was annotated with statistics, none of which made any particular sense to her. Next was a photograph of Reece's clothes—the makeshift Judge's uniform—and it was here that things got interesting. The report suggested that the legs of the boiler suit were steeped in raw sewage. No wonder he'd smelled so bad. She held the file open for Ramos. "Here. Look at this."

Ramos shrugged. "I guess they were old work overalls, from his time as a maintenance engineer?"

O'Shea shook her head. "No. Think back to the market. They were still *wet*."

"Suggesting he'd been down in the tunnels before Pennhouser and Hartigan had cornered him at the market," said Ramos.

Pennhouser got to his feet. "That does kinda make sense."

"Think about it. Reece knew those service tunnels better than anyone. He'd spent his life down there in that under city," said O'Shea. "It stands to reason that he'd use them to get around, to keep his head low."

"And the drainage pipes lead straight out into the Hudson," said Pennhouser. "That's how he could have disposed of the bodies." He sighed. "We've been looking in the wrong place all along. He wasn't hiding in the city, he was hiding *beneath* it."

"More than that," said O'Shea. "It's probably where he was holding his victims."

"Carrera," said Ramos. "He could still be down there."

"Then we have to go after him," said O'Shea. "We can use the maps from Reece's lock-up, try to narrow down the area to search."

"But the storm," said Pennhouser. "Those tunnels will be flooded. The storm drains run through there, back out to the river."

"All the more reason to move quickly," said O'Shea. "If Carrera *is* down there, he doesn't have long left."

"If it isn't already too late," said Ramos.

"There's only one way to find out," said O'Shea. She held the file out to Pennhouser. "Have an ambulance crew on standby, just in case."

Pennhouser frowned. "Hold on just a minute. I'm coming with you. We'll put a team together. The more of us down there, the better."

O'Shea shook her head. "The more of us down there, the more risk that someone's going to get killed. There's been enough death today. Ramos and I have got this."

Pennhouser looked for a moment as if he were about to object, and then took the file, gave a curt nod, and walked towards Flores's office.

CHAPTER FIFTEEN

THE MAPS IN Reece's lock-up gave little away, other than to suggest an entrance into the tunnels through an access point inside an old, abandoned warehouse in the Chelsea district.

The place was filthy, filled with rusting machinery that couldn't have seen service for a decade or more. Vegetation was beginning to poke through cracks in the concrete floor, and there was a pervading mustiness that suggested age and disuse. No wonder the place had been earmarked for development— as far as O'Shea could tell, it was beyond refurbishment.

At least, O'Shea considered, it was an opportunity for them to get out of the driving rain. The storm had now struck the city in earnest, battering the island with a ferocity that left O'Shea feeling small and insignificant. Wind gusted down the avenues, rattling parked vehicles and shaking windows in their frames. Traffic signals swung in their cradles, threatening to crash to the streets below.

O'Shea had barely been able to see as she'd slid down the road on her Lawranger, trusting the autopilot to navigate on her behalf. More than once, she'd considered turning back, all too aware of the acute danger she and Ramos were putting themselves in, trusting their safety to the whims of the storm. Even the Chief Judge would have ordered them back, she knew, declaring the circumstances too testing, the life of a single citizen—which might already have been lost—too small a prize to risk their lives.

Nevertheless, she pressed on. It wasn't just stubbornness; it was about tempering herself, testing her limits, measuring her determination to do the right thing. If she turned back now, she'd be admitting that Carrera's life wasn't worth the effort. She'd be putting her own life before that of a citizen and to her mind, a Judge had to be better than that. Despite everything, all the protests and the fear, all the circling doubt and the public rage, she still believed that they were there to *serve*. The Judges' charter spoke of serving the law, but what was the law but the will of the people? She was a public servant, and the day she lost sight of that was the day she'd hand her badge back to Fargo and call it quits.

The rain was thrumming on the corrugated tin roof of the warehouse.

"Give me a hand with this?"

Ramos had managed to pry the heavy cover from a manhole set into the floor in the far corner of the tumbledown warehouse. She dropped to her knees and helped slide it clear. There was a crust around the inner rim, suggesting this wasn't Reece's preferred route. In fact, it didn't look as if it had been used for some time.

A steel ladder led down into the dank tunnel below. She could hear lapping water, and the distant echo of movement.

O'Shea went first, swinging her legs over the edge and setting her boots on the ladder. She lowered herself into the hole and cautiously climbed down into the cold and dark.

The water level was above her waist, and she shivered as she dropped into it with a splash, found her footing and started wading slowly away from the tunnel wall. The only light down here was from the warehouse above, so she unclipped a torch and switched it on. The beam stabbed into the darkness, showing the tunnel bending away to the right up ahead. The water seemed to be flowing from that direction.

"Come on in," she called up to Ramos. "It's lovely down here."

She heard him grunt in amusement, and then his legs appeared at the top of the ladder, blotting out the light.

Cables and pipes ran along the red brick in both directions. She glanced behind her, flicking the beam of the torch from side to side. There was no way of knowing where Reece had kept his victims, even assuming they were on the right track. She fought the urge to give up, reminding herself of her earlier resolve. If Carrera was down here, they were going to find him.

Ramos splashed down into the water beside her. "You're right. Bracing." They'd been soaked through after driving in the storm, their uniforms stuck flush to their damp skin, so the water down here was more of a hindrance than a genuine discomfort.

"Which way?" she said, moving the torch back and forth so that Ramos could weigh up their options.

"That way," he said, jabbing his finger at where the tunnel turned to the right. "If my memory of those maps serves, the tunnels in that direction run straight under the main district. If Reece was bringing people down here, he probably used an access point down an alleyway somewhere."

"All right," said O'Shea. "Lead on."

They set out, fighting against the flow. O'Shea could hear the constant trickle of water down the tunnel walls, seeping in from the rain-swept streets above.

She wondered how long they had before the rising water level made the tunnels impassable.

AFTER A SHORT while—no more than twenty minutes, although it felt to O'Shea as if she'd been down there for hours—Ramos stopped and held up a hand to indicate she should follow suit. He turned at the waist, pressing a finger to his lips. Up ahead, around another bend in the tunnel, she could hear the sound of rushing water, along with a rhythmic clanging—the *bong, bong, bong* of something repeatedly striking a metal pipe.

She nodded to Ramos to indicate that she understood, and then followed as he moved closer to the wall, drawing his weapon. Slowly they crept forward, keeping pace with one another. The current here seemed stronger.

She stretched her neck, flexed the muscles in her shoulders. The water was frigid, and she was starting to lose feeling in her toes. She clenched her teeth, driving herself forward.

The roar of the water grew louder, and the sound continued unabated. She'd dipped the beam of the torch, keeping it low, but they'd already lost any chance of a stealthy approach—in the pervading gloom, even the slightest glimmer of light would telegraph their presence from some distance.

Ramos had come to a stop again. His arms were raised, weapon clutched in both hands. "Hello?" he called. His voice seemed stark and strange in the empty tunnel, echoing away down the passage. There was no response. She raised the torch beam.

She'd been right about the outlet pipe. Water was streaming in from a drainage point close to the ceiling, churning and foaming as it poured into the tunnel below. And there, directly beneath the outlet pipe, was a human corpse. It was a man, floating face down, dressed in what appeared to be brown rags, and his arm was knocking into a pipe on the wall, stirred by the constant motion of the water. A fat, brown rat sat on his shoulder, peering at them with black, beady eyes.

O'Shea glanced away, her eyes searching for something else—anything else—to look at. In the distance, further along the tunnel, was some kind of wooden frame fixed to the wall.

Ramos edged forward, making a hissing sound to scare away the rodent. The creature leapt from the corpse's shoulder, frantically swimming away down the tunnel.

She went over to join him. Clearly, they were too late. Carrera was already dead.

Ramos grabbed the corpse by its shoulder and turned it over in the water. The face stared up at them in silent horror, pale and staring, its eyes nothing more than glistening hollows, presumably chewed out by the rat. The man had a scruffy, unkempt beard, and his teeth were yellowed and uneven. His hair, too, looked as if it hadn't been trimmed for some time, long and wild, spread out in the water like a strange black fan.

"It's not Carrera," said Ramos.

"Another of Reece's victims?" ventured O'Shea, already coming to the conclusion that she was wrong. This man had nothing to do with Reece—his clothes suggested he was a scavenger, trying to eke out some kind of existence down here.

"A homeless man, by the look of him," said Ramos. He released his grip on the dead man's shoulder, and the corpse bobbed under the surface of the water.

"Cuff it to the pipe. We'll send a crew down here when the storm's blown over," said O'Shea. "See if they can retrieve the body. We'll have to be sure."

Ramos nodded. "Come on. The sooner we're done down here, the better."

They waded on, further down the same tunnel, until they came to the wooden frame.

"This is some kind of bed," said Ramos, the disgust evident in his voice. He pointed to the wall. "Look, a hammock here. This was some kind of shelter."

"So the dead man was living down here," she said, examining the wooden slats: salvaged pallets and old fruit crates.

"Some life," said Ramos. "Makes Reece's hole seem like a palace."

Around the next bend the sight was even more disturbing. More structures had been fixed to the walls, although some had collapsed with the rising tide, leaving fragments of broken wood drifting on the surface of the water. Bodies bobbed amongst them—a woman, three children, two more men... She couldn't count them all, for the tears that pricked her eyes.

This wasn't one poor homeless man who'd been trying to find shelter down here in the tunnels—it was a whole community of outcasts, all taken by the terrifying impact of the storm.

They came to the woman, who couldn't have been much older than O'Shea, although the skin around her face was deeply lined and ravaged. She looked eerily serene, as if she were finally at peace.

"This place is a nightmare," said Ramos. It was the first time she'd heard even a hint of reservation in his voice. "Look at it. Is this really what's going on beneath our city?"

"I think our job's just got a whole lot bigger," said O'Shea.

"It'll take more than two of us to put a stop to this," said Ramos. "If perps are hiding down here on this scale..." He trailed off.

"These aren't criminals," said O'Shea. "Or they didn't start that way. Something drove them down here. Circumstance, drugs... a political regime that doesn't give a damn. People don't make a *choice* to live like this. They do it because they *have* no choice. What we need to do is find the source and stop it, weed out the corruption, find the peddlers, the dealers. That's how we put an end to this."

Ramos sighed. "And Carrera?"

"We keep looking," said O'Shea.

"Then we're going the wrong way," said Ramos.

"How do you figure that?"

He looked down at the woman's corpse. "If these people were living down here, it's unlikely Reece would have brought his victims anywhere near them. Think about it—even if they didn't want to be discovered, do you think they would have stood by while Reece repeatedly tortured people to death? And besides, they could have freed them."

"Perhaps he threatened them?" said O'Shea, but she knew in her heart he was right.

"I don't buy it," said Ramos. "There are miles of these tunnels. Reece was a clever bastard, and he'd spent his life down here working maintenance. He'd have found a quiet spot, somewhere where he knew he wasn't going to be found—and he'd have known about these people too."

"Then I suppose we start over in the other direction," said O'Shea.

Ramos nodded. "For a while. But if the water level continues to rise, we're going to have to get out of here whether we like it or not."

CHAPTER SIXTEEN

HE COULD FEEL his life ebbing away with every breath.

The water had risen to just below his chin, and he was forced to hold his head up to breathe. For all of his earlier despondency, he couldn't bring himself to lower his face into the water and drown himself. It would bring an end to it all, but when it came to it, the thought of succumbing to that void, to giving in to it, was just too much to bear. He knew it was inevitable, but he was a coward. He was too scared. And so he went on, suffering, struggling with every breath.

He'd grown used to the ragged pain in his wrists now—so much so that he barely felt it—and besides, at least the water had provided some buoyancy, relieving the pressure on his wrists a little.

Water was still pouring in from above, however, and his delirium had continued—he'd daydreamed about being rescued, and been shocked to find himself still here, still chained to the wall, still dying.

Now, he wondered if he'd ever be found. Twenty years from now, would builders happen upon his mouldering corpse while tearing up the old tunnels to lay new foundations? Perhaps a maintenance worker would come to investigate the smell once the water had seeped away, and he'd be discovered here, his corpse bloated and half-eaten by vermin.

He laughed at the idea, sputtering in the water. A maintenance worker. That was what had got him into this mess, wasn't it? That's what the man had said. That was why he'd been battered over the back of the head in the street and dragged down here to the rotten heart of the city, amongst the detritus and the effluence: the deal he'd made.

The irony is that he'd done it for the right reasons. Of course, a few brown paper bags had exchanged hands beneath the table; but that was business in this city. And who really got hurt? Not the residents. No, they got to reap the benefits—a rejuvenated city, all shiny and new. They all knew it went on, anyway. It was just like tipping a waiter: a quick backhander to make sure the papers got signed. So what if some poxy maintenance worker loses a contract?

At least, that's what he used to think. Now, he'd do anything to go back, to do things differently. He'd seen the error of his ways. He'd had his punishment. Did he really have to die? Was that how this worked?

He sighed, and then choked on a mouthful of foul-tasting water. It seems as if he did. This storm—it was his doing. It had been sent for him. He knew that now. And he knew it wouldn't stop until he was dead and gone. Yet still he couldn't bring himself to let go. That was the sort of man he was, the sort of man he'd always been. Even now, staring death in the face, knowing that he had brought this storm upon the city, he couldn't bring himself to do the right thing.

And so he continued to hold his head aloft and cling on to the last vestiges of his life, wondering when God would see fit to end it.

CHAPTER SEVENTEEN

IT SOUNDED LIKE the rattle of old bones.

O'Shea turned to Ramos. "Did you hear that?"

"Hear what?"

"Like someone coughing."

They'd been searching the tunnels for over an hour now; the water was nearing chest height. They'd passed the ladder to the warehouse some time ago, and Ramos was beginning to get nervous that they'd be trapped down here, kept from their exit by the rushing water. They were battling the flow with every step, and more than once, O'Shea had nearly gone over. It was only through sheer force of will that she kept going. Ramos was right, though—they'd have to give up soon. It was almost certain that Carrera was dead. For all she knew, they'd already stumbled past his submerged body somewhere back in the tunnels they'd previously explored.

Then she'd heard the cough.

"I didn't hear anything," said Ramos. "Look, I think we have to call it. We've given it our best shot, and we need to report those civilian bodies. If we catch hypothermia down here, Pellegrino will tear us both new ones."

"I'm telling you, Ramos—I heard something. Just ahead, down there." She jabbed the torch. It was starting to flicker, and she guessed water must have seeped into the workings, despite her best efforts to keep it above her head.

Ramos seemed to mull it over. "Okay. Let's check it out. We head to the end of this passage, and then, regardless of what we find, we turn back. Deal?"

"Deal," said O'Shea.

They pressed on.

A hundred yards further on, the sound of rushing water became a roar. It was streaming in, cascading in a thunderous downpour. They were, she guessed, directly under a storm drain. The weather was incredible; she'd never seen anything like it.

But it wouldn't be her last—climate change had given birth to these super storms years ago and now they raged intermittently all across the globe, devastating cities, islands, communities. They were lucky the worst of it had blown itself out over the Atlantic, and this was just the tail end. At least the city would still be standing afterwards.

"Okay, time to turn back," said Ramos. "The rate that water's coming in, we won't stay on our feet much longer."

"Hold on," said O'Shea. "Just another minute." She passed the torch along the passageway. "Hello? Is anybody there?" The tunnel was empty. "Hello?" Something glinted in the torchlight: a metal spike, jutting from the brickwork on the curved wall. Connected to it was a thin metal chain. "Ramos. Over here."

She passed the beam back and forth again, wading over. "Hello? Hello?"

"Look, O'Shea, we've got to get out of here, now."

"I know. It's just—" She stopped abruptly.

"What? What is it?" Ramos sounded worried.

A man's head was bobbing in the water.

"Help me!" She said. She put the torch in her mouth and grabbed the man's head, lifting it free of the water. His eyes flicked open; he looked panicked, disoriented. He coughed, his body jerking beneath the surface.

She wrapped her arms beneath his shoulders and hauled him up in the water. His face was gaunt, his eyes sunken and bruised. His front teeth were smashed, reduced to jagged stumps.

Ramos was beside her, already getting to work freeing the manacles from the metal spike.

The man coughed again, and broke into a hoarse, spluttering laugh. "Judges," he said. "*Judges.*"

"Carrera? David Carrera?" said O'Shea.

The man's eyes flicked from side to side, and then settled upon her face. He grinned, looked utterly delirious.

"That's not Carrera," said Ramos, straining as he pulled the last of the chains free. "That's Governor Walter Adams."

CHAPTER EIGHTEEN

CAPTAIN FLORES DIDN'T seem to know where to look.

He kept glancing over at her, but then his eyes would flick away, embarrassed, as if he were unwilling to meet her gaze. She wondered if he was having trouble admitting to himself that they'd done a good job. Perhaps it was more that she and Ramos been divested their sodden uniforms, and sitting there in borrowed clothing, without their helmets, they both looked suddenly *human*.

That was the thing about the Judges uniform: it was a shield, but it was a mask too. Now, Flores was forced to see the people beneath the uniforms, and for the first time he appeared to understand that they were just like him—a man and a woman charged with upholding the law and protecting civilians.

"Pennhouser says you visited Adams's office. There was no indication that things were awry?" said Flores, after a moment. He rapped his fingers on his desk, distracted.

"Nothing," said Ramos. "His assistant told us he'd gone away for a few days to avoid the media, following his statement earlier in the week."

"Ah, yes," said Flores. "The *statement*." He sighed. "Well, I think we can assume his office will be issuing a retraction shortly. He's sedated at present. We've not had a chance to question him yet, to find out how he was picked up by Reece. The doctor said he was a wreck when you handed him over to the ambulance crew."

O'Shea and Ramos had managed to get Adams out of the sewer system and up into the abandoned warehouse, where they'd called in an ambulance and escorted it through the near-impenetrable storm before returning to the precinct. Adams was in a bad way, but they were assured he'd make a full recovery—in time.

"He's been through a lot," said O'Shea.

"Much of it of his own making," said Flores. "We talked to the perp you brought in—the man who shot Hartigan."

"And?" prompted Ramos.

"Seems he was in the pay of Adams all along. He and a few others—we've got names, and we'll round them up once the storm blows over—had been tasked with creating unrest. They were trying to provoke you, so that everyone would see you coming down on them at the protests. Adams was trying to control the story, to add weight to his position. It was a hatchet job."

"A hatchet job that led to murder," said O'Shea.

"Rohmer—that was his name—was never supposed to go that far. But that's what you get with people like that. He was hopped up on stims and out of control. Once he got fired up, there was no stopping him. Hartigan obviously saw things going south and tried to step in…" Flores shook his head. "Adams is in it up to his neck."

"He certainly *was*," said Ramos with a grin.

"We should have spotted it sooner," said Flores. "If we'd been working together, sharing information…" He trailed off. "I'm sorry. I can't condone what you did back at Chelsea Market, but the things I said—they were uncalled for." For the first time since they'd entered his office, Flores met her eye. He seemed genuine enough.

"Times are changing, captain," she said. "This is new, for all of us. But there's no going back. Not now. We're going to have to learn to work together."

Flores nodded. He looked out of the office window at his team, going about their duties. Despite the late hour, the precinct was still buzzing. "They're going to find it tough," he said.

"We all are," said O'Shea. "But we have a job to do."

Flores nodded. "Speaking of which—there's still the matter of David Carrera. We're no closer to finding out what's happened to him. Do you think he could be down there in those tunnels?"

"If he is, he's dead," said Ramos. "No one could have survived that. We were lucky to get to Adams in time."

"I suppose we'll know more in the coming days," said Flores. "We'll get a team down there once the water level drops. Take a proper look at what Reece was doing down there... and look into those other bodies you found, too." He grimaced at the thought. "A whole community, drowned in their beds. Poor bastards."

They lapsed into silence for a moment. O'Shea could still see the face of the woman, pale and staring, as she bobbed just below the surface of the water in the tunnel, eerily lit by the light of a torch. The image would haunt her, she knew, for years to come.

"Look, there's nothing any of us can do now. The whole city's holding its breath, waiting for the storm to pass. Get some rest, both of you, and I'll update you in the morning. You can use the dorm space out back." Flores rapped his fingers on his desk again.

"I'd feel happier if we had an answer on Carrera," said Ramos.

"We all would," said Flores. "But you've been out there, and you said it yourself—if he was down in those tunnels, he's already dead. There's nothing we can do for him now. We can pick it up again in the morning."

Ramos glanced at O'Shea, as if seeking her approval, or at least her agreement. She could see the tiredness in his eyes.

She nodded, rising slowly from her seat. "Thank you, Captain," she said. "Wake us if there's any news."

CHAPTER NINETEEN

A SUDDEN KNOCK at the door brought her round with a start. She stopped herself from reaching for her weapon. Memories came flooding—she was in the police precinct. She'd been sleeping...

A second rap at the door brought her back to the present.

"Come in," she called.

The door swung open on creaking hinges. It was Pennhouser, looking uncomfortable. He didn't look as if he'd slept. "The captain said I should wake you," he said.

O'Shea stretched, flexing her neck. "What time is it?"

"Six thirty. The storm's just about blown itself out. And Carrera has finally switched on his cell phone."

She sat up. "What?"

Pennhouser grinned. "We've tried calling it, but he's not answering. We've tracked its location to a house in Brooklyn. I'm heading over there now. I thought you and your partner might like to come along for the ride."

O'Shea nodded. "Give us five. We'll meet you out front."

Pennhouser nodded and withdrew, closing the door behind him.

O'Shea banged her fist against the partition wall by the side of the bed. "Ramos! Time to get up. We've got a lead on Carrera."

She heard a groan coming from the adjoining room, and laughed.

THE HOUSE IN Brooklyn was nothing like she'd imagined.

Having seen Carrera's office and apartment in the city, she'd been expecting something showy, a mansion hidden behind filigreed iron gates. This was a standard suburban house; she'd grown up in one just like it. She double-checked the data feed on her bike screen. It was definitely registered in Carrera's name, purchased by his company almost two years previously.

She swung her leg over the bike seat and slid down onto the sidewalk. It felt good to be back in uniform, although she'd yet to break it in.

She looked up at the house. It sat back from the road behind a small, informal garden. The boards had been painted pale yellow, but had bleached in the sun. An easy chair on the porch looked unused, and a hanging basket had been decimated by the storm, the flowers drooping on broken stems.

Pennhouser had been right—the skies were clearing, shafts of sunlight poking through the smudge of clouds, providing a welcome break amongst the showers that still trailed in the storm's wake.

"I didn't have Carrera down as the domestic type," said Ramos, from beside her.

"No," she said.

She turned at the sound of a car pulling up behind them. It had once been red, but was now so streaked with dirt it looked brown. One of the wing mirrors had been smashed, and was bound up with black duct tape. Pennhouser cut the transmission and clambered out, slamming the door behind him.

"You sure this is the right place?" said Ramos, as Pennhouser walked over to join them.

"So the tech boys tell me," said Pennhouser, with a shrug.

"Your guess is as good as mine." He looked to O'Shea. "How do you want to handle this?"

"Be our guest," she said with an expansive gesture. Pennhouser grinned, and set off up the path.

The door opened before he'd finished knocking.

David Carrera's face—familiar from the vid captures and photographs she'd studied—peered out at them in confusion. "Hello?" he said. "Can I help you?"

"David Carrera?" said Pennhouser. "I'm with the NYPD, and these are my colleagues from the Justice Department." O'Shea couldn't hold back her grin. The shift in Pennhouser's attitude had been marked; she wasn't yet sure if it was down to their retrieving Adams, or that he now had someone to blame for his partner's shooting. She supposed it didn't really matter.

"Yes, that's me," said Carrera. "How can I help?"

"Can we come in?" said O'Shea.

Carrera hesitated. "Well, it's a little awkward…"

The moment stretched.

"Well, all right then," he finished, standing aside to let them through the door. They filed into the kitchen, which smelled of rosemary and lemons, and he closed the door behind them. "What's all this about?" he said, as he joined them. He didn't offer them seats at the kitchen table. Clearly, he was uncomfortable, and wanted to get this over and done with as swiftly as possible. She could tell by Ramos's posture that he sensed it too: Carrera was hiding something.

"You've been reported missing," said Pennhouser. "We've been searching for you for some time. I must remind you, sir, that given the situation with Joseph Reece you were encouraged to log your movements with the precinct. Your assistant has been trying to reach you."

Carrera sighed. "Look, I'm sorry. I had… things to take care of here. A situation came up."

"What sort of situation?" said Ramos.

"A *personal* one." Carrera looked defiant.

"I don't think you understand the gravity of the situation,

sir," said Pennhouser. "We've been forced to assume you'd been abducted by Reece. My colleagues here have been dredging the sewer system in the hope of finding you before you drowned in the tunnels."

Carrera looked as if he'd been slapped around the face. He looked from Ramos to O'Shea. "I... I'm sorry, I didn't know."

"If you'd thought to leave word, none of this would have been necessary," said Pennhouser.

And we wouldn't have found Adams, thought O'Shea. He would have drowned in the tunnels, and they'd all have been none the wiser.

"I didn't have time. It all... it just happened so fast."

"What happened, Mr. Carrera?" said O'Shea.

His expression was pleading. "It's my sister. She had a fall. I got the call from a neighbour as I was leaving the office, and just hailed the first cab I saw."

"Your sister?" said Pennhouser.

Carrera nodded. "She's not well. This is her house. I had to make sure she was all right. And then I decided to stay to see out the storm. She gets scared when she's alone for too long, and I figured the howling wind..." His shoulders dropped. "Look, I don't spend as much time with her as I should, and her nurse was too afraid to travel over in case she got stranded. I came here in such a hurry I didn't bring anything with me. I realised I didn't have any way of charging my phone, at least until the storm broke this morning and I went out to pick up a charger."

"David?" The call came from a room down the hall. It was a woman's voice, slurred. "David? Who are you talking to?"

"Nothing to worry about," he called back. "They're just leaving."

"I want to meet your friends," said the woman. "Come on, bring them to me."

Carrera looked stricken. "I don't think it's a good idea," he called. "Better if you just leave," he said to the Judges. "I can see to her."

"It's all right," said O'Shea. "Let's say a quick hello."

He hesitated for a moment, and then nodded, and beckoned for them to follow.

The woman was propped in an armchair in the sitting room, her legs stretched out before the fire. She looked up when they entered the room, and smiled. For the second time in as many days, O'Shea was thankful for her helmet for concealing her shock.

The woman was badly scarred, her face misshapen, so that the flesh on the left side had bloated and drooped, as if the side of her head were simply sloughing off in layers of rubbery skin. Her left arm was swollen, too, her fingers curled into bony claws that rested on her lap.

"This is Patricia," said Carrera.

O'Shea mumbled a brief greeting.

"David's been looking after me," said Patricia. "He's such a kind man. I don't know what I'd do without him."

O'Shea didn't know what to say—how to respond. Everything she'd learned about Carrera, the picture she'd painted of the man during their investigation, had him as a womanising careerist, a man who trod on people to make his own way up the ladder. Seeing him here, like this, caring for this poor woman—it changed everything. More than that, it validated everything she had done during the last twenty-four hours, the lengths she had gone to find him. If he really *had* been down in that tunnel, if Reece had got to him, what would have become of his sister?

Carrera stepped back into the hallway, gesturing for her to follow.

"What happened to her?" said O'Shea.

"There was an accident," he said, his voice barely above a whisper. "Up until three years ago, she worked at a nuclear facility in Jersey. She has a brilliant mind. But something went wrong, a containment failure, and she was blasted with radiation. Most of her colleagues were killed. She survived, but this is what it's done to her." He swallowed. "I do what I can... but it's never enough."

O'Shea smiled. "I think you're doing just fine."

Ramos was standing in the doorway. "Pennhouser's just had a call. Adams is awake."

O'Shea nodded and turned to Carrera. "We'll be on our way." She made for the kitchen door, the others trailing behind her. At the last minute, she stopped and turned back. "Oh, and Mr. Carrera—you might want to give your assistant a call. She's worried sick."

He nodded and turned away, ducking back into the sitting room as they left.

CHAPTER TWENTY

SHE'D NEVER LIKED hospitals. Not since she was a little girl, and had shattered her leg falling out of a tree. She remembered stern nurses, and a doctor who'd wagged a finger in her face and told her little girls shouldn't be climbing trees, and all she'd wanted to do was tell him to get lost and that anything a boy could do, she could do too.

She'd buried her anger, though, channelling it into proving him wrong, showing how strong she was, how determined. And she'd done it, too—she'd been up and walking again in no time, and although the exercises had hurt, she'd gritted her teeth through it and pushed herself, harder and harder. It still hurt in the cold sometimes, but it only served as a reminder of her own determination. It had seen her through the Judges training programme, and it had seen her through the tunnels beneath Chelsea too.

Still, the acrid stink of disinfectant, the tiled walls, the *beep-beep* of the monitoring equipment—they all reminded her of that doctor's smug face, of her anger, and the pain she'd suffered as they'd slowly rebuilt the limb with metal rods and bolts.

A uniformed officer—a woman with close-cropped blonde hair and a swirling tattoo on her neck—showed them through to the side room where Walter Adams was recovering.

Reporters swarmed around the door, cameras flashing, hurling questions like weapons. O'Shea ignored them, shutting the door in their shining, expectant faces. She'd had enough of the media in recent days.

Adams looked pale and broken—the ghost of the man who'd been all over the television networks these past few days. His lips were a scabrous mess, his eyes blackened and bruised, and tubes sprouted from both bandaged wrists, twisting away to monitors, fluid bags and stranger machines.

In the far corner of the otherwise empty room, Adams's assistant, Richard Parks, was looking out of the window at the parking lot below.

"Governor Adams," said Pennhouser, circling around to the far side of the bed. "My name is Detective Pennhouser, NYPD. These are my colleagues, Judge O'Shea and Judge Ramos."

Adams twisted in the bed, looking up at her. He winced at the evident pain in his neck. "*Judges*," he said, scowling. "I suppose you're the two who saved me?"

"We are," said Ramos levelly.

Adams sighed, as if the very thought of it turned his stomach. "And thus am I tested. I suppose I owe you my thanks."

"You owe us nothing," said O'Shea. "We were simply doing our duty."

"Duty?" Adams laughed, a rattling, wheezing sound that ended in a spasmodic cough. "That's what you call it?"

"Call what?" said Ramos.

"The death of freedom," said Adams. The words sounded faintly ridiculous, coming from his ruined mouth. They'd grow him a new set of teeth, of course, but until then, he was stuck with a waspish lisp.

"Oh, I think you've done a very good job of killing your *own* freedom," said Ramos. O'Shea was impressed by Ramos's self-control—even she was fighting the desire to gloat.

"I don't know what you're talking about," said Adams. He turned to Pennhouser. "Get these people out of here, would you? I don't want them hanging around any longer."

"Oh, I'm afraid it's not that easy," said Pennhouser. He was having a harder time keeping a straight face—O'Shea could see the corner of his mouth twitching.

"The thing is, Governor Adams, you've been judged and found guilty of inciting hate crimes, along with conspiracy to murder. As soon as the doctors have finished with you, you'll be taken from here to a place of incarceration, where you shall serve a custodial sentence of no less than ten years." O'Shea couldn't stop herself grinning as she delivered the news, watching Adams's expression change from shock to red-faced anger.

"Of course, you'll be stripped of your elected position too, *Mister* Adams," added Ramos.

"What? You can't do this! It's a violation of my rights. I demand to see a lawyer!" Adams tried to sit up, but collapsed into a second coughing fit, triggering one of the monitor alarms. By the window, Parks had turned to watch, smirking.

The door burst open and a nurse bustled in, followed by a Latino man in a white coat. "Out, out!" he called, as they huddled around Adams's bed. "Give us room. We need to administer a sedative."

"I think we made our point," said Pennhouser. "Back to the precinct?"

O'Shea glanced over to the window. "Just a moment," she said. She beckoned Parks over, leading him from the room, past the press of reporters—who were now crowding around the window, trying to see what was happening to Adams inside—and along the passage to a quiet spot by a vending machine.

"Can I help?" he said. He was still smiling, having evidently enjoyed watching his former employer's sudden fall from grace.

"When we came to visit at the office the other day, you told us Governor Adams was taking some time out to avoid the media spotlight," she said. "Why did you lie?"

Parks shrugged. "The truth is, I didn't know *where* he was.

He hadn't been into the office for days. For all I knew he *could* have been hiding. I wouldn't have put it past him."

"You knew about Reece, though, and the possible threat to his life. You could have reported it." She sensed more than saw Ramos stepping up behind her.

"So what," said Parks, with an affected shrug. "So what if Reece had managed to get hold of him? You've heard the filth he spews. He's an odious little bastard, and he deserves everything he gets."

O'Shea glanced at Ramos. She took a deep breath, and then let it out. "Richard Parks, I'm sentencing you to two years in a state penitentiary for perverting the course of justice." She took him by the upper arm, ignoring his incredulous expression. "Judge Ramos and I will escort you directly to the holding facility now."

Parks gibbered something incoherent in response.

As she led him away down the bustling corridor, she glanced back to see Pennhouser, watching from just outside the ring of reporters by Governor Adams's door. He was beaming.

DISGRACED GOVERNOR WALTER *Adams today released a statement from his bed at Bellevue Hospital in downtown New York. No cameras were allowed into the hospital ward, but the audio was captured by one of our reporters:*

"I extend my thanks to Judge Ramos and Judge O'Shea, who did a commendable job in rescuing me from certain death. The work they and their colleagues are doing in New York, and throughout America, is of vital importance, and I regret my earlier statements regarding the Judges programme. I was wrong, pure and simple."

Adams, the final victim—and survivor—of lone wolf serial killer Joseph Reece, is to be stripped of his title as he begins a ten-year prison sentence on charges of inciting hatred and conspiracy to murder.

Adams's incendiary comments on the Judge programme last week were blamed by the NYPD for a number of public protests throughout the state, in which at least sixteen civilians were injured. It has also been alleged that he recruited people to deliberately promote violence at these protests, leading to the death of a police officer.

Adams, who had been abducted and held captive by Reece, was rescued from the sewer system by two Judges during the recent storms.

Protests continue, but with Adams's exposure, momentum

appears to have been lost, and the number of protestors has dwindled significantly in the last few days.

Could it be that public sentiment toward the Judges is changing?

Coming up next, we ask: is it time for a reappraisal of the Judges programme? Stay tuned for more.

In other news, the worst of the storm has now passed, and MTA officials are advising that services will be resuming as soon as possible, with the bulk of lines opening by...

ABOUT THE AUTHOR

George Mann is a *Sunday Times* bestselling novelist and scriptwriter.

He's the author of the *Newbury & Hobbes* Victorian mystery series, as well as four novels about a 1920s vigilante known as The Ghost. He's also written bestselling *Doctor Who* novels, new adventures for Sherlock Holmes and the supernatural crime series, *Wychwood*.

His comic writing includes extensive work on *Doctor Who*, *Dark Souls* (based on the massively popular video games), *Warhammer 40,000*, *Project Blue Book* and a creator-owned series based on *Newbury & Hobbes*, as well as *Teenage Mutant Ninja Turtles* for younger readers and a forthcoming series with Legendary Comics, soon to be announced.

He's written audio scripts for *Doctor Who*, *Blake's 7*, Sherlock Holmes, *Warhammer 40,000* and more, and for a handful of high-profile iOS games.

As editor he's assembled four anthologies of original Sherlock Holmes fiction, as well as multiple volumes of *The Solaris Book of New Science Fiction* and *The Solaris Book of New Fantasy*.

His website is at www.george-mann.com.

WHEN THE LIGHT LAY STILL

CHARLES J ESKEW

Dedicated to
the continued search for justice.

CHAPTER ONE

OFFICER EZEKIEL JONES watched as a puff of white smoke crackled from his partner's Glock in the near winter night. One body down, one weapon forward, and Ezekiel unsure if after that night—its cold promise, its absence of light—he'd ever really know up from down again.

"You saw—*holy fuck*, Ezekiel, I swear, it looked like a gun," Officer Williams cried out to her partner.

Later, Ezekiel would have a response.

He'd say that the moonlight hadn't glinted across the plastic in the same way it would steel. He'd say that it was uncommon for a gun to come so small, or in a pastel blue.

In that moment, though, there was only the body beneath them and the eyes that kept Ezekiel fixed. Ezekiel hadn't even budged when his partner jogged to the cruiser and began rummaging around in the trunk; for nothing Ezekiel could think would matter.

"Tank, did you *hear* me? Does. He. Have. An. ID?" Williams shouted over the clang of the trunk slamming under her hands. Ezekiel heard. But he shut his eyes, hoping they'd find a way to fall into themselves and never stop.

"*Tank?*" Williams shouted again, snapping Ezekiel's eyes open to the dark beneath him. This time he looked over to his partner, his Taco Tuesday compatriot.

"I... yeah, I got it, Williams," he said, and for a moment he took in the sight of Williams' sweat-soaked hair, thin blonde strands stuck slack to her trembling forehead, and forgot the body in front of them. It didn't last, though, when looking back at the memory of how he needed to serve in that moment.

He hummed loudly, to quash the tide rising in him, and knelt to the body.

The body.

The *fucking* body.

A body not unlike his own, carrying the same harsh history as most who were brown and beaten. While Ezekiel thumbed through the boy's pocket for a wallet, Williams flicked her flashlight on and began shakily scanning the empty parking lot as she walked back towards them. She stopped, mostly, when she reached Ezekiel and the thirteen-year-old corpse; Ezekiel holding up a puffed pleather wallet with a cartoon character on it.

When Williams finished searching through it, she tossed it to the ground. The *flap* as it struck the blacktop made Ezekiel flinch.

"What are you doing?" he asked, not sure if it was for Williams or himself.

"The... *shit*, Ezekiel. He's *thirteen*. He—if he wouldn't have run. If he'd just *listened*. Why didn't he just *listen?*"

The Grant High School drama club member—the receiver of countless embraces from a soon to be hollowed-out mother and father—Jeanie Jeffery's first kiss under paint-chipped bleachers—another bullet-riddled body—Dushane—was still bleeding as Williams knelt beside him. Ezekiel could finally make out what it was his partner had grabbed from her trunk when she set down her flashlight; and he knew, as he watched her place a clunky BB gun into the boy's hands, that this night would be the end of more than just one life.

"*No*... No, Williams, just... Don't do this. *Please,* you *can't* do this." Ezekiel's hand went to his pocket—for his walkie, not his firearm. His plea had come out as more a whimper than anything else, but Williams stopped. If that moment could have gone on, sliced out to infinity, maybe there would have been something to find. Maybe, Ezekiel hoped, something could catch her from falling.

She'd made a mistake; a horrible, indescribable mistake. Ezekiel didn't imagine, even if she had let his words dig rather than prod, that they'd be shooting the shit at Dewey's behind a couple piss-warm beers that weekend. If she'd just stop, take account of her actions even though it cost her career as a cop, then Ezekiel could plausibly hang on to hope: the most dangerous four-letter word in his lexicon.

"I made a mistake. I made *one* mistake, and what, I'm supposed to just let everyone *forget* about everything I've done up until now? No. *Fuck* that. This is happening, Tank," Williams said, as she propped the once-person into a pose that told a story not nearly as strange as the one they knew to be true.

When he joined the force, Ezekiel hadn't exactly been the pride of the Jones household. There'd been an understanding— or so his mother had thought—that her boy wouldn't be taken in by the stories of his father's glory days: glory days that everyone but the man himself had the opportunity to enjoy.

He'd grown up with a thousand uncles in the same line of work—his father used to say they had blue blood. Whenever they'd take him for the day, or stop by for dinner with what remained of their brother's legacy, he'd fall face first into the tall tales. He could tell a few on his own, now, as if he'd been there himself: the one about the standoff on the city bus, or the one about riding on the hood of a getaway car going fifty miles an hour (even if it'd been thirty in the first telling of it). There were also the wounds, the people he couldn't save, the mantra that put him back into the uniform every morning.

Even in the grip of that fantasy, Ezekiel entertained his mother's blueprint. Maybe he'd even fooled himself into thinking—from one stage to another, from high school diploma to masters—that he'd make it to the type of law that took place behind tables, as far from bullets and bravado as could be.

Reya, his mother, insisted it was just bubble guts and butterflies that kept him from pushing on past the LSATs, that the badge he'd come home with instead was just some twenty-something symptom he'd get past once he was done chasing ghosts. He tried to explain that even he hadn't known what it was that made him wake from a fever dream with a blue uniform and a job in his father's precinct. It wasn't fear, though: it was fulfilment. It was knowing his place was on the street, as close to their people who'd needed protection as he could get.

All at once, here in this crappy parking lot, Williams had stripped him of that, like the thief she'd thought she'd found in Dushane.

Ezekiel's gun had never felt so alien to his fingers than that moment, placing a hand over the Glock on his hip.

"The fuck are you doing, Tank?" Williams said. Ezekiel had grown up under the blue, under a revolving door of uncles that taught him respect for the badge, for the oath and the weapon. He knew enough to chide himself for giving Williams a chance, for being so obvious, for not pulling the piece in the six different ways he could have without her seeing.

"This isn't happening, Williams," he said. "I won't *let* it happen. I'm taking you in, and we're going to figure this out the right way, okay? Don't make this any worse than it already is." His breath misted, drifting over the body between them.

Williams was a quicker learner than he'd given her credit for. All those nights at the range, before drinks or dinner or softball (the EMTs were nigh-unbeatable), he'd shared some of the secrets he'd learned over the years. Her own draw almost escaped his eye.

Almost.

His fingers perfectly matched hers, unhooking and drawing

his own pistol. It flew into his hands as if magnetised. Earlier that day, sitting with Williams at Stu's Diner, a plate of pancakes and rubbery, overcooked turkey sausage links in front of him, the last thing he could have imagined was a standoff with the one person he'd thought *got it*.

"This is ridiculous, man. You know, you *know* how close I am, Tank. I have a—a—a fucking *week* before I start the Judge programme. Soon enough, we're going to be out here, all of us, Tank, making the choices. We'll say what's right, not the lawyers, not the politicians, not a—a—dickhole on Twitter or YouTube." She was pleading, but her grip on her pistol was steady as rock.

HE'D NEVER SAY it to anyone but the bottom of a glass, but he wondered, later—more times than Dushane deserved—what if he'd just gone along with it? What if he hadn't gone for the walkie?

Williams was closer than most Ezekiel had known to being accepted into the Judges programme, not that she'd told anyone outside of Ezekiel and her family. It was only a week earlier they'd celebrated it, and if she'd seemed to be going through the motions since then, Ezekiel forgave it as a late case of senioritis. She was proof, he'd thought, that Fargo and Gurney may have been right about things after all.

After the call, though, as Ezekiel sat across the table from Chief Cori, there wasn't anything *right* about it as far as he saw. After the call, as the chief scanned every social media platform he could find with Dushane's face, to *get a hold of the situation, and make sure the people know the truth about this kid before crucifying one of their own,* Ezekiel couldn't stop the thought bubbling up that the blue was covering something a bit more yellow-bellied. After the call, visiting Williams in her holding cell, crowded with the brothers he'd bled with, who wouldn't leave a policewoman alone with a traitor like him, his father's stunts seemed less righteous by the moment.

It would be nasty. Everyone knew that; no matter how much they spun things, no matter how they stalled before the media got hold of it. Williams was given a leave of absence with pay while they got to the bottom of the shallow puddle Dushane spent his last seconds choking in.

Ezekiel's own suspension, which felt less a matter of law and more of morale, was paid as well. He'd always been a frugal sort, though; his mother, a bank branch manager for most of his youth, had made it nearly impossible to do any summer fun spending without a guilt trip. As annoyed as he would be to ever tell his mother she'd been right, it proved more important than ever when those post-suspension payments, a bit cold and stiff and bloodied and dark, landed in his account. It meant it wasn't so hard a choice to send his weekly compensation for sitting on his ass anonymously to a GoFundMe campaign setup for Dushane's family.

At least, it wasn't at first. Because nothing on the net stays private, and when his contributions were revealed, the accusations followed; the insinuation that this was ultimately about the one thing it *couldn't* be, if anyone would take him, his truth, for anything more than that of a divisive, black, race-baiting traitor.

Jones had spent the better part of his short career being asked by a myriad of sides just *who he was loyal to*. He'd laughed it off, that ridiculous obsession with defining him, as if they were picking sides for a pickup game at the park. If he wasn't a Clarence Thomas or Uncle Tom, he was a radical in repose.

He'd have probably made a mistake sooner or later, erupted in front of one of the cameras that buzzed like gnats around his apartment after the incident. Thankfully, he'd always had two things to help him keep hold of the waning fucks he had left to give.

For one, he carried with him every voice, every face that he'd come across on his beat that offered love in one way or another. He remembered every peanut-butter-and-chocolate cookie Mrs. Sanderson sent him since he'd saved a high schooler from an after-school pummeling. He remembered the gratitude on Mr. Darzada's face when he popped into his 11th grade English class to explain and make amends after a video went viral of another officer choking Lanita Moore for mocking him.

For the other, he'd heard the voice of his father—like *Ghost Dad*, but less Cosby—over anything he did, and everything he tried to be.

His mother had explained to him that there was only one truth to know as a minor by way of melanin: to move from one day to the next.

There's another after this, and one more after that. It sounded like nonsense the first time he'd heard it, hell, it sounded even more insane when he started saying it to himself. It wasn't enough to simply *exist*, through a country that systematically deconstructed and parceled out black bodies; there had to be *survival*, and knowing that survival is just another turn of the wheel. Apathetic? Maybe, but Ezekiel leaned into it as a call to arms for the battle ahead.

There's another after this, and one more after that, he whispered on the day he'd taken the stand. The suit and tie, his *only* suit and tie, felt stiff and tight over a body that had swollen in strength in the years since he'd bought it. When he made his way to the stand, there were the expected murmurs of the misanthropes.

They may as well had been vapour, though. The only people Ezekiel thought mattered that day were Dushane's mother and father. The two of them glared tightly at him, *into* him. He almost missed his cue to swear to the higher power that'd let all this happen, as he was as fixed on them as they were on him.

It was far from the first time he'd stood in front of a grand jury. He didn't remember that old suit of his sticking sweat-drenched to his body like that, though. *This is the easy part*, he reminded himself, this was just going to get the ball rolling, to carry them all to court for the struggle that mattered. While the prosecutor shuffled through his briefcase, Ezekiel scanned over the Grand Jury. Most of them were white; not so much a conspiracy as the luck of the draw, but it couldn't do Dushane any favours.

Three of them are under 30, that could help... shit, well, at least it's only the one *red hat... is he* trying *to get bumped?* Ezekiel thought as he bounced from one face to another. He looked beyond the faces, seeing how they itched, how number 7 rolled his eyes when Dushane's family asked to be present, at the rising hate in the older tongues, ready to erupt at the broken boy on the road.

Eventually, Ezekiel was brought to the front and sworn in, the clerk's eyes never looking higher than his nose as she mouthed the familiar words.

Until that point, he'd not-so-accidentally found himself sat far, *far* behind Dushane's parents.

"You were present at the scene, Officer Jones, is that correct?" the prosecutor asked, his eyes unpeeled from the rain-worn legal pad on his table.

"Yes, sir," Ezekiel returned.

"Would you please elaborate on the events leading up to the incident?"

It took Ezekiel a moment to take his gaze away from the vibrating eyes of The Incident's parents before he responded. There was someone else with them, he realised, as Mrs. Reed doubled over at the mention of her son. It only took another glance to recognise Aaliyah Monroe; he'd seen her enough times over the last few months on TV. She'd usually be easily spotted in her ridiculous blue scarf, on the front line of a protest or behind the parents of pre-pubescent, plundered life. Ezekiel may have thought it noble, if she wouldn't always use the platform to push her own fairy-tale ideas of restorative justice.

Ezekiel took a slow breath before speaking.

"Yes, sir. Officer Williams and I responded to an emergency call: two teenagers involved in a violent altercation outside of the new Ump Tower. As we approached the two teenagers, Dushane Reed fled the scene on foot. Williams pursued Dushane first, I hung back to make sure the kid with the busted lip was okay. Williams ordered Dushane to stop, as did I. He was fast, and knew the area better than we did, so it took some time to catch up to him. While fleeing, he screamed back to us that we were chasing the wrong person. It wouldn't be until later that we'd learn, as I'm sure you're aware, that Dushane hadn't been the instigator of the fight, but the other individual, Patrick Powell. Regardless, the suspect continued to run from us."

Ezekiel stopped for a moment to compose himself. "I stopped running and doubled back for the patrol car; it just made sense in the moment. I caught up to Williams, picked her up, and we quickly caught up to Reed. He—as I cornered him, getting out of the car, and Officer Williams at his back, he started to pull out a cell—"

"Thank you, Officer Jones, that will be all," the prosecutor said, looking up for the first time and flashing a genial smile, as absurd as it was complacent. Ezekiel looked over to where he'd been used to finding a judge, and turned back to the prosecutor.

"With all due respect, sir, I haven't reached the point in the incident regarding Officer Williams' discharge," Ezekiel said, and bit his tongue back when the end of the statement trailed off on something close to a laugh.

"We appreciate your... *willingness* to testify, but as I'm sure *you're* aware, this isn't a trial. We simply need to gather details regarding the incident, and we've reached the end of what I believe that either I or the jury can listen to without consideration of your unique position in this matter," the prosecutor parried back, the words stale and sticky from sitting on his tongue for so long.

"My unique position? Sir, if this is regarding my donation to—"

"It's not *just* your charitable actions, Officer Jones. You are not under review—not here, anyway—but given the sensitive nature of this case, and yes, your contribution to the Reed family, we must also consider your actions during the Chicago riots two years ago. Forgive me, but we can't discount that you have had issue with proper judgement in the past."

It took Ezekiel everything he had to keep from sucking loudly at his teeth.

It always came back to Chicago. He'd not done anything illegal, a lifetime ago, during the riots. He served the badge he'd been given, against those who would abuse that power, against an industrial machine made for justice but malformed by fear.

He was a fool. It wasn't just Chicago they were thinking about. There was the media attention, the questions about whose side he was on. Perhaps most ridiculous of it all, there was that godforsaken nickname, *Tank*.

"You were suspended, weren't you? Ultimately, no formal charges were brought against you, but given that, and considering your recent contribution to the Reed family— and neither Officer Williams nor the boy you claim instigated the attack corroborate your version of the events—we must consider there is reasonable doubt to your account. We appreciate your time, Officer Jones."

"Okay, but I really don't think you're—"

"*Thank you*, Officer Jones, that will be all," the prosecutor said, looking up from the legal pad to Ezekiel. There was a moment then that would stick like a thumbtack in his mind: Ezekiel edged on speaking, his mouth open to collect flies or dust in the air, to collect all the things they were ignoring that hung in the air around them. Instead, Ezekiel closed his mouth, looking to the three of them; Aaliyah Monroe with arms latched around the Reeds' shoulders, one of many shadows that wouldn't be televised like the rest of the mess had been.

This wasn't justice, Ezekiel realised. This was just law. He'd never found anything grand in this part of the process: a prosecutor and a jury, free from the oversight of a judge, was nothing but an abdication of responsibility. There had to be a better way, and as he gave a jutted nod, and carried the eyes of the room with him on the way out, he knew he wouldn't find it behind the badge his father wore.

It would take months for the grand jury to officially reach a decision, but Ezekiel didn't need to wait with bated anything for an answer. Officer Williams was free to patrol the streets after a long staycation. The Reeds would have bullet holes and blankets carrying the fading scent of their son. Ezekiel, it seemed, got a light brown bagged lunch on the steps of the courthouse.

He didn't consider what to do after he ate, though, with the day or with the rest of his life. But the world hadn't finished with him as a woman in a trench coat and a perhaps-not-even-twice-worn suit sauntered up the steps towards him.

"This seat isn't taken, is it?" she said, with the savoury sweetness of a nurse, or death-brokering bureaucrat. Ezekiel glanced around the oversized steps of the courthouse and saw not a single person in sight.

"I guess not," he said, staring at the road and taking a bite of his increasingly unsatisfying bologna sandwich.

"Good." The woman settled. "What are you doing out here by yourself? Seems kind of a crummy day for an outside lunch."

Ezekiel shrugged. He watched as the woman pulled out a wrinkled pack of potato chips and a bag of Ump Chocolates and proceeded to dump the chocolates into the bag of chips and shake it up. He found himself sifting through the catalogue of legalese in his head in the hopes of finding some prohibition for such a snack food abomination.

"So, are you an officer?" she asked between mouthfuls of candied chips.

Ezekiel parted his lips to speak but looked at her again and paused. "Something tells me you already know the answer to that, ma'am. Is IA always so bad at interrogation?" he asked, before finishing his sandwich in one bite, defiantly forcing it in with a finger. Better to chew the fat he'd put together that morning than hers.

If he'd blinked, Jones would have missed the seamless shift from flustered damsel to smirking superiority. She poured the rest of the bag's contents into her face and swallowed, giving a theatrical sigh of satisfaction.

"You have a bit of paranoia about you, don't you, Officer Jones? Do you suspect every beautiful woman wanting your attention is out for your badge?" She leaned her elbows back on the long stone steps.

"Just the ones with Glocks under their coats," he returned. He glanced her way expecting to see defeat: that she'd concede and leave him to his unopened lemonade and sparkly disposition. What he saw, however, was the same look his Chief Cori had used, back before the shitshower that rained on their department after Dushane's murder.

"...Well, what else?" she asked.

Ezekiel blinked at the question, not sure what to do with it at first. After mulling it over for a moment, washing the sandwich down with his lemonade, he figured, *what the hell*. He was certain that there were seven different kinds of wrong in Internal Affairs approaching him like this, and it wasn't like there was somewhere he'd aimed to be. So, instead of rushing to an increasingly cold apartment to productively stare at a wall, he figured there wasn't too much harm in humouring his lunch companion.

"It's a little excessive, don't you think? The piece at your hip, a semi-automatic? Between that and the one under your coat I don't see much use for that switch blade tucked under your pants, left ankle." Ezekiel was showing off, but after the day he'd had, he didn't much care.

The woman chuckled.

"You *are* perceptive, aren't you? Granted, you missed the Taser, but three out of four isn't bad, *former* Officer Jones." She added a slow, slightly sticky clap at the end.

Ezekiel didn't flinch, or not outwardly at least. *Former*. He hadn't even the chance to tell a bottle of Jameson about his recent discussion, the day before, to no longer be associated with a system of problematic, pacifying pride. Even if he had mentioned it, anywhere outside the office, there's no way she could have found it out in such a short time—unless she'd been spying on him. The thought never occurred that she'd found out from someone at the precinct. As much as they now seemed hell-bent on destroying the oath, his brothers never gossiped about one of their own, with or without a shield.

"Who *are* you?" It'd come out more perp-oriented than he'd meant, but the woman only chuckled, longer this time.

"I'm not IA. I'm just someone who wanted to have a bite with you, *Tank*, and maybe a bit of substance-free small talk. For instance—oh, I don't know—what are your thoughts on Special Prosecutor Eustace Fargo?"

Oh, hell-fucking-no.

The thunder had been coming for a while, since the attack on the White House. Everyone in blue, everyone with a thrice-worn tie and briefcase, felt it on the wind as much as they did beneath their trigger fingers. Ezekiel, like most in his precinct, had felt some relief when an answer had arrived in the form of President Gurney and the proposed Judge system. After years of bumbling celebrities or other brands of idiot, it felt like a return to *sense*.

Of course, Fargo wouldn't get his way, not entirely. Gurney would rein him in, make something practical out of Fargo's pipe dream. He wouldn't let such a chaotic plan become anything more than rage bites for the masturbatory news cycle.

That was, of course, until it did.

Until officers were tripping over one another for what some expected to be a fast track to better pay—if not in pennies, then in power. Until red-faced co-workers filled the precinct, not-so-prodigal sons stung and singing, *Nah, I didn't get rejected, the whole thing is just a crock is all.*

Until this Jehovah's Witness of Justice had decided to pop a squat and ask him if he'd heard the good news about *Eustace Fargo.*

Of all the things he'd needed—an umbrella, another sandwich with more meat and a spritz of mustard, a bullet to the head—furthest from the top would have been anything to do with the Judges.

"All due respect, ma'am, you can get the hell on with that," Ezekiel told her. He began to gather his things, which seemed fewer and fewer by the moment.

"*All due respect*, you're going to check that attitude before we get anywhere near the Academy. I swear, if I came all the way to Cincinnati for some washout cadet with a hot head, someone's catching hell... I saw you in there. You did good, Jones." The woman's tone had softened but become more dangerous, reflecting a kind of kindling only those who handled fire could know.

I didn't see you, Ezekiel nearly responded, but he decided to tread lightly as possible.

"So, were you serious? Or just throwing a hissy fit?" she asked.

"What are you talking about?"

"Quitting. After all this, all you've gone through to get here, you're ready to call it a day?" she said, and this time it was Ezekiel's turn to chuckle.

"Williams... she saved my life more than once, she was supposed to be my partner, someone I could trust more than anyone to do the right thing, and she... Yeah, I'm serious. I worked hard to become an officer, like my father. More than that, though, I thought I was joining something that mattered. I'm not giving up, I'm just trying to find out where I need to be. Corny as it is, I want to figure out how to fix this, how to do the most good for the most people."

"You sound like Fargo," the woman said, bluntly. "You know, what happened at the White House?"

Ezekiel hadn't told anyone, save for Williams between burgers in other places they never went together, about his love or admiration for Fargo. While it'd be a bit much to say that he had posters, he did read every interview he'd had, few as they were.

Despite never having met him, Ezekiel felt that he could judge Fargo's integrity, his honour. Even after the Judges programme was announced officially, and the critics rose in droves, it never seemed all that bad an idea. If Ezekiel had to point to a reason, it was the same thing that got him the badge in the first place: that there was right and wrong and no room for deviations between. Just justice, that thing so free from the uncanny fucking valley that separated it from mere law.

"It's not like Fargo has some hard-on to be patriotic. He... There's something *different* about this. It isn't from the heart, or at least not as much as people think, Jones. The same thing could have happened at that coffee shop across the street and I'd still be here talking to you. The thing is, he is and always has been a judge. He sees everything, everyone, for what it is, *absolutely*, and makes the call he needs to make. He did the same thing with law enforcement, and I think if you stop, and consider what that means, you wouldn't have much of a reason not to check the programme out, at least."

Damn, she was good.

Looking at it through that lens, he had trouble offering up any kind of defence, but, from the look on the woman's face, she'd gathered that already.

"...Why me...?" Jones eventually asked, and the woman glowed with the unabashed joy of a fisher getting a bite.

"Well, you're clean, Jones. You're also damn good, you proved that in Chicago. Ezekiel Jones, the rookie who stopped a tank with balls and a single bullet. You saved lives that day, and more importantly, you showed appropriate judgement in dire circumstances. But I'm not here to stroke your ego. You're not *special*, Jones; but you're someone I think can see that what we're doing right now? It won't hold. The tumour within the body of law enforcement will only grow and grow if we continue to ignore it. So this is your moment, former Officer

Jones. Are you going to nut up, and *do* something about it? Or are you going to sit on the sidelines while the rest of us do the hard work?" She stood up and brushed the dust off her coat.

Ezekiel stared at his hands for a while as if they had an answer. He felt the rain from that night, pattering over them. He felt them clasping his partners' hands, on his first day in Cincinnati, in an unspoken promise that together, they could carry out justice. He looked up, finally, to see forward.

"Well, I think if you're going to be my superior, I should at least know your name, ma'am," he said, with a lightness his words hadn't known for months. The woman rolled her eyes, extending a hand to Ezekiel to help him to his feet.

"I'm not shit to you yet, Jones, but it's Marisa Pellegrino. You should get home and get packed. Our flight leaves tonight at nine. I slid your plane ticket under your front door when I missed you at your apartment earlier, so try not to get it muddied." She grinned, and Ezekiel laughed.

WAS HE INSANE, boarding a flight that night, with one bag to check and a million more unseen, to chase after a notion that could well be gone in a matter of months?

Probably.

But as Ezekiel watched the world beneath him grow smaller and darker by the moment, he hoped that there would be light to be found when he'd land.

AALIYAH

Friday, July 16th 2038
17:41

THE GUN RUBBED wrong in my hand. It promised to take everything and give everything, and it was all a fucking lie.

I didn't want to see him. I didn't want to remind myself of the *us* that was in that glance, behind those sunglasses. Those eyes, big brown shitstorms of all the mistakes Aaliyah Monroe could have avoided if she were the type to follow logic. I could fill this fucking moleskin with everything I *didn't* want, though, so I'll spare you, whoever you are.

"'Liyah, it's just us here. *Just. Us.* Isn't nothin' you can do ta convince me you gon' kill the fatha of yo' chil' while he half-nayki in bed. You aren—*ain't* no killer," he finished, lamely.

"Thurgood, what the hell are you thinking? What the hell am *I* doing here? What the hell is our *son* doing here?" I felt my fingers trembling against the trigger—*calm down*—I moved my index to the outside of the trigger guard as not to blow his head off his shoulders.

"You know you ain' gotta call me that," he said with a laugh to the woman now aiming one of his own triple-barreled contraptions at the thinnest target in the room.

299

"You just aimed at my dick, didn't you?"

"I just aimed at your dick, yes."

He scooted about the bed, his sunglasses making his grin all the more grotesque, somehow. "Kettle, you ain't eva hel' a piece this long in yo' life, jus' give i' 'ere," he said, reaching out. He stopped at an awkward angle when I stepped forward. Blind as he was, he always knew how to *find* me. The weight of the gun was cold and dead, and everything else I'd taught myself how to be at this point in my life—but, eh, here we are.

"Where's our *fucking* son, Colin." I didn't so much ask as order, taking a few steps forward with the pistol growing more embedded in my hand than I think you ever were to the things you threw away.

So, Aaliyah, how the hell did you get yourself wrapped up into Colin's dumb shit?

Maybe you always were.

Maybe, it'd eat up a decent amount of time to scribble in this little moleskin you found under the bed, tell the story of you to whoever ultimately finds your bullet-holed bones; of who you are.

Tell them why you fucking matter.

For the sake of your interest, it'd make the most sense to start with Colin.

So, naturally, as everything else in my life is fucking bonkers currently, I'll start with momma instead.

THEY JUST WOULDN'T stop shooting at us.

We wouldn't stop shooting at us. We'd made our voices known in one way or another. We'd told them to strip away the guns, strip away everything, to make Biology II and Trig the only things that killed us on the daily. It's as if they didn't know *how* to stop.

No, that's dumb.

They knew, because we fucking *told* them. We told them

with our goddamned words. They made a few adjustments, bump stocks were stripped away, and it helped. It grew in its reach, stood up to a crawl at one point, stumbling over and knocking shit off the wall, but ultimately, we got complacent. Enough of the world thought eventually that we'd just get over it. We weren't surprised, though, were we? We were the first generation to know what it felt like to be hunted and under a camera the whole time.

PS4 was pretty dope, though.

So, we did what any game could and bit back at the dogs. When we did, we were something to fear.

There was the insanity of a few short years separating us from having any real power to do anything about it. A boot over your neck, your body tied to the floor and the passersby sighing at your inability to just stand up. It's a hell of a place to be.

TL;DR? Our generation fell somewhere *during* Kill the Poor, *between* Holiday in Cambodia and Anarchy for Sale, all parts dead or dying.

"Ma, you don't have to worry. I'm safe, I'll always be safe, I promise."

I'd stood at the foot of my bed when I'd said it. Busted for trying to join the rest of my boxcar brethren in 'sneaking' me out, George's fucking car constantly set to ear-hemorrhaging death rattle. I'd dressed neck to toe in black with a stocking cap in my hand meant to slide over my clump of afro, with its too-easy-to-identify hot pink line running from the front to the centre and ending in a blue starburst.

Fifteen years old in 2018 was a tough time to call yourself safe.

A hell of a year.

A hell of a year filled with too many bad hairstyle choices, too many spins of my Bad Religion Spotify playlist, too many things we wish we could hold on to if we weren't tricked into seeing them as absurd.

It was the year Daddy died, not so much on a cross but

during a bout of throwing his life away yet again. Much as I'd like to save you from the cliché of me—and we can at least circumvent the deets—it *is* important to mention he wasn't around all that much. Mom said he gave me more weapons than I'd like to use; she wasn't a very reliable source, though.

Mom, like her mother, and her mother, and hers, and hers, and hers and hers all the way back to Eve, had been carrying that old tale. This misguided, miseducated, miseverythinged notion that by saving me from his darkness, only giving me those light-shimmered lies of who he'd been, in brief, staccato moments of teddy bears and belated birthday wishes, that I could have him, and he could have me back in a way he never earned.

I don't know why I'm setting it up as something that spurred the woman I never was. You'll have likely assumed that all sadness can do to a woman is break her. We are only visible by our scars, flesh proud and preaching on the atrocities of the heroes in all stories.

My father was never any of those things. After his absence I may have hurt, but only in the childish way anyone does after a supposedly broken heart before you learn that, at most, it leaves thin cracks to pick at.

I appreciated the name he gave me. Momma told the story often enough, like a sticky salve to numb certain welts, even after my body had built immunity to it.

"He can't dance, he thought he coul' and it was fuckin' adorable, he slipped up behin' me an' ma girls while *Rock the Boat* was playin'. Usually I'da not given him a second look but maybe it was my exhaustion at all the busted dudes who tried and failed. Or, I have a weakness for big cuddly teddy bear niggas that try to look hard wit' their Timbs laced up to the top."

The name was supposed to be a gift, but it was just *their* story, lacquered over my bones. Just narcissism.

It's probably the only beautiful thing he's ever given me, though.

There was a likeness we shared, and probably always will in being both too big, and having too-black-to-love-but-bold-enough-to-leave skin tone.

"I luh' you, *so* much, 'Liyah, I jus' want you to be *safe*, I can' *keep* you safe if you keep chasin' down dis shit," Momma said to me, as if it were something a teenager could comprehend.

"I love you too." It came out more like code, like everything we weren't supposed to say without sacrificing something else, like blood in my throat, thicker than warmth could allow. I promised her that night, after she begged and pleaded and did everything short of holding me back, that I wouldn't risk the part of him she hadn't lost.

Of course, twenty minutes after she was done dealing with the sight of me—and an additional fifteen minutes after I texted George to turn his damn engine off—I still went. I was a bit of a bastard in that way (and don't read too much into 'bastard'; we all have the ones we lose to themselves, mine just happened to be my daddy).

If I'm being real, going that night to protest half-peacefully was mostly to do with making a tangible display of the fucks we no longer had to give, but if I'm also being real? My first girlfriend, Becks, maybe had something to do with it.

Six months of dating meant we were still filled with all the fire of a new couple, but made the mistake of thinking that we'd got to know each other. We stayed up late, talking about how we'd change the world. Stories we unlocked every time we played our game. We knew each other's middle names. We knew the best parts of each other and only a fraction of the worst. We knew filters, and how they trick you with forever. We knew how much we loved to learn something new about ourselves, together.

We weren't exactly the prophetic anarchists our playlists had promised we could be, but we did aim to make noise. The thing is they talked, and talked, and talked so much about the importance of the future, of our votes and our vast numbers and our anything-but-lives to live. So, we decided the best way to be heard was by whispering an absolution to the one thing they supposedly cared about.

Us.

Just us.

Our target was the Gospel Gut Mac's Mess-'Em-Up Gun Shop out on Wabash. The plan was simple enough: we would break in, take what our nigh-voting-age arms could carry, and lay it out in front of the shop. Afterwards, Frank, who shook the whole drive, and shivered the whole time we'd moved the stores stock out front, would call the news station, and 911, in that order.

The cameras did what they were supposed to, and captured us. The nearest news station was closer than the nearest police station, but even knowing that, we made sure to give them a thirty-minute buffer. We used the ignorance they thought we had and slapped on our buffawed, befuddled, be-*ohshitdon'tcallourparents*-ed faces before lining up behind the weapons. Those of us untouched by melanin held in each of their hands a rifle. They were empty, of course; we needed them to see how easy it was to seize their means, to take back the production of things that killed. I, and the only other POC with us, Felicity, held our hands flat and filled with bullets.

Neither the reporters, nor the cameramen, nor anyone that wasn't us dared cross the weapons sprawled out in front of us, nearly twenty feet long and filling the parking lot. We chanted our chants as they tried to call out their questions.

Stop killing us!

Why are you doing this?

Stop killing us!

Are you affiliated with any of the local street organisations?

Books not bullets!

What are you hoping to accomplish here?

That last question almost caught me. *This*, sat on my tongue ready to pounce, but I swallowed it back. The police arrived in record time for the street we'd been on, and immediately tried to take care of the press when they arrived. It, thankfully, hadn't worked. Local news hadn't been much of an ally before, but it seemed if you give them a meaty enough story to bite, they'll fall in line like any well-trained carnivore.

I just wanted to be heard in all the ways no one has time for, and other drugs they couldn't load us up with. It wasn't exactly a take-to-the-streets-with-your-pitchforks-and-pain rebellion, but there was a message beneath all the romance.

That message was nearly lost, though, when one by one we lost the twenty of us who'd gathered through the night. The revolution, it seemed, only took a few appeals to parental authority to dismantle. It was when the standoff had reached three hours that the first domino fell. Patrick Bradley's dad had seen us, who told Lisa Fogworth's uncle, who—well, dominos.

One by one we were turned back to the children they wanted us to be. As each of us tapered off, in some fucked-up equilibrium, another local media outlet would find their way to us. By the third hour, when it was just Becks and I left, hand in hand, the major networks started to spill in.

In the end, though, under the tenderly livid but maternally sound threat of excommunication by her mother, Becks folded too.

Becks, the last one holding a rifle in one hand—holding mine in the other—let both free, before crossing the picket line of guns and ammunition.

The hardest thing about that moment? As they drew my first love, my first punk, my first kiss behind the Saint Nitchell Mance Recreation Centre (while snorting back a viscous ball of amber snot I'd coughed up at the worst imaginable time). The *hardest* thing was to remember all the YouTube videos I'd watched on making myself cry on demand a week before.

You know what, how about *you* try it? Try to force yourself, right *now*, to cry. *First*, however, you'll have to imagine a few things, dear reader.

You must imagine that second-year senior George Ravinski called each of our parents at the appropriate time, selected in relation to their driving speed and distance from the gun shop to ensure the best staggering effect.

You have to imagine that a month prior, Greg, Thomas, Jacqulyn, who were down for the cause enough to bleach and blacken their hair like the good ol' untroublesome White youth Mac would speak in length with, made entry and exit a breeze.

You also need to embrace a reality in which Tammy Jean made her way into the CEO of Stronghold LLC's home, or more importantly his rolodex and media contacts. This was thanks to her mother playing golf with the wife of his second cousin's polo instructor, who'd been tennis companions with insert-other-white-privilege-nepotism-shit-here.

You need to imagine that I hadn't fought Becks tooth and nail to be the last of us standing in the end. You need to imagine a world where I didn't tell any of them I was ready to die.

"Put the bullets down!"

You need to imagine a world where, okay, I'm not telling you I *wanted* to die, but I saw the gain if shit hit the fan on *my* body over one of theirs. I hadn't told them about my father, how he was gunned down by a police officer while running, unarmed, after buying a pack of cigs for some seventeen-year-old. I didn't mention how I couldn't bring myself to see him at the funeral, when I'd seen him so little elsewhere in my life. I didn't say how his story didn't have enough bite, or enough merit to be much of anything on its own.

Shit ain't easy, right?

I let the bullets spill from my hand, all except one, which I held up between thumb and forefinger.

"Fuck you! You want us dead so bad, don't you? You want us dead so fucking bad, how about I just do it for you!?"

As I raised the bullet to my lips, I glanced to Becks, who as expected grew her eyes twice as large as I'd ever seen them. It was off book, far from the derivative shit Ronald 'Well, *I* am in AP English, Aaliyah' Vickston came up with. I closed my eyes then, just in case, so I at least had something beautiful in her, saved to crop on the wallpaper of my eyelids if they'd never open again after.

I could have told them, or even just Becks, at any of our twenty meetings, about the research I'd done, about discovering just how likely I'd be to pass a bullet and what it could do to me. I could have told them that I wasn't so much being brave, just confident in the medical professionals who'd discussed the topic online thanks to the unabashed ignorance of the few who had done so for far less meaningful reasons.

"*Aaliyah, don't!*"

I could have told them that every tear was spilled not from panic but from a lease on my poppa's bones. That the last thing he gave me was something to pick at inside, an emptiness in me, a maddening frustration at the world we'd never stay alive long enough to inherit.

"*Crazy ass bitch.*"

I could have told them all the steps it took to become their Bullet Bitch.

It had to ring true, though. The problem with a movement is that you have to do something truly fucking *dumb* to get people to move in the first place. The truth was there, in the margins, in the things that led me there, but everything else was just a show. They wouldn't see our calls, they wouldn't see our blog posts. They wouldn't see the empty caps, the still-packaged gowns. They would only see what we shoved down their throats, even as they complained about our immature tactics the entire while.

Granted, in the end even that didn't do much. It got me in front of a few TV screens, and a full ride scholarship, and a less-than-regal moniker. Eventually, everything about that night faded away into upvotes. It did remind a few people, though, that we wanted our lives back, and maybe that much made it worthwhile.

CHAPTER TWO

"*So, this is the worst mistake of my fucking life, how about you?*" Judge Jones screamed at the deputy beside him, not that either of them could make anything out over the roar of gunfire.

While Ezekiel's training at the Academy had taught him much, he'd learned this trick—to feign a connection with what amounted to a glorified citizen with a gun—much earlier in life. The two were crouching—cowering—behind a row of shattered lockers, and Jones was trying to calm the kid who'd insisted on getting involved in the Judge's business. It might have worked, if not for the glint of death in the officer's eyes. It was a look that reminded Ezekiel that nothing at the Academy could possibly undo the one truth of the world: stupid will always find a way.

McCandless High was among the last remaining 2A Schools, which armed educators with semi-automatic weapons to protect their students. Ezekiel had found himself in the midst of a D- decision over a C+ student.

The call that'd brought Judge Ezekiel Jones and Deputy Einstein together was one of the many, *many* wounds left by a former president. Unfortunately, the details of that time are murky at best, and those who are keen on mental disability and development history know why, although the illness known as "Collective National Ubiquitous Trauma" wouldn't be described and named until decades later. The disease is marked by a selective amnesia, sudden bouts of existential dread whilst looking up, and uptake in dopamine production when snapping tiki torches in two.

Far on the other side of the hallway, the student who'd kicked off the whole ordeal after flashing his side-strapped pistol at his English teacher was a mouthy GenSlag Gang member. Roy 'Fuck Y'all' McElroy had decided to educate his teacher, Mr. Reynolds, with the back end of his pistol after a subpar grade for his paper on Samuel J. Battle.

Bullets thundered, and tore. They shattered. They forestalled any chance of communication.

"I... I think we should charge, sir—or, um, Judge, sir? I—I—I can take out the one on the left if you—" Deputy Aristotle was stopped when the side of a ricocheting bullet clipped a chunk of his ear off. Judge Jones snatched at the Deputy's neck, yanking him down below the line of fire.

"You mean my left, the fifteen-year-old with a pea shooter? Or your left, the English teacher who has, at best, three shots left, and hasn't stopped shooting to realise we're not with the gang member who probably isn't even here any more?" Judge Jones asked Deputy Sagan, who trembled, and shook, and held onto his bleeding ear.

"Well?" Judge Jones asked even more loudly, but still, Deputy Newton didn't have an answer. He let the young man stew in his embarrassment; embarrassed was a whole hell of a lot of heartbeats better than the alternative. It also hadn't hurt to give the English teacher a chance to run out of bullets.

When he had, Judge Jones unclipped his helmet and hurled

it at the student, who'd apparently figured out how the safety worked on the gun he'd claimed.

The student shot his embarrassingly small load of bullets and stopped short of anyone's lost life—and, to Ezekiel's satisfaction, not a scratch on his helmet.

Judge Jones hopped up in the bullet-broken air from behind the lockers and bolted as fast as he could for the student. He slammed into the GenSlag runt, shoulder first, full of force and a dash of nostalgia from his offensive line days back in college. The chump slumped, wincing the whole way down. When Ezekiel turned to the teacher, a thirty-something with a tweed blazer, the man twitched and clicked at the trigger in nothing like logic.

Deputy DeGrasse Tyson sprung up from the hiding place, mimicking a guy who knew what the hell he'd been doing, his pistol clutched in hand and his sanity slipping free. He aimed it at the teacher, who naturally had another firearm tucked underneath his tweed jacket. He yanked it out, ready to fire. Ready to make mistakes of them all.

Ezekiel was tired of mistakes.

Maybe he shouldn't be so hard on the old guard, or the young genius. It was one of their tools which Fargo took control of that brought him to the 2A school in the first place, after all.

"*Shots fired.*" It was the automated voice system chirping to life in Judge Jones's helmet that had brought him to the school. Back sometime before 2020, the Chicago PD had instituted a system that responded to the noise of bullet fire. The system, Shot Spotter, utilised an amalgam of audio and visual surveillance set up in key areas throughout the city to respond faster to gun violence than eyewitness reports.

When the Judges came to the public, one of Fargo's first initiatives was to place his new avatars as the primary gatekeepers of all such technologies. Like everything the plebs couldn't process, there was a resistance to the new oversight. There was that hope again—hope that swelled their superstition of Chief Boogeyman Fargo—that he was amassing too much access, too much technology that was meant for the masses, and not for a trumped-up army of vigilantes. The truth of the matter, though, was that they were all playing a part: that Fargo had stuck to the same ideals that had—bit by bit, bullet by bullet—garnered him the popularity he'd needed to become Chief Judge under President Gurney. Judge Jones learned that well enough at the Academy, where he was free to learn all he'd ever wanted about Fargo.

One of the Academy instructors made it a point to open his class with a review of three principles that Fargo once discussed that would change the future forever.

For control, technology.

Nuclear, biological, biblical or otherwise, the means and progress of production must be maintained by those detached and trained enough to understand it isn't superiority that guides them, but wakefulness.

For peace, blood.

You cannot hope to have their cooperation if you don't offer something equivalent in turn. Judges must be prepared before anything else to give their lives, to bleed themselves of the idea they are worth more than the machine.

For progress, power.

They will never save themselves, but they don't know how to, do they? They only know that there is an end, and everything they breathe or hear or fuck or fight must be in the service of preventing just that. They have too much power. They are smashing sandcastles and pulling cat tails; they don't deserve power, not yet. You must take it, if only for a while: they will understand one day, if you can keep the order intact enough for that day to eventually come.

Another saying came to mind, though it'd been an old acquaintance of his father that'd given him it: *God made men, but Samuel Colt made men equal.* That wasn't exactly true. Ezekiel proved that with the nigh-invisible draw of his left-hand weapon: being a southpaw himself, he made sure to keep the one with non-lethal rounds in that holster. He fired first at the deputy's hand. It was a small target, but compared to the crud his weapons trainer back at the Academy had him shoot at, it may as well have been a parked car. While the plastic round tumbled towards the deputy and cracked into his hand, Ezekiel rolled across the ground and came up a handful of feet away from the teacher, close enough to lift him from the ground with a well-aimed roundhouse kick to the chin.

This is going to be a hell of a report to write, Ezekiel thought, and it broke his tight lip, his tight everything, the laugh bubbling from a part of him he'd written off as terminal long ago.

There was a knowledge in that moment, that he'd carried with him all this time. It all amounted to busy work. It was reassuring, sure, to read articles month after month, year after year, documenting the decline in violent crime since the Judges programme rolled out. It wasn't enough, though. Would it ever be enough? It didn't feel like anything was changing, or not by any vast degree. This had been the fifth school he had to intervene at that year, which wouldn't have been so terrible if they hadn't all been in the same quarter. He persisted, though, or at least something like it. He remembered that every gym teacher with a revolver he took down, every eighth-grader with a semi-automatic, every art 'guide' trying to make a scarlet Picasso with pedantic paints, was one less he'd have to worry about killing a citizen.

The gang member—Judge Jones wasn't even sure he was a student—started to rustle about the ground, wincing like anyone would who had been hit with a perfectly aimed inch-thick helmet. Ezekiel went over to him, knowing there wasn't a bullet left in the gun by the perp's side, and picked up his helmet. After latching it back on, he cuffed the kid; young as he was, he'd decided to play an adult game, and as such Judge Jones may have tightened the cuffs so the only thing that could pass through, barely, was the blood in the boy's veins.

"You think this was a good idea, punk?" Ezekiel said.

The strangest part of Ezekiel's training in the Judges programme was their public relations techniques, which pretty much entirely contradicted the training he'd received as a police officer.

When he'd been an officer, he'd have chalked up maybe five weeks of mandatory sensitivity training for talking to a suspect like this, but as a Judge? It was *invited*. It was important to separate them as something *less*, not by colour or creed or anything else that didn't put that gun in his hand. As schoolyard as it seemed, name-calling boiled their blood, kept them off balance. Any amount of reckless rage was easier to deal with than steely resolve.

"I think that you don't know what you put yourself into, you fuckin' Rambo-ass fascist," the kid said, spitting at what he'd probably meant to be Ezekiel's eye. *Reason 35, Article B, to always have your helmet,* Ezekiel thought, and grinned as the spit ran down to the edge of his visor.

"I think you're going to tell me where the others are. I've only taken three of you down so far, report said there were eight," he grunted.

"That what your report says? That what they tell you? Eight? Nigga, we a fucking *army*. We a fucking maelstrom of the end. We are a brotherhood, *The* Brotherhood, you couldn't hope to stop, not any more. Once we rise—"

Ezekiel stopped the ramble with a swift backhand to the face. It did what it was meant to: the student sucked in his lip and started sobbing like the child he was. Jones grabbed at the boy's forearm and dragged him to his feet, before grabbing the back of his shirt and pushing him ahead. This was generally the part where the excuses would swell, or the attempt to tug at the old heartstrings as if Ezekiel hadn't worked his ass off to burn those away. What Ezekiel got this time, however, was chuckling.

"Laugh it up, punk. Gives me more to work with to keep your ass behind bars."

"You ain't gonna ask why? You ain't thinking, why the hell would anyone try to shoot up a 2A school?" the kid said, still laughing his bruised, beaten ass off.

It had crossed his mind, but Ezekiel just attributed it to the same old shit he'd dealt with in any suit, blue or black. Reckless hormones and a weapon to fire them through. Fear. It was what he'd hoped for, this whole experiment, which was becoming less of an experiment every day and every crime prevented. The emotion was what drove them, on either side of the lane, to be utter dumbasses.

"No. I'm not," Ezekiel said, which only made the boy laugh more. Ezekiel tried to ignore it as they walked through the halls—cautiously, not sure how many other teachers were in wait, hiding behind their classroom doors ready to pop out of them before blowing a Breakfast Club's head off.

The 2A schools were never a firm idea, more like a rattled, taco-bowled brainfart that affixed onto recorded law like a malformed tumour. Like an angry scab, they were one of many things left around by the hazy yesteryears. It was the simple fix, like many, to show tolerance of the intolerable. Years ago, when Ezekiel was still as old as the cackling perp he wandered the halls with, he was privileged enough to see the seeds of 2A schools. There was, as always, protest, resistance, hashtags and heartfelt monologues. It was a hell of a surge for weapons sales, of course, teachers arriving at ranges in droves to complete eight hours of weapons training for the right to tuck a firearm in a desk formerly reserved for cell phone confiscation and flasks.

While Gurney had worked to break down the practice, it didn't change that the schools who had come to rely on the aid weren't apt to give it up.

"Hope you know you're not gonna get far, you think I'm in this shit alone? You think a teacher can wave a gun in my nigga's face and get away with that shit? You think—man, you think I'm the only one tired of this shit, tired of *your* shit?"

"You learn any other words in this school, or is *shit* about the end of my tax dollars?" Ezekiel said, twisting the perp's arm as they walked, closing in on the door. He would have laughed, if the perp hadn't first, when he opened the doors to the outside world at the end of the hall. He would have laughed, if not for the three kids standing in the doorway, clad in black jeans and grey robes. He would have laughed, if the firepower each of them held in their hands squashed every thought that didn't serve to keep him alive.

The punk laughed, though. And laughed. And laughed as the hooded three raised their weapons. *Move*, Ezekiel thought, staring desperately around at his surroundings.

Lockers, four without locks, the closest ten feet to the right.

Loose papers on the ground, one text book

One woman, two men... boys? Boys.

Only one of them is holding their weapon right—priority target.

Ammo low. Unfamiliar firearms.

Left boy, trembling, fear.

They swarmed, like Ezekiel's thoughts had when on the other side of the reaper, at once and with a cyclical kind of chaos. He kicked the cuffed kid forward with the flat of his boot, sending him soaring off the ground, slapping face first on the terrazzo flooring. A small part of him was curious to see how the new bullet-proofing would work out, but he tabled that inquisition to cover his ass. As one of the hooded men took aim, Judge Jones had already darted to one of the unlocked lockers, opening it to allow the door to shield him.

Then?

God bless the educational system's inability to progress past back-breaking text books. Ezekiel snatched a small brick of a book and chucked it at the closest armed, hooded suspect. It stuck them in the face, making them fall back for a moment.

"Gia!" one of them screamed, because Gia couldn't.

Judge Jones tumbled out of cover, snatching at the text book on the ground. He popped up again and chucked the other text book at one of the hooded punks. It cracked against their skull, making them keel over and lose grip of their gun; Ezekiel never felt as indebted to Algebra II in his life. As the weapon skidded across the ground, Ezekiel made a note where it stopped then leaped forward, coming down, like the hammer he was, foot-first on the prone thug's knee. It popped. The punk screamed. There was still work to do.

"You're dead, yo—" *And you should have just taken the shot*, Ezekiel thought as he thrust a flat palm into the next thug's throat, snatching their gun hand and ramming his head and helmet into the hooded punk's face. Teeth shattered, and a saliva string tinged with maroon trailed from the thug's mouth and across Ezekiel's helmet. He wobbled for a moment, but Ezekiel helped him on his way with the steel toe of his boot.

The last one, the scared one, who couldn't have held a gun more than a handful of times, took aim at Ezekiel. Death filled the hollow of him as he considered his waning options. For a Judge, this wasn't such an uncomfortable position to be in. For peace, blood.

He felt the sharpness of the air, a promised heat like the red phosphorous on a matchbox waiting for the strike. Judge Jones waited with as the threat grew stale, his hands raised. From the hooded one, the click, and then? Nothing.

Your lucky fuck, Judge Jones thought, staring at the empty gun in the punk's hand. He slowly let his hands fall to his side, and unclicked one of the pouches on his belt, drawing his reserve pistol.

"Put it down, now. Not gonna ask twice. I'm well within my rights to blow your ass to hell. Don't make me," Judge Jones said, taking aim, but the punk didn't seem too scared of it. They pulled back their hood, the sides of their head trimmed and nearly shaved with a spindle of pink at the top twisting down. Whoever she was, she was young; no older than twenty from what Ezekiel could tell.

"Gia? Ray? Get your asses up, only got one shot at this. Get the kid on my signal and haul ass." She didn't flinch, but her finger wasn't even over the trigger. It rested over something on the weapon's side, a red button he'd never seen on a firearm.

"You're not going—"

"*Burn,*" the young woman said, low. She clicked the button

and a line of flame tore out of the weapon. Judge Jones did the only thing he could, and leapt to the side. He dodged the worst of it, but as the heat licked across the whole of his left leg he screamed out, the searing pain breaking the supposedly unmalleable grit for which Judges were known.

The pain. It tumbled across all avenues of his mind while he twisted on the ground, the steel of the locker at his back cool through his uniform in all the wrong places. Get up, he commanded, but his body—like the hooded punks helping up the kid who called them—didn't give two shits. He tried to fight the darkness, the blinking black that rode on a pain he'd never tasted. For as long as he could, he fought, but as they kicked the door open to the light outside, his vision slipped, his everything fell, and the darkness came.

AALIYAH

"GOTTA SAY, GETTING shot down by *the* Bullet Bitch may make all of this worth it."

Colin cackled, more than he laughed. He hovered there for a moment before sliding back into a chill he hadn't earned. I rubbed a finger at my temple as if it'd ease the headache he'd been in my life.

"You're trying to piss me off. You're trying to make me irrational. You're trying to—"

"See the woman I fell in love with," he said, and I don't think it was a lie.

"UGH, DOESN'T THAT just like, irk you, Aaliyah? I mean, I think open-mindedness is important, but you have to be *livid*."

"Yeah?"

"They probably love each other, but Black men, they can just be so blind to your beauty, your hashtag-Black-girl-magic, you know?"

Nah, Rebecca, I don't. Please teach me, though, O great interpreter of Melanin Maladies.

"I don't think that's necessarily true, not all the time at least."

"You're so brave, Aaliyah. I want you to know that."

Reb had chosen a contemporary African-American course, over the Women's Studies option that she would constantly remind me was completely filled before she'd switched courses.

She said it just felt like the right thing to do.

The fragility of a White woman walking her first steps against her own privilege is a precarious thing. There was something that—I don't know—I wanted to protect in their innocence. Their tight eyes seeing a sun for the first time, talking like a two-year-old about the ways it can burn. *Yeah, honey, it's hot, that's what it does,* I want to say, but they wouldn't hear anything in my exhaustion than a judgement, a thing that I had which they could never accept if they couldn't own it, a knowing that would send them back to the dark.

I heard a laugh from behind my table, but I wasn't ready then, and not quite ready yet to discuss him. Rebecca couldn't stop staring, her stank eye. I tapped her shoulder and thankfully she let the two be.

"I'll let you in on a little secret…" I didn't quite whisper it, but kept my voice hushed. "Most of us? We don't really give a shit. It's true! I can get you the meeting minutes from the last black-girl-magic conference call." I pause for laughter. She takes her cue.

"Now, that's not true," she said. "No offense. I mean, it's not anything you need to *justify*, it's your right to be angry. You're *allowed* to be angry about it, don't feel ashamed."

"Thank you?"

"You're doing that thing, the one where you think I don't know you're making fun of me."

I broke for a moment, laughing until I realised she wasn't. I sighed.

"I mean, dude is a dude. Who knows what problematic shit that woman has to deal with? Maybe there isn't any. Maybe there are half a million ways this isn't a problem I can afford the time to dissect before the other things in queue. Like making as much money as him, like literally not knowing if saying *hello* will somehow alchemise a dick in my phone, like learning the specific decibel range to stay in, in order to not be thought of as angry, or emotional, or nasty. But also not hood, and also not militant, not a sellout, not a hoe, not a prude, and like any other women of colour, but also a singular individual, but also not 'alt–Black' as if that does anything but separate me from my own community, like having to get the good white folk like you, you exceptional butterfly, to keep asking questions. Yeah, that about sums up the first twenty minutes of my day."

"Shit... but you *do* have a nice smile though, you should use it more," Rebecca teased with Cheshire eyes and a play-play smile.

"I'll take that note, thanks." I laughed and rolled my eyes. She nodded, once, in approval she thought was hers to give.

I took another look at the interracial couple and wondered about the caveat that pushed into the forefront of the irksome shit in Aaliyah's day when they looked at me looking at them.

When they defined, ironic-as-fuckily, a glance as something more.

They hurried and half stepped with their eyes in a kind of dazed waddle from me to her, from her to me. His eyes were filled with hope.

I'd like to say it was only some exceptional level of chill that filled me, but that'd be a bold-ass lie. I'd have to say that beneath that chill, there wasn't anger at the absurd idea that I'd somehow lost something, but that he looks at me as if he is something so exquisite to be lost.

I should probably move along, though, because there are too many sightseeing expeditions I can take you on of shitty things brothas do and I can't afford not to get you to the end on time by stopping to take pictures of Jittery Jamal.

So, on to the next?

The reason we've come here on our Black-girl-magic mystery tour is him. The thing is, when I met Colin, he hadn't been some card-carrying pseudo-rebel with an H&M Dashiki or woke-weary brow furrowed by the burden of blackness. Maybe it's why I slipped up.

If I die here, if I never escape, and you find this before anyone else, Colin? Know that I'm not saying here that you are at all special, you weren't and never *will* be a prophet, that Melanin Moses these vanilla-skied sycophants pumped your head up to be.

You were just tired. The same way I was, filled with all the things that would make you sink, but left you standing at the edge of the sea not quite ready to dip your toes.

"Could be his sister, or an old friend, or hell, even *classmates*. Trying to take care of Professor Ez's group project early," said Thurgood, on the table behind us—Colin—dusty-ass nigga with the world not on his shoulders but on the tip of his ring finger. Anywhere else, it might have been a bit more creeper-level omega to come so bold onto our conversation, but at *Skrrrt's* it was hard to avoid eavesdropping.

The spot was too small and too shallow for the volume of bodies that filled it to have much of any breathing room. You'd think, with all the business they got, there would be plans for expansion, but the money kept coming in, so why fix what's not broken?

Rebecca hadn't known what to think, it seemed; she stared blankly to the black man who had opened the conversation so blatantly with the name drop of a professor at the university, as though to dissuade any thoughts of him being something *lesser*.

"You know, that is just the brilliant concept that my friend and I—the ones who are actually having this conversation?—well, it's something we just couldn't have got to," I said.

"Thanks." He grinned in response, somehow picking up on my extremely subtle sarcasm.

"You know, I see your point. I mean, if I was sitting on the outside of a group, making decisions and judging who they are? Well, I *might* have seen that someone doing the same to me was completely unwarranted. I appreciate you keeping a man honest," he said, bowing in our direction.

I smiled, and fuck if he didn't have a point.

"I'm Pot," he said. "It's nice to meet you." He straightened in his seat, resting as suavely as he could in a hotdog print, short-sleeved button-up.

"Kettle. It's nice to meet you too."

CHAPTER THREE

"SO, ARE YOU going to quit then?" Cadet Ocasio, Ezekiel's bunkmate asked, straining to keep his eyes open after a long, *long* day. Ezekiel hadn't meant for the conversation to lead to something so absolute, as he sat on the hard slab of a bed in the housing quarters of the academy. Ezekiel had, one day before, made it two months longer than most of the washouts, but he nonetheless found himself only a few wrong words from the same end.

"I'm just starting to wonder, where the hell is all of this going?"

"You're still pissed about the exercise earlier, aren't you? That's just what they do, E, this is just Boot Camp 101: get in your head, break you down, build you up." Ocasio groaned, leaning back to what they dared call pillows.

"It's not just the exercise, though it didn't help. Judge Stein wasn't teaching us anything today, he was trying to take something *away*. What the hell are we here to become then, hm? I wanted to be *part* of something, something that would—I don't know. I do know I ain't here for some voyeurism shit."

325

The exercise weighed on him more than he was willing to admit, even to Ocasio. It wasn't often they left the academy grounds, part of the philosophy being of course to control the narrative Fargo's new avatars would be filled by.

No TV, recorded calls, a library filled only with approved texts devoid of any objective poisoning from any side: up, down, left or right. Even the food, which was the hardest thing for Ezekiel to swallow about it all, was specially designed for each cadet's needs to gain muscle mass and lose the useless fat from a life they would never have again.

Earlier that day, Judge Stein took a class of twelve first-year cadets out. The world felt too bright in some places, too dark in others. Littered, cracked blacktops scarred by separation from the only thing that would hold it together. Judge Stein rode beside the bus on his Lawranger, dressed in the uniform they all sought to wear themselves one day.

Eventually, Stein sped up and crossed into the lane in front of the cadets, raising a fist to let the bus driver know to stop. The bus pulled over and crawled to a halt, and the cadets fell into a tense silence.

"Fall in, cadets," Judge Stein ordered as they disembarked, and they all circled their superior, hands clasped behind their backs, standing exactly two feet apart from one another.

"What state is Academy 3 in, cadets?" Judge Stein called out, and the cadets bounced confused glances between one another. It seemed too simple as they *were* Academy 3, one of five camps established to teach the programme.

"A… Alaska?" One of them called out finally.

"Correct. Now, why *is* that? Why would we have one of only *five* academies situated here, of all places?" Judge Stein asked, and then more murmurs, more nothing. For a while, at least, until one of them spoke up.

"W… Wyatt Earp… sir?" Cadet Simpson stuttered, and then another silence while Judge Stein gave a strange, huffing laugh and strode to the erudite cadet, and stopped a few inches from Simpson's face.

"Wyatt. *Fucking.* Earp?" he asked, the laugh fading into something sharper. *Just shut the hell up*, Ezekiel thought, watching a grown man nearly simper in front of the Judge.

"W... Wyatt Earp, he served as a lawman for 10 days in Alaska once, he was one of the most dangerous men to carry a gun, a fearless—"

"Revenge nut who hunted down the murderers who killed his brothers and lit 'em up. That what you here for, Simpson? To be an individual? You get a hard-on about being in the history books? *Wyatt Earp*... I could beat your lily ass for that shi—"

"Alaska, *sir*, like the other stateside bases for cadet training, holds one of the highest rates of violent crime in America," Ezekiel chimed in, and immediately regretted when he realised he'd interrupted an increasingly annoyed superior. Judge Stein smiled but didn't turn his eyes away from the cadet Simpson.

"Correct,   Cadet-Who-Gives-A-Shit-About-Becoming-A-Judge. Why do you think that is?"

Trick question, Ezekiel thought, before what he'd wanted to say reached the top of his tongue. Before the consideration of the Native American population and its invisibility to the powers that be had, maybe, possibly, resulted in lackluster consideration for the overall epidemic of crime throughout. Shit, Ezekiel had been here before, *the old white dude who only wants to hear you repeat his sage wisdom back to him*, but at the Academy there were so many creeds they slung around he couldn't keep track of them all.

Does he want,
Perception not affection!
or
We Are the Answer Not The Question!
Wait... wait maybe
We Are the Order!

"Judge Stein, it is not a cadet's place to find the reason for the lawlessness, but to bring the hammer down on the lawless," Ezekiel said squarely.

"Correct. You see that, cadets? That is the difference between a future *Judge*, and a future washout," Judge Stein said, his eyes never leaving Cadet Simpson.

"Judge Fox! I think it's time for our guest to join us, don't you?" he finally belted out, turning his attention away from Cadet Simpson and towards the darker edges of the park. The rest of them, including Ezekiel, turned to see a Judge dragging out a cuffed man, bloody-nosed but otherwise fit enough, from the darkness. Judge Fox said nothing as he passed the cadets, shoving the reluctant, ragged civilian forward. Ezekiel couldn't help but dig, to try and unearth whatever it was they were looking at. A drunk, that much was apparent by the reek of hooch as Judge Fox passed them, shoving the tied man forward, who spat obscenities the whole way.

They stopped when they reached the centre of the cadet circle. Judge Stein shook hands with Judge Fox, before Judge Fox wrangled some keys from a pouch at his side, readying to free the nameless man. Ezekiel squirmed. Was this a simulation? It had to be, Ezekiel resolved, and it helped quiet the shaking throughout, if only for a moment.

Judge Stein reached down to his boot, rolling up his trouser leg to snatch a short-bladed knife from an ankle strap. There was a flinch, a shudder straining from the criminal. What the shit is this? A smaller, terminal part of Ezekiel bubbled the thought. He let it scratch, let it bite and do all the things immaturity could before letting it settle down into the black of him.

"What's the last news you remember, cadets? About Fargo's progress with our little social experiment here? Hm?" Judge Stein asked. It wasn't the easiest thing to remember, at least not where Ezekiel was concerned. When they'd arrived, it wasn't without condition: it was stated, drilled, lectured, and delivered by any means necessary that the outside world was a pollution, a *sickness*. What would turn them into the face of a new society, a *better* society, was to trust emphatically in the one thing that couldn't be marred by the affliction of sight.

WHEN THE LIGHT LAY STILL

There were times Ezekiel thought about his mother. He thought about the way she couldn't think about him, couldn't think about his father—or maybe she could. Maybe if he would have stayed, never breaking from the light of her in the assisted care home, at her side while the darkness came, if she would know his name. It was childish, and as such belonged with the other things he packed away to barter with Fargo's vision.

It was too much for some cadets, that separation from friends, from family, from the annual school gun fairs or Sunday mornings and the milky rot breath of everything laying with them in bed. Then there was of course entertainment, news, and the mangled line between them. Generally, those cadets washed out in week two or so, but it didn't make it any less hard on those that remained.

"Sir! The ongoing debate against our cause, the *plebeian's* struggle to retain due process! The ignorance of citizens, well-intentioned but obsolete, to fight the future!" This time it was Ezekiel's bunkmate, Ocasio, who had spoken up. Ezekiel wanted to chuckle, but kept it inside. There was, perhaps, more than one occasion the two men would laugh about the anachronistic way their instructors would speak about the law. It at least made it easier to throw the words back at them upon request.

"That's correct. So, as none of you cadets, you *glorified plebs*, have any idea what is happening in the world, I'd be remiss to waste such an… interesting opportunity. This squirming little shit you see in front of you? Judge Fox apprehended him two hours ago. This… scum, murdered a woman while mugging her—"

"*Itwasanaccidentitwasanaccidentitwasan*—I just… oh, god…" The criminal, the scum, rambled, he shook, he sobbed, and perfectly played the part of something more human than he deserved to be. Judge Stein grinned to Judge Fox, who only shrugged his shoulders in response.

"We are the order in this world, boys and girls," Judge Stein started, before kneeling behind the criminal, using the knife to cut off the ties behind his back, and returning to his feet. "I, Judge Stein, hereby sentence you to death for the crime of murder."

"You... you can't just—what are you—?"

"I grant temporary authorisation to you cadets to carry out my order," Judge Stein continued, pulling his weapon and aiming it at the criminal's head, letting the cool of the steel barrel rest against his skull to deliver what would save everyone from the cursed, criminal drain on society.

"Which one of you is going to step up and execute my order?" Judge Stein called out to the group. No one moved. It wasn't uncommon for a cadet to have a mental break, but for an Instructor Judge, to use the technical term, to *lose his goddamned mind*, was something new. Insane as it seemed, though, Judge Fox didn't seem surprised in the least. This was real, Ezekiel realised; they want us to kill this man.

"Sir! I—I will complete your order!" Cadet Simpson said, walking up to the Judges in the centre of the circle, and the criminal shuddered at the sound of his approach. Judge Stein smiled, handing the weapon over to the cadet, who pushed it against the back of the weeping murderer's head.

"What you maggots don't know—well, that could fill the Justice Library—but what's important to know is while you've been twiddling your dicks, the world keeps moving, and by executive order from President Gurney, we now have full autonomy to bypass the court system, and carry out judgement, trial, execution as we see fit. Trouble is, I guess... you have no real way to confirm this, do you... *Simpson*, right? You could be carrying out the request of a madman, you could be killing a very profitable tool in prison labour. *Or...* you could be disobeying the request of a Judge, and the new world order, the *law*. Got to say, kid, I don't really envy your position." Stein lathered the words with a kind of sweetness.

Cadet Simpson looked back to Judge Stein, then to Judge Fox, who only waited with crossed arms and straight eyes. The criminal felt it, then—the pause, pregnant and palpable—

before taking his chance to turn around and latch two hands over the mile-long barrel.

"You don't have to do this," he said, through salt and snot, but Simpson said nothing, not with his mouth anyway. Ezekiel and most of the other cadets could read the rest of him clearly enough. He was panicked; the sweat, the wordless part between his lips screamed.

"So, you're not going to do it? Shit, kid, this one is easy, you didn't even have to make the judgement. You get to do the easy part here; that is, of course, if I'm telling you the truth," Judge Stein said, and for all the moments of hard-ass hell he would inflict, Ezekiel felt a fire for the first time in this one. *He's enjoying this,* Ezekiel thought. Cadet life wasn't filled with doves and chocolate fountains, sure, but the tether that kept Ezekiel—all of them, for that matter—from slinking into the old ways of life was that every breath could only be in the service of building something more.

Ezekiel broke from the circle, walking towards the centre, paying little mind to the other cadets, or to the Judges who eyed him cautiously. By the time Cadet Simpson turned to him, Ezekiel's hand was already over his forearm.

"What are you doing?" Simpson whispered. Ezekiel stared down to the criminal. He swung the steel toed tip of his weighted boot into the man's chest, making him flail backwards against the tall grass. It took little effort for Ezekiel to pull the weapon from Simpson's hand, and it seemed even less so for him to place the flat of his foot over the criminal's chest, to lean in with the weapon, and to pull the trigger.

Click.

Silence. Then, from the Judges, applause.

"Good work, Cadet Jones," Stein said, patting the back of Ezekiel's shoulder.

"Sir! The only truth in this world is the law! The law cannot lie, the law is above fallacy, the law is—"

"—the Judges," Judge Fox finished from behind. Ezekiel turned, giving a stuttered nod to his superior, before returning the weapon to him. Judge Stein helped the struggling perp to his feet and dragged him away.

While they rode back to the camp, swept away once more from the outside world to the only home that mattered, Ezekiel stared out the window to catch as much of it as he could. There was a beauty to it, but only by accident. As much as Judge Stein seemed more of a fraternity hazer than anything, Ezekiel couldn't say, while they rode back, that he hadn't learned more than one truth that night. He knew that Stein was a symptom of an old world, a superior that would one day need to be purged from the body of justice. He knew that Simpson wouldn't be in the mess hall in the morning to follow. He knew that he was growing; that fear, day by day, would call out less and less, and in that existed a future without something so pedantic as beauty, but calm.

AALIYAH

"YOU KNOW I'LL never give up on you, Kettle," he said, as if it meant a thing in that moment.

"You know our son never stopped not-knowing-who-you-are, Pot. You know neither of us *deserve* this? You know that—"

He slammed a hand against the wall to stop me. It worked, but not out of fear, *Colin*. I'd been dealing with little boys for about eleven and a half years, so I knew when they were struggling to use goddamn words.

"You know, more than *anyone*, what was taken from me. You know that I'd have never got here if not for expulsion, for losing my funding, for being lumped in with criminals for— I'm right. You don't see it now but I'm—I'm just trying to get back what's *mine*, Kettle. Is that so insane?"

"IT'S... I JUST don't see why you enjoy these, is all."

Colin walked beside me, an arm over my shoulder, the other holding his cane. He, moreso than I, was still reeling from the cinematic 'masterpiece.' His coat smelled of college-grade weed, nights in the winter curled up at home had let the skunky scent sink into his tweed blazer, but I was pretty high at the moment, so the fuck did I care?

He'd taken me to see a movie.

In May.

I'd not taken him as a superhero fan, but thinking back on it as you carry everything wrong with this world inside of you, Colin, I really should have. Since about 2021 it was impossible to find a movie from May through mid-September that didn't stem from the same universe. It's not that I didn't enjoy myself, but by the end of it I felt more like I'd chugged a two-litre of Mountain Dew, thirsty for another in the sad realisation that my quench was never the goal in the first place.

"Would you rather see some indy director wank off for two hours in an 'original film' that is a lengthy testimonial to all the directors they stalked through their life?" he said, and I could nearly see the many times that particular splooge of troll juice had been posted online.

"It's not that, it's just the action is so… empty. Hell, half of it is visual effects, I don't know how the hell you like these things at all." I stopped to throw away a half-eaten popcorn tub into the bin and slipped for a moment from Colin's reach.

"Empty? You're *so* wrong! They are consistent, always, with powers and fighting ability and—well, even down to the damn jokes! I don't need to *see* to enjoy phenomenal storytelling." I rolled my eyes just as unaware, just as unprepared for the eyes that hung over us as you were.

"I suppose I can concede that. I concede that you are no superhero and I should be conscious of your shortcomings as a human being and more importantly, a film critic."

"You're such an empath."

"It's… it's a struggle, fam."

I've been through the moments that followed far too many times, Colin. The men who were watching us, or watching me. The same shit I'd been through over and repeatedly when anyone recognised the girl who held a bullet up to the world and swallowed it whole. The thing is, I know their tactics, I knew their threats against my body or my life, and I knew when they were worth batting an eye at.

You knew something too. You knew that when they came with their thin threats, like tiny $13.99 tiki torches they thought could burn our world down, the only thing that mattered was their threat against what you thought was yours.

You may have gathered I don't want to spend much time here, on the blood of your knuckles and cane. The hunger you had to defend your item, the affront that is Black and mouthy, and the transfiguration into the blue-and-red-and-lackluster narcissism of a nigga to stay it. I'm done reliving it, and that's okay. There was a slap on my backside, there was Colin, using those push-ups of his in the worst possible way. There were the officers just doing their job. There was just woefully and wilfully driven to the fatal preoccupation to not be wrong. When they broke you away from me, when they let the wrong man go to tell you your rights after a fist flung too much to the left clipped a government paid chin, maybe you could have apologised. Maybe you could have bit back something I attributed more to rebellion at the moment than rage. It wasn't your fault, Colin. What comes next, after your name was added as a potential gang associate? Well, that shit's on you.

"YOU KNOW I *deserve* this, and I'm taking what I *deserve*. You can't hate the player—"

I take a step forward with the gun. "You think something about this—This isn't funny. People, Colin, fucking *people* are going to—*have* died for this. For *you*. You think they would do the same if they knew the truth about you? If they knew how you use them when it is most *convenient* for you?"

He won't wipe that fucking smile off of his face.

"You know," he said, unfazed as he hopped up from the bed, and walked to the blinds, tugging them up by the string to let light into the room.

"I am just doing what you wanted me to do, Kettle. I'm just—how did you put it, in that BuzzFeed clickbait you did?

Not the one where you bravely took on the task of trying multiple hot sauces: *Hot Sauce In Her Bag,* if I remember the thumbnail correctly. The other one." He turned back to me. *Yeah, I was clout-chasing, fucking sue me,* I wanted to say, but instead let the steel fill the space between us.

"*Right,* right, I remember now, *The cost of being in a country that constantly taxes your body, is only as much as you're willing to pay.* You know, I've never been a fan of leftist propaganda behind a chill-hop tune, but I have to say, *that* part, that resonated, Kettle," he said, and as sarcastic a prick as he was I can't say I didn't believe him.

"I am done paying, Kettle, I'm done being taxed for *their* mistakes. I am ready to take back what's mine."

"So this is, once again, about *you*. It's about what Colin needs, and Colin's little ego, and Colin's little sob story. You got off *easy*, Colin. You are *alive*. You could have fought back, got your scholarship and grants back. I told you we should appeal the school, we should use my platform to—I tried. I'm not going to feel sorry for you when you didn't lift a fucking finger to save *yourself*." The words stunk from the expired carton I'd stored them in.

Colin shook his head and laughed.

"Yeah, and then what? Do you think I'd have found a job, even if all your fighting paid off, even if, somehow, your way had worked? What do you think would have happened if I tried the *fair* way under the circumstances?"

I'd seen enough, lived enough to know the answer, but I gave him one anyway, if only to cut.

"You would have had *us*, Pot."

CHAPTER FOUR

THE TRUTH OF pain is at the end of every fire.

There is the cost for an unbearable kind of light. Pain that pilfers all thought and leaves something resembling your favourite pop song on the fifth listen, and a string of profanity you hadn't realised you'd ever learned. There is the ash. The great unifier, black and grey and bled of hope.

There is the inescapable. There is the moment when we're all judged the same.

There is, also, a senior dude named Braden who can't seem to understand that the obsolete analogue television set in your shared hospital room can't connect to his BlueFang auditory implant but yeah, sure, Braden, go ahead and turn the volume up to twenty-holy-hell-man-can't-you-turn-off-those-old-ass-syndicated-episodes-of-*Bum-Brawls*-and-get-some-sleep-it's-three-in-the-morning-oh-okay-let's-just-turn-it-up-more-instead.

In an older time, it would take months to heal from a third-degree burn that enveloped 18% of the body: at least that's what the thinly-skinned doctor with more crust than clairvoyance in his eyes had told Ezekiel while he stared more at a chart than at his patient.

It was a game they both knew they were playing as soon

as Ezekiel said the word *Judge*. It would have been so much easier if they just accepted the truth of their reality, but maybe it wasn't their fault, maybe it was just the natural ebb that hadn't yet flowed from the hands that once clutched the steering wheel. He'd seen it his first time in the hospital with a Judge's badge, though Ezekiel had been too green to realise it. What had it been? A bullet to the cheek? No, a knife wound? Yeah, probably. Whatever it was that'd put him in an oh-so-dignified hospital gown also meant the cherry faces of every medical professional assigned to him telling him he was wrong at every turn about how long it was going to take him to leave. He was able to fire off a round at the temple of a man while still in cadet clothes, but telling a doctor that, as a Judge, he had access to medical care beyond that of a civilian irked him in every wrong way.

Maybe the world was fucking insane after all.

This time, though, he'd been around and around more times than they could know. He'd learned how to pull rank, how to demand primary care, and how to expedite a recovery plan for a flame-broiled leg down to three weeks.

The skin grafts rubbed in a gritted drag. He had thrown on the triple-weave Kevlar tunic, but the pants tickled across the freshly false skin like half a million icicles that never learned how to melt. He made his report, and the pain migrated from ice to fire as he rode to the local precinct in Chicago. While healing, he'd received a summons, and as the Judges hadn't yet got their own bases in the same quantity, Fargo had mandated that the already-outdated law enforcement make room for them whenever required.

It wasn't the first place he wanted to be, but the rules are the rules are the ridiculous things that kept him from hunting down that unique tech. The question of *what the hell was that gun* had rustled around his head for the entire stay in the hospital. It was so slim, and chimed in a bizarre way when the word *burn* was whispered to it.

He arrived at the precinct, knowing the eyes to expect. The officers, formerly fraternal, now seemed so far away.

Judges weren't new to Chicago, but no matter where Judge Jones parked his Lawranger, they gawked, and sneered, and did anything that they didn't realise Ezekiel had endured for years as a queer black beat cop in a world constantly promising to progress past, well, *the fucking past*. He bit back at the idea of taking his helmet off. It was childish, or worse, civilian; it was the part of him that died in a street, that lost his cable bill in a poker game, that took a few twisted flats filled with scentless bud to the Snoop-Dogg concert and added to the haze. Parts of him that believed too hard and too long that people are only that; sum of zero and welcome to the seeds of indiscretion.

He decided to keep the helmet on while approaching the front desk. They *needed* to see, instead of eyes, the dark tint of his visor that reflected the hope etched into their faces and left in the lines a gravelled fork in the road separating them from what they could never be.

"Judge Ezekiel Jones. Your superior is expecting me. I'm thirty-seven seconds early, I can wait if you'd prefer." The officer at the desk didn't perk his eyes from the magazine laid in front of him until he'd heard the word *Judge*. When he did, he surveyed Judge Jones from head to holy-fuck-that's-a-big-gun before stuttering out directions to the chief's office. Judge Jones nodded and made his way to meet the man on high as yet another pair of eyes latched onto him.

He counted while he walked, slowing his pace to meet the door one second prior to their scheduled meeting, and twisted it open, letting himself in.

"Shit." From behind his desk, Chief Chalmers had been stolen from his conversation with a woman sitting across from his desk, half his ass hanging from his cracked leather chair.

"I take it they ain't teach none of you how to knock on a goddamned door in *Fuhergo's* little summer camp?" the chief said, his brow furrowed. No, they hadn't, Ezekiel *would* have told him if he cared to waste his valuable time on the man. He could, of course, have explained that if anything they are taught the opposite: that a Judge's presence should be expected any and everywhere it needed to be. It wasn't worth it, though—and then Jones saw Marisa Pellegrino, sitting with her back to him across from the chief, and nearly put the man out of his mind completely.

"You can leave us, Chief Chalmers," Pellegrino said. "I'd like to speak with Judge Jones privately."

Ezekiel almost broke the stone crusted over his face. It'd been over a year, and of all the places he'd thought to see her next, a Chicago police chief's office was among the last.

Her eyes stayed narrowed until the door clicked close behind the chief, at which she rose and embraced him: not for long, but long enough to say what was needed, before she walked back to her chair, nodding for Judge Jones to sit in the empty one beside her.

"You've had a busy week, haven't you, Jones? What was it, Saturday that you rescued the Mayor's son from an attempted kidnapping? Good PR right there. Then not even two days later you executed three founding members of the Crimson Dragons in a raid—that hurt the bastards. Lastly, we have the sixth shooting this year at one of the last remaining 2A schools, but I guess we can't call that one a total victory, now can we?" Marisa glanced down at his leg with a smirk.

Ezekiel remembered when Marisa's knowledge of his ins and outs was still a shock. There was something innocent in not knowing just how far and deep and rooted Fargo's—and by extension Marisa's—access to information went.

"Yes, ma'am, I failed. They escaped custody and are undoubtedly terrorising more innocent citizens. Are you here to reprimand me?" Judge Jones asked, and felt silly after Marisa's chuckle.

"You're so—*no*, Tank, I'm not here to *reprimand* you. As quick as you usually are, I'm surprised your assumption is that I of all people would be sent to slap you on the wrist. No, I'm here for something else." She pulled a handful of folders from beneath her chair and watched Ezekiel sit. "How's the leg, Judge?"

"Well, what's left of it is fine, and what isn't is getting better by the moment," Judge Jones said, and Marisa nodded lightly.

"You think you're ready to get back to work, Judge Jones?" she asked, and Ezekiel found himself thankful for the helmet and its power to obscure eye rolls.

"Yes, ma'am. You running field assessments now? Seems a bit beneath you."

"You say it as if you know what the hell is above or beneath me, *Tank*," she said with a smile. Then, "Judge Jones, we have a new mission for you, and it involves what happened at the 2A school."

Ezekiel cocked his head. "The 2A school? It was routine, wasn't it? Hell, there's a reason we call 'em shop class, ma'am. Too many accidents, not enough steady hands."

"No, I'm talking about the pint-sized flame thrower," she said, and Jones was suddenly back to the pain. It never left him, really.

That type of power in the hands of some do-nothing street gang held the potential to tip the balance. Of course, it was just a street gang: place enough pressure on them and they always fold. "They seemed a bit more organised than some, but also... detached. They'd been trained together, a little; there was familiarity between them. What are we dealing with, ma'am?"

Marisa leaned back, looking tired. "They call themselves The Brotherhood. Why can't we go back to the world of single syllable shitheads? Thing is, they've been growing, and not through competition. From everything I've gathered, members range from your run-of-the-mill sob story to long-time known lowlifes, and even otherwise squeaky-clean citizens with a few too many visits to the Huffington Post website. We also know, those weapons? All in-house. Make 'em themselves. The information we've collected points to a figurehead, which is the only good thing about all this. If they have a head..."

"Then we have a bullet," Judge Jones said. It was one of the sayings back from his Academy days.

"Exactly. Thing is, week to week we're seeing more and more of these designs in the hands of thugs; they are growing, and more and more, we are fucking dying. By the numbers it's not much of a loss, but you know how thin we really are."

Ezekiel nodded. "So, we do what we always do: hit 'em in the pockets, they get sloppy, we get back the order."

Marisa shrugged. "That's just it. Their motive isn't something so simple as that. The tangibility, or lack thereof, is their greatest weapon." She paused for a moment, before picking up the coat from her chair and the four manila folders. She slapped them on the chief's desk, save for one, and nodded for Ezekiel to look through them.

"What am I looking at?" Ezekiel asked, and fought a wince as he moved towards them, his pants prickling at the bandage.

"Everything. We haven't been this blind before, if I'm being honest. They operate so sporadically. In New York they helped take down a hate group, skinheads—will those fuckers just *die* already? They aided a local gang—trumping up their numbers and arming them to the tits. In LA, a month ago, an annual benefit put on by the industry titans, the Kach brothers, was decimated. Again, a local gang, augmented like no one has seen before, robbed the guests and gave a glorified TED talk about the victims' 'declining morals.' Then—"

"I think I get it," Ezekiel chimed in weakly. Anyone else may have registered it as rude, but Marisa saw how fast Ezekiel picked through the folders, faster than she'd been able to tell him, and nodded.

"So, what can we do, then? Radical group, fighting the Man. Sounds a bit tedious, for the Judges anyway. Why not tap into the FBI? Dust off COINTELPRO, is that still a thing? They're more meant for the espionage stuff. Subterfuge isn't practical when you're running around looking like a comic book character."

"Listen," said Marisa, "we're tapping into our... law enforcement brethren, for help with this. It's recent, though, they closed ranks on us pretty hard in '33. What we've gathered, or at least can piece together, is there is something more tangible, even if most of them don't realise it. See, their leader—"

"Thurgood? That can't be a real name," Ezekiel said, holding one of the folders open.

"It's what we *have*. A Judge recently apprehended someone with one of The Brotherhood's firearms, but for the first time the perp wasn't one of the zealots choosing incarceration over betraying, as they say, the righteous justice of their leader. The perp talked. He hadn't stolen the weapons, but bought them..."

"So, if he's slipping up so bad, why haven't we caught him yet?"

"I didn't say he slipped up. He isn't an idiot, at least from what we've gathered so far. The sales are slow and sporadic. The only real way to get in on one is either be a member of The Brotherhood, or high up enough on the shit-eater chain to get word of a sale."

While Ezekiel listened, he combed through the folder, gleaning what details he could that Marisa didn't have time to touch on.

"He's not alone." The next folder she handed Ezekiel had a familiar name in the indent: *Aaliyah Monroe*. He didn't know her personally, but it was hard to see any footage, any picture of a protest against police brutality, without her standing with a fist raised.

She would have still been a grad student when he'd seen her in person, back at the indictment hearing when Dushane's family let her in to sit and watch his failure play out with them. He remembered seeing in her something like paradox, something like fire, everything like not having a choice but to try and do *something*. At least in that, Ezekiel couldn't help but respect her.

Ezekiel scanned through the pages of her life. She was a mother, though the boy's father hadn't taken the time to pen his name on the birth certificate. She now worked as a civil rights attorney out of Chicago, and aided, quite openly, a social action community which had over the years had multiple name changes.

"What does Aaliyah Monroe have to do with this? She's a pain in the ass, but she's not a criminal." Judge Jones closed the folder.

"I would have said the same thing, until two nights ago. She was brought in for questioning after they'd found one of The Brotherhood's weapons on her person. She wasn't exactly... cooperative with the authorities." Marisa sighed.

"She's a notable member of Black Lives Are Important But Not MORE Than White Lives Or Anyone's For That Matter," Judge Jones said, pausing to draw a breath. "They aren't exactly known for their great relationship with the justice system."

"Yeah, and her reason for having the weapon wasn't so unbelievable either. But none of that mattered after Thurgood sent a group of his lackeys to bust her out of an interrogation room the other night. Listen, the CPD is focused on her, they've got pins in their dicks about her most recent stunt, but don't get distracted by it, *Thurgood* is who we're after. If we get Monroe too, then hey, woohoo for us, but stay the course."

Everything always came back to Chicago. Aaliyah, and the bubbling tension of class and race threatening to call home the clucks. Of course, that last one may be less a city-wide epidemic and more sewn into the fabric of the very flag.

"Just curious..." Ezekiel started to ask and thought to stop. Thought that his answer was given in Marisa's sad, sad smile.
"Yeah?"

"Am I the first of the twelve you came to?" He asked it slowly, trying to pick any glass from it before it reached her.

Ezekiel was one of twelve Judges of a separate but equal nature. While the Judges programme was possibly the *only* enforcement bureau that had been fully inclusive from day one, there was inevitably an imbalance of white male officers, who were a clear majority over, well, everyone else. It should have been expected, at least Ezekiel thought as much. Women, minorities, LGBTQIA, anyone with a qualifier affixed to their name wouldn't exactly rush in droves to the building burning brightly, that promised so many times over to light them all away.

There were also the qualifications. The psychological evaluations meant to weed out the biased, those with either an overabundance of empathy, or a signal lack thereof. There was the hope that hope could be bled out.

"You're the *first*. I won't bullshit you, Tank, one day it won't matter who brings in assholes like this. Today? It does. We'll laugh about this shit, but right now we don't have the talking stick. *They* do. We play by their rules, for now. So, yeah, one of the reasons we need you is the press looks a hell of a lot better than if we went with Judge John Manifest Destiny Smith to take down Diet Black Revolutionary, but also you're a Judge, and that's what the public really needs to see."

Truth, for any Judge, felt more a fiction than something to waste the man hours searching for. It was so dependent on the other; on some shitty, shifting negation of survival.

"You practise that?" Ezekiel finally answered, grinning at his old not-quite-friend.

"Go eat a dick, *Tank*." Pellegrino looked at the last folder, the one gripped tightly in her hand as if to lose it meant napalm and worse. She sighed and handed it over to him.

"You won't be alone. Judge Poet will be working beside you. He has some background with The Brotherhood, though if I'm being honest not much more than you."

Ezekiel leafed through the dossier. Judge Poet, one of the first class. Though, as the same was true of Judge Fox and Judge Stein, Ezekiel didn't count that for much.

What did count, though, was his list of accreditations, of apprehensions, of other small-print, all amounting to a record that made Ezekiel wonder how he'd never heard of the man. It wasn't his place—or any Judge's—to know, though. Hell, the woman who'd handed him the document was the very embodiment of secrets. It was a Judge's place to understand,

and obey. Looking through the file, Judge Jones understood that even Fargo, for all his proclamations about the truths we hide from one another, knew there was something to be said for the dark.

"He was selected... no way, he was *handpicked* by Fargo? I mean, I figured he'd approved most of us in the end, but this write-up was done by the Chief Judge himself?" Judge Jones looked back to Marisa, seeing the crooked brow, the crooked everything, and knew he'd sounded more pained than he'd meant.

"If I'm not mistaken, Judge Jones, you're jealous?" she said, enjoying it more than a fistful of Ump Chocolates. She picked up her coat while Ezekiel continued to thumb through, staring at him until he returned to the world of the living again.

"No, not jealous," he finally managed. "Just a bit... lacking, I guess."

"You shouldn't. I think you'll complement each other well, he's been working out of this precinct for about two weeks now. Just... be careful, Tank."

"Careful?" Ezekiel asked, following Marisa out of the chief's office. The pink, puffy-cheeked man grew even riper and stormed back into his office.

"Well, files aren't everything, you know? I'm not trying to be coy or anything; it's just I don't really know how to prepare you, except to say that Judge Poet is... an interesting Judge." She was picking her words carefully.

"Thanks, but I think I'll be fine... I've had my share of problematic co-workers in the past." He saw something pass behind her eyes, but she let it drift off before saying it. She held a hand out, and he took it to shake, leaving in the same way they had the last time he'd seen her, a year and a half ago when he was still at the Academy.

"Oh... *fuck me*," Marisa said, hand still latched to Ezekiel's, though her eyes were locked onto something behind him. She looked like a scared child. Then, she didn't. She gripped tightly, and smiled even tighter, looking back to Ezekiel.

"Sooo... I may have forgot to mention—or, okay, that's bullshit. I might have waited until the last minute to also let you know that your old, um, bunkmate Ocasio happens to work here and is currently approaching us now but anyway make sure to call me if you need anything, okay? Okay, buh-bye!" She snatched her hand back and darted as fast as she could from the building.

There was a moment when Ezekiel saw his former bunkmate, and something scraped across the lining of his stomach.

It was common that some cadets had slipped up, caught a case of the cold that drove them to a touch from someone near. Ezekiel had assumed he was above it, silly schoolboy shit that only detracted from the mission, robbing time better suited for studies.

Ocasio hadn't planned on it either. When he'd met Ezekiel, he hadn't initiated some master plan set to seduce his grumpy bunkmate that didn't know how to keep his side of the room clean. Maybe it was the way Ocasio talked about what he was trying to gain from the Judges programme, to finally have the means to bring change in his community. Maybe it was the way, after Ezekiel shared it with him, that Ocasio hadn't offered condolences for the body in the street, the nothing that came after it, and instead discussed how he saw in Fargo's vision a solution to the infinite fuckery of the system.

Maybe it was something like light and something like dark and something like the moments they could find each other in between.

Maybe it was a weakness that Ezekiel thought he'd bled out with the rest after that body bled out in the street. Ezekiel had never been any good with men—women either, for that matter—but with Ocasio, if he'd have taken a moment to track him down after the accident, it may have, just that once, ended with beginnings. It was all the more reason to stay away; the world had a way of giving and giving until the punchline sank in.

"You look well, Officer Ocasio," Ezekiel finally said. Ocasio rolled his eyes and took Judge Jones's hand.

"You working out of this precinct? Bit of a coincidence, or maybe..."

"It is. A coincidence, I mean, that I'm here, it's just a—"

"A coincidence, got it," Officer Ocasio said with a chuckle. Ezekiel did the same, noting that he still could. Ocasio pulled Ezekiel in for a hug that lasted a moment past comfortable and platonic, but when they stopped, they became shields all over again.

"So I'm guessing you're here about The Brotherhood? Honestly, I'm glad to have a Judge with some sense in your damn head." Ocasio nearly whispered it.

Judge Poet, Judge Jones thought.

"I'll be working with Judge Poet to subdue the leader of The Brotherhood. Will he be back soon? I tried to radio him, but he hasn't responded."

Ocasio grinned slyly. "Yeah, he wouldn't. A report came in about an hour ago, bank robbery downtown on State Street. Six armed, seventeen hostages."

"How many men were you able to send with him?"

"Yeah... that's not a thing, not for that dude. He said some weird shit like 'A Judge doesn't do for the people with the people,' or something."

Judge Jones nodded, starting out the door. He couldn't find a fault with Judge Poet's assessment, and as a Judge himself he couldn't ignore the call of duty.

...In no way whatsoever could it possibly have had anything to do with escaping awkward encounters with the man he never texted back.

Judge Jones distracted himself with the information he'd requested on the robbery in progress screeching over his helmet's radio. Judge Poet's file indicated he'd interacted with the public rarely since arriving in Chicago, though had full autonomy to do so under the Judges programme. Ezekiel found it reassuring. He found the company of heroes more tiresome than anything the Academy could throw at him. The press had tried to paint *him* as a hero on more than one occasion; they just couldn't see what the Judges had strived to create. Heroes fail. Heroes would have tried to go above and beyond the mission, *their* mission. The Brotherhood.

They didn't understand.

When he arrived and climbed off his Lawranger, he'd half expected a police cruiser or two defying Judge Poet's command. But there was silence: there were half-hung doors and there was the sight of the robed white dude crawling out from the bank and down the cement landing. The man had been cursing the heavens, the sky, the earth, anything that would perhaps alleviate the new reality that was having two legs that pointed to the same side. The shiver of pain that rattled up through his body, from his unsocketed knee and shattered ankle, persuaded Judge Jones to investigate further.

Another Judge stood by the ramp as though waiting. His hair was dirty, blond and blood-splattered, but most importantly, Judge Jones could *see* it. He wasn't a huge fan of the bulky helmets himself, but rules were rules. Too many punks and thugs had filled their heads with first-person-shooter games and the promise they held of headshots. The helmet, silly as it fit, mattered. It was the line between the law and the last thing most of them would ever see.

"Judge Poet?" Ezekiel called out, but it stopped nothing.

The other man in the diorama was a wall of muscle, and a face of hate. He kept pacing back and forth, back and forth, except now, with another Judge on his ass, the corner tightened, and his fists clenched at his sides. Ezekiel drew his left-holstered weapon up, training it over the pacing criminal, and finally Judge Poet took as much as a breath to acknowledge his new partner's existence.

"*Judge*, respectfully, I must insist you lower your weapon, and stop interrupting."

"Respectfully, he's going to kick your ass," Judge Jones said, his hand loose over his weapon to easily follow the pacing cultist, who'd not turned his gaze from Poet even after Jones had walked in with a pistol.

"Hah, maybe, but maybe that would be *justice?* In the scope of this building, this patch of nothing we find ourselves in— you, he and I—who is to say what is the most good for the most people right now? I've successfully evacuated the building, not a casualty on the side of the innocent. I've enforced my power of lethal execution across our friend—I'm sorry, Frost Dog was it? Right—I've taken out all of *Frost Dog's* accomplices. Now? Just the two of us here. No offense intended there, Judge... Jones? ...but you don't really factor into this experiment. *So!* Where was I? Ah, most good, *most* people..." Judge Poet finally stopped his rambling to pull out a firearm. *Well, at least he's not doing anything—nope, no he really is, he's doing something completely stupid. That was his gun, and now it's across the room. Shit...*

"...Dumb fuck... Goanna kill me a fuckin' Rambo today... you think you getting out of here al—"

"Shhhh, now, Frost Dog, I don't remember giving up the talking stick. As I was saying, Jones, I don't know if it serves the most good to execute this overgrown cock goblet. I don't see any immediate threat he poses, but he did blow one of his own men's heads off about fifteen minutes ago..."

"I was aiming at you, if you wouldn't have got out the fuckin way I—"

"Would have killed me, yes, Frost Dog, remember the talking stick? Do I need to have a literal stick for you to get that concept? So, we have a murderer, an admission of guilt to attempted murder on a Judge, also armed robbery. That was all in the past, though, all stuff of the dust. What can I say about the you of the now, this stalled fucking trolley in front of me? I mean, don't get me wrong here, kiddo, you've done some very, *very* heinous shit, your ass is mine. But who does your *death* serve in the here and now? Care to weigh in?"

"I don't think that now is the time to—"

"Judge Jones, *less* respectfully, still not speaking to you here. Frost Dog? Your answer?"

Frost Dog, or Theodore Groggins, wasn't a man of words.

This isn't to say he didn't have them; he just learned, at an early age, a lack of concern for the ones he knew. He learned that his body was more often than not the thing people cared about, and decided that he'd give them a hell of a body to deal with.

He used his body, his monstrous form, to spear into Poet, taking him down in a single tackle. Ezekiel sucked at his teeth; he may have been a good shot, but no one would take the chance of killing a fellow Judge.

Frost Dog snickered as he struggled with Poet, although he fought, to Ezekiel's eyes, like he was stalling. Presumably he'd worked out that if he just snapped the Judge's neck, Ezekiel would most definitely cap him.

In his caution, he'd perhaps overlooked something more important: Judge Poet, while smaller than Frost Dog, wasn't a pushover. He found a vice grip of Groggins' testicles, twisting them until the man winced, before latching his teeth over the criminal's face, tearing off half his cheek. Ezekiel couldn't ignore the sharp huff of laughter.

There was blood. There was the gasping, broken chain of a breath unhinged, there was Poet's hand snatching at Frost Dog's neck, there was everything but what they lied to themselves that their badge promised to protect.

When Frost Dog had finally faded away into the black, Judge Poet rolled him off, panting as he climbed to his feet. He twisted his body, driving a closed fist with everything that he could muster into Frost Dog's chest, startling him back to the living with a few coughs. Before the behemoth could come too much to life, however, Judge Poet used the same hand to club Frost Dog on the chin and back to a between-place.

He cuffed the man and rolled to his feet before making his way to Judge Jones.

Judge Jones watched, not aware himself that he'd never lowered the weapon, even as the blood-drenched Judge hobbled his way over to him, hand outstretched, smiling ear to ear. Judge Jones felt a fire in his fingers. He wondered in that moment how Pellegrino thought—*could* think—matching him with this Judge Poet, this death machine, could make sense.

"As we've established, I am Judge Poet. Looks like we'll be working together. It's a pleasure to meet you, Judge Jones."

AALIYAH

ALL THE BEAUTIFUL things that I've been a burden for came to me in a storm.

Elijah came to us two weeks early. His tiny bones and tiny hands and tiny worth in this tiny, tiny world bore a kind of magic, that somehow turned into something massive in that same breath.

The Uber driver drove us through the rain in his PT Cruiser with the bald tires that was one of three things filled with reckless abandon on the road that night. God, we were so fucking young. Young in that way that believed there was a kind of terminality to our mistakes, if only we could escape our twenties alive, if only with a few broken teeth, if only with bruised bone. The downpour was thick, *clat-clatting* on the car so heavily that the voice recognition app on the driver's phone kept chirping to life with *I'm sorry, I didn't understand that*.

I didn't understand it either, none of the shit that brought me there with him that night, a week or so after he'd made his choice, and I'd told him to get the hell out of our lives. Colin was like that, maybe it was some macho shit, chasing things that didn't want to be found all the harder. Maybe it was hope, that thing Momma said shows its head in the dark, that four-letter word we must carry but can never say aloud or give form or do anything but swallow into our bellies to flutter and lay in wait. Or maybe it was just that part of him that I always wondered was there until I couldn't do anything but see it in rusted smiles.

We made it to the hospital. We rushed through the storm, me swatting away Colin's hand as he tried to carry us into the hospital, as he tried to force me into a wheelchair, as he tried to take control of the situation he would later abandon, of my Elijah.

He cried, and for a moment I thought he was terrified, angry that we were so selfish to bring him into a world that would take him from us one day.

I cried too. Not so poetically, more from pushing eight pounds of *just us* from my vag.

Colin leaned into my ear and whispered that no matter what, no matter the cost, he would always be there with us.

There isn't much beyond that. You were born, no twists or turns, just the story of the only thing that will ever matter to me in this eroding, cursed earth that I need to force somewhere here.

You were named Elijah, because mom loved her Bible. Because even as a heathen academic, I do too. Because we give you what armour we can. I always wanted you to go your own way, though, because what's the point of a god without faith? What's the point of a church you are dragged to kicking and screaming?

Regardless where you find your belief in this life, Elijah was a pretty badass dude, so you're welcome. He was a prophet, a real one, who opposed a king, who knew what it was like to lose and to give up, who wasn't allowed to. That... may set a pretty high bar for you, so, sorry about that.

He was blessed, and he was made a miracle worker. He went to the dead son of a widow, he brought him back to a life he'd left too soon. He did all those things we wish we could do.

I mostly just want to say here, Eli, that if this ever gets to you, I'm sorry I didn't get to tell you these things myself.

CHAPTER FIVE

"So, HAVE YOU ever seen rot, Judge Jones? True human rot, that is, not the shit you see in the movies—toilet paper and latex, usually."

Judge Poet was… an interesting man.

Judge Jones stared blankly for a moment, content that the darkness of the visor would keep his thoughts to himself. "I—are you *okay*, Judge Poet?" he finally asked, with more concern than he'd expected.

"Are *you*? We're going to be working closely, Judge Jones; who knows how long this will take, how many shots will get fired at our asses? I'd like to know who it is I'll be working with. I mean, I read your file, I'm sure you read mine, but did it tell you about the time I stole Ginny Rumple's chocolate milk in kindergarten? No? Well, point Poet," the Judge said, smug about a contest no one else was competing in.

Judge Jones knew what he'd needed. He knew that Judge Poet dominated any given conversation. He knew that, since they'd met, there hadn't been a moment's hesitation, from one bloody hand to the next. He knew the Judge was nothing like he'd been expecting from his report.

Poet's background file indicated high emotional intelligence; it mentioned a former medical career. It suggested a man who could use a colder set of hands, to do the things his own conscience couldn't bear, but Jones revised that opinion as they carted the severely beaten men away from interrogation rooms 1 and 2.

"Is Officer Wilson back yet?" Judge Poet asked the desk worker, who never seemed quite comfortable when addressed by a Judge.

"Y—Yes, sir, told him you'd need some help with some old tech. He said he'd be in until 8," the officer said, turning away before Judge Poet could acknowledge the reply.

Judge Poet brought Ezekiel to the back room, where Officer Wilson had returned from his forty-five-minute lunch. "My new partner here hasn't seen the footage of Aaliyah Monroe's interrogation yet. We need to take a look," he said.

Officer Wilson nodded and led them to the back room. Dust filled everything, floating in the air to land in the grooves of their helmets.

"Yeah, anything that'll help take them down," Wilson said, digging up an honest-to-god VHS tape. "The Brotherhood needs to go down, anything I can do to help you Judges to do that, I'm happy to." He took a moment longer staring at Judge Jones than Judge Poet. The two of them nodded in unison: it was something Judges tended to do, and more comforting than Ezekiel expected. "'Course, the *real* problem is his little nappy-headed hashtag-starter," Officer Wilson added, snorting a gumball-sized lump of mucus to the back of his throat and swallowing it. Aaliyah Monroe, Ezekiel recognised, remembering Marisa's warning: *don't get distracted*.

"I think she has a name," Judge Poet remarked, and Ezekiel felt a kind of lightness at not having to say it himself.

"Don't get all PC on me now, you know what ah mean."

"Yes, we *do*. You can play the footage now, officer," Judge Jones said in a neutral tone. Under his composure, he was shaking, fingers trembling by way of a chemical heat. Ignorance rattled across his bones in the same tune it had years ago.

Officer Wilson leaned in, and pushed the tape in with a grunt, evidence of a lard-heavy lunch.

"Never seen one of those in person before," Judge Jones said, staring at the black brick.

Wilson shrugged. "It's an old piece of crap, but we haven't got much in the way of funding since, well, you all. The interrogation room we had to use for Monroe was never updated. Maybe you boys can put in a word for us sometime?" He sounded more pleading than Ezekiel thought he intended. After a long moment of dust and silence, the officer shrugged it off. "The Judges have complete control over CLEAR, though, don't they? You greedy bastards are just digging your nails into everything, now," the officer said with a huff of something beneath it that Ezekiel couldn't quite read and didn't quite care to. He knew when he was being baited, though. The CLEAR biometrics database, and other systems like it, were held on to so tightly by those who formerly had them that they'd been too close to see what they had. When Fargo claimed the system as his own, they took it as more personal than the Chief Judge was capable of being; as a slap on the hand to put them in line. The truth of it was, as it is most times, much simpler.

It didn't work.

A computer was only as good as the data it received, as far as Fargo was concerned, and the people entering the data were only human. The trick was to fix the humans.

"Aaliyah Monroe, now that's a hell of a woman there. Hope you give her what's coming to her. She oughtta rot, not trend." Wilson laughed.

Judge Jones had seen and heard all he'd needed to know of Aaliyah Monroe. Her first act of protest, swallowing a bullet while even her fellow social justice whiners called for her to stop. That riled them up for a while.

Her true nature was revealed later, in a college arrest report. After an officer had dared to ask her for an ID, she stood, cheering, as the thug accompanying her cracked two officers' skulls wide open and urinated over their prone bodies. Without their courage and suffering, the thug she'd been with may never have been added to the CLEAR system.

Of course, there was this latest incident, the one that had brought her under interest to the Judges in relation to Thurgood.

Officer Wilson popped in the tape and let it play.

"So, you can let me go, or we keep going on in this until you say, or maybe even do something stupid, and very indictable? The choice is—"

The video cut out for a moment, and Judge Jones fixed his eyes on the time stamp, the minute clock not skipping forward.

"I want you to bring all of them in here, I want to look them in the eye and tell them I'm not afraid of their bullshit."

"Play that bit back," Judge Jones asked the officer, who rolled his eyes but complied. Judge Jones called for it to rewind again, and once more before they finally let it play on.

"You're not going to tell us? What will you say then, hm? If you're not going to ask for a lawyer, if you're just going to throw out slanderous accusations to distract from your own screw-ups, why waste the taxpayers' dollar?" the detective asked, taking a sip of his coffee.

"You can go to hell," Aaliyah said, but the resolve, the heat in her eyes from a moment earlier had faded.

"I guess we'll just see, won't we...?" the detective asked, turning away from Aaliyah. Before he could reach the door, though, Aaliyah opened her mouth and gave the officer exactly what he'd been looking for.

"You can't stop him. Thurgood can't be stopped, he... he is... he is the true voice of the underprivileged and overkilled, he is the only judge that matters in today's world. You think you'll stop us? You think I'd do anything to give away the whereabouts of my... love? I think you need to—oh, come on."

"We need to what, Ms. Monroe?"

"You need to leave me and my love alone, let me go or we'll...

we'll go straight Bonnie-and-Clyde on yo' ass," Aaliyah said, finally raising her head back up to the detective, who nodded slowly.

Her face crinkled. Play it back. Her face crinkled. Play it back. Her face crinkled. Okay, keep going. Her face crinkled, and then the door burst open from the hinges. The detective spilled over to the ground, clutching at his chest when a smoke bomb erupted.

Then, they came. Five hooded individuals swarmed into the interrogation room, slipping a mask over Aaliyah's face before helping her to her feet. One of them kicked the detective and would have likely kept going if Aaliyah hadn't shoved them off and screamed something. Play it back. She screamed, *No time for that.*

She somehow found time before leaving to snatch a seat, stand on it near the camera, and briefly remove her mask.

"You brought this war, pigs are going to die, if we all are going to fry. Dreams and reality are opposites. Action synthesises them," she said, eyes teary from the gas and a cruel smile painted over her face.

"Stop it here."

Officer Wilson obeyed, quickly hitting Stop on the tape, and watching as Judge Jones leaned in to view it.

"Might help if you don't wear a tinted visor indoors," the officer scoffed, and Judge Poet laughed for a moment, before leaning in to Wilson.

"Just for clarification, I'm laughing at *you*," he said, in a near-whisper. "Figured I would spell that bit out for you. We aren't wearing sunglasses, Officer Wilson; you honestly think Fargo would arm us with something that didn't allow us to see better than you lot?"

The officer groaned, scooting up clumsily from his seat and storming out of the room.

"So, what do you see with your elven eyes, Judge Jones?"

"What?"

"Not a Tolkien fan, then, noted. What is your analysis,

Judge Jones?" Judge Poet clarified, scooting into the seat beside Ezekiel.

"Well, I see why Pellegrino didn't want us too concerned about Aaliyah," Judge Jones started, rewinding the tape back before the glitch. "This is such sloppy work. I don't know how she thought I'd buy it, even with that BS about old equipment." He played the tape back.

"Good eye, Marisa wasn't being too gracious with her praise of you I see. It took me a few more watches to catch it myself."

"Really? Well, I guess they didn't do too bad, but someone should teach them how long a second lasts..." Judge Jones smirked. "There's also the quote."

Judge Poet crossed his arms, leaning back in the chair with a raised brow. "Oh?"

"Part of what she said: it was a bit too performed, too detached from the rest. Her voice is trembling, but through it she's trying to remain cold, stone. She's no actress. It just... it doesn't fit like it should."

"Doesn't it, though? You read the file, about her case against the CPD? She posted a video of... Well, you've seen it, haven't you? Imagine you're Aaliyah Monroe, bleeding heart and what were there, six children in that video? You don't think there was something there that could have snapped? That made her stop hiding the fact that she was an associate of Thurgood's? She mentions him by name, calls him her lover."

Judge Jones leaned back with a sigh. He ejected the tape and stuffed it under his belt. It wasn't worth much more than what he'd already seen, but it didn't belong to the police any more. He thought of all the arrests, of all the accolades his new partner had acquired in a bullet-bolstered life, chosen by Fargo himself. Maybe he'd been digging too deep for something he hoped was there, and Aaliyah Monroe, for all her pacifist proclamations, was just as bloody as the rest of them.

"Where are you going?" Poet asked as Ezekiel started walking out the room.

"Review old reports, see if I can dig up anything on The Brotherhood, or any connection to Aaliyah Monroe."

"You mean the gang database? Thing is a fucking maze drawn by a three-year-old, good luck." Judge Poet waved him off.

"So, ARE YOU going to just act like I don't exist, or are you going to have the balls to spend more than thirty words on me?" Officer Ocasio stood at the door of Chief Chalmers's office, where Judge Jones had decided to work. Ezekiel's eyes tightened on the computer screen for a moment, not sure if he could answer how he'd like, but decided it was owed and detached his helmet, setting it beside him on the desk.

"I think this is the first time I've seen your face since you got here," Ocasio said with a laugh, walking to one of the empty seats across the desk and settling in.

"Part of the job, remember?" Ezekiel said, immediately wincing. Like there was any chance he could forget one moment of Academy.

"Right. How else are we supposed to respect you if you're not walking around like a BDSM biker at all times, right?" Ocasio said in mock-earnest, and Ezekiel couldn't quite stop a laugh.

"Officer Ocasio, I don't quite know what you're expecting me to say here..."

"I think that has to be a first for you, Ezekiel: not knowing what to say, what to do. It's freeing, though, no?" He spoke lightly, but not so lightly as was probably intended.

It *was* a first, but saying that would take Ezekiel back to what they'd burned away, he decided.

"It's problematic, Officer Ocasio."

Ocasio sighed low and long. "We're not at the Academy, Ezekiel. There aren't boogeymen monitoring your every move, this isn't some psychological test to measure your— well, fuck, I don't know, your inability to go above the emotional range of a robot?" He laughed, this time all by his lonesome.

Ezekiel scooted the chair back to see Ocasio better, with enough of the desk still in his line of sight to obscure his old bunkmate's left hand.

"So, what? You want to throw insults at me, talk about what we could have had until I get all weepy?" Jones said. He thought he'd score a point, but Ocasio only gazed at Ezekiel with an unsettling chill.

"I'm sorry about your mother, Tank. I never got the chance to tell you that in person, I thought I'd see you again after I caught wind of the funeral…"

"You 'caught wind' of it?"

"Well, I may have kept tabs. Don't get all Sherlock about it or anything, I was just concerned. Why weren't you there?"

Ezekiel wanted to tell him there wasn't any reason to be there. He wanted to tell him that if he saw her there, frozen from rot by the fluids and the makeup and the desperate ways they tried to make her corpse exquisite… that it all felt a bit grotesque.

"I was on a case," he said thickly.

"Ah, right. Okay, well, while we're being chatty, then, why haven't I heard a single word from you since I left the Academy?" The question had clearly been tucked away, folded and frayed, in Ocasio's pocket for some time. Ezekiel's answer had the same crinkles and tears.

I was going to leave. I was going to tell them all to go to hell and find you and I was also going to make a Big. Fucking. Mistake. We BOTH were.

I was going to resent you. You were going to try and convince me, and yourself, that we'd be okay with a consolation prize that would have made for a few good nights and a few good mornings until eventually it wouldn't. Until we realised that the only real thing we had in common was everything we lost.

I was going to choose you, until I was reminded it was never really a choice.

"I didn't get your number," he said weakly.

"Says the Judge with every conceivable access of public and private data to the lowly citizen." Ocasio was void of beats or bullshit.

"Officer Ocasio, as I'm sure you're aware, Judge Poet and I are here for a very specific reason: the leader of The Brotherhood, and his accomplice. If you don't have anything to say regarding the matter—a case, if I'm not mistaken, you have no connection to whatsoever—I'd request you give us the appropriate space to complete our directive," Jones said then, reaching for his helmet, sliding it on.

Ocasio didn't break eye contact; he flashed a genial smile, heaved himself to his feet, leaned over the desk, and reached out to shake Jones goodbye with his left hand.

The Judge took the hand, shook it firmly, and turned his attention back to the computer screen, which took an alarmingly long amount of time to boot back up from sleep.

"Listen," Ocasio said, standing near the door, "I didn't mean anything by coming by like this. I just wanted to say, what happened was excessive; it wasn't a part of a grand plan, or some Mr. Miyagi shit, it was just wrong. You know it was wrong, and despite whatever they scramble your brains with, I hope you know that it wasn't on you."

He left, and Jones continued to watch the black screen as it reluctantly lit up. He stared at it unmoving for minutes, though he was unsure how long exactly. He never expected to be so thrilled to see, reflected in his own visor, Poet standing in the doorway.

Frost Dog had folded. Unexpected, perhaps, but neither were inclined to kick a gift gang-banger in the face. Another mission, another trip on the Lawranger, another way to snuff out whatever it was Ocasio was so hell-bent on finding.

AALIYAH

"ARE YOU TRYING to be a superhero or something?" I asked Colin, who'd been using three chairs to do push-ups in the small living room. He laughed, slouching a bit and nearly losing the thick Textbooks stacked on his back.

"Nah, just staying prepared," he said, easing back onto his feet.

I'd been rereading *Assata* for the third time. I usually ended up on his couch on Thursday nights. We were two months into dating, almost at the point of making the one thing I'll always live for.

There would be times I read aloud, for his benefit and mine. For me, it meant practicing my speech reading, while Colin, as he put it, was able to hear what weighed on me most, what gave me peace and what gave me pain, what built me.

That night, he'd spent the bulk of his time doing push-ups as I read. I kept losing my place while he grunted out his count— keeping his voice low, but not so it fooled me into thinking he didn't want me to hear.

"So, I think I want to tell you I... I *want* to tell you something I'm supposed to, but I can't without letting you know the truth." I wasn't ready, not to hope, not yet.

"What do you want to tell me?" I asked.

Colin opened his mouth as if I'd somehow summoned the words from his gut, leaping through his small intestines and out through his throat.

"I think I love you," he spat out.

We sat there, blank in the silence like it we could hide from it.

"...*So what are you so afraid of?*" I weakly sung.

We both, as if on a sitcom, let loose on the Partridges for a few bars. It was a good moment, and I can't take that away from us.

"I'm afraid, of—I want to show you something, Aaliyah. Can you follow me?" He was nearly pleading.

I set my book down and rolled up slowly, nodding at first like a moron who hadn't been dating a blind man. "Yeah," I added weakly.

When he took me to the back room, a small part of me expected a grey-shaded shitshow I'd need fifty ways to escape from.

"Just... let me explain before you leave, okay?" he said when we reached the door; his hand over the handle. I stared, unwilling even to blink.

All men, all women, all *everyone* had shit stored in the darkness, things they feared both to lose and to be found. In your case, Colin, this turned out to be more literal than most.

I thought of all those things I'd yet to open for you—for anyone, really. I'll at least give you that: you turned on those things most of us don't care to see.

"So, this is me, Pot," you said, almost an apology, weaker than promised by the fifty or so firearms hung over the walls. The smells I'd both known too well and understood so little stagnated in the air. I didn't expect to feel, of all things, regret; at least whips and chains would have made for a conversation with Reb over tea the next day.

"So... " he started, and trailed off, shrunken and still.

"This is... *something*," I said. I found myself laughing.

He sighed, making his way to a workbench in the middle of the room, sitting behind the only surface not covered in weapons.

"To start with… I'm not a psychopath. I know how this all must look, especially to *you*."

"'Especially to me?' You know, then. I wondered. How long have you known?" I lifted one of the larger rifles off the wall.

"I'm only human, and the internet is still *mostly* free." He chuckled and I smirked, forcing out a snort for his benefit.

"Of all the dudes in all the—I mean, what the shit?" I said, and this time didn't have to fake the laugh, and neither did he.

"None of these are loaded, and I don't carry, ever. I just think of all the things we've poured ourselves into, these… tools, they're so primitive. All this time and we're still just throwing stones at one another."

I nodded, because I still slipped up from time to time.

"So, what, then? You want to make it easier? Make them kill 2.0?" I say, with less mirth this time. I just wanted to understand.

"No, not exactly…"

I sat on the other side of the workbench, and bit back the urge to wave a hand in front of his face.

"How—?"

"Does a blind man fall into this area of interest?" he finished.

"I mean—*yeah*. That. I know that you *can*, I know that being blind doesn't prevent you from being an engineer or—well—anything really, but why?" It was invasive to ask, and I knew that even then. The thing about Colin and I, though? We both knew bullshit and the ways to read it. So, we had an unspoken agreement to not waste time on it.

"I like to understand how things work. It's—I've never been good at people. Firearms make more sense. But there's an… indifference to them. Everyone cares about what is done *with* them; nobody cares about the tools themselves. I want to make significant improvements on them. Non-lethal, mostly," he added, and I appreciated it for what it was.

I toyed with the anything-but-a-toy in my hand, moving it back and forth, feeling its weight and its war.

"You're... actually taking this rather well," he eventually said to break the silence.

"I don't know how I'm taking it, really."

"That's fair."

"I've never been... afraid of them, they are bits of metal and coil and plastic and they can't do anything we won't do ourselves, if we don't see a human being in front of us."

Release the safety by pressing in the button under the hammer on its right side, as viewed with the barrel pointing forward. Pull the trigger to release the firing spring.

"... But?" Colin prodded, and I sighed.

"But... why?" *Find the hinge pin, or the screw that is located where the lever enters the receiver. Unscrew the hinge pin and pull out the lever.* "Why do we need yet another method to destroy one another? Why continue to separate the act of taking a life from the proximity of that life, literal and otherwise?"

"It's a semantic point, Kettle."

Pull out the breech bolt.

"*Is it?* I think not. I think it ties to our desire, our constitutionally-backed right to take a thing that liberates us from the weight of murder. I mean... swords were pretty rad, but it's the *efficiency*. It's a moral dysmorphia. Why not remove them altogether? Why not approach enforcement in a restorative sense rather than buying into this old stagnant shit?"

Colin, much as I could see him fight it at the corners, nearly cackled.

"I—*no*, Kettle, the consideration of *self* is paramount. We can't hope to spread this idea of—of compassion if we've never been shown it. The why of it is the protection of self, of *I am important, I matter, and there's nothing wrong in making sure that I protect that life*." He truly believed that I had been on the opposite end of that argument, I think.

"I'm impressed, by the way," he added, and for once wasn't condescending. He ran a hand over the disassembled gun parts

I'd laid out on the table between us. "Who taught you how to do that?"

"The internet," I shot back, and it wasn't untrue.

"Hm. So, my turn to ask... why?" he asked, sliding the pieces over to himself and beginning to reassemble the gun.

"YOU'RE WELCOME. NOT that you thought to thank me. You really don't see it, do you? Of course, I know what you were working on, Kettle. You have to do everything in the light, don't you? You can't just, oh, I don't know, use a little goddamned subterfuge every now and again?" He was almost yelling. I wasn't afraid, not of him—not of you, Colin—but I was fucking confused. You'd clear that up, though, wouldn't you?

"Where is my son, Colin?"

"*Our* son, and, hey, can I just finish? Elijah is fine, he is safe, and you'll be holding him... five minutes after I'm done speaking with you. Just chill the fuck down for a moment."

You motherfucking cocksweating taint-faced speck of shit-covered navel lint, I would have said, Colin, just so you know.

In the moment, however, I raised my hands up, tightly closing my lips, and waited while you dangled our boy out there like bait.

"Thank you. You throw the word 'sociopath' around a lot, Kettle. Like, I'm not the one who sat here and tried to shoot someone's face off, jus' sayin."

"It wasn't loaded."

"Well, just not for *you*, but—you know what? Moving. Along. I know how kidnapping would make you look, Kettle. That was the whole point."

"What?"

"You've pissed off a looot of people. People that I need to work with, for instance. They don't know about us—not yet, anyway, though I'm sure they will soon. You posted the video on YouTube, for fucksakes, from your account!" He laughed thinly and watched me for a moment, as if waiting for me to work out what the hell he was getting at, but I only stared. Why make it easy for him?

"I didn't ask for any of this, Kettle. I just wanted to build. I lost everything, you *saw* me lose everything, and you still wanted to tell yourself we could win by their rules. Or maybe you wanted to play like we're not all running around on borrowed time. The Brotherhood I've created reaches further than anyone realises. It may have got a bit out of hand in the whole… black power thing." Colin threw up a weak fist for a moment and became the only person laughing in the room.

"You're starting a war, a literal race war, and you… you… just—just wrap this up, dude." I shook my head all the way down into the palm of my hand.

"I'm brilliant, Kettle. I *defined* brilliant, and I was stripped of everything, because some list of names told the world I was a threat? I was put here, though, wasn't I? They put me here, and now they are hurrying to work with me, to put an end to their 'thug' problem. The quickest way to do that, of course, is have them blow each other all to hell. That's just a bonus, though; this is a lot more *precise* than that. There are targets: troublemakers, loudmouth preachers, idealistic officers, and not to mention now two Judges to add to the list. Oh, also, funny enough, a five-figure salaried civil attorney who moonlights as a political activist. You should know that it's not smart to publicly broadcast a group of police officers, just being good ol' boys, Kettle…"

Fuck if he wasn't right. I knew when that video was shared to me by one of the men in it, I should have practised some level of patience. I should have taken more than a second to decide the whole world, or at least the part of the world that clicked on that YouTube vid, would be more apt to do something about what they did than I could.

When the video was released, I didn't hide. I put it on my account for a reason, Colin, and you would have seen that, if you weren't so busy trying to claw your way up, up and away from it all.

* * *

"Eustace Fargo's Judge system is morally bankrupt," I said, to no one in particular. I knew they were there of course, but the skin-searing lights of national news blinded me to everything.

I was asked by the school to join a panel on the recent, frankly blatant attempt by Fargo to strongarm his way around due process. We huddled in a room to duck and cover like the academics we were, and at least get paid for talking about things that we knew were already decided behind closed doors.

"How so?" asked the host of the panel, some forgettable famous dude whose 'woke' reputation was tarnished a few years before by sexual assault. His question irked me, because his existence on a panel of people who actually gave a shit *irked* me. It'd meant the school, like everything else Fargo could reach by way of Gurney, was compromised. I'd been there a semester and a half and already I was picking up nicknames; granted, Aaliyah 'Clout Collector' Monroe was a hell of a lot better than my more permanent moniker.

"It's the same thing we've been fighting since the *first*, is why," I said. "What's worse? *It's our fault.* We, the people who actually are *affected* by these policies, knew—*we fucking knew.* When Fargo used the death penalty as a loophole for his Judges to become government sanctioned hitmen, to hop and skip over due process in 32 states, *that's* when we should have fought harder."

After a moment of nothing, there was applause.

As the clapping subsided, as the space between us swelled, once more, with the distance denied in epidermis, I waited for the mistake, on both sides.

"That—If I'm being honest, sounds like more rhetoric we've come to expect," he said, and the room giggled. The lights lay alive across me, snatching from the crowd their individuality, bleeding them into an amalgamated terror of all things right and white.

"There's nothing more dismissive, sir—or, frankly, lazy—than the label of anger, of *rhetoric*. I don't know if you know this—or, well, *anything*—but as someone who has seen the families of those lost, who has sat and listened to their hurts, I can tell you confidently that more firepower, blood, and bodies of any hue, aren't going to fix this country."

He rolled his eyes to that, and the crowd chuckled on command. They were fewer laughs this time, though, so at least that was something.

"What *is* needed, then?" came a voice from the crowd. I couldn't see you any better than I could the rest of the crowd, Colin, but I didn't need to.

"I'm sorry, I—I'm... I'm going to go."

Of course, I didn't think of the consequences, the tweets and the blogs and the everything that would tell the world I was as empty as they'd thought all along. That all it'd taken was the right opinion on the right side to make me show my ass. They weren't exactly wrong though, were they, Colin?

I jogged off the stage, up the aisle and out of the auditorium, to a place I'd expected to find something other than daylight.

"You MADE A deal," I finally whispered.

"I made a deal. They still wanted their pound of flesh, but if they hoped to get any access to my weapons after this all wraps up, we had to come to an agreement regarding my child and ex-wife," he said, trying to place a hand over mine and proving that he hadn't been as brilliant as he imagined. I snatched it away.

"We were never married," I shot, and he rolled his eyes.

"Yeah, I know, but calling you my baby momma in this getup feels too cliché."

"So, is this it? We take Elijah from hideout to hideout and never give him a life?" I asked, trying to appeal to something I wasn't sure existed any more.

"For a time. We all are making sacrifices. I'm not delusional,

Kettle. I don't expect anything from us, you and I specifically that is—not that I would mind it, of course—but when we had Elijah, we had a deal. We were in this together and would always put him before any of our shit. I can't have you two running out there right now, not unprotected like this, and you made your choice, Kettle, and sticking it out with me for a while, until I know you're safe, isn't all that much to ask for."

I go to speak, I go to tell him every way he is wrong, for every moment I've known him, but then he says a word, one that brings the world bursting through the door and into my arms. I fall into my boy, on the ground and twisting across the ground. In a house full of firearms and men undeserving of their cost I can't help but forget it all, if only for a night.

CHAPTER SIX

"TODAY, CADETS, IS brought to you by the letter K. Anyone want to guess *why?*" Judge Fox shouted from the centre of the cadet circle, a large brown satchel hanging over his side. They'd been on the Marsh Pit that day, one of six 'mini-terrains' meant for combat training. It wasn't half as much a pain in the ass for Ezekiel than the Sand Box or even the Sea Circle, but it didn't come without a heavy toll on manoeuvrability.

K is for knife training, Cadet Jones thought, glancing around the circle at the other cadets. Knowledge—bartered with the senior cadets—was the only real power at the base. Barter wasn't permitted, of course, but permission is only a consideration if you were caught. For Cadet Jones, who worked the kitchens and could sneak sugar and spices out beneath the waistband of his uniform, it was a constant stream of what to expect in the coming classes, traded for the invaluable chance to stomach bland potatoes and boiled chicken with a bottle of sriracha. Before the Academy, he'd never expected condiments to be worth their weight in gold.

"Knife training sir," one of the cadets shouted out.

"*Nice*. Cadet Jordan, was it?" Fox said with a chuckle. "The scum-lickers you'll be protecting our citizens from will sometimes be too close to get your gun out, or you'll be caught out of ammo, or a million other things you will fuck up because, tragically, we can't bleed out all the old failures you brought here."

Jones and the other cadets began to unsheathe their blunted daggers from the gear belt around their waist, but stopped when Judge Fox raised a hand for them.

"No, you little turd-nuggets. Welcome to year three; time to take off those training wheels." Judge Fox dropped the sack to the wet ground beneath his boots and kicked it open, spilling out a pile of uniform onyx blades with silvery hilts. One by one they came and selected their freshly sharpened blades, before returning to their place in the circle.

"We don't get long with you maggots; or not now, at least. If Fargo had his way, we'd get a hold of you before the world dulled you down with its lies. As it is, we'll work with you gash-sweats until we can hopefully weed a few of you out that won't die your first year in the field. To do *that*, you'll have to take risks! Are you sorry butt-brownies ready for that?"

"Yes, sir!"

"*Are you ready to make yourselves the order of the world?*"

"*Yes, sir!*" the cadets cried.

Considering he'd been the only cadet amongst his peers to use lethal force prior to graduating, Jones didn't think too much of using live weapons, be it a gun or something more archaic like the blade in his hand.

The exercise was less chaotic than Ezekiel hoped. They partnered up and ran through drills meant to quickly take down a criminal beast by non-lethal means. Ezekiel and Ocasio, per the usual, deciding to work with one another. It'd been four months since they'd first found one another in the same bed, generally Ocasio's of course, as Ezekiel had some sort of allergy to bedding sheets, or the alien concept of 'pillows.'

Generally, in the night, after they finished falling into one another, there was something to see by in the darkness of their room. When the light lay still, there was something like illumination, of a truth that Ezekiel felt foolish for finding each time.

There was Ezekiel's mother, and he'd shed the slate face he'd held for hour after hour in the training ground, lines breaking as he spoke about her mind wandering in a concrete coffin of a home while he gambled on Fargo. There was Ocasio's brother, who ran with a local gang in Chicago; who died so cold, so far and so unbearably heavy that even as tightly as Ezekiel's arms were around his fidgeting body, they felt inconsequential to anything.

Beyond the bunk though, in the sand box, or the mess hall, or the Marsh while running through drills, they were just cadets, and terrible liars.

Judge Fox strode around each of the groups, giving them direction, or something a little less kind. Cadet Jones focused on his training partner, not batting an eye at the instructor, ignoring the sound of a broken finger to his left, a sliced ear to his right. Hearing the harsh cries of his peers made knowing Fox's alphabet of arms in advance worth every trade.

When Judge Fox passed Ezekiel and Ocasio, he'd not said a word. They relaxed, at first, but Fox's attention returned to them again and again. He'd wander around the two, sizing them up, a kind of pleasure tucked under the ginger mustache.

The rest of the cadets had continued, but their eyes eventually drifted away from their partners and fell over Ezekiel, Ocasio, and the Judge who stared at them so intently. The trick to the Marsh was in the footing. If a cadet could properly adapt to the sinking land, how it stole speed and balance, then it became a simple dance of precision. Though Judge Fox, knowing this, and prizing hazing above orgasms, decided it was time to see what the two could really do.

Faster, he'd command, and they would obey. *Faster.* The two obeyed again. *Faster!* Again, they obeyed, and the knife grew closer and closer to Ocasio's face as he lurched back to dodge, closer to his hand as he avoided Ezekiel's disarm.

Faster, you turtle-dicks!

Ezekiel obeyed.

Which isn't to say Ocasio wouldn't, but he didn't have the nights sneaking out in black to train. To understand.

To judge.

Ocasio fell back as Cadet Jones's feet plucked effortlessly from the sinking bog, bringing the blade up with the same speed Cadet Ocasio fell. Ocasio raised a hand over his face, and Ezekiel couldn't help but grin as the blade stopped centimetres from Ocasio's fingers. The cadets cheered, the rare sound jarring Jones for a moment before he reached a hand out to help Ocasio up.

"Show-off." Ocasio chuckled.

"I guess K was for *kiss my ass*," Jones whispered, through a smile, under everything that could take them to dust.

"Stay down, cadet!" Fox screamed from five feet away. Ezekiel seemed to weigh the order for a moment, but ultimately returned to a stone stance, hands at his side and bunkmate slowly sinking into the muck.

"Cadet Jones, why did you stop your attack?" Judge Fox questioned, taking steps between them with his back to Ocasio.

"Sir?"

"Did you not hear me, cadet? I guess some of you maggots lied on your physical exams, then? Here I am thinking I'm teaching future Judges, Judges, who have no room for hereditarily unfit citizens that—"

"Sir, I hear you, sir! I finished my attack; the target has been subdued!" Jones shot back, his eyes struggling not to fall over Cadet Ocasio.

Judge Fox held a hand out flat. "Your weapon, cadet."

Ezekiel broke through the pieces of steel and brick and harder things he thought couldn't be blown down before glancing down at the empty hand. He complied with the order.

"Cadet Ocasio," Judge Fox started, before turning to the muck-covered cadet. "Please, share with your classmates the brilliant strategy you used to protect yourself from an oncoming attack." Ezekiel's eyes spilled down, bulged and begging that through some kind of telepathy he'd never had, he'd be able to tell Ocasio *No, take a reprimand, take a week in the Cube, take anything but that order.*

Cadet Ocasio slowly, carefully raised a hand to cover his face. It happened so fast, blood bursting out with Ocasio's screams before he keeled over, half his face folding into the wetness of the mud.

Judge Fox spun to meet Cadet Jones's eyes, expecting him to make a move against him, to reach for his training partner, to do anything but be the good little cadet he was. Cadet Jones stayed solid, staring forward and pushing everything into a small brushfire in his mind.

"*This* is a subdued aggressor, Cadet Jones. Do you see the difference?" Judge Fox asked innocently, as if he'd only smacked a ruler to the back of Ocasio's hand. Cadet Jones nodded eventually, unsure if he even had that much in him.

It wasn't enough for Fox, it seemed, who leaned in to Ezekiel's ear, dropping his voice for only the two of them to hear.

"Take your *bottom* to the medical wing. Your *new* bunkmate will be assigned within the hour."

Spit clung to Ezekiel's ear. Jones met the Judge's eyes, filling them with every mistake they tried to strip away, and then nodded once more, taking one of Cadet Ocasio's arms over his shoulder, carrying him off to the medical wing without words, only knowing that he'd be packing for more than one cadet's departure that night.

AALIYAH

I'D JUST FINISHED a TED Talk when it happened. Another attempt to remind people that we were human, beneath the badges and bad associations; another thing you thought didn't matter, Colin. They approached me, from behind, before I could unlock my car door, before I could pick up *my* son from my next-door neighbour, Ms. Branden.

They asked me questions about a gun, of all things, saying a tip had brought me up for questioning, and nothing at all to do with the video I'd acquired a few nights before.

"I've done nothing wrong. I have no *idea* how that weapon ended up with me. Well, I *do* have an idea, but it's not one you assholes will ever admit to, *is* it?" I said, and the officer rolled his eyes.

"You want to get under my skin, don't you?" he said. "You think bringing up what you've done to the good men who protect *you* and *your* right to protest in the streets *against* them... You—I'm not going to bite, lady."

I can't quite find the word to explain what I did next. *Laugh?* No, that's not enough. *Cackle?* Hoot and holler like a hyena? Still too conservative a description.

I kept going for two and a half minutes.

Then I wiped my tears away, not aware the moment of joy

would be stolen from me soon enough.

"You think lives *spent* on you is *funny?*" he spat. "You deserve all that's coming to you."

That quieted me for a moment, but not for the reason he thought. "No. I don't think *that's* funny. I just find it interesting that you can't see it. You *do* know that I've protected officers, *detectives* like yourself, don't you? Maybe you don't. Maybe you think I'm just out to slam every cop who shows up and does their job. Yeah, you have some *bad hombres,* don't you? But hey, they aren't all bad. Some of them are rapists, some of them are—"

"Okay, laying it on a little thick now, aren't we?" he said.

I flung my hands up, but he was kind of right. "Listen, detective, you're only hurting yourself. I know what you're really doing, bringing me in here on some bogus shit. I know you're trying to threaten me, but I think we both know I didn't do anything *wrong* here. The only thing I did wrong was share a video."

"I don't know what you're on about, ma'am."

"Oh! Well, *that's* embarrassing. For a moment, I thought you may have me in here for putting up that clip of the Chicago PD beating the holy hell out of 12-year-old Chicago resident Presla Bonck, in front of one of your cruisers, no less. I mean, *that* would mean you were, yet again, abusing your power. You all wouldn't make that mistake twice, though, so I guess we're both just riled up for no real reason, now aren't we?" I said evenly. The officer, who I'd recognised from a video that made its way into a friend of a friend of a friend's inbox that eventually popped up into mine for better distribution.

"You're an idiot. You don't know it, but damn, you've really gone and fucked yourself this time." The officer laughed, which was unexpected but didn't much shake me. What he did next, though? Scooting from his chair, hunching over me, undoing my handcuffs? That may have thrown me a bit.

"You can cut the tape now, Encinia," he shouted to the two-way mirror as I rubbed my wrists. Before I had a chance to respond, he'd flopped open the manila folder on the desk between us, pulling out a piece of paper and scooting it my way.

"What the hell is this?" I asked, too confused and suspicious to even touch the paper.

"Your lines, Ms. Monroe," he said with a grin from ear to ear, before the door behind me unlocked and two other officers made their way in. They were men. They were hungry in the way men were told they had to be. There was an absence of everything that mattered in their eyes.

"Don't worry, they ain't gonna do nothing to you. Not the way they *should*, anyway. They just want to see your face for this next part." As if on cue there was a chortle from the studio audience.

"The hell—?"

"Read, bitch," one of them interrupted from behind me. I swung my head back, and burned as much of myself into him through my eyes as I could. He was too cold to know the heat, and I was too preoccupied with, I think, plan… *34* on how I would get the hell out of there, to care.

So, I read.

Fuck.

"Are you—you really, *really* don't know who you're *fucking* with do you? I've been ready to die, ready for whatever shit you think you can put over me, for my entire *life*. You think you can *scare* me? You think you can make me read this shit aloud to—?" One of them stopped me, pressing his fat finger against my lips. I stopped. You would have too, or at least, that's what I tell myself. As I was surrounded by the possibility of a great many mayhems, at the fringe of everything *they* care about. With all my tweets, all my clout, all my class, they still held the match.

It lasts for a second, that hope, that fear, until I remember one of many lessons I've had to learn through corpses I've aligned myself to. I've learned that if you have the ego to call yourself a revolutionary, you have to be prepared for a revolutionary suicide.

"Fuck. You," I said, taint of pork and things that were made to destroy me still slathered over my lips.

They laughed, one after another in a domino effect.

"Yeah, fuck *us*. You got some balls on you, lady... What about your son, though? Have his even dropped?" Officer With-A-Death-Wish said. I see red. I see the promise of meat lover's pizza I forgot I made about and opted for McDonald's again, on the way home the night before, filed away in the overstuffed folder of 'Mother I Wanted to Be.' I see every child's body I'd seen in one photograph or another over the years. I see Emit. I see Eric. I see George. I see Trayvonne. I see Cameron. I see VonDerrit. I see Laquan. I see all of them that I should list with every bit of ash in every bit of tomorrow, if I wanted to fill this moleskin with things that make you close it. I see them all because I want to see everything but Elijah.

I see the paper.

"You won't threaten—"

"We aren't *threatening* anything. Not *yet*. Thurgood, though? He ain't as gracious. See, we didn't quite know what to do with you. I mean, what *could* we? You're the *Bullet Bitch*. You have people *fooled*, don't you? See, we had a few ways to get rid of you here, ways even the *Judges* couldn't deal with. Thurgood though, he knew that whatever evil little cop-hating spawn you bled would be the one way to shut you up, to make you shut *yourself* up."

I fought back the vomit. I fought back my free hands, ready to wrap around one of their pistols, ready to end them, then Thurgood, then everything that wasn't Elijah. I was their Bullet Bitch.

That was, until he said my other name.

"He told us to let you know—shit, one sec..." The officer rustled in his back pocket, pulling out a piece of paper, scrawled in your shitty handwriting, and squinted to read:

"*Let her know to read from the kettle, read from the pot, read from everything that will give her the black*. I mean, I'm not going to sit here and say he's not a weird fuck, but you get the point. Read the paper, and then? Then you *might* see your kid again."

I wanted that smile of his between my teeth. I wanted to tear away all the power he held by way of his dick. I wanted everything, if it meant breaking him.

I also wanted to rewind to the point of my day before the words *kettle* or *pot* weren't uttered. A point at which Thurgood was still just a boogyman.

"Where is he?" I demanded. To your immense surprise, I'm sure, they didn't answer me.

"This is what's going to happen," the officer said, signalling for the other two to leave, now that he'd imagined I'd be a *good girl*.

"I'm going to clap my hands, and then the camera will start again. You will *read* that script, and not long after? 10 seconds or so, that door"—he pointed off, keeping his eyes on me—"will be blown to hell. You'll follow along with the other thugs that come to get you, and you'll never be a pain in our ass again. Oh! You'll also see your son, maybe teach him to not make the same mistakes his momma has. You do this, you're free, *we're* free. Unless... you want to keep going? Thanks to Thurgood, we have more than enough to put your ass in orange, and honestly? It seems more fitting, if I'm being honest, but, here we are." He looked solemn, poor guy.

I thought for a moment, but any more than that would be a betrayal to Elijah. So, I glared, tight-lipped, scanning through the paper I'd been given with my lines, nearly finding a way to laugh again when I reached the one, I knew, he'd thrown in to *really* piss me off.

"Something funny?" the officer said, worried—almost.

"Everything," I said. I smiled. I clapped.

"Well, that is interesting," Colin huffed, rolling off the other side of the bed. He listened to every click while rustling through his dresser drawers, taking his time to find the perfect outfit for random Tuesday afternoon inside.

He could spend hours choosing between a button-up and a graphic tee. That should have been a warning, if nothing else.

Colin smiled when he heard the clicks stop, when he heard a stream of swearing I can't even piece together any more.

"You're a sociopathic prick, Colin."

That seemed to sting him. He raised his weary head in my direction.

"That… hurts, Aaliyah," he said, lightly, before turning his grin up to his ears. "I thought I'd been the dropout here. 'Sociopathy' is such an antiquated term, it's just the same traits of a psychopath without the fun, Hollywood vibe."

"What happened to you, Colin?"

"Awwww, now, come on… it's been so long since we've seen each other, Kettle, I needed to see if you were still in there. The you I *know* you can be." He slid on a t-shirt and shuffled his legs into jeans twice the size I'd ever seen on him. He finished it off with a wave cap still in the Wal-Mart packaging, tearing it open with his teeth and stretching it over his skull before turning to face me.

"Why the hell are you doing this, Colin? Huh? I—I was… you ruined my life. I was finally, finally getting some traction with the case. I had them, I had them and you kidnap me from the fucking *interrogation room?* Do you know what that looks like?" I screamed, no bullets, no Muay Thai, nothing but what he'd stripped me down to. "You know, when that jackass detective slipped me that paper, your instructions? I didn't know it was you until I reached that final bit of shitty dialogue. Oh, and by the way, having me quote *Assata?* Bet you thought that shit was *reeeal* fucking clever, didn't you?" I said, not meaning to compliment him, but I should have realised he wasn't capable of seeing anything I said for anything but.

"Yeah, I almost wanted to order my people to get a copy of the tape to see that bit myself. I thought you'd be happy, don't you live on that hotep shit?" he said smugly, as if he ever understood the insult.

"Where is—?"

"—'my son, Colin?' Christ, you're *really* repetitive with the dialogue, aren't you?" He picked out a pack of flats from his back pocket and sparked the nothing, growing too comfortable for my liking. "You remember what happens, Kettle? When you pull the trigger? I'm just curious. I never went into academia like you, had the chance to *mold* the minds of the youth. Never had the *chance,* now did I?"

"Whose fault was that?"

"Ah, right, that again." He laughed. "Let's not change the subject. What happens when you pull the trigger, Kettle?"

I sighed, but also, I wasn't going anywhere.

I guess if you got this far, neither are you.

CHAPTER SEVEN

CARL 'CATASTROPHE' PATTERSON Was A Cold Motherfucker.

When Carl commissioned to have the words etched into his headstone at twenty-three years old, the artist saw the address on his ID and rushed the order at no extra cost. Carl didn't scrimp, even back then before Thurgood saw his potential began paying him accordingly. Black granite, double upright, plated with white gold, and at its foundation wrapped in a cloth dipped in Chameleon paint. Being the brute enforcer for a mid-level street distributor of Halcyon Daze had its advantages.

He placed it on the front lawn of his six-bedroom house that he'd inherited from his grandmother. She'd been the rock of his life and quite possibly the only person brave enough to tell the 6'6" walking-stop-and-frisk-justification where to go. Tragically, for both Carl and his neighbours on West Nuohlac Street, sweet, Catastrophe-wrangling Geneva Patterson died in her hospice bed, by way of a street-side bullet meant for her grandbaby.

I'm not afraid.

She would use the word 'cold' often—it was an adjective that described much of her life—so it felt right to Carl that it be adopted.

That cold muhfucka Rick James could have been your granddaddy if I ain't git stuck with Cindy's fucking nightshift and missed tha' sho.

This one cold ass beat, why they call it Capture rap again?

This ain't how shit supposed to go for you, Carl. You tryna end up like that fucking spuhm donor that dipped on you and your momma? You smarta and betta than tha'. Now hush, and pass grandmama that cold ass kush.

She had faith that young Carl would become something more than the accumulation of the bodies he'd broken in his hands.

Granted, Thurgood had the future gunrunner surrounded. He'd graduated from strongman to hitman, which ultimately only meant more class and more corpses.

Six months prior to Judges Poet and Jones descending on his humble town, Carl would take on a job that would change the rest of his life. The newest monster was only known by the name 'Thurgood.' While he'd been a seller of a different kind of death than the ones Carl generally dealt with, he'd been just as detrimental for the chemical capitalism running over the streets. This *Thurgood* was denying access to his weapons to any drug pusher that came knocking, but with the specific set of skills Carl had to offer, well, maybe he could have been persuaded to open his marketing plan.

What he was, however, was *impressed*: not by the body but the breathtaking lengths he went to, to make his way into the same room as Thurgood. It wasn't a trail of bloodied faces and chipped teeth that'd put Thurgood and Carl in an ill-lit parking garage together, Carl seemingly unfazed by the circle of guns around him. It was a *correspondence*. E-mail after e-mail, gratuitously praising retweets and shared status updates from the fake account of @MarketingManJohnSmith, led him after some time to the inbox of one of Thurgood's inner circle. Once there, he'd mapped out a plan to market Thurgood's product in a way that would yield a 300% influx of members.

Unfortunately, when this information was brought to

Thurgood, he'd proven not only a genius of engineering, but of the criminal sciences. With a deft ear he'd been able to perceive that *John Smith* was, quite *possibly,* a sign of foul play. The ability—known in a better time as *fact checking*—that Thurgood employed was a relic in this day and age, and it wasn't one Carl could have possibly accounted for.

Thurgood had the sense to make a meeting... and to bring the appropriate level of protection. Two armoured gunmen sourced out to ensure they knew what they were doing. Three sharpshooters, each with nocturnal introspective, grafted, gas-augmented scopes courtesy of Thurgood.

Halcyon Daze.

An unregulated street drug that sells cheap, with immeasurable worth.

A side effect of the euphoric dopamine dump was the loss of the ability to see pigmentation; the skin of other organisms took on a trippy, translucent sheen.

There was a reasonable argument for its legalisation: it reduced high blood pressure, reversed type II diabetes, even reduced intolerance to lactose. In the end, however, it proved too dangerous for the youth of middle America.

It *did* help catapult president Gurney in the polls, giving him an altruistic mission to rescue America's best and brightest from those who would poison and indoctrinate them.

For Carl, the high *was* nice, but it proved more valuable that Halcyon Daze made him more of a businessman while using it than anything else.

It took ten years of falling in and out of love with Halcyon Daze, and other drugs more dangerous in the long term before he made the first objectively informed decision of his life. He didn't kill Thurgood; he listened to him. Thurgood listened, too. He listened to a tired hostage, under-galvanised. He listened to the qualms, and watched the charm, of someone who had a hell of a lot more in common with the suspicious and cowardly lot of lowlifes than he'd had.

He listened to the beginning of something that would carry

on for years, and hopefully fill the air with not just words, but *action.*

"So, JUDGE JONES, what do you think?" Judge Poet asked from the passenger side of the 2019 junker of a car they sat parked in for cover, after releasing a colossal fart.

"Who benefits?" he continued. "Vegan chili, by the way, in case you're wondering. I've expelled a Franklin, and you, being stuck in this car with me, are burdened by it. Granted, I am too, but I am rewarded in divesting myself of the chaos of beans."

"Oh. Oh, god, that is—Who the hell is Franklin?" Judge Jones shouted, his nose filling with justice.

"Benjamin Franklin of course. He penned one of the most succinct articles on the importance of releasing gaseous waste from our body whenever we can. The man deserves his just due, and I for one will give it to him how I can." Judge Poet looked proud, and as far as Ezekiel was concerned, was far too prepared for the speech.

"Well, we *both* have to deal with your rancid ass, so I can't say any of us benefits. You've just nearly shat yourself and you could have held off until we're more than a foot or so away from one another. You made a choice, and it was a shitty one at that."

"Yes. Yes, I suppose I could have waited. Though, *Tank*, you haven't really done much other than tell me that the inconvenience to you is greater value than mine. It isn't wrong necessarily, but it makes you a bit of a hypocrite, doesn't it? I, in my time of Franklin, have done nothing more, in making a choice to take care of my person." Judge Poet took a long, Oscar-worthy sniff at the air.

"Your argument here, then—just to make sure I have it—is that, by asking you to not fill a very enclosed space with your… *Franklin*, which we are both occupying and just need to get through, that I am only considering myself in this scenario?"

"Not so much an argument as a statement of fact. You consider your pain more important than mine. Do you deny it? Do you hold, like the old guard does, to some feigned altruism? I have to say... so far, I don't quite understand what Marisa *sees* in you, Judge Jones." Judge Poet hadn't broken eye contact with Judge Jones.

An hour, and a second Franklin, passed—in each case, faster for one man than the other.

They spoke again when running through, for the umpteenth time, the file of Carl 'Catastrophe' Patterson. To Judge Poet's credit, they didn't veer away from the clunky dialogue Judges generally used, at least as long as they were discussing facts.

Jones didn't judge the bone-breaking brute's selling history of Halcyon Daze. He bemoaned, like any liberal, the harsh enforcement, the ways in which the decriminalisation may have helped his mother. He made the novice mistake, the *old* mistake, of injecting an anecdote of experience, against the more important things. The things that mattered.

"You confound me, Judge Jones," Poet said solemnly, and Ezekiel couldn't do much besides survey him blankly for a moment, before a laugh leapt from his mouth and latched longer than he'd thought capable in years.

"That's... *Okay*. Fuck it, I'll bite. Why—no, *how* do I confound *you*, Judge Poet?"

Judge Poet's features hardened behind the sad smirk.

"Because you've *seen* this, you watched a boy bleed out in the street. You, who has seen a world I won't pretend to know, ran to the law. Yet, somehow, you still question the law's worth."

"It didn't do all that much for the people, though, did it? Halcyon Daze—*that* did something for people, and I don't think it's wrong to admit that." Jones looked back out onto the street.

"Never said I thought he was wrong; do you think something so simple as right and wrong exists, Judge Jones? Do you also collect unicorn horns to power Santa's sleigh?"

"Believing that some things are wrong isn't inherently ignorant, Judge Poet."

"No, not ignorant, but… fatally optimistic."

Two hours, three and a half Franklins, and one regurgitated debate on the importance of 2A schools passed between the two.

Judge Jones was saved from Poet's ramblings when their prey finally arrived. Two Brotherhood members had been patrolling the area.

More importantly though, two fairly sized, one-size-fits-all-cloak-wearing Brotherhood members.

The Judges left the car in unison, tumbling out to the pavement and slowly closing their doors without a sound. For all his ramblings, Judge Poet knew how to shut the hell up when it served a greater good.

Left, left, left, right.

Right, nod, left-eye blink, right-eye blink.

The Judges had seen the benefit of sign language, but saw no use in a system anyone else could read, so they'd made their own. Ezekiel noted Poet's nods, took out a large, black ball from his belt and tossed it to the side of the building, where it vibrated loudly.

Startled, the hooded strangers shuffled in the darkness, away from the halogen lights. Judge Poet struck first, while Jones darted to position; they made contact in the same moment; Jones striking his target's throat with the side of his hand, stealing his sound, before cracking the top of his skull with the butt of his pistol. Poet's approach lacked Jones's precision, grabbing the back of his target's head and feeding it into the side of the building, silencing his victim before the ensuing wail.

As Poet released his target's head, Judge Jones's heel was already en route to the back of his skull, the crunch of a patriotic boot liberating society from another Brotherhood layabout.

"*Shit,*" Ezekiel mouthed, as he quickly stripped one of the targets, Poet the other, hoping to get their robes off of them unbloodied.

"What is it?" Judge Poet asked, muffled by the robe he'd slid down over his uniform.

"Fatality... I was hoping to avoid—"

"Coulda been worse, coulda been two. Let's go."

Judge Jones nodded in reply before shifting the bodies into the shadows.

They entered the warehouse, keeping the grey hoods low. Clearly, the enigmatic Thurgood had got the word out to the lowlifes. The subterraneans, the inhuman scourge of food stamps and unearned freedoms.

In the robes it was hard to make out how many of the street gangs the crime lord had corralled together, but in the few glimpses the Judges allowed themselves—risking discovery every time they raised their faces—it seemed his reach had extended beyond the walls of the city. It didn't line up, though; what sort of tech do you offer to competing dealers all at once? Thurgood was undercutting his own market.

Of course, the man himself was nowhere to be seen. From the whispering around them, the arms dealer had opted out of attending: according to some because he was on his third felony, to others because he was a coward. Most had no idea one way or another, beyond tales of an eight foot, two dicked Mensa member who knew kung fu.

The bulk of the similarly-garbed gang-banging trash was, as expected, the Brotherhood themselves. Even as they stood in that greyed robe from head to toe, Ezekiel read them by all the things not to be seen.

Desk worker, bad posture—Black
Female—Indian
Black—Janitor—Felon
Mother—Incel—Sugar addict

Then there was movement behind him, and he and Poet shifted to see what was happening next.

*   *   *

THE BROTHERHOOD SPLIT down the middle in obeisance to Carl 'Catastrophe' Patterson. The former enforcer was wheeled out on a podium, waving grandly as he paraded through the crowd. When the podium stopped, he straightened his tie, allowing silence to fill the warehouse, because—as he'd put it to Thurgood earlier that day—*Niggas gonna put some respect on my suit, if I'm expected to drop stack on it.*

"Welcome my brothas! My sistas, my cousins, my wiggas, my niggas, my bitches, my thots and my hoteps, to the last weapons sale you'll ever need!" There were murmurs, and chuckles.

"Where is the real leader, where is Thurgood?" an 86-Scarlet gang member asked from the safety of the crowd.

"Ah, *Thurgood*. Y'all niggas stay on that enigmatic figurehead bull, fam. There ain't no Thurgood. How about that? How about there is just the Brotherhood, and we ain't got no leader, don't need no leader. We just got the message, and the means to deliver that good news." More murmurs, less chuckles, and the kindling within Catastrophe to show how cold a motherfucker he was.

"Let me tell you what this ain't finna be. Y'all taking turns talking in the back of class or some shit!" Catastrophe shouted, and stopped, until someone got their mind right and remembered to bring him the mic.

"You all have a unique opportunity, a promise for the most minimal of effort on your part," the gangster continued, and the Brotherhood members chanted the word, *opportunity*.

"We came here for an auction, my nigga, not some dashiki shit," Jimmy 'Jank-A-Motha-Fucka-From-Behind' Frampton said from the back of the crowd. He'd led the Cheddar Chips, who'd spent their days cornering the market on academic grounds, slinging Vyvance to pre- and post-grads.

Jimmy was also known for his chronic *use* of said product, which at times led him to precarious situations, such as challenging a dude named Catastrophe.

Catastrophe wasn't patient in many things, including outbursts from hopheads. He descended from the podium in a slow, slick promenade to Jimmy, and smashed the microphone into Jimmy's mouth.

Carl didn't pay much mind to Jimmy after that, turning his smile to the rest of the Cheddar Chips behind their tooth-alleviated leader. When he felt his point had been made, he turned to his own two-hundred moderately-trained Brotherhood members.

"Nigga, my nigga, if you do not want the talking stick, you shouldn't have asked for it, my nigga," he said sweetly. Judge Poet chuckled caustically for a moment, before looking around and restraining himself.

"Niggas be on some real nigga shit, but I see you niggas, I see you. I am not a prophet. I cannot tell you the way niggas on the west is gonna watch the sunset with niggas on the east, but no one can. I *can* tell you, though, that beyond the colours and the package and the fu'n-fu'n *Godfather* vendetta ish, that we all respect that all y'all just tryna survive, my niggas. Why is we just *surviving*, though, ya feel? Why we just okay with them corralling us against one another, my nigga? Why ain't we just doing this our way, in our *homes?* You hear me, my niggas?" Catastrophe cried out, his exuberance received and reflected en masse by his niggas within this warehouse.

"Buh… buh, yo, Catastrophe…" ventured another thug. "I ain't tryna get my face busted and shit, but that nigga Jim had a point. I'm hearing what you sayin', nigga, but you ain't being practical about this. Yo' fallacy lies in the method, my nigga. Say we all, what, put down our primary revenue source, therefore losing our footing of real, tangible *control,* my nigga, we lose the majority of these fake-ass, halfway crook-ass weekend niggas 'cause we also lost our executory powers over these niggas. All for some Huey P. Newton ish, my nigga? Like, yo, I done heard you got a fuckin' arsenal, but 'less you got fuckin' *tanks*, and fuckin'-fuckin' controlling interest of Ump Post, then we just throwin' our lives away, fam." There were murmurs sprouting, as they do, between everyone's feet. But Catastrophe was more than just a cold motherfucker: he raised his arms, fanning down the scatter-shot conversations. When there was silence, he delivered a snapback.

"Nigga, my nigga, you speak true, my nigga. However, I must stress criticality upon letting a nigga finish, my nigga." Catastrophe laughed, and it spread throughout the warehouse.

JUDGE JONES THOUGHT to join in the laughter, mostly hoping he'd remembered how. But he just grunted as a Brotherhood member behind him shoved a foot behind his knee. He caught himself and straightened again, but the gang-banger behind him seemed hell-bent on dicking with him. They shoved Ezekiel's arm forward, and it hung for a moment in the air as if he'd had a question for Catastrophe.

Jones remained calm, though if he hadn't turned for a moment to see the face beneath the hood, he may not have stayed as composed.

"Nigga, my nigga, you think of a minor portion of our retail, my nigga. A fundamental analysis of our programme, of what we really offer, my nigga, will surely change your mind. Nigga, I ain't gonna sit here and say I came prepped with an EPS, my nigga, but there isn't even a fuckin' margin of investment to consider, my nigga. You could argue that high volatility is something to consider, but the stability of Thurgood's—of the Brotherhood's—reach comes into play when you see that he also has the information to put behind the weapons. Y'all niggas, sittin' up here scared of the police... psh... y'all ain't even seein' bey*awnd*, my nigga. Y'all ain't on our level, that futurist ish my niggas, what if we told you it ain't gonna *stop* on the streets? What if I told you we even gonna take on tha Judges, my nigga?"

"*Preach that shit, Catastrophe!*"

"We got the only Judge on these streets behind us," Catastrophe shouted. "The Judge that holds the most important weapon of *all*, my niggas. Thurgood is *that* nigga's name. *Thurgood* has the means of production, my niggas. We ain't giving you no bullshit, and I got proof!" He snapped his head up to manically laugh. "See, you join us, you commit a *dollar*, a name on a paper, a tangible display of yo' heart in this game, ya feel? You do that? Then you stand behind someone that knows how they work. Someone who knows about them punk-ass Judges that are even here *tonight,* in this *room*, my niggas!"

It was already too late for either Judge Poet or Judge Jones to attempt any kind of escape. The woman behind Ezekiel latched her hands over him, and he didn't attempt to struggle.

"I see in the dark. You will lay still forever in the garden of our dismay. Sleep now, sweet boy, know the fruit will fall in time." As Marisa uttered the words beneath her hood, she began shoving Judge Jones ahead through the crowd, pulling his hood back to show his helmet. He fought back, of all things, a pang of nostalgia as she led him to the Catastrophe ahead.

She'd said the words loudly enough for Poet to hear, who chuckled as he was pushed alongside Ezekiel by another Brotherhood member. He seemed less concerned with the strapped, sadistic criminal buttcrust than he should have been. If the vagabonds of violence had been to the Academy at all, they may have understood why.

I see in the dark, she'd said. I am with you, Judge, but must stay unseen.

Jones and Poet suffered through the wads of spit, the petty names and threats, as they were tied up beneath Catastrophe at the podium, by Marisa and the others. They were good soldiers, though, and made sure to do as they were told.

You will lay forever in the garden of our dismay. Follow my lead, play chicken, head down, eyes open.

If he'd just had a heads-up that he'd be sitting stiff and full of piss for two hours while every gang member followed Thurgood's ritual, signing and paying a monetary pledge, he may have planned his time in the car with Poet more appropriately.

The upside, however, was the expeditious nature of the trade; the gangs excited to move along to a promised demonstration of the weapons, using a couple of Judges' heads as targets.

There were so many choices, and it gave them time at least to consider how best to build a corpse. The dorsal and ventral rounds equipped to the weapon were engaged by four buttons above the grip: fire, bullet, poison dart and electrocution.

There was an Instagram post of the Judges with a gun aimed at each of their heads by Shaquan 'Reverse-Bachman-in-this-bitch' Arnold for three and a half minutes before a Brotherhood member had to force him to take it down. The spectacle, as far as Judge Jones could see, was worthy of a photo. The Brotherhood members walked the grounds with forms, collection bags and tablets affixed with credit card readers.

One dollar, Judge Jones thought while observing them sign and pay. Even in a crowd that large, there wasn't anything that Thurgood couldn't have achieved through a dozen other means. How did production even continue at that low price point? Judge Jones wondered, if only to keep from pissing himself.

There was a familiar obedient freedom about it all, Ezekiel considered, watching the not-so-free market. Anyone too proud, too individual, was turned away. It seemed Thurgood had no room for the non-believer.

"He got the same e-mail as everyone else," Ezekiel overheard a Brotherhood member say to two members of 'The Subversively Named Gang' gang.

"Listen, bruh, he's—we came all this way, my boy's just new," said the senior of the two.

"New? To... to *readin'*, my nigga?" The Brotherhood frowned.

When the guns were properly distributed with all-sized grey monk's robes folded neatly beneath them, the Judges were dragged forward again.

Catastrophe waited, with his microphone in hand, raised high until his audience stopped their calls for the Judges to burn and bleed and everything else.

How the shit did they know? Ezekiel wondered as Catastrophe looked the Judges over, and after a requisite cold-motherfucker glare, flapped the flat of his palm over their helmets. After a full minute of slapping at them like they were bongos or something, he brought the microphone back to his mouth.

"Woop-ditty-woop! The *law* is here, my niggas! See, the thing is, the Judges? These muh-fuckas think they somethin' speshal. They just you, though, feel? They just on some IR Roth shit while we out here—Y'all hear me out there? We. Out. Here! On some majority high-risk shit, my niggas!"

The warehouse obliged with a bull-penned, rancorous applause.

He looked them over again with a hand scratching under his thin beard, as if pondering, as if he or Ezekiel would be surprised when he ultimately decided to start by blowing away the Black dude. He tore away Judge Jones's helmet, kicking it aside and letting it rattle and roll a few feet from them.

Well, at least there's that, Ezekiel thought, staring at his own worn, piss-filled, sleep-deprived form in the reflection of the black visor.

"Y'all thought y'all was so slick, *didn't you?* Y'all fuckin' Rambo-ass niggas in here tryna fuck tha game up for us hard-workin' folk 'cause Gurney signed a piece of paper, my nigga? How that paper hollin' up now, hm? Yo people ain't get you ready for this, did they? Ain't get you prepped for this Viet Cong shit you done stumbled yo bitch ass into." Catastrophe paused for the laughter, the sky-scathing gunshots, the Cheddar Chips leader finally shuffling back to his feet.

"First thing we go'n do is show you what we can do here..." With that, Marisa scooped up Judge Jones's helmet, tucked it under her arm, and took a few steps back to let Catastrophe through. Judge Jones almost sighed in relief seeing the helmet in Marisa's hold.

Carl's teeth, studded with steel, glittered harshly against Jones's eyes when he grinned. Catastrophe clasped a hand beneath Jones's chin and spat a long, stringy clump of phlegm in his face, watching it run down his nose.

"See, you are *just another nigga under siege*. Their siege. You think you know that this is just an issue of order, but this shit life and def, my nigga. Your life, our life, anyone that ain't what they want this world to be. How many of us gon' exist if we ain't taking care ah us, if we ain't—?"

Carl paused for a moment, and Ezekiel saw in the flinch in his eye that the truth in black bodies had returned to him. He wasn't just speaking to Ezekiel, but the massive swell of the Brotherhood that his Thurgood had enlisted, and those yet to be swayed. He'd excluded every non-black body in his declaration of pain, of the things that had been taken, of a fire in rise.

"You see," Carl started after spinning to the rest of them. "By nigga, I refer to *all* my niggas. I refer to the nigga in you, Terry, and you, Jared, and you Kevin, and you! Yes—yes, you, Chadwick. You all are in this, with this. We Brotherhood, we brothas, we niggas are all, in the end, in *some shit* if we do not unify as a niggahood."

There was silence, and then, as Ezekiel readied for Carl's swansong to fall flat, there was an encore from the crowd.

"This nigga is soundin' real lit!" screamed Sean Smith, a former tennis player from Ohio.

"Thank you, thank you so much, my nigga," Carl said, before turning back to Ezekiel with a grin.

Shit, he's good, Ezekiel conceded. Judge Jones hadn't expected the sloppy play to work, but trading off the word *nigga* proved to be a hell of a play.

"So!" Carl started, taking a few steps back and pulling his gold-plated pistol, courtesy of Thurgood, from his back waist. "What do y'all want to see? Y'all wanna see him *melt?* Y'all wanna see him bleed out? Or y'all want to see him electrify like a cartoon in this muh' fucka?" His adoring audience filled the room with laughter, shouting out suggestions.

Jones had never been one for ruining a good time—mostly because he didn't know much about them to begin with—but he knew, as Marisa moved the helmet into one hand and pulled a small, round grenade out of a pocket with the other, that the show was soon to be at an end.

Sleep now, sweet boy, know the fruit will fall in time.

It's been an honour, Judge; know your sacrifice won't be in vain.

Before Catastrophe could fire the winning munitions, Marisa dropped the helmet and threw the grenade as hard as she could through the warehouse. The explosion roared, sending the bodies of the belligerent and brash scattering.

Carl eventually climbed to his feet, shaking off the thin sparkles of light and fuzz swimming across his eyes from the jarring spell of utter catastrophe. He cast about for Jones, hoping to find some solace in taking his life, but saw Marisa freeing both Judges. One more thing the law had taken from him that day.

The masses, armed with weapons they could barely begin to understand, began to shoot at will at the sparse targets of Poet, Jones and Marisa. The *booms* reverberated throughout the building, as Catastrophe hid beneath his podium from the haze of hell.

"Y'all niggas need to calm this—fuckin'—*fuck!*" Catastrophe couldn't so much as finish a sentence. The podium gradually crumbled under the onslaught.

JUDGE JONES KNEW what had to be done as soon as the first fire blazed. It was messy, it was a titan of paperwork, but if it'd ever been necessary, it'd been then.

"ARE YOU FUCKING NUTS?"

Judge Poet, it'd seemed, wasn't so keen on the idea.

"We have another plan? You know how important this is, how *fucked* we are if we don't. He *knew we were here,* he has more information than us, his technology is more advanced than ours, this became—*cover!*" Judge Jones threw himself back as a bright line of fire came at them from above. They split, Marisa falling away from the two Judges.

"*This became,*" Judge Jones started, as he and Judge Poet crouched behind a conveyor belt in the warehouse, "more important than a couple of militant thugs as soon as that happened. We can't risk—"

"Okay, just—just fucking do it, then!" Judge Poet spat.

"We'll need to get to the centre of the room," Jones grunted.

Poet spat out a string of obscenities, but finally found something inside, something insidious within to temper him back to form. "Well, let's go show these fuckers some *Rambo* shit, Judge Jones."

Poet laughed, and Ezekiel nodded back. Then Poet reached into one of his pockets, took out a smoke ball and squeezed it in his hand to activate it. He hurled it forward and began his attack, Jones following behind.

"Raven Georgia," Poet said, reaching out to Judge Jones, who implemented the manoeuver—drilled into them in the Academy—without so much as a blink. They clasped wrists and fell backwards, catching themselves before they hit the ground, guns drawn and ready. The bullets meant for their heads missed, even as they dispatched the targets behind each other's backs.

They pulled each other to their feet, and threw themselves back into the battle.

His hands grew weary of the pull of the trigger, of the hammer, of the things that broke through skulls while he fought through the smoke. He and Poet kept tossing them out, as they worked towards the centre of the room. When they arrived, Judge Jones at least was relieved to see Marisa jogging up to meet them.

"Initiate the LBRAD!" Marisa shouted, only a few feet away but pressed by the ongoing rage of fire and bullets and everything the maggots of mire and street life threw against peaceful justice.

The *LBRAD* system was developed a year or so after the Judges programme was founded. It was one of a few crowd-control tools the Judges had at their disposal, an enhancement on the previous LRAD system, which weaponised sound to halt unruly protesters, now shrunk to pocket-size and heightened from annoying to paralysing.

"Initiating," Judge Jones screamed, waiting for death. He knew the risks without his helmet, but it was necessary.

He and Poet pulled palm-sized disks from their belts, slapped them on the ground and dived as far away as they could before the machines began their culling song.

Screams echoed through the warehouse. Judge Jones sprawled on his back, trying to wrap his hands over his ears but feeling the sticky blood popping out of it, seeing Pellegrino doing the same. He watched, in the distance, as some began to hemorrhage blood from every available orifice, as if trying to escape their own bodies.

Judge Poet lasted a little longer thanks to his helmet, but as close as he was to the devices, the noise pierced even him.

Ezekiel's eyes, while waiting for sweet death to arrive, finally fell over Catastrophe, who seemed more resistant than some of his cohorts. The gangster was still on one knee, with what little wits the death noise left him. He tore the shirt off, ripping one of the sleeves free and wrapping it around his ears, knotted at his forehead to keep his line of sight clear. A few others tried, like Catastrophe to fight back, though with less thought, still firing their weapons indiscriminately. It didn't take long for a stream of flame to reach Catastrophe's podium, igniting the hastily applied varnish. The fire roared and raged, leaping through the dusty air to the stacked boxes littered throughout, tickling against everything, licking its lips and hungry to sate itself.

In the heat and the haze, Jones felt his body breaking down in the sound, until, suddenly, it wasn't any longer. The first thing he heard that wasn't from a vortex of eldritch terror was the crunch of Catastrophe's foot over the shattered LBRAD tools.

Catastrophe clutched Ezekiel by the throat, dragging him around to meet his gaze.

"You niggas think you *winnin'* this shit, my nigga? You think we ain't already won? You ain't fuckin ready for what about to happen, for us to take this shit over! Hm? Oh, you can't *breathe*, muh'fucka? The fuckin *law* can't breathe, ain't *that* jus—"

Catastrophe, with at least two paragraphs left of monotonous grandstanding, suddenly stopped short. He dropped Judge Jones and turned, looking down to see the slim, serrated glee over Jimmy 'Shank-A-Nigga-In-Tha-Back' Brown's face.

"You… shady-ass nigga," Catastrophe spat, scrabbling for the knife wedged deep into his back.

"Talkin' stick, bitch!" Jimmy shouted, darting as fast as he could to the exit.

Judge Jones struggled to stand, throat raw from the smoke and the strangle. Pellegrino shoved him to his feet from behind.

"Ma'am," Judge Jones croaked as Poet helped from the other side.

"Judge Jones," she returned.

Ezekiel eventually took his arms as he found his own strength to move again. The gauntlet of gang-banging vermin proved harder to cut through amongst an engulfing flame. However many were foolhardy enough to delay their escape found the Judges were just as tenacious. They pushed, they fought, they judged.

Poet stumbled as a bullet clacked into his helmet, but he rolled and sprawled himself out, weapon aimed, and fired a single shot at one of the hooded figures towering over him.

The twenty-one-year-old pit bull shelter worker's head exploded. The splatter distracted the surrounding thugs long enough for Poet to steal the sawed-off from the fallen corpse, spinning upwards from the ground. He made quick work of the thirty-two-year-old mother of two, and the local mailman who once found your dog when you left the door open.

"We have to get the hell out of here, Poet!" screamed Jones, grabbing the older man and shoving him through the door ahead of him.

It was nearly the last thing he said, as a burning slab collapsed towards him. But before it made impact, Jones was shoved forward by Pellegrino. He stumbled and turned to the suddenly flame-filled doorway.

"She's gone! Go! GO! FUCKING GO!" Poet hollered, yanking Judge Jones away. Jones followed him out the building. But before they reached the night, a wayward explosive detonated in the hall behind them, launching them through one of the frosted glass panels lining the entrance.

As the fire fell, Carl 'Catastrophe' Patterson contemplated the potential oversight in not keeping a tighter eye on Jimmy 'Shank-A-Nigga-In-Tha-Back' Brown. He crawled in search of life, coughing and screaming "Nigga!" as loud as he could, nearly two thousand times, one for every time they'd reduced him or his brethren to that word in the place he'd been born, year by year. It was fitting though, and his laughter filled ever corner, echoing across every corpse the proud were no longer burdened with.

The truth of life and death, those things, the only things he'd ever seen truly separate-but-equal, had style to them. Maybe it was that Old Testament, that part he should have feared, but damn if it wasn't poetry. As the last of the fire washed over his prone body, melting away the sin to leave the beauty, Carl 'Catastrophe' Patterson left this mortal coil as anything but a cold motherfucker.

AALIYAH

A HOUSE FILLED to its tits by mayhem—and the means to produce it—is not a home. It's what we had, though.

Thurgood made good on his promise. He let me hold my boy, *our* boy, as if it was a gift for him to give. I wasn't sure which one of us was the child as I held Elijah. I told him I loved him. I gave him kisses and I gave him lies.

I ate the food they brought to the room they promised I wouldn't stay in forever; eventually they realised I skipped on the bullshit that'd come on the side. Elijah did what Elijah does, and made everyone fall in love with him. I wanted to forget their humanity, though, to bleed them of it, but as is probably evident from most of the things I've touched on, I will ultimately fail.

I held out for a decent amount of time. The first week, I would snatch Elijah away by the arm, dragging him off if one of Colin's hooded 'Brotherhood' members so much as breathed in his direction. This was, admittedly, ill-conceived; the preoccupation of pre-teens is to find all the ways their mothers are monsters. I eventually relented, slightly, knowing if one of them so much as spoke about Thurgood's weapons, his quote-un-fucking-quote 'mission,' that I would show them the terror of a mother loaded up on a lifetime of punk music and three free Jiu-Jutsu classes.

They—Thurgood's in-and-out associates—seemed to get the message. It was another week before I ventured past monosyllabic responses to their questions. While I stewed in a petty piss mood, Elijah was making new friends. The closest was Feng, who I minded the least as she rarely bothered with that ridiculous monkish robe. She wore a smock most days, when I'd watch out the window of my room in the garden out front of the house.

I'd forgotten the light for a time. I would wilt away in a room not my own, glad for the reprieve when Elijah insisted on helping Feng outside. In the moments he spent away I could stop pretending, if only for a while, to have any idea how I could protect him from the world.

Colin would come by, but his visits slowed around the second molar I relieved him of. His lackeys would try to play sweet, butter me up, to no avail. I decided if they wanted me here, they'd have me on my terms or not at all.

That was, until I heard Elijah screaming from the garden.

I bolted out the room, down the stairs, unaware of the footsoldiers trailing me for fear I was attempting my fifth escape. I didn't even realise they were behind me until I reached the garden.

Feng had been letting a caterpillar scoot along her palm while Elijah watched in disgust. She'd smiled, but that soon faded as she saw me standing there with a knife in my hand I must have snatched on the way out from the kitchen.

"I see you're awake, Professor Monroe," she said, lightly dropping the caterpillar as Elijah came over to hug me tight. I watched Feng give a nod to the men who'd chased me out the house, signalling them to leave. Elijah leaned back, told me I stunk like Billy 'Pee Pants' Jordan, bringing one of those moments of truth when a laugh is hard to bite back.

I let my gaze weigh on her for a moment as she approached us, as if it had any power in that place.

No one had called me *professor* since I taught two semesters at Harlond Washington as an adjunct. More than one student commented on the vanity hire of the famed Bullet Bitch. Of course, the little shits could have been right; I fucked up too early on to say one way or another, though.

"Professor... so he has you *aspiring* youths doing your research on us, I see," I said sweetly as Elijah tore away from me, remembering someone else was around to see him hugging his mom.

"Yes, although we've met before, professor," she said, with a smile for a friend I wasn't interested in being. "I took your class once—well, for two weeks. Realised it wouldn't count towards my history credit, so I dropped." As she mentioned it, I *did* remember her face, the crescent-shaped birthmark over her right eyebrow. I felt crummy for staring at it for a few seconds too long, the first day she popped into my class.

"Fei...?" I asked.

"Well, *Feng,* but I'm surprised you remembered me at all, ma'am."

"I'm good for remembering faces. Comes in handy for attendance during lectures, police line-ups, not much else," I returned with a diabetic sweetness.

She only smiled and nodded, looking back to her garden.

"We are growing one of our research projects here in the garden—one of *mine* anyway. Elijah was helping me until we came across our little friend." She laughed, and glanced in 'Lijah's direction. She knelt down then, to a group of lumpy tomatoes, gingerly snapping one free from the vine and bringing it to me. She dug her nails into it, red pulp staining her fingers as she bit off one half and handed me the other.

I looked down to the pulpy mess and raised a brow at her way, and she urged me on with a flutter of her eyebrows.

"You all unearthed the 23,000-year-old art of food production. What the hell was someone like you doing at a community college, Feng?" I asked, less innocently than my tone suggested as I rolled the vegetable in my hand for a moment. She smirked, waiting in silence as I took a bite. I felt everything tighten in my throat for a moment before it went down; I hadn't eaten much since I'd arrived, just enough to stay strong, just enough to not tempt Elijah to starve himself.

It settled down through my stomach and I felt everything inside snatch at it in wanting. It only took a couple of moments to feel the effects: I felt calm, but not in a way that robbed me of myself, just the clarity of dopamine.

Feng recognised the wonder on my face and chuckled a bit.

"I haven't got the flavour sorted yet, but someday, sooner than I could have without Thurgood's resources and capital, we can use produce to alleviate chemical imbalance, rejuvenate niacin receptors in nicotine addicts, stimulate appetite. A world of hurts, fixed by a tomato." She was clearly impressed with herself. I was too, but I wasn't inclined to show it.

"Neat," I mouthed, dropping the rest of it to the ground.

We'd reached the end of the adolescent boy's attention; Elijah left us to find another cult member's brain to pick. I watched him run off and turned back to Feng.

"If you fill my boy's head with your Brotherhood bullshit, I *will* kill you," I said, half expecting some form of retribution. More than her polite nod, anyway.

"I understand your concern, truly," Feng said. "The others... they don't want to cause you any harm, professor, not the ones Thurgood posts here, at least. To tell you the truth, we couldn't use these weapons against you, or your son, even if we wanted."

She saw my expression, spun her gun out and aimed it at the ground. I'd never thought they could be so silent as they were in the movies, even with the bulky silencer on the end. She slowly raised it my way, other hand raised as though to reassure me. My fists tightened at my side, but I wouldn't give her my fear. I waited for whatever she thought she had to deliver my way.

Click!

The gun stuttered and fell silent, and she refastened it to her side.

"Pretty nifty, right? You and your son are *safe* here, professor. The chamber utilises a biometric—"

"I'm not *safe* anywhere. I was *working* towards safe, my fucking *life* was working towards safe. Now what? Now, as far as the public is concerned, I've aligned myself with some fucking Black Panther Party wannabes. I'm *this* close to really, *really* bein' the Bullet Bitch, and worst of all? I think I hate hot Cheetos now. So, fuck you, and fuck *safe*," I said.

Feng recoiled at this, but big ups to her for keeping that sweetly condescending smile.

"Ma'am, we aren't the monsters you think. We're just *people*. Did you know that most of us here are college educated? Even the men. I'd say at least twice as many as have been incarcerated. Did you know that 52 percent of us here are women? That we have a voice here?"

"Talking points, seriously?" I laughed. "You have done your research."

"I'm just trying to illustrate that maybe, if you took the time to stop hating him, you'll begin to see us as people, trying to prove that we're just that, *fucking people*," she said. It was the first thing she said that didn't sound rehearsed.

She asked me to follow her through the house, to listen, and see her cohorts.

She was wrong, of course. I did, and will forever see them as human, tragically so, which was all the more reason to hate them for being so wilfully blind.

No pun intended.

Eventually, she took me to the basement of the house, where other members of the Brotherhood were floating about. They would pop in and out of half-made rooms separated by tarps.

There were smells, some familiar, some not so much. There was dank weed, there was gasoline, there was baked bread, they were as contradictory as their leader.

"*This* is what we're really about, doctor. Thurgood hasn't just given us some frail promise of tomorrow; he's backing us with the means to pursue it. We are all misfit toys, broken by a system that neglected us in one way or another. Stu over there? He's working on a drone that can scan public record information instantly to avoid disasters," she said, as a death less scattershot was somehow worth more.

"McMahon, there? He is working to isolate the effect of Halcyon Daze that alters pigmentation perception. He hopes to weaponise it against the Judges and officers. Officers like the ones you yourself have been battling in a... more *passive* way." She watched me for a reaction.

"And... what? This is the *wow* moment that Thurgood cooked up to sway me?" I asked, breaking through the moment she'd no doubt thought she'd had. "You've ruined my career, you've ruined the credibility I'd built up, trying to stop this shit. You've done nothing but fall for someone's shit about wanting to 'fight back.'"

There was the sigh, there was the smile, for a moment the empty, frilly, unbound things fell from her eyes.

"And... I don't know," she said. "I'm trying here, ma'am, I'm trying, but I don't think I can get you to see beyond *your* shit."

It jarred me a bit, even if I'd felt just as relieved to hit something real in her.

"My *shit* is something that *matters*, Feng. My shit just wasn't as flashy, as punk as yours. You know, Blacks made up—"

"Talking points? Seriousl—?"

"*Blacks made up* 34% of all people incarcerated in 2014. Did you know that? Do you know what the rate was after that?" I asked, and paused. Feng tried to wait me out, but if I was expected to play Thurgood's games, she'd give me my fucking turn.

"No," she eventually said.

"No? I don't either. *No one does.* Back in the teens, they slashed funding to collect data like that. Shit like that is what renders us *unseen*, things like that are what skew our pain. Patriarchal, racial, socioeconomical, any fucking 'al' you want to pick, are bit by bit laying still. Thing is, while you all are out here playing college philosophy majors who shoot people in the fucking face, they are *winning*. There is a *reason* flash dance anarchy won't work, Feng: it's because the powers that be, *are the powers that be*. That power has to be redistributed before you could ever hope for something new." I was monologuing, but I didn't give a shit.

"That's just... No, professor. I'm sorry, I wanted you to see the truth of it all, more than Thurgood, I think. Our revolution isn't opposed to yours." She gave a nod to two cloaked crassholes, who made their way towards us.

"Doctor Monroe is tired," Feng said. "Please escort her to her room." She tore her eyes away from us before I could look into them with my own any longer.

Two men came up behind me, clutching me under the arms, but I darted forward before they could get a firm grip. Feng tried to spin round, whipping out the gun that she'd promised could do nothing to me, but she was too slow, or I wanted it more. I landed on top of her, clawing at her and seething obscenities through spit.

"Crazy ass—!"

My hand across her face cut her off. I thought of Elijah. *Slap*. I thought of everything they wanted me to be in that house of blood and bullets, and all the things I thought I was above. *Slap, slap!* I thought of a lot of things as they tore me away.

I was tossed into my room and locked tight like a hog in a pen.

While, in my humble opinion, the display lacked the subtlety of my Bullet Bitch days, it worked well enough. To believe in a peace, a world uncursed in the tomorrow, in all those punk albums, doesn't mean sitting still and turning cheeks. It means fighting—sometimes, in times like this, more literally than others.

I waited until the night fell before reaching to my backside to take out the phone I'd pilfered from Feng.

I made a call.

CHAPTER EIGHT

"He would have had a birthday next Thursday."

When Cadet Jones heard Marisa's voice behind him, a small, unseared part of him was impressed. Had she been in the room the whole time?

Ezekiel considered her for a moment, the increasingly tattered trench coat, the increasingly tattered eyes, and then forced himself to continue packing his scant belongings.

"Why are you here, ma'am?" Ezekiel asked, done with games and arguments and anything that wouldn't put him in a plane to the first city he saw on the departure screen when he went to the airport.

It hadn't been a full hour since Jones had dumped his former bunkmate in the medical ward, bloody hand wrapped in a paper towel.

"His mother and father have divorced, they sold the house. Can't blame them, seeing what he could have been if some dumbass hadn't killed their son."

"Stop it."

"The asking price is pretty shit, might be worth renting out, so, if this whole most-important-thing-of-your-life doesn't work out, you can get into real estate maybe." Marisa shrugged.

"Did you know this would happen? Is this another test, ma'am?" Jones demanded, tossing the last T-shirt into the duffle bag.

"Officer Williams is getting a Merit Award for excellent arrest. Your old drinking buddies are proud of her too. Guess you may not have got the invite to the celebration tomorrow at your old station."

Marisa was unfazed as Ezekiel's eyes bored into her own. He walked to her, to Ocasio's bed, close enough to taste her.

"Why. The fuck. Are you here, ma'am?"

"What the fuck are *you* doing here, cadet?" Marisa said, startling Ezekiel with her sharpness. "You were my first recommendation for this programme, did you know that? No, of course you didn't, and you don't know why that is a big enough deal for me to occasionally check in on you, either. You think, what? This shit was going to be boot camp? Police academy? You think you just get straight As, put on a bitch face and boom, you're a Judge? You think there wouldn't be *sacrifice*, little boy?" Her laugh did nothing to betray the lightning building behind her eyes.

"So, what? You telling me that Fox's or *Stein's* homo-murderous bullshit is something new? It was more gratuitous, more—"

"Oh, for chrissakes, Tank, do you think we give two craps who you're banging? You think we don't know, in more detail than I like, which of you entitled emo rabbits are screwing each other over here? Getting laid doesn't stop you becoming a Judge, Cadet Jones. What *does*, however, is Valentine's Day shit. *That* will compromise you.

"Tell me, how is Cadet Ocasio's brother? We have video surveillance, Tank. We have the goddamned search history, so don't tell me you haven't accessed private record data under the guise of a superior—which, while impressive, is a gross misuse of access you shouldn't have had."

It was Ezekiel's turn to hold back a flinch.

"You're saying, what, then? That this was for *me*? You're

saying that I was your choice, and this gives you the right to—"

"What *we're* saying, Ezekiel, is that Cadet Ocasio was shown to have too much baggage, too much held over from the old guard. He was never going to make it. We saw a cadet break reg for said space waste, and thought it important to evaluate their resolve—"

"'Resolve'? What the shit does that even *mean?* He cut his *hand* open."

"That… *wasn't* what was discussed. Fox will be removed from that post, I swear, and I'm sorry, Ezekiel. But only for that." She was honest, she was vulnerable, but she wasn't at any point ready to concede that all of it was, as Ezekiel saw it, fucked.

"So, what? You here to ask me to stay?" he said, nearing the door of the room.

"I'm here to remind you that you were *always* going to stay. That… that's *okay.* I'm here to remind you not to let this moment obscure what you are doing here, Cadet."

"*Wooowww,* you really—I'm not an idiot, ma'am. I'm not—"

"—anything, Cadet Jones. You. Are. Nothing. Okay, you were gifted, that's not—you were and *are* barely a citizen, Ezekiel. What did you do? What was it you were fighting for? You lived in an empty canvas, you didn't have so much as a TubeFlix account for us to measure interests by. You just had the night. When the day went dead, you became something, the only thing that meant you were *here,* alive."

He wanted to laugh. He wanted to do anything but acknowledge that his hand had left the doorknob.

"How do you create a new guard, Cadet Jones? Better yet, how do you create a new guard from the scraps of the old? We can't enlist children—not *yet* anyway—and we can only work with what we have. Most of them come with baggage, including the ones who have a shot in hell of making it. Brass tacks, though? You're different, Jones. You are a single, highly accredited officer who at most could *pretend* to be one of them, who could play in a softball league or grab a beer or talk at a fucking school career day, for their trust. For them to leave you alone and complete your directive."

"Fuck you."

"Fuck me?" She smirked. "Well, never said you were a wordsmith; but more importantly, why are you pretending right now, Cadet Jones? We both know why you're still here, and we both know how this ends. Because you need someone else who sees, like you did back when you took down a tank with a single bullet. You didn't care about the protesters when you jumped in front of it, did you? You cared that there was an inconsistency, that order was being grossly ignored."

"They always say it was a tank, it was just an armoured truck—"

"You're right, that completely counters my point," Marisa said drily. She rose from the bed with a groan. "Truth is, Tank: if you leave? This all continues. Truth is, Ocasio *is* going to go home, a little light in the digits, but alive. And you are going to stay, because you're done with them, you're done trying to reason and empathise with them, and you know what they really need is for us to take control."

Cadet Jones, somehow, grew more solemn.

"The riot was destroying the city, and you didn't quite know if that was a *bad* thing, did you? You didn't need to, though. You knew that what was happening was chaos. The protesters, the police, they were all *afraid*. They had power, and they had bad intel, but they also had the full authority to use what force they needed to stop a group of dumbasses from tagging their building."

"Stop it… "

"They called you a hero, a goddamn genius. You had, what? A 9mm? You told them to stop too, right? You forgot about protocol and fired a single shot, one *impossible* shot that through the grace of leprechauns or whatever, to make it fall apart.

"You only cared about the *law*, Jones. You only cared about doing something to make you matter. That cold? That blind adherence to what is *right* over what is *easy?* That is what makes you what this country needs. We don't *need* any more Ocasios—or, if I'm being honest, any Foxes, either. You know that, don't you? The truth is, if you leave, it continues, and we're stuck with schmucks like Fox who are still *afraid*. He'll be dealt with. Trust that. Don't let a hookup ruin everything you are here for, everything we *need*."

Cadet Jones waited for the time to come where the hand would move, and let him fall from the high ground he'd lived in his whole life and into the pit with the rest of the citizens. It didn't. He walked back and sat on the bed, slumping down and burying his head into his hands.

"What do I do, ma'am?" he said, after a time he couldn't measure.

Pellegrino sat lightly on Cadet Jones's bed beside him. She placed a hand over his back, rubbing slow circles over it and letting a smile strain out.

"You do what you're told, cadet," she said sweetly, and, looking up, Judge Jones nodded.

CHAPTER NINE

WHEN POET TOOK his first life, he had, only moments before, wrapped up the final edit of his high school valedictorian speech.

He heard the cries for help, for something as silly as justice, Poet made his way to his mother's bedroom in the hopes that for once it would prove to be a mistaken case of carnal cries.

It wasn't. It was the same thing that sent his sister away to boarding school in escape. It was the same thing his mother told him to not pay any mind to. It was his mother's face, cratered swelling.

His father, whose last breath bore that clichéd stench of weakness and whiskey, had seemed surprised when Young Poet came in with death in his hands. He held the gun lightly, more carrot than stick, before passing the ultimate judgement on his father.

When his mother decided to defend the dead man rather than her son in court, Young Poet had the composure of a man who'd never had a free meal ticket. The more surprising development, however, was his choice to defend himself; the papers called him insane.

Tragic as it'd been to lose the opportunity to give a listless valedictorian speech, there was some victory in what he gained.

He learned that the only thing that really mattered, at the end of the day, were the words; pretty words in pretty books to defend his less-than-pretty soul from conviction. If not for that, scouring night after night through texts on law, on philosophy, on an asphyxiated understanding of life, he may never have become the man that dragged Ezekiel Jones from the wreckage of the warehouse.

He would have never been approached by a former classmate, some scrawny whelp who'd taken up the school honour of valedictorian after the whole 'murder' thing disqualified Young Poet. The young man had made good use of his life, more than Poet had—or at least, that was his thought meeting the Harvard Law student who changed the course of his life forever.

"Why did you do it?" he asked, sat across from Poet in the diner. "You know—that doesn't matter. Do you think it was right? Do you ever wonder if you should have done time for taking a life?" It wasn't a question you would ask someone you've only shared one class with. Asked it he did though, and Community College Student Poet mulled it over without so much as a frown.

"I suppose I could understand that, but no. No, I don't. The law is a blankie. It's—"

"Trivial?" the law student asked, or demanded. Poet only smiled, if with something a bit more magnetic than was there before.

"No. Shit, no. It's the most terrifying, powerful bit of nothing. It's only trivial, like any story, when there are too many inconsistencies. I was told time and time again that what I did was *incredible*, defending myself with no prior experience; that I'd earned people's respect. That's where I find my why, and how, at night. I saw something wrong, I made it right. Justice isn't just words, it's what we *do* with it." He wasn't sure why he needed the man to hear him.

The law student smirked. "I think that's very poetic, apologies for the pun. Granted... it's a bit of a mixed metaphor there, is it a story or a tool?"

"Oh, well, I don't know about that. What is any story if not a tool of one kind or another?"

Both men assumed the meeting would be their last. But one story led to another, that led to another, that led to Judge Poet pulling Judge Jones from the firelit warehouse, burning more brilliantly than could ever be expected by daylight.

It also may be why all the new weapons to account for, the death of Pellegrino, and the ash and debris finding its way into Judge Poet's ass-crack led him to suggest a coffee after his partner awoke.

"DESTINY HEAD. WE were... utter fucking garbage. I didn't know how to play my bass, but I did know how to look really into it. If I look back at it, though? I just had a bit too much college at that point, and was sure that anything I vomited would be important to the world," Poet said, twenty-five minutes and a bad coffee later.

"The hell does that even mean? Destiny Head?" Ezekiel laughed.

"Hell if I know. If you were to ask me then, I'd of probably freestyled something about us being at the head of a change that was necessary for the world to survive, that we were ultimately the one thing that can be the start of a new destiny, a reprise that would finally bring balance. All bullshit, of course; honestly, I joined three weeks after they'd started jamming together and was too excited that someone would let me play to even ask."

Judge Jones laughed again, watching across the diner table as Poet sprinkled his fifth pack of sugar into his cup.

"Well, maybe you can go back to it after we send in this report," Ezekiel said, sighing into his coffee. "Here's to 'Destiny Head,'" he added, raising his coffee ironically. "And to Marisa Pellegrino, who gave her life for—*holy jelly bombers.*"

When Marisa, still sporting singed garments from the night

before, slid her butt into the stall next to Poet, their glasses stayed raised high. She took a long sigh that ran down the back of her throat, not stopping until it hit the seat beneath her.

She grabbed a cup of water from the table while the Judges' eyes were too occupied to remember their coffee, searing their palms as they gaped.

Her hood was hanging by a thread; Ezekiel stared at it, trying to work out how in every multiple-choice hell she wasn't burned from head to toe.

"Well, that was a fucking show, now, wasn't it, gentlemen?" she said, slamming the water back down to the table.

"Ma'am...?" Judge Jones prompted, peeling his skin away from the ceramic and returning the cup to the table. She eyed him, and would have more than likely responded, if not for Poet's sudden cheer.

"Rein it in," she said with a huff, sliding her hand across the table to grab at Ezekiel's coffee, taking it down with the same endless swig as she'd done the water.

"Yes, ma'am," Poet said, sliding his helmet on and clipping it tight.

"I'm glad to see you made it out, ma'am," Ezekiel said. "We—*I* thought something may have happened." He turned his eyes down to the flat of the table. It'd been a long few hours without his visor, without the protection it gave from the rest of the world, but knowing Marisa, Ezekiel figured his relief wouldn't have gone unseen either way.

"Yeah, I'm okay. I mean, you know, waking up to the sound of thirty sirens while a partially burned skull stares lifelessly into your eyes wasn't, existentially speaking, a great start. Oh! At least I had the pleasure of speaking for two hours with Officer Dennison, who married a woman named Denise! It was such a fascinating story to hear *fully seven times* while they fixed the Wi-Fi to confirm my credentials."

"Well, at least we have the weapons. I'm sure there's a lot to sift through, but hopefully they lead back to—"

"We got shit, Poet. Thurgood is clever. The weapons that were seized melted in a soppy mess of hot steel by the time we reached the station. I'm not sure how he—well, how he *anything*, but it seemed in the handling, either the fingerprint locks, or something else, activated a failsafe." Marisa leaned her head back and closed her eyes.

Judge Jones remembered the heat of the flamethrower, the seared flesh, imagining the sight of that same heat turned inward.

"Well, at least we have our lives, right?" said Poet. "At least we have—apologies, ma'am, but Judge Jones and I were having a rather productive lunch before you returned from the dead to remind us we've got nowhere."

Marisa brought her head back from the ceiling.

"Well, it's good that I have actually brought something more to the table than shitty jokes and an allergy to wearing my goddamned helmet like a Judge is supposed to," she said with another sigh.

"What *do* we have, ma'am?" Judge Jones asked, dropping his voice. Marisa leaned in, a flash of a smirk passing by at the sound of Poet's helmet clicking.

"Not here," she said. "Clubhouse, gentlemen."

The Judges nodded, standing up and following their superior out of the room.

During Fargo's first hundred days of appointment, the Judges had had to move fast and steadily, sometimes ignoring the proper processes of government. Conversations caught on body cameras had been leaked, leading the new Chief Judge to make a public vow to never again bypass consultation with the Senate.

Sometimes however, time was not on his, or their, side. To avoid the possibility of Washington ears connected to Washington mouths from picking up on anything too sensitive for comfort, all discussions deemed classified were to be handled within codename 'Clubhouse.'

It was archaic, but held unfortunately true for Washington,

or for anywhere in the country where men held power and diners were sort of shitty, that statistically a women's restroom was the safest place from eavesdropping.

They entered the restroom, Judge Poet leaning against the door after they scanned it for lingerers.

"The truth is, gentlemen, that our numbers aren't strong enough. Not by half. A tip was received that you'd been set up, but no Judge in proximity to aid. Unlucky for me, I was still in Illinois, out in Elgin on business. I'd infiltrated the meeting by force, and that brings us up to speed."

"Why couldn't you communicate all of that to us with, you know, *a phone?* Or do anything else that would have helped us *before* we arrived?" Judge Poet asked, and Marisa shot him a glare from beneath slightly singed eyebrows.

"I had every means of communicating this information to you, I also had the means to withdraw you from the mission, but—"

"The mission mattered," said Jones mechanically. "The mission is the only thing that matters. If we were aware, we could have compromised the acquisition of Carl Patterson, and the largest black-market distribution of arms in Chicago's history."

Marisa smirked proudly. "Precisely."

"Well, lot of good that did, *ma'am,*" parried Poet. "We have none of Thurgood's connections, the Brotherhood members who didn't die escaped, and quite possibly the largest militia in history is gathering while we sit in this shitter."

"We have what we've *always* had, gentlemen. We have the Law."

Judge Poet sucked his teeth. "But do we have anything *else,* ma'am?"

Marisa rolled her eyes before making her way to one of the stalls, opening it and standing on the toilet seat. She pushed up the flimsy ceiling tile, allowing the thick briefcase she'd previously stored there to fall into her hands.

She heaved it to the sink countertop.

"*Whew.* Well, Judge Entitled, I do have a new helmet for

Judge Jones, and a bit of fun for you boys," she said, unlatching the combination lock with a pair of 20s.

She first tossed the helmet to Ezekiel, who wasted no time in stuffing it over his head. What was left in the black briefcase were two weapons, not so different from their own weapons, slightly larger, augmented somehow from within.

"We're no Thurgood, but our boys in R&D do what they can. A disclaimer? Don't break these, *please*. They are prototypes. They come equipped with a doubled capacity on your standard issue weapons, as well as"—she paused, taking one out and flipping it upside down for a moment to read a serial code etched on the bottom of the handle—"two additional munition options. Two buttons. One initiates a strobe light—"

"A *strobe* light?" Judge Poet interrupted, picking up the other weapon.

"Yes. A fucking strobe light. The other, which is activated with the second button, is a grenade launcher." She lazily handed the weapon over to Ezekiel, who checked the scope and measured the weight in his hands.

"What grenade, ma'am?" he asked, setting the weapon down, pulling out his old one and emptying what was left in his clip.

"That's a question for the nerds, but I'm told it makes the Milkor look like a little bitch." She chuckled.

"Well, this is all good and admittedly *cool*, but what are you aiming us at, *ma'am*?" Judge Poet asked.

"We storm Thurgood and his annoying-as-shit street monks," Pellegrino replied. "We take them out, we do the hero thing."

She noticed the rally hadn't fired them up as expected, so she changed tack. "He has them strapped to the tits. You know what order *isn't*? This shit. This is that *other* thing." She clacked the suitcase closed. "Someone got caught slippin' up. The call was made from a cell phone. GPS puts it in a local house in the name of one Mrs. Patterson. Who was the grandmother of—"

"Catastrophe," Jones finished.

"Precisely. The call was short, Aaliyah Monroe has been abducted; at least, that's what was said. The call included the address, not that we needed it, but she couldn't have known that."

"Well, now what? Why are we sitting here, ma'am?" asked Poet. "Shouldn't we be mobilising all Judges active in the Illinois area and ending this crap once and for all?"

Ezekiel nodded in agreement.

"Well, that *would* be protocol, but I don't know what the hell we're walking into there," Marisa said with shoulders slumped and nearly burned body ready to shut down.

"What do you mean, ma'am?"

"The information wasn't given freely. Protocol is for local law enforcement to surrender any pertinent information about ongoing cases to us. The location of one person of interest in the largest technological revolt is pretty fucking pertinent, don't you think? The old guard kept it from us. They are *still* sitting on it. I thought that, at first, they wanted to be heroes, swoop in and make us eat crow."

"But?" Poet asked.

"But we're still sitting in a bathroom trying to figure out what to do about this," Jones said.

Pellegrino smiled wide, with one finger on her nose and the other pointed at him. "Two for two."

"Why the hell would they do that?" Poet asked, and she shrugged.

"All I know is that they're not moving, *at all*. My theory? They *want* Thurgood to win, whatever he's doing; they're compromised. Maybe not all of them, though," she amended, as she saw Jones flinch.

The thought of Ocasio being part of something like that hurt him more than he'd expected.

"So, what's the move, ma'am?" Judge Jones asked, composing himself.

"We fight. We take this right to them, and we do it *alone*,"

Marisa said, and this time it was Judge Poet who flinched.

"Well, that worked out *so* well for us last time."

"You think you came here to *live*, Judge? Get your shit together, we have a job to do."

THE JUDGES ARRIVED on Nuohlac Street to find it silent and peaceful. The door was cracked, sweltering a heat out into the world beneath the light.

Judge Jones was first. A thug in grey robe started reaching for something that looked enough like a gun, enough like a reason, and Judge Jones answered in kind. Ezekiel stepped over his body from the door to the corner of the den. Poet followed.

The next room was filled by one couch, a zebra-print throw rug, a TV affixed to a hastily-fastened wall mount, and not a single Brotherhood member.

"They know—" Judge Jones started to whisper, but he stopped at a footstep from above. He pointed to Judge Poet, and then at the steps at the end of the room leading to the basement. Judge Poet nodded, making his way to clear it out.

Judge Jones made his way to the flight of stairs leading up, before tapping the commlink at the base of his helmet.

"*Justice blind, ma'am,*" he whispered, and after a moment heard a quick "*Affirmative*" from Marisa crackle through the comm.

Three seconds later, the lights throughout the house—and the entire street—were shut down. Jones tapped the side of his helmet to initiate the dual night vision and body heat sensors through his visor.

When he reached the top of the flight of stairs he paused, unclipped a rattler from his belt, and slung it down the hallway.

There were the expected shots of gunfire in response. The flashes of fire, the boom of bullets, told Judge Jones of five firearms waiting through the hall for him.

"Come on, you pussy!" he heard one scream, and being a civil servant, Judge Jones obliged.

Tumbling forward, he sprang upwards, wrapping an open hand over the closest cultist's face and twisting his head round with a *snap*. As the body began to fall, Jones tapped the button at the side of his new weapon, directing the strobe light at the rest of the cloaked trash.

As they blinked in the staccato light, Jones fired true. Nothing in the world seemed as fair or consistent as a centre-mass shot, and it didn't disappoint as Ezekiel fired round after round, stopping only at the faint *click*.

"You murdering sonofa—" A man lunged at him from the darkness. Jones snatched a weapon from a corpse and hurled it as best he could at the voice.

When it connected, and the body toppled back with a wince, the rest of them opened fire again: a line of flame, the *thack* of bullets against the walls, and the familiar *tic-tic-tic* of a taser.

Ezekiel fell flat to the ground, smacking visor-first against it and losing the augmented sight.

The light from the fire was more than enough to see, so he popped back to his feet, snatched the wall-hanging mirror next to him from the wall and hurled it at the ceiling down the hall.

It impacted, and the glass shattered in jagged pieces over the remaining cultists, and they looked up.

Their screams blossomed in Jones's ears, but there was still work to be done. He reloaded, weighed their crimes and granted them their due, one bullet at a time.

"Judge Poet, rooms scanned upstairs, seven down, report," he said through the communicator.

POET, WHO'D BEEN indisposed by the Brotherhood members filling the basement, decided to apologise for not answering late, if he made it out alive. The Brotherhood members down here were less panic-prone than those his partner dealt with; one of them had thought enough to use her weapon's flame mode to give her fellow cultists a fighting chance.

Poet deactivated the night vision mechanism in his visor, regaining clear sight as a robed gangster darted towards him, and quickly dropped a smoke bomb.

The Judge crouched low as an arm swung to lop off his head, then popped upwards, letting his helmet crunch the thug's nose into his face. The lowlife sprawled out flat, and Poet shoved the heel of his boot through his throat.

He took off his helmet and hurled it at another thug's head. The cultist ducked low, evading the helmet, but not the butt of Poet's pistol, cracking into the waste's jaw.

He flipped the gun back around before the remaining thug could respond. His aim was never anything special, but thankfully, the crescent-shaped birthmark on her face was target enough, and he laid out the probable drug addict and dropout with a merciful bullet to her face.

JUDGE JONES, STILL waiting for his partner to respond, continued dispatching the Brotherhood in the rooms along the hallway. They were easy enough game, and he'd judged them each within two seconds flat; just as the old guard would a pellet gun in a Cleveland park.

Clearing them out, one by one, bullet by bullet by bullet, was taxing. He wasn't sure, as he reached the final room, that even the upgrades Marisa had provided could keep up; by his count, he had at best five rounds left, at worst three. It was immediately academic, though, as he was tossed across the room by a robed thug that tested their tailor's one-size-fits-all strategy to the limit.

Jones had dealt with bigger, badder, and less breakable, but he *was* tired. The demon lumbered at him, and he tossed his weapon aside and rushed the thug, tackling him to the ground. It had little impact, as he plucked Jones off him with a grunt and slammed him against the ceiling.

"Fuck what you think," Judge Jones wheezed, as he scrambled to his feet, closed in and swung a knee under the beast's chin. It wailed and fell to its knees, gripping at its mangled, mandingo chin.

As Judge Jones leaned in, trying to grasp at the thick wrist, he felt like a five-year-old taking on Hulk Hogan.

"What the hell *are* you…?" he asked as the *thing* snatched its arm back, dripping thick, foamy spit, like a streetwalking waste who couldn't be bothered with a sidewalk.

It drove its foot into Jones's jugular, sending him sprawling.

The beast heaved itself to its feet again, and Judge Jones reached for his pistol, only then realising it had fallen to the floor when he'd come in. He resigned himself to a hopefully swift death.

"Martin?" A woman's voice, an incantation that made the creature turn. Before it could reply, something smashed into the behemoth's face with a heavy *thwack*, rendering it unconscious even as it fell to the ground.

"*Marisa, showtime,*" Jones said into his communicator, and as planned, the power came back on throughout the house.

Judge Jones turned off the night vision of his visor to see the person of ever-growing interest, Aaliyah Monroe.

He looked to the weapon across the room, and then to the woman once more. She dropped the pistol in her own hand and reached down to him.

"Could have shot him with that, you know," Jones said as he climbed to his feet.

Aaliyah looked at the prone hulk for a moment, nudging him with a foot to confirm he was out. "No, I couldn't. These weapons, only specific people could use them. Also, not much of a murderer, *Judge*."

"Not what I hear."

"You heard fucking wrong. I'm—I was set up, I haven't done anything *wrong*, not the way you all wish I did, anyway. My son was taken, I gave testimony under duress… your honour."

Jones retrieved his weapon and checked the room for any remaining danger. "Where is your son?"

"Not here. I don't know what Thurgood did with him; if he's been hurt, I swear—"

Judge Jones stopped her before she could finish, clapping a hand over her mouth and shoving her back to the room's closet. He watched her slump to the ground.

"We intercepted your call to the Chicago PD, Dr. Monroe," he said. "We are here to *end* this. Keep yourself hidden." He tossed her his old pistol, with half a clip.

He slammed the door before she could respond, muffling her parting words, and made his way to the now-illuminated hall, seeing his partner waiting with Pellegrino at the end of it.

As he ran to meet them, he wondered about the quality of his new helmet, most importantly the sound input settings. While it was able to pick up Aaliyah's fleeting words, it made them into nonsense.

I never called the cops...

He couldn't see how such a blatant lie could serve her.

"Status, Judge Jones?" Poet asked.

Jones tapped the bottom of his gun, prompting Poet to produce a spare clip.

"Fine," he said as he loaded. "Last room. You ready to meet Thurgood?"

"Drokk, yeah." Marisa laughed.

The two stopped.

"The hell?" Judge Poet asked.

She shrugged. "I heard a kid at the precinct say it the other day."

Jones shook his head and stepped back to thrust a foot at the door, smashing it open.

After the mass murder, nightmarish night terrors, and poor grammar, Jones was open to endless possibilities: a monster, a robot, a living god... he was almost disappointed at what he saw. A sunglass-wearing, quivering minority on his knees, with his hands stretched up in the sky.

"Who are you? Where is Thurgood?" Judge Jones demanded, marching in with his weapon. He noticed the man didn't flinch. Pellegrino and Poet surveyed the room, finding nothing but the simpering man in front of them.

"I—I'm just—*oh, god, don't hurt me!*" the man whined.

"Answer. Him," Judge Poet added, pushing the lip of his weapon against the shivering man's head.

"I—*oh, oh, god,* I'm—I'm *Colin Jobee*. I am a-a-a-a engineer. I was brought here by Thu-Thu-Thurgood, I crafted his weapons for the Brotherhood," Colin wailed.

Judge Poet took a step back, lowering his weapon slightly before giving Judge Jones a shrug.

Judge Jones looked him over, and raised his own pistol. He caught the twist of Marisa's face and held out an open palm to reassure her.

He turned the strobe light function on, and, after a moment, shut it down.

"He's blind," Judge Jones said, holstering his weapon, and continuing to search the room.

"Yuh-yes… is that… is that against the law, or—?"

"Shut. It," Judge Poet spat, aiming his weapon at Jobee. He kept it there for a moment, registered Pellegrino's grimace, and awkwardly shuffled the weapon against Jobee's head for him to *feel* it. Pellegrino gave a condescending smile and flashed a thumbs-up, then continued her search of the room.

"Seventeen down in total, ma'am," Jones reported. "Aaliyah Monroe is armed in a closet next door. She isn't here of her own volition."

Marisa glanced back to the door, to the suddenly stilled blind man, and back to Judge Jones. "What did she tell you…?" she asked, meeting Jones's eyes and nodding back to Jobee. Ezekiel nodded back.

"Everything," Judge Jones said, hand over his holstered weapon.

Colin Jobee's shaking fully stopped at the word *everything*. He began towards the door, but was stopped by Judge Poet's forearm.

"She… she told you lies," Colin said, writhing on the ground for a moment before composing himself, on his knees.

Jones nodded thoughtfully, but stayed silent. He waited,

and waited, and as Judge Poet rolled his eyes, waited for a bit longer.

"She told me that you'd say that, *Thurgood*," he eventually bluffed.

Colin, keeping his hands raised, sighed, long and low, and slipped into a smile. "Whatever you *think* she said is circumstantial at best. Yes, though, let's take time to mull over the rantings of a confessed consort of *Thurgood*. More importantly, I'd like to speak with your superior about your *brutal* methods, officers."

"Yeah, I'll call HR in the morning. Get the fuck up," Pellegrino commanded.

"Well, *thank you*. I have to say though, there is a more pressing matter to attend to, *Marisa,* was it? Excuse my impertinence, but if I may explain, *lives* hang in the balance!" Jobee wailed.

Jones noticed Marisa eyeing him and turned to meet her gaze for a moment, before turning back to Thurgood.

"Talk."

"The *weapons*. I—as disclosed in the contract I've distributed to my customers, the weapons have a… a kind of kill switch, excuse the pun. As they were, and still *are* in production, it was only ethically sound of me to do so, in case they were found ill-suited to private use."

"Of course," Judge Poet huffed.

"Thurgood, from what I've overheard, is a kind of prophet to these people. Meanwhile, even as this 'Brotherhood' marches as one on every police precinct in Illinois, I remain but a humble entrepreneur and a concerned citizen," Colin said, letting tears spill. "I am also, a—a friend to all human kind. And what you do for friends is… you cherish your friends, look out for your friends, lift up your friends, love your friends." He was sobbing now, and for a moment, Jones wondered if Colin Jobee really *wasn't* Thurgood. Anyone who would carry the name of a Judge with such entitlement couldn't possibly blubber like this.

"For cock's sakes man, stop with the bullshit and say your words," Judge Poet groaned.

Jobee winced. "What... what time is it?"

"Quarter after eight, why?" Pellegrino said, glancing at her watch but keeping her gun aimed tightly over Colin.

"Oh! Oh, no! It's already started... the TV, please, it has to be on some local station."

Marisa glanced over to Judge Jones again, jerking her head towards the TV. Jones obliged.

Jobee had fortuitously left the TV last on a news station. 'It' had, as promised, happened.

"What is this?" Judge Jones asked, heavily.

Jobee grinned for a moment, unable to see the broadcast, but listened along with the rest of them, his hands still stretched to the sky.

They heard the description of the Brotherhood members surrounding multiple police stations throughout the city, each armed with the weapons he'd built for the cruel 'criminal mastermind,' Thurgood.

"They were ordered by—by Thurgood to take... retributive justice for all the wrongs made against them, by blood. God forgive me, they can *do* it too, with my weapons, with my— *listen*. I can stop them. I can—"

Judge Jones stepped out of line, his body filling with a rage, threatening to drown. He felt pushed the cold steel of his weapon against Jobee's head, against what could only be Thurgood's head, and felt no hope at all.

"Judge Jones!" Pellegrino shouted, but he didn't respond.

"Well, I don't know how *that* is going to help anyon—"

"How can we stop this?" Judge Jones snapped before Colin could finish.

The blind, black, bent man shrugged, slowly lowering his arms from a surrender he'd never intended to give, and carefully climbed to his feet.

"As I mentioned before, I have integrated a kill switch—oh, what's that sound? Are the officers on their way out? Not long now… " Jobee cooed.

He was right. Judge Jones turned briefly to the TV, watching as the helicopters recorded the officers emptying out from the back of the building, strapped in the weapons of old, weapons that held no hold over the future.

"I—and excuse any implication here—I don't quite know how to *trust* this won't result in yet another false accusation from the Justice Department on my character? Now, if I had *assurance* that I would be free from any unconstitutional handling of my person…"

"What do you want, Jobee?" Jones demanded.

"Well, I want to be *wanted*, like any rational businessman of the century. You see, I was unjustly made into this… beggar you see before you, when I was catapulted from a budding future and—"

Judge Poet fired a round into the ceiling, putting a halt on Jobee's speech. "Not the time for the whole 'Sympathy for the Devil' speech, citizen. Answer my partner's question."

"Yes, well, I don't want—or, I don't want to give this *Thurgood* control over anything. I am a proud taxpayer, I don't even deduct for political donations, so, you know, good guy here. I admire, and want to play my part in continuing this tradition of protection, of *service*. What I want most, though, is a form of income. So, I leave the choice here to you…" Jobee seemed almost pained, almost human.

Pellegrino lowered her weapon, and ordered the other two to follow suit.

"What choice?" Jones asked.

"Well, speaking in hypotheticals here, of course, but… this is not going to end well," Colin said slyly. "People won't walk away from this… But I wonder who you would want to remain? We have the intrepid, tenacious police force of Illinois. They aren't all that bad, are they? But they aren't going to go without a fight. What if you don't *have* to fight? What if, by way of an unpressed button, the fight was finished for you?"

"And door number 2?" Marisa questioned, paying no mind to Jones's incredulous look.

"The weapons are deactivated at the opportune moment, after a shot or two, and two-thirds of those contributing to the murder capital of the country are taken out in a heartbeat. There is the start of, if not justice, at least order," Colin said, mouthing the last word slow and sticky.

Judge Jones looked back to the TV: the gangs were there, some sporting the robes and some not; not that it seemed this Thurgood, this invisible man, cared much for their unity.

The officers did just as Colin said they would, emptying out and readying themselves for a death they couldn't begin to comprehend.

"What would you require, citizen, to give us the tech?" Marisa asked.

"Ma'am?" Jones prompted, without reply.

"Well, skimming over the whole trust-but-verify speech I had planned," Jobee replied, "I've... prepared for such a possibility. If one of your dogs wouldn't mind—the dresser over there? Top drawer."

Marisa nodded to Judge Jones, who went to the dresser and pulled out a single black folder. When he opened it, there was a contract, filled with the familiar legalese he'd always hated dealing with.

He couldn't help looking at the letterhead, though: a company logo that only read G. A. *Manufacturing* and nothing more.

He took it over to Marisa, who glanced it over and laughed hollowly.

"You. *Assholes*. I can't believe I didn't see it earlier..."

"What is it?" Poet asked, but Pellegrino didn't acknowledge the Judge's question, instead glancing at the TV for a few moments before turning back to Colin Jobee.

"So, Mr. Jobee, I don't expect the CEO of General Arms Manufacturing will be joining us as well today, will she?" Marisa asked, and treason danced across Jobee's face like a child proud of his trickery.

"No, unfortunately, you just have me. Though I do speak for her. We trust each other entirely. You, though—*tsk*— you haven't been so trustworthy, have you? We know, for instance, that you've been flirting with Metal Storm about their weaponry developments behind our back. For shame, Pellegrino, for shame. You should know that we aren't *angry*, but saw it only as an opportunity to *show* you our developments. While Thurgood, wherever and whoever he may be, hasn't been the best business partner, he has done everything legally."

"One dollar..." Jones said.

"Oh, you're familiar with our price point? Well, if you don't spend you don't win, bit of a business 101 tip for you there. I digress, call this a signing bonus, in one sweep Fargo gets whatever he values more, or call it *Operation Revelations,* we know how much you love your code names. Call it whatever you want, frankly, but make your choice fast, we don't have much time." Colin Jobee seemed to relax, lowering his hands and leaning back on them.

Marisa grinned, looking at the papers, looking at the insignia of her future business partners. She looked back to the TV, withdrew her weapon, and sent a round through its centre, letting it flash to nothing but wires and darkness.

"Judge Jones," Marisa started.

"Yes, ma'am?" Jones said, staring still to the television.

"A pen, please."

Jones and Poet holstered their weapons, and Ezekiel withdrew with a pen from his belt, clicking it to wake and handing it to her. She worked her way around Jones and used his back as a surface to sign on.

"Well! That's that. Thank you for your patronage. So! Moving along, what would you like to do?" Jobee said as the scratching of the pen stopped. He reached to his back pocket and pulled out an inch-long, circular device with a button fixed in its centre.

"I'll have that, Mr. Jobee," Marisa said. Jobee tossed it

underhand towards her voice, and she caught it. She looked over to Ezekiel and Judge Poet.

"What happens, *exactly*? If I press the button?" Marisa asked.

"Hit the button, the signal goes out. It takes roughly two minutes, unfortunately," Jobee said.

"Ma'am, you can't... you know, you *know* what will happen. It won't be mercy."

Judge Jones, *Ezekiel*, was the cadet on his bed again.

"No, it won't, Jones, but it will be *order*."

Marisa tapped the button.

They heard a sizzle from within the weapons littering the room, and the hallways. They didn't hear, of course, the last breaths of the men and women in the street.

"Judge Jones, make sure to—"

"You... you—"

"*Judge* Jones. Judge Poet. Please escort Mr. Jobee out of the house. He'll need medical attention for that shoulder."

Judge Poet gave a quick nod and helped Jobee to his feet, while Judge Jones kept his eyes on Marisa.

"Judge Jones?" she asked, mildly.

"Affirmative, ma'am," he eventually replied.

As they walked the halls, Judge Jones was careful to avoid the bodies. Judge Poet seemed too weighted by Ezekiel's gaze to try and nudge him back to the man he'd met at the diner earlier that day. They stayed silent until the end of the hall, until a sound in one of the rooms drew their attention.

Aaliyah, Judge Jones thought, but then realised it'd come from a different room.

Poet rushed towards the room, leaving Jones holding Jobee.

He heard Poet screaming in the distance, but nothing returning to him, only words he'd heard so many nights, the catalyst of so many mistakes.

"Put the weapon down, *I won't ask twice, kid*."

It was the first time Colin seemed truly rattled. "No!" he screamed, attempting to rush to the room, until Jones kicked him in the sternum, knocking him to the ground.

Jones jogged past the wheezing engineer, his weapon out, entering the room to see a young boy holding one of Jobee's weapons.

"Judge Poet! Weapon *down*. This isn't—the weapons have been deactivated."

"We can't know that, not for all of them. Kid, let's not do this, let's not—"

Given more time, Poet could have explained why pointing a gun at him wasn't a great idea. He could have talked the little black boy out of killing himself through a Judge's gun. He could have done many more things, if not for the sound from across the hall. If not for Aaliyah Monroe, gun still smoking and still in her hands; if not for the bullet that split Judge Poet's eye socket, leaving him in darkness.

CHAPTER TEN

AS POET LAY there, at the end of everything the Judges' severance package promised, Ezekiel's eyes watched Elijah. Another boy dead, in one way or another. The boy hadn't breathed, standing so still for so long Ezekiel wondered if he'd been drowning in the air, stale with death and lingering between them all.

"Judge down, Judge down!" Pellegrino called out over her wrist comm. She darted to Judge Poet's side.

Ezekiel's arm shot up, dead-aimed at Aaliyah Monroe's head. Aaliyah had, true to form for a militant, readied her weapon at Judge Jones in kind.

"I—I didn't... I—"

"I hereby sentence you, Aaliyah Monroe, for murder in the second-degree—"

"Ouch. I'd say manslaughter in the second at best, if we're—"

"Colin Jobee, you are wilfully impeding an arrest." Judge Jones said without looking Jobee's way. The engineer shrugged with his arms still raised high in the air.

"Ezekiel..." Judge Jones heard Marisa call from below him, but he didn't take his eyes off the murderess who had shattered a man's life. "Ma'am?" he prompted.

"Will—Judge Poet is breathing," she said. Ezekiel didn't

remove his aim from Aaliyah's centre mass, but his finger slackened on the trigger.

"What are we doing, Judge?" he heard Colin say. He didn't have an answer. He could only wait. Wait for Poet's last breath, wait for an ambulance, wait for something, anything, that could lead to judgement.

"Cuff her. And the kid," he finally spat, not taking his aim away from Aaliyah Monroe, or the child that made his way to her, tightly clutching his mother's waist.

Marisa fumbled the cuffs as she pulled them from her trench coat, and did as directed.

When the first cars arrived, Poet was rushed away. While Chicago offered many adequate options, the Judges would see that Poet got the very best care possible. He might not be very pretty, but none of them were getting out of *Operation Revelations* unscarred.

Judge Jones made it out in a fairer condition than most of the others in the house, but he still felt a loss. There was an imbalance, in that hate burrowing into the hollow of the boy Elijah's eyes as he'd watched his mother, in a separate car, torn from his life. In that child being sent home with his remaining parent, Citizen Colin Jobee.

Aaliyah's aunt, the family lawyer she'd called before the Judges' arrived, met her niece at the precinct.

Officer Wilson was thrilled to have his perp back in custody, and the chance to protect the American public from her hysterical, abrasive rhetoric.

The law had persevered. The judgement had protected all of us. A father reunited with his son, a radical threat neutralised. There was peace.

But Jones had difficulty seeing it as earned.

Was it the bodies a button-press had broken? Was it a partner that had saved his life, seen something of worth in him, and paid a price for that humanity? Did it have something to do with the tattered moleskin he'd found that night in Aaliyah's room?

It was most likely that first thing.

Regardless of what it was, after the nigh endless paperwork, Judge Jones would seek refuge in something that mattered.

In favours he hadn't earned from boys he never took the time to love at police stations he hoped to never see again.

As he sat in that post office, sending his third letter to Officer Ocasio, dancing around what mattered and asking about the… *refugee* he'd agreed to harbour after their escape, he knew the choice he made was the right one.

That even where the darkness lay, he could be worth something; could be human.

EPILOGUE

"WE'RE CLOSED," THE waitress called back, as the bell on the door jangled. B&W's was a good place to find diner coffee in the pot that had sat around less than three hours, an award-winning tuna melt sandwich, and the rampant swell of bar-hopped bros and bastards that didn't always agree to the 3 a.m. closing time. What B&W's wasn't known for, however, was genial customer service.

"No, you're not," Judge Poet said, letting the door fall closed and twisting the lock. The waitress yelped at the sight of the Judge, or at the crinkled skin substitute, and the way it peeled at the edges around the eye.

"Holy shi—sir, your associates are waiting in the back." The waitress spoke as fast as her feet moved, as she lunged for her coat and purse behind the bar. She nearly fell over her feet as she passed the Judge, who was fortunately alert enough to catch her.

"Th—Thank you, sir, Judge, sir," she said, carefully looking away from the string of bloody puss he hadn't wiped away from his newly-robotic eye.

"The keys, Tanya?" Judge Poet said genially, before letting the woman go. She shuffled the jangled mess of keys to Poet and ducked out.

He watched her leave, or at least he meant to. The mess in the reflection of the door caught his attention, and he winced.

Judge Poet had one eye, something he found himself forgetting at times. There were things he didn't overlook, of course—the way the wind hit the synthetic nerves sewn into his grated face. His new distaste at his helmet, where it rubbed at his unreal skin. The truth of his mission, of what had always been his mission.

He eventually dragged his forty-five-minute-late ass to the women's restroom. When he opened it, the two associates he'd been expecting were just as much a gaggle of chattering dicks as he'd left them months prior.

"—not going to go that way. You can't trust the Ump Brothers, I don't care if we stay in the red for fucking ever, there isn't a world where we align ourselves with the immoral. We don't need a lobbyist, we need more taxation." Judge Stein, ginger-haired and ruddy-faced, leaned against the bathroom sink as he spoke. When he noticed Judge Poet enter, a grin flashed over his face, and the other two turned as well, if looking less pleased.

"You are late... again, Judge Poet," the other man said, leaning against the closed bathroom stall.

"How's the gardening, Morty?" Judge Poet asked, taking a piss in the stall next to him.

"It's Judge Mortimer, Poet."

"Right, well, I'm late, apologies. Where are we, gentlemen?" Poet asked, shaking and zipping.

"We've already been updated on your report; we received it last night from Fargo. It was peculiarly slim regarding your primary mission, Judge Poet." Stein watched Poet hop on the sink counter and pull out a pack of cigarettes.

"Well, I figured you lovers of repetition would only ask me about it again," Judge Poet said, drawing from his cigarette to feel full of something other than shit and sore nerves.

"Well, I suppose we should begin. Judge Poet, we'd like to know your findings in your reconnaissance mission," Stein said, officially and obtusely and probably less offensively than Judge Morty would have preferred.

"As believed, Colin Jobee was using the alias 'Thurgood' in establishing the now-defunct Brotherhood. Ultimately, his aim wasn't to incite a racially-motivated rebellion. He wanted us to see him," Poet said, stopping when Judge Stein chuckled.

"Clever fuck," Stein mouthed, and Judge Poet shrugged.

"Clever, and useful. Pellegrino—"

"Bitch," Judge Morty spat, prompting a brief, awkward silence for the rest of the Judges.

"Eh, some days more than others," Poet eventually responded. "But she's Fargo's right hand, and you will respect her accordingly." His eyes tightened and bored into Mortimer's.

"Please, go on, Poet," the other Judge eventually replied, weakly.

"Thank you. As I was saying, thanks to Pellegrino we were successful in acquiring a vital resource that will, I propose, fully assuage Gurney's concerns."

The other Judges nodded and murmured. Judge Poet waited, patting the puss accumulated below his eye socket.

"Judge Poet, we haven't much time. Please, what of your primary directive?" Morty eventually said, winding his hand to hurry things up.

"Right. In observation of the candidate, Judge Ezekiel Jones, I found much of Judges Fox and Stein's report... *fairly* accurate," Poet began, taking a moment to pat his eye with a napkin. "Jones met all physical assessments. To be completely honest, I've seen stronger Judges, and... weaker. Rarely as many with his precision in aim, but they are around, and with less baggage."

Judge Morty smirked. "Yes, we're aware of Jones's... history. Would you consider him viable, though? You seem less than impressed with your field assessment, it contradicts your report."

It was Poet's turn to chuckle. "Never said that, now, did I?

What I was getting at, in my assessment, was something far more valuable. I know the ins and outs of... what I do likely bores you, gentlemen, but please, if you would entertain me for a moment?"

Judge Stein stuck a thumb up, and Morty followed.

"Splendid. On first contact, I tested Judge Jones's resilience. He'd arrived immediately prior to my execution of a Brotherhood member. He observed, and as I'd not broken protocol, did not intervene, regardless of my eccentric performance. He never submitted a report of my behaviour at any point, as long as I operated within the confines of the Law."

"So? He's a good boy, we've got plenty of those," Judge Morty said.

"Yes. Yes, we do, Morty. What we *don't* have are those who not only revere the Law, but see that it is the *only* way to save this country, this *world*. Judge Jones never acted recklessly. I tried to... connect to Judge Jones. I gave him personal anecdotes; I waxed philosophic. I gave him an enemy."

"An... enemy?" Judge Stein echoed with a frown.

"Yes. As Officer Jones quite infamously turned against his own men in court, I needed to find a way, somehow, to ascertain if that stemmed from something so silly as racial politics, or from something more useful." Judge Poet paused as if in anticipation of a fanfare, and when none was forthcoming rolled his eye and hopped down from the counter. "Do you know much about psychopathy, gentlemen?"

"This is going to take forev—"

"*Psychopathy*, in brief, is most *commonly* marked by a lack of empathy, heightened aggression, recklessness. Back in the beginning of the millennium, there was research that showed that in the mind of an average tax evader, it was common for the amygdala to light up when shown certain... disturbing images."

"Pussies," Judge Morty said, a verbal high five no one wanted to receive.

"Genitalia aside... in psychopaths, we see something different. We see that their amygdalae is where the light lay still. Empathy—specifically the way it constrains—the psychopath is *free* from that. Judge Jones showed these patterns, in the scans we've conducted whenever he's been in hospital."

"So, he's a psychopath. Huh. If anything, then, that makes him *more* unfit than before. How the hell did he even pass the psych eval to get in?" Judge Stein asked.

"Psychopathy isn't necessarily genetic, and is inherently variable. Also, the psychopath doesn't *necessarily* lack a conscience, they just have a weak response to its call. Some can mimic empathy well when needed; others... not so much."

"Fascinating. This bathroom reeks. Get on with it, Poet," Morty said.

"Yes, well, as I'd been saying, Jones exhibited these traits, not that he's the first officer or Judge to do so. It took losing my eye to really get what I really needed for my assessment. Granted, could have done with keeping the eye; maybe a leg wound...? Or, you know, anything else. I digress. When Pellegrino ordered Judge Jones to stand down, there was *no* sign of conflict whatsoever. When he nearly killed Aaliyah Monroe, there was no conflict until after I showed signs of life."

"Okay..."

"The Law, gentlemen. It's the *only* thing that mattered. It's what will *save* them. All of them," Poet finished solemnly.

"It's settled, then. We fast-track him, use him as a model for the next round of training." Judge Stein glanced towards Judge Morty. "You've done well, Poet."

Poet laughed, thin and reedy. "Yeah? Let's hope."

They ended as they always had, with a show of kinship, forming a circle.

A thing of no end, and of no beginning.

Of forever.

ABOUT THE AUTHOR

Charlie J Eskew is a writer from Columbus, OH. He
a professional comic book shop lurker, and tenured
Black dude in America. He is the author of *Tales of the
Astonishing ~~Black~~ Spark*, and enjoys movies, long walks
on the beach, and punching Nazis in the shnoz.

Twitter: @CJEskew
Instagram: @Author_CJEskew
www.askeweskew.com

INTERVIEW WITH MICHAEL CARROLL

RICHARD BRUTON

Judges: The Avalanche is your fourth Dredd-related novella (following *Judge Dredd Year One: The Cold Light of Day*, *Judge Dredd Year Two: The Righteous Man* and *Rico Dredd: The Third Law*). After the far-future world of the first three, how did you find working in an era so much closer to the present day?

It was a little strange at first, I have to admit! My first step was to look back over the established material that covered the foundation of the Judge system... and I was surprised to see how *little* there was. In *Judge Dredd: Origins* there are only three or four panels that cover the first few years of the Judges. So I had to pin down the year in which I wanted to set the story. I chose early 2033 because I figured that the first Judges—culled from the police force, the Army and the legal system—needed some retraining.

2033 was only sixteen years in the future when I started work on the book (fifteen years now) so we can't have technology that's *too* advanced, and the stories have to be clearly rooted in the present day. For a Dredd tale, the reader knows it's far in the future so they're willing to take a big leap to get there. Flying cars, aliens, atomic wars, etc., are all acceptable. But only *fifteen* years? That's a different matter. That's not a leap, that's a single step. Electric cars, no problem. Giant animated billboards everywhere? Again, that's possible with today's tech. But household robots and flying surfboards are out, unfortunately!

The biggest differences between our present-day world and the world of *The Avalanche* are societal and political rather than technological. It's a world where the Judges are seen as a necessity, where The Powers That Be have devolved into The Powers That Were: they have lost control of the nation and it's only staggered on this far through momentum, like a massive dinosaur with a slow-acting nervous system that keeps lumbering on long after its head has been chopped off (by an alien ninja-viking wielding a laser or something: you don't know that's how they *didn't* die out).

The idea behind the Judge system is simple: sacrifice some liberties in the name of stronger security. It's all for the greater good, which is of course the battle-cry of heroes and fascists alike.

Throughout *The Avalanche,* this transitional period—the embryonic Justice Department inserting Judge teams into existing police districts—is explored in two ways. You have the smaller-scale interactions of the investigation in St. Christopher, Connecticut subtly (and sometimes not so subtly!) mirroring the gross societal and political transformation sweeping the USA as the Justice Department sweeps away the concept of due process, altering the constitution forever. We read of the changes in St. Christopher, see how it affects Judges, cops, perps, and citizens, and can easily extend upwards.

Part of this duality of storytelling comes in those small details that litter the novella, all adding to the concepts you're introducing. One of my favourites was the small conversation between one Judge and the local cops as they offer a coffee to start the shift. It's not banned yet, but the Judges discourage using it already as it's a stimulant. Simple, effective.

Although the ideas of what you were doing in the novella, and with the overall *Judges* series, were clear from an early point, I didn't fully get the title until getting to the line, "You can't push the avalanche back up the mountain." And that's just perfect, because as I was reading *The Avalanche* I realised the novella is all about a society that's reached, and passed, the tipping point. All of the changes instigated by Eustace Fargo, changes that we know will eventually lead to world of the Mega-Cities, and to Dredd, are impossible to turn back, no matter what.

In many ways, this puts you in a unique position with the world of Dredd. Yes, we've seen many references to the early days, but as you say, never really in depth or in any detail. So being there at the very earliest moments gives you a lot of say in what happens.

It also gives you the chance to introduce small but important aspects we've come to accept when reading Dredd over these years. Just to name a couple, you covered Fargo's reasons for keeping the Judge's helmets at least half-open, and also got to have potentially the very first historical usage of "Drokk" and "Grud"! How much fun was that?

That sort of thing is the gold-plated cherry on top of the icing on an already delicious cake that has sprinkles and chocolate-chips *and* a shiny sixpence hidden inside! I love including tiny details that might not mean anything to the casual reader, but even if only one devoted fan picks up on them, I'm happy.

The novellas give us a lot more space to play with than the comics, so I like to throw in plenty of such Easter eggs. My first Dredd novella, *The Cold Light of Day*, has the story flash back to Dredd's days as a cadet, along with his clone-brother Rico and several others who've been named over the years, including Cadet Gibson. Long-time readers will know that Gibson grows up to become a corrupt Judge who operates under the name Mutie the Pig (*2000 AD* progs 34-35, September 1977). Dredd realises that Mutie the Pig is a Judge because of his skills, and deduces that he must be Gibson because there's only one left-handed Judge who holds his gun in that manner. In *The Cold Light of Day*, I included a seemingly throw-away line about Gibson reaching for his gun with his left hand.

Speaking of left hands: I had similar fun with the second novella, *The Righteous Man*, in which I introduced a character called Brian O'Donnell, nicknamed Red. He and Dredd become friends, and towards the end of the book O'Donnell's right arm is badly wounded. If you take a look at the first episode of "The Cursed Earth" (*2000 AD* prog 61, April 1978), you'll see Dredd greeting his old friend "Red"... and shaking Red's left hand. When that prog came out it struck me as very odd that they'd shake hands with their lefts, because that's not what happens in the real world. Presumably, it was either a mistake or a stylistic decision by the artist, Mike McMahon. Whatever the reason, thirty-seven and a half years later I took the opportunity to provide an explanation for that hand-shaking anomaly. I love including stuff like that!

But these things are not *all* left-hand related, I promise! *The Righteous Man* gave me the opportunity to provide a (cough) "scientific" explanation for the "Death Belt" that was a major element of "The Cursed Earth" and to explain why the Death Belt didn't appear in subsequent stories. Plus I was able to link that explanation to Mega-City One's weather control, which was a bonus.

Knowing where the overall story (or at least the world) will ultimately end up is less of a burden when writing about 2033 than it would be closer to Dredd's time: we have some room to play around. We know from *Judge Dredd: Origins* that Fargo is authorised by President Gurney to establish the Judge system, but exactly *how* the system is managed has never been established. You can't replace all the country's police forces, military and judiciary overnight, so how long is the transition period? What about the cops who are forced into retirement? The lawyers who've spent years studying for their now-worthless degrees? What about the covert-ops military teams currently operating on foreign soil? How does the rest of the world react when they see that America, once the land of the free and home of the brave, is deliberately adopting a paranoid, ultra-restrictive hard-line stance?

As for "Drokk" and "Grud": well, I figured they have to come from somewhere! I had wondered for a long time what it would take for new swear-words or expletives to seep into everyday vernacular and replace the more familiar naughty words, but a couple of years back I noticed that the exclamation "Oh, my days!" was becoming very popular in the UK, particularly with the youth. It's not even profane! So if that can happen, then why not "Drokk" and "Grud"? (Purists and pedants will thank me for pointing out that "Drokk" actually first appeared in issue #1 of *2000 AD* uttered by Dan Dare.)

You're overseeing the other books in the series... How did that came about, and where do you see the future of the series heading?

The editor, David Thomas Moore, asked me to kick off the series and to shepherd the other two books that have been contracted so far: it's not a particularly difficult task—mainly, I just have to make sure that we're all steering our boats in roughly the right direction.

From the outset it was made clear that the stories should not directly feature Chief Judge Eustace Fargo as a main character—he's John Wagner's creation and we don't want to plant anything that might later scupper John's plans—but that suits me fine: I want to focus on the street-level Judges, not the political offices. Politics can be deadly boring: the *impact* of political decisions on ordinary people is where you find the good stories!

The other writers—Charles J Eskew and George Mann— are very accomplished. There was never any doubt that they'd produce excellent, thought-provoking work: I just had to make sure that they adhered to established continuity. Each of the novellas is effectively a stand-alone tale, and we each created our own sets of primary characters: this means that readers will be able to approach them in any order.

My plan for the future is that we move on a couple of years for the next round of books: the Judges are more established, though they've not yet taken complete control of the USA. The nation is in a state of flux, where even the Judges' most vociferous and adamant supporters will be thinking, "Damn, *that's* harsh!" and their most ardent opponents will be thinking, "Okay, yeah, I kinda see where they're going with this."

At some stage, assuming that the series is popular enough to keep going, I'd like to start bringing everything closer to Dredd's world. That means covering the atomic wars, which is going to be fun. I did have the idea very early in the development stage that the first three books would be set in the 2030s, then the next three in the 2040s, and so on, ultimately ending in the mid-to-late 2070s, taking us right up to the *Judge Dredd Year One* series.

I also have vague, tentative and somewhat nebulous notions of looking at the formation of Judge systems *outside* the USA. A tale set in Moscow in 2040, for example, might be very interesting indeed! I don't think that the early days of East-Meg One have ever been explored.

You do have quite a few stories dealing with either East-Meg or those displaced Sov cits heading off to Mega-City Two. The three stories "Black Snow," "Echoes" and "The Shroud" being just the latest. Is there a grand plan behind all this?

I do indeed have a grand plan for the Sov stories. Well, it's grand-*ish*. In fact, I also have several emergency back-up grand plans waiting in the wings just in case the main grand plan has to be scrapped. This, I've learned, is very important with a series like Dredd where there are several writers involved. First, because another writer might come up with a similar story to something I've got planned (that's already happened more than once), and second because it's equally possible that a writer might change something in Dredd's world that renders a part of my plan obsolete. That's also happened, the most spectacular example being "Day of Chaos" which took everyone by surprise with its ferocity, extent and sheer audacity... Only John Wagner could improve a fictional universe by almost completely destroying it!

With the "Black Snow" trilogy, though, I didn't have a plan from the beginning to have them play out like this. "Black Snow" came about because I wanted to explore the Dredd-world version of western countries riding in to "save" beleaguered institutions that just happen to be rich in minerals, plus I got a chance to take a look at the way the Sov bureaucracy works: in the aim of increasing efficiency it's become so micromanaged that it's actually now vastly *in*efficient. Sort of like the way most countries' civil services seem to work: they centralise everything for greater efficiency, then decentralise to remove the bottlenecks caused by everything being in the one place, then centralise again for greater efficiency... That's how the Sovs work in Dredd's world, but with fewer union-related problems and more state-sanctioned executions.

It was as I was developing "Black Snow" that I realised I could add a twist to the end of the tale and lead straight into another adventure, which became "Echoes." See, one of the more tricky aspects of writing a Dredd story is that he's got the Justice Department of Mega-City One backing him up: it can be hard to put Dredd in a position where he can't just call for help if things get too hairy. So since "Black Snow" already had him out of the city, I figured I'd make the most of that and lead directly into the "Echoes" story (otherwise, I'd have had to come up with a completely different reason for why Dredd gets stranded in that region).

Same thing happened with "The Shroud" except that this time the story wasn't one that I'd planned. However, it did allow me to return to a minor character I'd created a long time ago, as well as introduce the antagonist Maul, who's been lurking in the background of many of my stories for years. I had some fun with that, where Maul sees himself as Dredd's arch-nemesis, but Dredd has no idea who he is.

Talking of grand plans, is there some overarching plan somewhere for Dredd, perhaps a secret 'bible' somewhere in John Wagner's possession?

The existence (or absence) of a Wagner-written Dredd-bible is something that I'm asked about quite often!

But either way, I'm sure that all of the regular Dredd writers have their own ideas as to where they intend to (and where they'd like to) take Dredd and his world. I certainly do: I've got several ongoing storylines, and sometimes maybe only one of them is lightly touched upon in a particular story, but that'll be a seed that germinates somewhere down the road. For example: the 2014 story "Traumatown" has Dredd (and, later, the rest of Mega-City One) plagued by odd visions and nightmarish creatures. Well, some of those visions were actually premonitions... So it's worth revisiting that story, folks, not least for Nick Percival's gorgeous artwork!

When John was writing "Day of Chaos" he gave us all a heads-up, letting us know what was going to happen to the city and the Justice Department. Some of us had stories already lined up so they had to be tweaked to take John's changes into account. I don't want to speak for the other writers, but I think that was a good thing: Chaos forced me to come up with ideas that would never have occurred to me otherwise. Essentially, what John did to us other Dredd writers was the same thing we do to our characters: move them from their comfort zone and into terra incognita, and see if they've got what it takes to cope.

It's tempting to pretend that there's a Big Plan that we're all working towards, but the truth is that we're all given a go at steering the boat and none of us have been told where we're supposed to be taking it. Occasionally, the Mighty One might give the wheel a nudge or say, "No, you can't go that way," but that's all. This is about the journey, not the destination.

Looking back on your Dredd tales, I'm beginning to feel that you're doing something of a Dredd-verse equivalent of a land

grab, looking at characters, places, possibilities that haven't been explored or have been neglected and taking them for your own. I'm thinking particularly of your adoption of the entire Sov world, whether that's the ruins of East-Meg 1 in this latest trilogy, East-Meg 2 post Chaos Day, and the SovSec you established in Mega-City 2. Is this way off base? Or is it merely a case of you going wherever the ideas have taken you?

I love the idea of finding—or creating—new and different aspects of Dredd's world. That was part of the thinking behind SovSec: an attempt to create a diplomatic solution to a very tricky problem. The Sov-descended Meggers didn't want to relocate to East-Meg Two, but they couldn't stay in MC1. So the creation of a new state in the middle of MC2 was seen as a workable compromise. However... MC2 was not completely empty. There were people (mutants are people too!) already living in that sector and they were forced out in order for SovSec to be created. If there's one thing we've learned from history, it's that people don't much care for being displaced.

I'm not saying that the SovSec situation is *deliberately* allegorical to any real-world countries, but there are certainly aspects of it that have parallels. One of the things I love most about science fiction is that it allows us to explore such things from different angles. In fact, it's arguable that *that* is the greatest strength of the Judge Dredd strips and novellas: the Judges are almost completely fascistic in their approach, yet they're usually presented as the good guys. Certainly, that's how they see themselves. (But then, *everyone* thinks that he or she is the hero of their own tale... I'm sure that even modern-day monsters—like, say, those loud-mouth right-wing migrant-phobic racist bigots who are given proportionally far too much air-time simply because the networks know their presence will all but guarantee an audience—think that their own lives are filled with good deeds and positive energy.)

But, yes, I guess what I'm doing could be seen as a sort of land-grab, in a way! Not because I want to get there first and plant a "Mike Was Here" flag, but because Dredd's world is not just Mega-City One. That's just a tiny part of it. Sticking only to MC1 with Dredd stories is the equivalent of going on holiday to Spain for two weeks but never once leaving the hotel.

On a related note, another lost character you seem to enjoy championing is Judge Dolman, one of Dredd's younger clones, but lacking some of Joe's more obsessional law-above-all traits. Any plans to bring him back again, and possibly take him further?

When I originally brought Dolman back I did have a very specific path I wanted him to take, but when I pitched it to Matt (I mean, Tharg) he shot it down for reasons that I can't go into because that would spoil the idea, and I might get a chance to use it some day! But it was probably a good thing because it forced me to re-think Dolman's fate. I came up with a second idea, which I think was better, but that one was rejected too.

That sort of thing can be annoying, but it's to be expected: they're not *my* characters. Even the characters I've created for the Dredd universe don't belong to me. I knew that going in, so I'm happy with it (that said, I probably *wouldn't* be very happy if another writer killed off one of my characters without asking me, but that's not too likely!).

Your work is notable for the emphasis on the political and social aspects you include. Is there a concerted effort on your part to avoid making them too action heavy, concentrating instead on the fascinating socio-political issues of Dredd's world?

For me, it's usually the other way around: making sure there's *enough* action in the story! I do love the political stuff, particularly the way the politics impacts the average citizens, and the idea of a more "cerebral" Dredd tale is enticing, but it wouldn't necessarily be very engaging for the readers. It's not that they need to have a regular dose of action every few pages to keep them interested: action scenes can move the story along very rapidly and *show* the impact of the political machinations rather than just have the characters talk about them.

Because Dredd only has six pages per episode (ten in the Megazine), it's important to keep the story moving, whereas in US-format comics the creators have the luxury of allowing the characters more down-time (including that adorably quirky thing you sometimes get in superhero comics where the characters spend half an issue sitting around their headquarters discussing the more mundane aspects of their lives while still wearing their costumes and masks). Action is also important for keeping the story interesting for the artists, too: just as the readers don't want to see page after page of talking heads, I'm sure that the artists don't want to draw that.

When I'm plotting a story I got into a *lot* of detail with the whys, hows and wheres and all that, just so that I know exactly where everything stands, but I generally keep my notes for the action scenes sparse—just something like "Dredd escapes" or "Dredd fights the bad guy"—and then at the scripting stage I have fun fleshing them out.

I've found that if I have too much action in a story, it'll be criticised for being too "thin." Not enough action, the critics complain because it's too slow... It seems that in this game you just can't win. But you can *quit*: I no longer read the reviews!

Taking the socio-political aspect of your tales to an extreme, and setting aside the *Judges* series, have you ever thought of pitching a multi-part epic where you ignore Dredd completely, relegate the action to a tiny part, and focus exclusively on the minutiae of the politics of Mega-City One? Do you think Tharg would buy into *Judge Dredd: Adventures in Admin*?

I did mention once (on a convention panel, I think) that since the Judges are in charge of every aspect of the running of Mega-City One—there are no other politicians or civil servants—that means there's some Judge who's spent fifteen years in the toughest academy on Earth, who has the authority to dispense instant justice and whose words is law, and it's his job to oversee the department's supplies of ball-point pens and toilet-paper.

I love the idea of a series based around those Judges! The Judges who maintain the other Judges' Lawmasters but never get to ride one themselves. The Judges who man the Sector House desks and spend all day dealing with queries about lost robo-pets or collecting parking fines. The Judges whose sole job is watching the city's countless TV shows and movies to make sure that they're suitable for their intended audience. And even the Judges who maintain the robots that maintain the pop-corn-makers for *those* Judges.

Seriously, though, what is it about Dredd's world that fascinates you?

Story-wise, the possibilities are limitless. There is no genre that can't be made to work in Mega-City One or elsewhere in Dredd's world... and yet, at the same time, there *are* rules and restrictions. No reset-buttons, for a start. We're not allowed to wipe out past continuity and start again. And with a few tiny exceptions—mostly from the strip's earliest days—anything that's happened in Dredd's world is part of the canon. It all progresses in real time, too.

Anyone unfamiliar with Dredd might think that makes it all very daunting for new readers: how do you jump on board when you've got *forty years* of back-story to catch up on? Especially when the Big Name superhero comics keep resetting their time-lines so that you don't need to know that, say, fifty-eight years ago ClownDog killed Significant-Chap's step-half-nephew by using his Disguise-O-Ray to make a plugged-in toaster look like a bar of soap. Instead, you get to see ClownDog and Significant-Chap meeting for the first time.

So, yeah, it seems easier to get into a comic like that because you have the illusion that you're coming in fresh.

But the truth is that all those resettings of time-lines, and the undoings of those resettings, and the alternate realities, and the parallel universes, and the imaginary stories, and the endless multi-title crossovers, and the past-altering time-travelling adventures... Well, you end up not with fresh continuity but a jumbled mess that's all but incomprehensible to anyone but the most attentive (and forgiving) reader. Seriously, I'm a huge superhero fan but I find it almost impossible to follow the comics on a month-to-month basis. Instead, with each new Battle of the Century (seriously, guys: how many centuries ahead are you now?), I just keep out of the way until it's all over and then buy the collected edition.

With Dredd, you can tell any new reader, "He's a cop in a huge futuristic city." That's all they really need to know to start reading. But if they *do* want to know more than that, you simply direct them to the Case Files graphic novels. No need for "Oh, you'll love *this* one—it's an absolute all-time classic, the Crisis of the Parallel Alternates! They all get killed at the end, but then they come back in the next one, but it doesn't count because that was on the Alpha-Earth which was nulled out of existence when Singularity The Living Universe averted his gaze at the wrong instant because VeryFastCyclistGirl pedalled so hard that she broke the reality barrier."

Hmm. I seem to have wandered off for a little rant there! But the point holds, I think: Dredd's unbroken continuity is a solid foundation rather than a minefield.

Every Empire Falls was your first Dredd epic tale, complete with the complex machinations of Chief Judge Oswin and Texas City, the behind the scenes involvement of Brit-Cit, and the continuing post Chaos Day realisation that Mega-City One is no longer the untouchable powerhouse it once was. How enjoyable was it to finally get the chance to give the readers that first "epic" Dredd storyline?

That was tremendously fun to write—but at the same time it was exhausting and head-wrecking because it was five stories spread over twenty-two separate issues, and two different publications (one of which was monthly and the other weekly), with four artists and three colourists, plus it was the culmination of several different story-lines.

Ideally, I'd have planted certain plot-seeds a lot sooner—I should have established Pamelina Oswin as the Texas-City Chief Judge a year or two in advance, for example—but on the whole I think it holds together pretty well. It was certainly nice to see the collected edition bringing together many of the earlier tales that set up a lot of the elements.

It was massively satisfying to see *Every Empire Falls* become the #1 best-selling Cult Graphic Novel on Amazon (and the #1 Crime & Mystery Graphic Novel at the same time!), but I don't allow myself to think of it as *my* graphic novel: the artists, colourists and of course the letterer Awesome Annie Parkhouse all did absolutely outstanding work. My job as the writer is to tell the story to them: they have the much, much harder task of telling that story to the rest of the world. I still can't believe that I'm permitted to work with such talented people—legends, they are!

Your Dredd stories are notable for your avoidance of using Dredd as a blunt instrument, cracking cases by cracking heads. Is this a deliberate decision on your part, to move Dredd away from the oft-used fist of Justice to a more measured, investigative solution from a seasoned lawman?

It's tempting to write Dredd as a sort of superhero—and there certainly have been times when I've pushed his physical abilities a little beyond reality—but I prefer to present him as a cop first, hero second. He'll use his fists if necessary, but it's a lot more fun when he doesn't. (I had a story a couple of years back where a bunch of perps come across Dredd asleep and they have the opportunity to kill him, but in the end they're so scared of his reputation that they end up arresting themselves because that way it's safer.)

Right from the start I always intended to show Dredd as more of an investigator than a door-kicking-in grunt, but there's not of a lot of room in the comics to have Dredd attending lectures on the latest forensic techniques or meticulously scrutinising piles of evidence to find that one tell-tale grain of HyperSand (or whatever) that will point to the killer. Plus, again, it wouldn't necessarily lead to interesting comics.

So there has to be a balance: other writers have, occasionally, presented Dredd as headstrong and, well, a bit thick, but I try to write him as someone who's dedicated and driven but doesn't have much of an imagination and pretty much lacks any form of ego. Certainly, that's how I have him in the Year One and Year Two prose novellas, especially in contrast with his clone-brother Rico: really, the only difference between Joe and Rico is that Rico *does* have an ego.

Now, onto artists... I won't ask who your favourite artistic collaborator has been, that's pretty much like asking you to name a favourite child. But what have been your artistic highlights amongst those you've had the pleasure to work with?

You know, I don't *have* any kids so picking a favourite child is no difficulty for me. Therefore, I can and *will* name my favourite artistic collaborator, and if the other kids don't like it, well, they should bear in mind that every bout of whining brings them another step closer to the orphanarium.

Working with Carlos Ezquerra on the final part of the *Every Empire Falls* storyline was an absolute joy, and without a doubt it's the highlight of my career so far. Not only have I've loved his work since before *2000 AD*, Carlos co-created my three favourite *2000 AD* thrills: *Judge Dredd*, *Strontium Dog*, and *The Stainless Steel Rat*. My most prized possession is an original *Stainless Steel Rat* double-page spread!

I've been massively lucky to work with some incredible artists over the years. Paul Davidson, Henry Flint, Paul Marshall, Steve Yeowell, David Roach, Paul Jason Holden, John M. Burns, Leigh Gallagher, Ben Willsher, Karl Richardson... My most frequent collaborators are Chris Blythe on colours and Annie Parkhouse on letters: two vital aspects of the comic-creation process that don't receive nearly enough credit.

And there's Colin MacNeil, too. Absolute legend, that man. I have a friend who regularly phones me up to remind me how unbelievably lucky and undeserving I am to be working with Colin—and he's right. (I named the main protagonist of my *New Heroes* books Colin Wagner, after Colin and John Wagner.)

I've also worked a few times with that other legend John Higgins... The weird thing about John is that he's one of my closest friends so I tend to forget how good he is. But I was certainly reminded of his talents last year when I edited his book *Beyond Watchmen and Judge Dredd*: it's packed with stunning examples of his artwork from his forty-year career in comics (plus it's a great primer for upcoming artists: all the tips and tricks you need to know!). John is unequivocally among the very best in the business, the sort of artist that makes *other* world-class artists go, "Bloody hell, I wish *I* could draw like that!"

Going back to the beginning... what was your first Dredd work or *2000 AD* work?

My first published *2000 AD* strip was a one-off *Time-Twister* called "Back to the Führer" which was published in prog 1566, back in December 2007. So just over ten years ago now. It was drawn by Gary Erskine, which blew me away: I'd been a huge fan of Gary's work for years and to have him illustrate my first professional comic strip was just overwhelming. Gary's one of the great unsung heroes of British comics, I think: I've never seen a page of his artwork that didn't make me go "Wow!" at least once.

My second published strip was a *Future Shock* drawn by John Cooper—the man who co-created *One-Eyed Jack* with John Wagner (a character who is, arguably, a prototype for Judge Dredd), as well as drawing countless gorgeous episodes of Johnny Red in *Battle Picture Weekly*. I swear, when I saw that John Cooper had drawn my strip I nearly cried. So it's safe to say that I've been very lucky indeed when it comes to artists.

How did you land that first work at *2000 AD*, and can you give us an insight into your comics history and background?

I've read comics all my life... But the first comic I clearly remember was issue #5 of *The Mighty World of Marvel*, from November 1972. So that means I was six and a half when I first encountered superheroes. I fell in love with the Marvel characters instantly! Not long after that I discovered Batman and Superman and The Flash through imported DC issues—superhero comics in *actual colour*!

I was almost eleven when *2000 AD* was launched, and it felt like it had been designed specially for me, because it combined both my loves: science fiction *and* comics! Amazing! So I've been a reader since prog 1. Even when my friends began to grow away from comics, I stuck with *2000 AD*. It's never let me down yet!

I desperately wanted to be a comic artist, but I quickly learned that drawing is harder than writing, so I chose the easy path. My first ever attempt at writing a novel was an adaptation of the first appearance of Judge Death. I managed about a page and a half before I concluded that writing can be hard work too.

But I never gave up on the idea of creating comics. My very first published comic strip was in (I think) 1994, in an anthology published by the Irish Science Fiction Association. That was a superhero tale called *Overman*, drawn by my mate Johnny Rothwell (who is massively talented and should have stuck with the comics!).

473

After that... there was a bit of a lull, I have to admit. I was still writing short-stories and novels, and occasionally pitched a few *Future Shocks* to *2000 AD*, but it wasn't until 2004 that I had another comic-strip published, a one-page story called "The Curse of the Were-House" published in *Solar Wind* and drawn by small-press maestro Dave Evans.

I eventually broke into *2000 AD* through persistence more than anything else—like talent. I'd gotten into a cycle of sending in *Future Shock* scripts, having them rejected, sending another one, and so on, but with "Back to the Führer" when Tharg rejected it (rightly!) I replied with the tentative suggestion that I might make some changes in line with his comments and re-send it: he agreed to permit that, I did so, and a few weeks later I received a letter saying, "Great, send me an invoice."

I had to look up how to do an invoice.

What's coming up next for you, in *2000 AD* or the *Meg*?

Coming up soon is a project that's been some years in the planning: John Higgins and I are collaborating on a crossover between Judge Dredd and John's character Razorjack! It's a three-part story for the *Megazine*, and I had an absolute blast writing it. I know Razorjack pretty well—I've written a *Razorjack* novel, and I did some work on the recent collection of John's original RJ stories—so it was a huge amount of fun putting them together.

Also in the pipeline is some more Dredd strips and a couple of other novellas. Outside *2000 AD*, I'm working on something that I can't talk about. But I *wish* I could. It's one of those "Everything I've ever done has led to this point" life-changing projects!

And finally, the Dredd movie question... Which one did you prefer? And was there anything at all in the Stallone version that you can be nice about? (Personally I'm quite fond of it in a poor relation to take pity on sort of way)

There's a lot to like in the Stallone version, but there's so much that could—and should—have been done better. The helmet is the most obvious thing. Once he removes his helmet it stops being a Dredd movie and becomes a Sylvester Stallone movie. Such a shame, especially since I hadn't realised that he hadn't removed his helmet until he did, if you see what I mean.

But they got Mean Machine Angel right, and the ABC robot was pretty cool. And any movie that features Ian Dury automatically gets raised up a notch. Sadly, they also decided that Dredd needed a comedy sidekick and a love-interest, so that lowered the movie by *two* notches.

The 2012 *Dredd* movie, though, is a modern masterpiece. *That's* how you do Dredd on-screen! The story didn't need to hang on a world-ending scenario—it was a day in the life of an ordinary cop. Dredd's comment at the end sums it up perfectly, when the Chief Judge asks him what happened, and he replies, "Drugs bust."

Karl Urban understood something that Stallone failed to grasp: we never see Dredd without his helmet because a Judge is *all* that Dredd is. The helmet *is* his face. It's not a mask that he removes at the end of the day, a persona that he sheds when he's not fighting crime. He's a Judge twenty-four hours a day, every day.

Some people might see that as being an element that makes Dredd less than human, but those people need to step back and take another look: here's a man who has dedicated his life and sacrificed any potential happiness to the pursuit and implementation of justice and the protection of the innocent. He could choose to step down, or even just ease off the throttle a little, but sitting back won't get the perps caught. If he takes a day off, people that he could have saved will die.

No other comic-book hero is so selfless. Almost all of them have alter-egos to hide behind when they need a break. They allow themselves to have other lives, and to bask in their accomplishments. Superman has a trophy room. Spider-Man has been married. Batman has a searchlight bearing his symbol that illuminates the night sky.

Judge Dredd isn't driven by the need for vengeance or the desire to be a hero. He's utterly altruistic. That doesn't make him less than human: it makes him *better* than human.

FIND US ONLINE!

www.rebellionpublishing.com

/rebellionpub   /rebellionpublishing   /rebellionpub

SIGN UP TO OUR NEWSLETTER!

rebellionpublishing.com/sign-up

YOUR REVIEWS MATTER!

Enjoy this book? Got something to say?

Leave a review on Amazon, GoodReads or with your
favourite bookseller and let the world know!

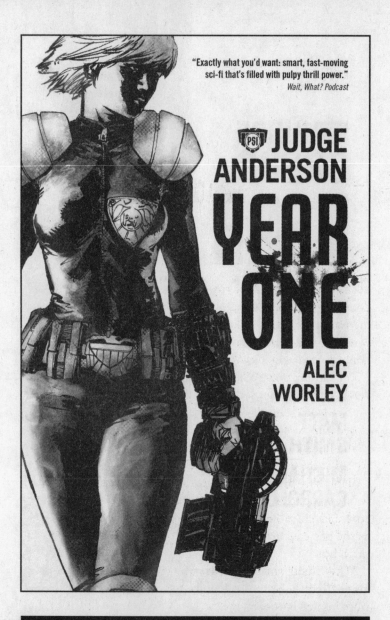